CW00573600

GOLDEN APPLES

Paul Heiney

Hodder & Stoughton

Copyright © 1999 by Paul Heiney

First published in Great Britain in 1999
by Hodder and Stoughton
A division of Hodder Headline PLC

The right of Paul Heiney to be identified as the
Author of the Work has been asserted by him in
accordance with the Copyright, Designs and Patents Act 1988.

10 9 8 7 6 5 4 3 2 1

All rights reserved. No part of this publication may be
reproduced, stored in a retrieval system, or transmitted,
in any form or by any means without the prior written
permission of the publisher, nor be otherwise circulated
in any form of binding or cover other than that in which
it is published and without a similar condition being
imposed on the subsequent purchaser.

The author is grateful for permission to reproduce the following:
Lake Isle of Innisfree; *The Song of Wandering Aengus*;
He Wishes for the Cloths of Heaven by W.B. Yeats.
Reprinted by kind permission of A. P. Watt Ltd
on behalf of Michael B. Yeats.

All characters in this publication are fictitious
and any resemblance to real persons, living or dead,
is purely coincidental.

British Library Cataloguing in Publication Data

A CIP catalogue record for this title
is available from the British Library

ISBN 0 340 69549 8

Typeset by Hewer Text Limited, Edinburgh
Printed and bound in Great Britain by
Clays Ltd, St Ives plc
Hodder and Stoughton
A division of Hodder Headline PLC
338 Euston Road
London NW1 3BH

For Libby, who first took me to Ireland

Acknowledgements

Although the crisp factory in this story is completely and utterly fictional, I was greatly helped by Stephen Hutchinson of Tayto who make crisps of the highest quality in Tandragee, Northern Ireland. In return for much time spent explaining the production of crisps, followed by fine hospitality, all I can do in return is direct you to his web site (www.tayto.com) where his excellent crisps are available by mail order.

1

It was too wet to be planting potatoes. Any fool could have told him that. You didn't have to be born and bred in the far western fringes of County Mayo to know that when the rain ran down the furrows with the energy of the River Moy at full spate, there were better things to be doing than dropping seed potatoes one by one into the sodden soil. Anyway, it was a Sunday and no God-fearing man should have been on the land on the Lord's Day.

But nothing would ever persuade Pat Tierney to be anywhere other than on his patch of land on 2 April, Sunday or no Sunday. He had done it every year since he was a boy, and even though the aches of 67 year old muscles and bones made it ever more of a chore, the tradition was upheld. Whatever obstacles the unpredictable weather might put in his way, the planting of his small potato crop at this time of year was as immutable as the feast days of the church. It was as likely as the ringing of the Angelus bell down in the town being forgotten that Padraig – or Pat for short – would not be bent double on this day of the year, shuffling along the furrows he had painstakingly dug with a spade, dropping seed potatoes from a wicker basket hooked over his arm.

Some years the weather was kind. The year before had been warm with a welcome hint of sun which he'd felt on his back through the thick, black woollen overcoat he wore year round, whatever the weather, like his own skin. One year, he recalled, there had been sleet and by the time he was back in his cottage after seven hours' continuous planting, his fingers were chapped. The black, peaty soil got under his skin in every sense. It had needed a slug of strong poteen before he had been brave enough to put his hands under the hot water tap and scrub them clean of the filth. It always amused him that poteen, the illicit spirit he distilled from fermented potatoes, should be the medicine which relieved the pain potatoes had inflicted in the first place; the cause and cure were, paradoxically, the same thing. Having taken a stiff draught before washing, and several after to ease the pain further, he was sufficiently mellow to allow his conviction to waver, and vow he would never plant potatoes again. But twelve months later he was inevitably driven back to the field by ghosts he could not ignore, spirits which demanded annual homage, history which his conscience told him should never be forgotten

This was just an average, teeming, sodden, bloody Irish west coast year. He had dug his furrows from north to south, up and down the slope of the hill, so that should they ever be blessed with a sight of the warming sun, it would shine equally on both sides of the growing plants as it crossed the sky. And so as he worked his way up and down the field, first his left cheek and then his right felt the wrath of the west wind as it whipped around his face and neck. To ease the muscles of his back, he occasionally straightened himself up and with narrowed eyes looked to windward, hoping to see an improvement. But the storms which had brought this deluge had formed long ago on the far side of the Atlantic and, wearied by the long crossing, the rain wanted instant relief from the journey. So it fell exhausted, here on Ballymagee, and no power on earth, thought Pat, could ever persuade it to do otherwise.

If there was anything to be said for the persistent westerly blast of air, it was that it kept the atmosphere on the move and, coming from the Atlantic had none of the taint of the air originating in the town. It was all the fault of the factory; a sprawling complex of sheds, yards, and a high chimney over which hovered volcano-like, a permanent cloud of steam. Trapped beneath this blanket hung the oily smell of food being cooked on a grand scale. Pat could just about come to terms with the way the factory had blighted his view by pointing its chimney high into the sky, marring the graceful, natural lines of the saucer-shaped valley in which huddled Ballymagee. At least he could turn his back on the factory buildings, or arrange the chair by his hearth so that he did not have to see them from his window. But the smell, when the air was still or the wind in the east, carried the two miles up the hill and came creeping under his door and between the cracks in the loose window frames of his low cottage, until it was so strong he might as well have been down there on the factory floor, standing next to the bubbling cauldrons of cooking oil. It was a foul smell, to Pat's mind: a cloying vapour which came to rest at the back of the throat, coating his mouth till it was as greasy as an incontinent diesel engine. It made him want to retch.

And it made him all the more determined to plant his potatoes every year, whatever the weather, and no matter what the personal cost. For this was his way of apologising. Without his help, that vulgar factory would not have been there in the first place, the landscape would not now be blighted. To be partly responsible for its very existence was the greatest sin of his life. So the sowing and harvesting of his potato crop became a penance, to be ignored only at the risk of his eventual absolution. And although he cursed the westerly wind as it drove the rain before it, soaking him to the skin, he loathed the east wind even more, for the constant reproach of the foul smells it brought in its wake.

Above the noise of the wind, Pat heard the stutter of a reluctant engine trying to make its way up the hill towards his cottage and guessed it must be about ten-thirty. It was one of the few fixed events in his day. He knew that exhaust, there was no other like it. It had more holes in it than a drunk's alibi; so little steel left you could wave a metal detector over it and the machine would barely register. For a moment, the continuous moaning of the the wind did battle with the sporadic fire of the exhaust, till eventually the engine won. As the car drew nearer Pat was forced to stop planting and look round. It was a rusty old Volvo saloon, hand-painted a sickly shade of green. With one windscreen wiper missing, and the remaining strip of perished rubber hardly able to shift a dollop of cuckoo spit, let alone a torrent of Atlantic rain, it made for a sad sight in the downpour. He saw the car slow down and come to a halt so close to one of his gateposts that the driver could reach out and touch it without leaving the comparative shelter of his seat.

'Will you ever get that damned car of yours fixed? Noisy machine,' Pat shouted grumpily at the driver, cowering beneath a woollen hat of a shade of green even more sickly than his car's. 'It's nothing but bloody pollution. Spoiling what bit of peace and quiet there's left up here.'

'Can't hear yer for the wind,' the driver replied. 'Shout louder or shut up!'

'Shut up your bloody self,' Pat bellowed above the wind. He watched the driver shove a rolled newspaper into an old drain-pipe, tied with a length of farmer's twine to a gatepost built of whitewashed breeze blocks. He didn't push the paper far enough, noticed Pat. He knew that by the time he came to retrieve it at the end of the day, the rain would have returned it to pulp. Best thing for the *Tribune*, perhaps.

'Push the t'ing all the way, yer messer of a boy,' he barked at the driver. Then he noticed something different about the familiar car. It had sprouted white lettering down its side; gleaming, boastful words, brilliant against the green paint.

4

Pat screwed up his eyes in a watery attempt to focus. He could make out *Cars*, but the other word was too long.

'Taxi, are we now?' he shouted mockingly. 'More like a stinking cattle waggon, I would have said.'

In a desperate attempt to keep the engine running, the driver gunned the throttle till the air was filled with the sound of rattling from the perforated exhaust. Before winding up the window he shouted, 'And if you want your papers bringing in future, you can pay the bloody fare, understand?'

The driver chortled as he turned the car in the middle of the lane, then gave Pat a friendly wave: it had all been part of the daily joshing, the banter that flowed between them, the wise-cracking which concealed their unaccountable pleasure at seeing one other. This was the sum total of Pat's social contact for that day, or any other for that matter. He might not see another soul till the driver appeared the next morning, and even then they would only exchange further insults above the roar of the wind. He looked into his basket and guessed there was not enough seed to plant a further row, and so he walked to the end of the furrow where the sack stood, grateful to be upright. He looked down the valley, saw the car disappearing into the mist, taking the corners too quickly, and hoped that the cheeky driver would not be taught a painful lesson about driving too fast.

But if he had a certain fellow feeling for the driver who bothered to bring him a newspaper every morning, he had little for the rest of the people in the nearby town. The whole damned miserable pit of a place that was Ballymagee needed to be taught a painful lesson or two, he thought. Of all the small towns on the Atlantic coast of Ireland, there was none so smug as Ballymagee. And *they* had the cheek to laugh at him for planting his potatoes every year on the hillside, not having the wit to understand why anyone should bother to be growing their own when only two miles away their town had more potatoes for the asking than any person could consume in a lifetime. It was the potato capital of the entire country. The place grew potatoes like cats breed fleas. There was no stopping them. Potatoes flourished here on a grand scale.

Not that Pat would ever have allowed one past his lips. He saw them as tainted by the greed of the people who had grown them, stored them, then sold them to that cursed factory which cooked them and turned them into packets of potato crisps. It was almost beyond understanding how something as innocent and ephemeral as a potato crisp could be the focus of such intense loathing. But if Pat Tierney could have had his dearest wish, it would have been to stand atop the hill on which he lived, and with an Old Testament wave of his stick, consign the whole factory to perdition.

He growled in disgust at the thought of the place, and then filled his basket from the sack of sodden seed potatoes. Some, he noticed, were growing shoots, which was a good sign. He was careful to transfer those without damaging the delicate, soft growth. It was a miracle to him how one seed potato could flourish and multiply in the short span of six months so that when fork or spade was taken to it in late-September, where there had been one buried potato there might now be six or more. It was a true miracle. The potato, he always thought, was a wonderful plant.

By four o'clock in the afternoon he had finished. With no chance of frost it was safe to leave the seed potatoes uncovered in the furrows. The only risk was from birds who might target the juicy, sprouting shoots for their supper, but it would take at least half a day's work with the spade to cover them and Pat didn't feel like starting now. No matter; if the birds did get the shoots, new ones would grow again and if his crop was a week later because of it, that didn't matter much either. Pat was his own master.

He had only one more job to do before he could call it a day. Stumbling from tiredness, he made his way to a wreck of a shed which leaned for support against the back wall of his cottage. The roof was made of rusty sheets of tin, the walls of crumbling brick, the glass in the mean windows was cracked and the holes laced with cobwebs. Pat pushed open the door against the grip of the rust which was trying to keep the hinges closed, and felt with his hands in the gloom till he found a wet and festering piece of sacking draped across a mound of putrid potatoes. Far from being disgusted by the sight, he smiled as he peeled back the cloth to reveal the full extent of the rot. The worse it smelled, the happier he was. He moved a few potatoes aside and placed his finger into the heap. It was warm. They were rotting fast. Pat was happy with that. He replaced the cloth, wiped his hand on his coat and pulled the door tight shut behind him. This was a secret place, for his eyes only.

Pat stumbled back towards his cottage, the rigours of the day leaving him exhausted, and was just about to remove his leather boots when he remembered the *Tribune*. It would be mush by now and if he had any sense he would leave it there till the wind took it, for the chance of gleaning anything from its smudged print was now remote. But on this day of all days, the day he planted his potatoes, he judged it an ill omen for the *Tribune* not to be brought into the house, and so with a curse he set off down the muddy track to rescue the half-drowned newspaper.

Rid of his boots, and with the door closed behind him again, his wet coat hanging sodden on the hook, the spongy newspaper lying in a pool of inky water on the table, Pat collapsed into a high-backed wooden chair by the hearth.

'Jesus, thank you for letting this day be over,' he muttered, then sighed with exhaustion and closed his eyes. He had only dozed for five minutes before he woke, shivering. A torrential cloudburst hit the corrugated tin roof of the single-storey cottage like a hail of bullets; the door rattled as a blast of wind swept down the hill and passed through the house without hindrance. Pat would have to light a fire.

In the small back yard, beneath a heavy canvas sheet, stood a pile of turf; solid lumps of peat which he had cut from the hillside the previous spring, stacked and dried in the summer air, and laboriously brought home in a sack carried on his shoulders. This, he thought, was another miracle; the way that the warmth of the sunshine which had shone down on plants and trees ten thousand years before, could now, by the mere application of a match, be released to shine again and warm him by his own hearth. Every time he placed the fibrous lumps of peat in his grate, he could not rid his mind of the thought that the vegetation within them was alive at the time the Ice Age was coming to an end, four thousand years before any human being dwelt in Ireland. A sense of history, had Pat Tierney.

Kneeling before the grate, he tried to strike the first match but it was damp. He tried another, but drops of water falling from his wet hair extinguished it. The third burst into life and he quickly applied it to the crumpled sheets of yesterday's copy of the *Tribune*, hoping it might catch before the gale of wind which was blowing up the chimney could extinguish it. With the paper ablaze he added a few lumps of peat. Not too many or the fire would be killed; too few and it would be no fire at all. A fine judgment, one more balance to be achieved.

Everything about the way Pat lived was a struggle. Even the peat, which could just as easily be bought in the town, had to be cut by his own hand, piece by piece, stacked, then hauled home by his own efforts. He could have had an electric cooker connected but shunned it and settled instead for a solitary electric light bulb hanging from the centre of the ceiling in only one of the three small rooms. To hell with an electric cooker, the television, or even the radio. He turned his back on it all, and preferred to do his penance by taking no easy option. For that reason, the sharp-tongued lads in the town had nicknamed him 'the Monk'.

Just as the flame was taking hold of yesterday's newspaper in the grate, Pat glanced round at the table, remembering there was something he must read in today's. News rarely mattered to him, but on this day of the year there was one piece of information he always sought. Most days, his tired eyes passed over it, but today it must be read and considered. He saw the sodden copy of that day's *Tribune* lying in a puddle of its own making, fast returning to pulp, and grabbed it to see if any of it could be salvaged, but the pages fell apart in his hands as he tried to turn them. Cursing, he spun round, reached out and grabbed the blazing newsprint from the grate. It was yesterday's, but it would have to do. As urgently as if they were bank notes he had absentmindedly flung on the fire, he smacked the singed pages between his hands till the flames were out. Pat fell to his knees, gave a sigh of relief, then immediately regretted what he had done. He squeezed his eyes tightly shut and clenched his teeth in anger, not because the act of burning yesterday's paper was anything in itself to get worked up about, but because a darker obsession had triumphed once again. A self-indulgent habit of which he had tried to rid himself over the years had proved itself master of him. That was what hurt more than the flames that licked his fingers for Pat believed himself to be a truly weak man, and had just proved it again. The truth was that the information he sought would be just as valid if taken from tomorrow's paper, but on this day of the year especially it was something he *had* to know. He screwed up his eyes to decipher the numbers on the charred corners of the pages. The one he was looking for was usually near the back, 26 or something like that. His eye dismissed a parade of headlines: *Archbishop Speaks of Shock in Aftermath of Priest's Conviction; Accused was at Funeral of Slain Friend Court is Told.*

'No horses stolen, then,' he muttered mockingly. 'That's all right then. So long as it's just a bit of sex on the side for the priest, or a murder now and then, we can assume life in Ballymagee is following its usual course.' He threw the page back into the grate.

The next had the racing results from Downpatrick, and Pat was beginning to think the news he was seeking had already gone up in smoke. Then he spotted the familiar layout of the only page which ever caught his full attention. The headline read *Faltering Wall Street Hits Euro Recovery*, and below it were the closing prices on the Dublin stock exchange. The light was fading and he had not bothered to switch on the single electric bulb. He slanted the paper towards the small window, one pane of which was missing and had been blocked off with a ragged piece of plywood, allowing little light through. He could just make out the numbers on the page if he screwed up his eyes very tight. He read them aloud to himself: 'Bank of Ireland . . . up 5 pence. Good. Everything seems to be up a little bit.' The company he was looking for was, annoyingly, on the fold of the paper where it had been rubbed. He could just read it. 'ChipCo – sod the buggers – are up 8 whole pence. My God!' he declared with a broad smile on his face. 'Pat Tierney is *still* a rich man, and richer than ever as the days go by!'

He enjoyed his joke; relished the irony of circumstances which had made him a man of some substance. He could have had every electric cooker in Ballymagee connected, running at full tilt, and still afforded the bill! Or so he thought. Exactly how much he would be worth if he sold his shares, he did not know. Nor cared. He had no interest in the sum, no wish to spend any of it. It was the devil's money, in Pat's opinion. But he enjoyed his occasional glance at the stock market closing prices, and it had become a tonic. It made the long days easier to bear, sugared the pill of a hard, lonely life. But it did not make Pat any fonder of ChipCo and that damned factory which he could see and smell from his cottage. It was still a blight on the town of Ballymagee, an atrocity, its very existence a sin. To hell with how much profit it made, and to hell with his own prosperity. That factory he would always despise.

Pat crumpled the sheet of newspaper and set about lighting the fire once again. He forgot all about the ChipCo market prices as quickly as you might forget a football result in which you had no interest, and thought once again of his potato crop. It was a special day of the year, he must not forget that, and it had been a satisfactory one though planting potatoes by hand became harder work as the years went by. In three years' time he would be seventy years old. Pat wondered if he would still be able to do it then. The flames of the burning newspaper caught the edges of the turf, the smoke changed from black to grey, and the sweet, emollient smell of burning peat wafted into the room, buffeted by the downdraughts which a gale of wind occasionally flung down the chimney. When Pat was satisfied that it had caught, he took a pair of bellows from beside the fireplace and blasted the sods of turf till they sparkled like the coals in a blacksmith's forge. Then, over the very hottest part of the fire, he placed a blackened kettle and fell back into his chair to wait for it to boil.

In his relaxation, he must not forget that this had been no ordinary day. It was Potato Planting Day; a milestone in his year, as important to him as Christmas to a child. It was to be anticipated, enjoyed and celebrated as tradition demanded. And now he must perform the final customary act. He rose from his chair and went across to his bookshelf to remove from it an old prayer book, a leather-bound missal from which his mother, and hers before her, had read the words of the Mass on every devotional day of the Catholic church. He glanced at the kettle. It had not even begun to sing. He had time yet.

He opened the fragile book with great care and from it withdrew a folded piece of lined writing paper on which a few lines had been written in a flowing, antique hand. The ink was beginning to fade and what had once presumably been dark blue was now as pale as Pat's aging eyes.

Written across the top in a disciplined and formal hand were the words: 'Copied by Kathleen Tierney in 1871 from a copy of the Tribune which bears the date 5 April 1847.'

He kissed the piece of paper lightly, in memory of his great-great grandmother, Kathleen. Then he read aloud to himself, reciting the words as if they were a prayer.

'With regret we have to add another name to the melancholy catalogue of the dead from starvation in this district, in the person of a poor aged man named Padraig Michael Tierney who, while on his way on Wednesday last to seek admission to the workhouse, expired on the side of the road near Bally-magee within about a mile of the town. When he was discovered life was found to be extinct, and his remains were taken to the warehouse where an inquest was subsequently held upon the body by Michael Crowley Esq., deputy coroner, and the verdict returned of "died from want".'

When he had read it, considered the grief the death must have caused Kathleen, and said a prayer for his ancestor Padraig Michael, Pat carefully folded the piece of paper, returned it safely to the missal and placed it on the shelf. With the passing of the years he had learned to control his bitterness, and the annual ritual of reading the notice copied from the local newspaper no longer made him angry. The paper would stay there till next potato planting, and every one thereafter for which the Lord spared him. He would take it out every year on the anniversary of Padraig Michael Tierney's death and read it aloud. He would never forget. He had heard the story many times from his own father, and from his grandfather too – the story of the long, hungry, desolate, heroic walk of Padraig Michael. In bleak moments, Pat wished he had a son or daughter to whom he could pass the legend. Instead, on dark nights, he sat by the fire and told the story to himself. Resigned to the fact that when he died, the legend would die with him.

He wiped dampness from his eyes on the sleeve of his flannel shirt and heard the kettle coming to the boil. He stood up, gasping at the pain in his back and leg muscles inflicted by the potato planting. He limped across to a dark green cupboard in the scullery and from next to it took an old stoppered bottle which was half filled with clear liquid, then picked up a mug and took it back to his chair. He uncorked the bottle and poured out a heavy slug. It was poteen: potent, illicit, impure spirit distilled, improbably, from potatoes. The crop which had caused him so much pain today would now relieve it. Pat topped up the mug with scalding water from the kettle and sniffed the sharpness of the scented steam. It would not be long before this kindest of all painkillers was being shunted through his body to relieve every aching muscle. The fire was glowing hot. He closed his eyes, and just before falling asleep heard above him the drone of an approaching aeroplane. Pat opened one eye to glance at the clock. The evening flight from London was half an hour late. Nothing unusual about that.

The most rundown aeroplane of the world's ultimate 'no-frills' airline, Aer Shamrock, was ten minutes from landing at the airport which stood ten miles outside Ballymagee. The slab of concrete they called the runway had been laid on the top of a flattened hill which, from a distance, made it look like a boiled egg from which the top had been roughly sliced. They called it Ballymagee International Airport. Some joke. True, there was the daily flight from London, and one from Glasgow, if you could call those international. And, yes, there was once, years ago, a slim chance that the Pope might have landed here on his visit to Ireland *if* the weather in Dublin had forced his plane to be diverted. It had caused a crisis for the worshippers in the town who felt it their duty to pray for the safe arrival of the Pope in their capital city, but at the same time thought it might do no harm to pray for a little fog and have him first come down from the heavens into their very midst. Given just the slightest chance of His Holiness dropping in, they'd upgraded the technical facilities till they were beyond the comprehension of anyone who had to operate them. So they switched off most of the stuff and got by on what they understood.

Never having set foot in Ireland, let alone Ballymagee, Kathy McGuinness, the young woman travelling alone in first class, knew nothing of what to expect. She had no idea what Ballymagee International held in store, although the aeroplane might have given her some clues. It was a craft of two distinct halves, separated by a curtain embroidered, she noticed, with the predictable shamrock symbol. A plaque fastened to the bulkhead announced: *Welcome to Aer Shamrock. A subsidiary of the ChipCo Corporation.* Crisps were complimentary and came in generous quantities at the slightest excuse, giving the aircraft the permanent stale odour of a fast food outlet. Spillages gave the carpets a greasy, and occasionally crunchy, texture. Aer Shamrock existed primarily to enable ChipCo to get its executives in and, more importantly, out of Ballymagee as quickly as possible. They were immune to the sight and smell of potato crisps. The few fare-paying passengers were forced to endure them.

The forward half of the aeroplane was plush by comparison. In the back sat the non-ChipCo travellers, a predictable gathering of the people most likely to be found on any transport in or out of rural Ireland. Amongst them there was usually a priest, sometimes a nun, inevitably a student with a rucksack and a fat, rich American seeking his roots. There might well be a farmer who wore the expression of a man bitterly missing his pigs, or a woman looking twice her age and festooned with children from the age of seven downwards with hardly a year between them.

Up front, on the first-class side of the shamrock divide, drinks were served with ice. The stewardess opened the bottles for you instead of leaving you to struggle for yourself, gave you more than a passing glance, and tried to pretend that flying with this airline was a pleasure. There were free copies of the Dublin newspapers, and the annual report of the ChipCo Corporation, in case you couldn't find anything more tedious to read.

Kathy McGuinness did not bother with any of them. Instead, she pressed the button above her seat to summon attention. With impatience written bold across her face, a surly girl ambled reluctantly from the plane's galley, where Kathy had noticed her making a sneaky coffee for the young steward past whom she had been assiduously squeezing herself throughout the flight, far more often than mere duty required her to.

'How long to landing?' Kathy asked.

'Oh, not long. Nothing to worry about,' the girl replied, mindlessly mouthing words of reassurance as she had been taught to do.

'I'm not worried. I just want to know how long so I've time to get changed before landing.'

'I'll ask the pilot.' The stewardess sighed, and went to open the door which divided the cockpit from the cabin. Dropping all pretence of a cultured accent, she shouted, ''Ow long?'

'It's blowing a bastard and a half down there,' came the non-aeronautical reply. 'It's right across the bloody runway. I'm not landing in this. She'll bounce all over the bloody place. I'll go round a couple of times, see if the wind drops. Say fifteen minutes.'

The stewardess closed the door, switched on the shallow smile and turned on the patronising voice. 'The pilot says we are on schedule and expects us to be safely on the ground in fifteen minutes.'

Kathy tried to read the *Irish Times* but was distracted by the stewardess's watchful eyes which were once again fixed on her, as they had been for much of the flight. Their expression was critical, thought Kathy, and it made her feel uncomfortable, as if she shouldn't be up here at the front of the plane but at the back with the rabble. Mind you, she admitted to herself, it wasn't often that a young woman's travelling companion, strapped safely into the seat next to her, was a scuffed black guitar case. Up front, she presumed, it would usually be leather briefcases and not instrument carriers. And certainly the front cabin customers, who were usually drawn from the upper managerial ranks of ChipCo Corporation, did not usually dress in revealingly short denim skirts, black tights and boots, or wear black canvas combat jackets. They were used to seeing a bit of tailoring in first class, with neatly cut and combed hair, not a floppy mass of jet black curls that went halfway down a girl's back. A nice, tight cut, shaped to the head, was more the sort of thing, and a skirt that came decently down the leg and didn't cause the wide-eyed young steward to make four unnecessary visits with the duty-free trolley.

Fifteen minutes to landing. Kathy decided it was time for her to change and unbuckled the seatbelt holding the guitar case firmly in place. She undid the catches, and as she did so the stewardess unclipped her own belt and came towards her.

'I'm sorry,' said the girl vacantly, 'but the playing of instruments isn't allowed.'

'Why not?'

The stewardess looked blank then replied, 'Because it might interfere with the aircraft's navigation system, I suppose.'

'Lucky then, isn't it,' replied Kathy, with a laugh, 'that I didn't bring the drums as well? Or the poor confused pilot might keep us up here going round in circles forever.' She opened the case, trying hard to keep her face straight, and mischievously showed the contents to the girl.

'Clothes. Nothing but clothes!' Unsmiling, she went back to her seat. The stewardess wasn't used to this sort of thing in first class. ChipCo management usually flew with tidy cabin luggage which fitted standard-sized overhead lockers and came in either brown or black leather with polished brass fittings.

The plane juddered as it hit turbulence and Kathy McGuinness imagined the pilot summoning up the pluck to get this heap down on the ground. She delved into the guitar case and grabbed a handful of clothing. God be praised, she thought, for crush-proof fabric. She got up, clutching it to her like a washerwoman trailing bits of blouse and skirt behind her, and made her way to the toilet compartment which was next to the galley where the stewardess was sitting.

The girl looked up. 'There are smoke detectors in every compartment, and may I remind you that the consumption of prohibited substances is not allowed on any Aer Shamrock flight,' she said, mind and mouth on autopilot again.

'Including the in-flight food?' remarked Kathy, one eyebrow raised. She slammed the door behind her and drew the catch across. The toilet stank of piddle. With little enthusiasm she removed her shoes, skirt, tights, then her jacket and T shirt, and fumbled through the clothes to unearth a sponge bag. 'Shit!' she muttered. It was her mother's, accidentally grabbed in haste. She unzipped it and tipped the contents into the basin, staring at the expensive foundation creams, perfumes, hideously coloured lipsticks and other cosmetics which were all unfamiliar to her.

'Mother!' Kathy said to herself. 'You keep a fair old bit of kit, don't you?' She picked up a lipstick, twisted it to reveal a colour far too vivid for her, and winced as she held it up to her face. 'This may be your sort of colour, Mum, but it certainly ain't mine.' She dropped it into the waste bin. It made a heavy, metallic clunk which alerted the stewardess. There was a knock. 'Landing soon. If you'd resume your seat in the next five minutes, please.'

Kathy discarded most of the contents of the sponge bag, except for the deodorant which she quickly smudged under her arms, then started to climb into the clothes. First, new tights of a respectable beige colour, then a black skirt which had received more tailor's attention than the denim rag she had discarded. It fitted her like a dream. Then came a white, silk blouse which buttoned to the neck, on top of which she put the tidy black jacket which fastened with two brass buttons. It draped itself round her body like a second skin. Then she fumbled in the pocket and pulled out her pearls. This was the only part of her managerial uniform which she enjoyed wearing. It was a double string of the finest milky South Sea pearls, given to her by her mother on her twenty-first birthday. Strangely, although Kathy was the last woman in the world likely to enjoy such a reminder of a more decorous era in ladies' fashions, she felt secure wearing them, as if they were somehow a talisman or protective charm. Fumbling with the clasp, she was buffeted by the turbulence outside. Twice she stumbled and fell painfully against the edge of the basin.

Another bang on the door. 'Five minutes to landing. Return to your seat, please.'

Kathy rummaged through what was left in the unfamiliar sponge bag, found a brush and hastily waged war on the tangles in her hair, then swept it back and fastened it with a band till it hung down her back as neatly as a show pony's tail. Then she polished her black shoes on the paper towel, and was done.

'Please! Resume your seat. The aircraft is about to land.'

She slid back the catch and threw open the door, determined on a dramatic re-entry. As she had hoped, the stewardess's eyes opened wide, like a child who had just seen a magician pull off an amazing sleight of hand. Into the cubicle went an urchin of a girl. One wave of a magic wand and out she came a besuited young manager, perfect in every detail down to the pearls.

'Er, excuse me,' said the stewardess, with more deference than Kathy had noticed up till now, 'but you seem to have left some things in the toilet.'

'Just rubbish,' she replied, closing the guitar case. 'They can be thrown away.'

'You sure you won't be needing 'em?' the stewardess asked. 'Jesus, those clothes look as though they've still got a bit of use in 'em.'

Kathy McGuinness looked at the girl and said sadly, 'Has anyone in ChipCo ever had any use for a denim skirt?'

'But the perfume and stuff,' said the stewardess, wide-eyed. 'There's Hermès in that lot you've left on the floor. That's real pricey, that is.'

'At ChipCo, sweetheart,' said Kathy breezily, 'we just put a dab of cooking oil behind our ears, and that has to do. The Hermès is yours.'

She settled back in her seat and snapped the seat belt shut. Looking out of the window, she saw the low cloud surrounding the aeroplane as it lowered itself from the sky. The further they descended, the darker and more threatening the cloud seemed to get, until finally the plane burst through the thick cover and in the twilight she caught her first ever glimpse of Ireland. It was wet, windy and very dark. No blue hills, no emerald grass as she had imagined, just moorland as black as a tinker's kettle, like a landscape in mourning. She spotted no trees, no sheep, no fences, no walls. The only landmark was the string of overhead power lines which marched across the bog, marsh and moor, presumably towards the airport.

But as the plane descended further, she saw that the terrain was not quite as uniformly black as she had at first thought. It was criss-crossed with channels running with water or puddles the size of football pitches, and piled everywhere with lumps of black earth. Peat . . . that's what it was! Now it made sense to her. She had heard how, in Ireland, they cut lumps of earth from the ground, dried them and burnt them in the winter. That was what she must be seeing. She'd imagined the plane itself might be landing in the bog, for there was no sight of any airport, and was relieved by the heavy bump of its wheels on concrete, which she had convinced herself could just as easily have been a sickening squelch.

'Welcome to Ballymagee International Airport,' the stewardess gabbled over the public address. 'Our partner hotel here is the Crowley House Hotel where a warm welcome awaits you. Crowley's car hire have all classes of vehicles available. Please take all your belongings with you. Thank you for flying Aer Shamrock.' Click. Kathy watched her push the microphone back into its clip and then come towards her. She spoke in a half whisper.

'Did you mean it when you said you wouldn't be wanting any of the stuff you left in the lav?'

'Sure.'

' 'Cos some of it's real good. That perfume. That's *real* Hermès, you know.'

'It's Mother's, not mine. She won't miss it. And I don't care for it much.'

'Thanks, I'll have it then. You don't get many bottles of good perfume out of what they pay us here. ChipCo manager, are you?'

'What else?'

'I see a lot of people like you, coming in and out of here, and I always reckon there's two kinds of people come to Ballymagee,' the girl confided. 'There's the ChipCo people and the desperate.

Stay one and don't become the other, that's my advice. Best o' luck now, and thanks for the smellies.'

Kathy McGuinness looked out of the window as the plane taxied to a halt. It was guided to its parking place by a drenched man wearing a baseball cap from the brim of which ran a cascade of rain. He was signalling to the pilot with two orange baseball bats which he was struggling to keep vertical against the blast of the wind. A less formal announcement came over the plane's loudspeaker:

'You'll need your coats on, now!'

First mistake. Kathy had brought no overcoat, and if ever she'd needed something to protect her from an unremitting monsoon, it was when visiting Ballymagee. Rain drenched her in the short walk from the bottom of the steps across to the shed they called the terminal building. Less than a minute and the merciless dampness was through that smart suit and into the silk blouse, chilling her skin. As Kathy sprinted across the tarmac she caught sight out of the corner of her eye of one lone, relaxed cow grazing by the runway, unfazed by the roar of a departing jet. Other travellers joined her in the rush towards shelter, their booze-laden carrier bags clinking heavily as they jogged. Once or twice the wind caught the ridiculous guitar case and almost spun her right round. It had been a bloody stupid idea, bringing it in the first place, but at least she didn't have to wait for the painfully slow baggage carousel to get itself up to speed, or the even slower baggage handlers to unload the plane. In shelter now, she stood still to catch her breath. Most of the other passengers, she noticed, did not even bother to linger by the baggage reclaim. Old hands knew how long it took and instead of standing around, headed straight for the bar.

Kathy McGuinness had no clue where she might go next. She knew she had been booked into the Crowley House Hotel, and ChipCo had told her she would be met, but not by whom, where or how. A baggage trolley would have been useful but there wasn't one to be seen. To her left was a desk – Crowley's Car Hire – but it was a Sunday night and there was no one behind it. To the right was a bureau advertising trips to a local shrine where a statue of the Holy Mother was once said to have burst into tears. The distinctly unspiritual Miss McGuinness was not surprised; she thought this place would have made anyone weep. She dropped the guitar case and shivered.

Behind her was a flurry of air and a resounding bang as the glass door of the terminal hit its stop. The devout, queuing for trips to the shrine, turned to see what kind of a Coming this might be. The gale worked its way across the floor of the building, lifting paper cups and empty ChipCo crisp packets, till it blew itself out somewhere near the entrance to duty free. And blown in with the wind came a man with a green wollen hat pulled down so far over his face that he could hardly see the way forward. He had muddy, sodden plimsolls on his feet, and wore a pair of jeans which were streaked with black sludge and a flimsy sweatshirt which was ripped across the front, showing he had not the sense to wear a vest on a wet night like this. He staggered across, aided by the following wind, which forced the strong odour of farmyard ahead of him.

'Oh, bejasus! You'll be the new lady at ChipCo – Miss McGuinness,' the man gasped. 'There's you standing all alone, and me ever so late. Damn and blast it. Hi! Morrissey's Cars. I'm your chauffeur.' This was her first earful of the lilting tones of Mayo, a melodic accent with the rhythm of a calypso and the charm of angels. And on the lips of this very intense young man sounding like an Irish comic telling a joke – too Irish to be true. He dragged the hat from his head, pulling his wet brown hair with it till it stood on end, and Kathy noticed he was younger than she'd thought at first glance. About her own age, she guessed. He offered her his hand. It was smeared with grease, filthy and uninviting.

'Oh, God, I'm sorry,' the lad gabbled. 'The fan belt . . . it went just outside Michael Flann's farm – when his cows were going into milking too. And there's me, lying on me back in the road trying to fix the damned t'ing when they go galloping by, never botherin' a bit about me under the car. Jesus, I could have been trampled to death, so I could.'

'Crowley House Hotel, I think we want,' said Kathy, not taking his hand. He laughed out loud. 'Ah, yes. It's the least worst hotel in Ballymagee. I'll go and stand by for yer bags, if you like? The car's a big Volvo, green. If you try and get in on the right you'll have no luck. Handle's lost. So go round, will yer?'

'There are no other bags,' Kathy explained. 'Just this case.'

'A guitar? Now what's a young ChipCo manager doing landing at Ballymagee with a guitar and nothing else to her name? Sure, it'll be all over the town by the morning. You'll be the talk of the place. If I were you, when you get to the Crowley House, you just tell 'em yer bags are comin' on later.'

The lad picked up the guitar case and led the way to the entrance.

'Do you pluck it or plug it in?' he asked as they walked.

'Sorry?'

'The guitar. Is it one o' them acoustic t'ings, or electric?'

'Neither,' explained Kathy, smiling, enjoying the melodic chime of the lad's accent. 'It was the only case I could find at short notice. Mother's gone abroad and taken all the suitcases. I didn't realise till I had to leave for the airport.'

'Well, there's me thinking that all women concentrated on nothing else but packing for weeks before they went anywhere,' said the man incredulously. 'And here's you, lookin' for a case while the plane's standing on the runway, waiting to take off.'

'Depends how keen you are to go, I suppose,' replied Kathy, quietly.

'Well, anyway, it's good to see a nice, fresh face in Ballymagee, miss. And to be sure you're very welcome.' He gave her a broad grin, which made her feel better about life.

The car was a bit of a disappointment even by Kathy's easy-going standards. In London, she had been used to the occasional ride in one of ChipCo's Jaguars; a Volvo with the rear bumper missing, one side mirror hanging like the limp wing of a shot bird and a windscreen wiper which was missing its companion on the passenger side, was a new experience for Kathy. The only smart thing about the vehicle was the white lettering which announced *Morrissey's Cars* down the side. And the colour! It was the vilest shade of green, enough to make a sailor sick.

The driver went to open the boot and had to bang down hard on the lid before it would open. Only after struggling and scraping could he get the guitar case inside.

'It's these spare tyres,' he explained. 'I picked up a set goin' cheap the other day. Damn' good tyres. If I can find a car that'll fit 'em, I'll buy it, so I will. And then I can have two cars on the road.'

'Bit Irish, isn't it? Buying the tyres before you buy the car?' Kathy enquired.

'Irish? I'm pleased to hear you say that it sounds Irish. Thank you very much,' he replied, as if grateful for the remark.

'Is this the only car?'

'At the moment it is,' he admitted.

'So Morrissey's Cars, plural, is a bit of an overstatement, then?'

'You could say that. But I thought at the time that if the feller just painted "car", I'd have to go back later to have the "s" put on if I got another as well, see? And since I've plans for this business, I thought I might as well have it done there and then. Even if it is a bit of a lie, God forgive me.' This was getting Irish beyond belief, Kathy thought.

'Plans?'

'Sure, I've got them. There's no decent taxi in town 'cos most people have their own cars. But there's visitors lookin' for lifts all the time. Smart folks like you. Executives.'

It came as a shock to hear herself described as an executive. It felt like a tight suit of clothes or new leather boots which pinched.

'So long as ChipCo's here,' the driver continued, 'there'll always be some money to be made in Ballymagee.' Kathy reached out for the handle of the front passenger door but he got there before her.

'There's a knack to it. I'm lookin' for a spare but yer man over the hill who might have another'll charge the earth, so he will. It's cheaper just to give it a twist, if you know how. Anyway, I guessed not many passengers would want to travel in the front. They'd prefer to ride in state in the back, wouldn't they?'

'Travel sickness,' Kathy explained, and got into the front seat.

The driver churned at the engine and it showed no sign of life. It was as dead and as damp as the bog around them. He persevered, unfazed. As the wind buffeted the car, the multi-coloured rosary beads draped round the rear-view mirror rattled, as did two Guinness bottles which were lurking on the floor between the driver's and the rear seat. Against all the odds the engine fired. A cloud of thick, blue smoke briefly filled the view from the rear window before it was snatched back by the gale, and then the car pulled away.

'Been here before?' asked the driver.

'Never,' replied Kathy.

'It's a grand place. The people are grand . . . the music's grand. Would you like some music? It's half an hour at least to the Crowley House. It's not quite ten miles but the road's awful bad. I'm trying to work out from your guitar case if you'd prefer the rock or the folk.'

'Neither, really.'

'Well then, shall we have a little bit of old Ireland, eh?' He pushed a tape into the cassette player and waggled the volume control up and down to get rid of the crackle. The tape was wrinkled but through the distortion a wavering flute could be discerned, playing a predictably familiar tune.

'*Danny Boy*! My song,' said the driver, beaming. 'My mother, God bless her, sang it to me when I was a kid. All day long.'

How corny, thought Kathy.

'Is that your name – Danny?'

'Wasn't then, I think she just liked the tune. But the name's sort of stuck. Danny Morrissey – that's me.'

The rain was easing and Kathy tried to make out some features in the passing landscape, but all she saw through the raindrops on the window was black bog merging seamlessly with darkening sky, and tidy piles of cut peat standing guard by the road side.

'It's grim this side of the hill, sure it is,' explained Danny. 'But on the other side, well, that's where the money's made.'

'It's where the potatoes grow, I assume?' said Kathy.

'To be sure they do. Spuds as far as the eye can see. Two thousand acres of the blessed things. All sitting under that soil waiting for the day when they go into that factory of yours to be made in crisps. Do you like crisps?'

'Do I have to?'

'Everyone here loves crisps. Even if they don't eat 'em. They think they're grand. Best thing that ever happened to Bally-magee.'

The faltering tape wavered its way through *Danny Boy*, the rosary rattled, the Guinness bottles clinked together and Danny's Irish accent grew thicker with every word. Too thick sometimes, Kathy decided. It made her wonder who this creature sitting next to her might really be. Was she safe? She listened to more of his banter. It was too much, too Irish; like getting into a

London cab and finding a Beefeater behind the wheel. The trouble was that she had grown up unable to fathom anything about men and so found it impossible to work out if this driver was an amiable fool or a risky travelling companion. Certainly he was filthy and malodorous, but didn't his friendly eyes make up for all that? Deciding about men had always been her problem.

'Are those the lights of Ballymagee?' she asked, after about fifteen minutes.

'They are, yes, the lights of Ballymagee. Quarter of an hour and we'll be there, miss. Would you like any more music?' The tape had finally expired halfway through *The Isle of Inishfree* and she spotted Danny's hand moving dangerously close to a tape of Irish tenors singing *Songs of the Homeland*.

'I'll skip on the music, thanks.'

'A drink? There's a bottle of Guinness in the back?'

'Nothing, thanks.'

'A smoke? Would yer ever like a smoke?'

'I'm fine.'

Having been mistaken about men before, Kathy gave some thought to the nature of this driver for no other reason than to pass the time. Something about him didn't add up. If he'd shaved and washed his hair, got some of that grime off his hands and put on a set of clean clothes, he would be a halfway decent-looking bloke. She imagined him in well-cut jeans, Calvin Klein or something like that, and enjoyed the thought. She dared to take a fleeting glance at the rip across the front of his sweatshirt. Nice chest, young and fit. And no hint of the premature beer belly that was a sure sign of indulgence in many young Irish men.

'Oh, God!' Danny cried, steering the car towards the grass verge and switching off the engine. 'That bloody belt's gone again. Damn it! The ignition light's on. Look at the damned t'ing.'

'Won't the battery get us into town?' asked Kathy, nervously.

'Most batteries would but not this one. You see, I bought it off a farmer and it's got as much juice in it as a dried plum. The headlights wouldn't outshine a candle by the time we hit town. I had to bump start her this morning to get her going. Damned t'ing! I'll have to get out and fix it.'

'Would it help if I said a prayer?' joked Kathy, reaching for the rosary beads. Danny didn't smile. He opened the door and got out. Just as he was abreast of the headlight, she heard a yelp like a pup's which had just had its tail trodden on, and saw Danny falling head over heels by the side of the car, followed by a splash as his body fell into a puddle. She had to waggle furiously at her door handle for some time in order to get out, but he was still lying there, groaning, and soaked to the skin, when eventually she got to him. Kathy put out her hand to pull him to his feet.

'If I ain't had it up to here with this mother-fuckin' country . . .' her mouth dropped open, but not at the language '. . . I'll get out of this goddamn' place as fast as I can!' Then he fell silent, suddenly realising not what he had said but how he had said it. The accent had gone. The Irish had vanished as fast as a glass of Guinness down the gullet of a parched drunk. There was no trace of it, no shamrock on the breath, no blarney on the tongue, no lilt, no melody. All that was left was pure mid-American.

'What's happened to Danny Boy, then?' asked Kathy, cheekily. 'Turned into a bit of a cowboy, has he?'

'Ah, shit,' replied Danny, wiping his eyes, all trace of his brogue evaporated. 'First job for Morrissey's Cars and I have to blow it. Sorry, ma'am. You'll have guessed by now I'm new around here.'

Kathy grinned. 'I thought you might be. I didn't want to say anything but the turn for Ballymagee was half a mile back. *I* worked that one out by reading it. I was giving *you* the benefit of the doubt. Open the boot, please, there's a good lad.'

Kathy opened the guitar case and, having felt around in it for a while, pulled out their saviour: an international mobile phone, a status symbol in ChipCo.

Getting assistance took some time, especially on a Sunday night. Danny remembered that O'Mahoney's Garage in the town had a breakdown truck but when Kathy tried to discover the number, directory enquiries only had a number for a 'Flynn's Garage' listed in Ballymagee. When she got through to Flynn's Garage it was explained to her by a fast-talking woman that this was indeed O'Mahoney's Garage but the phone number was under Flynn because Gabrielle O'Mahoney had been left the garage by her father, God rest his soul, and had gone and married Dennis Flynn with her poor dad's body hardly cold. *That* Flynn, he'd had eyes on that garage for years, it was explained to Kathy as if she were a family confidante, and had his feet under the table before the coffin was out of the door. Anyway, he had the phone put in his name 'cos it cost him nothin', but he didn't have the name repainted over the garage because he was too damned mean. Now how could they help her?

Neither Kathy nor Danny was quite certain how to describe their precise location, although there was the sign that Kathy had spotted half a mile back which gave a good clue. Having guessed where they might be, the woman then announced the breakdown-truck driver had settled down for the night in a pub and extraction might take some time. And even then there was no certainty of his being capable of getting behind the wheel of a truck, even assuming she could find him. The woman thought he might be there within the hour, or he might not. If she couldn't find him she'd come out herself, provided she could find a bit of rope to tow them back to the town. Kathy thanked her and told her she was very much looking forward to seeing either of them.

'Do you want to walk?' asked Danny. 'It's a straight line into town from that signpost. An hour's walk, though.'

'Nah, haven't got the shoes for it.'

'I'll come with you,' he offered.

'And carry me?'

They sat in silence for a moment.

'I've got some more tapes . . .'

'Please, no. Anything but the *Isle of Inishfree*,' Kathy replied. 'Have you got any Billy Joel?' Danny shook his head. 'There's a bottle of Guinness, if you'd like?' he offered. 'Funny stuff, but you kind of get used to it. I'm more a Michelob man myself. Always drank that at home. Or Miller Lite.'

'Miller Lite!' said Kathy, growing animated. 'Now there's a real drink. Colder the better.'

'Don't get carried away,' warned Danny. 'There's two bottles of well-shaken, lukewarm Guinness in the back and no chance of so much as a sniff of a Budweiser for at least fifty miles.'

Five more minutes passed. Danny was still not saying much, but at least what little he did say was no longer cloaked in that phoney Irish accent. The shamrock on his tongue had finally curled up and died.

'So where are you really from?' asked Kathy after a while.

'Kentucky, USA. Louisville. Birthplace of Colonel Sanders of Fried Chicken fame. Muhammed Ali, three times world heavyweight champion. And Tom Cruise. And me, of course,' he boasted. 'Polk. Raymond Polk. At your service, ma'm.'

'It's none of my business,' Kathy replied, 'but as we might be waiting some time, if you feel you want to explain your presence here, don't let me stop you. And I think we'll have it in American. We've had enough blarney for one night.'

'Well, it's like this. Louisville is a great place providing your dad's not a hot-shot lawyer who finds God, joins the Baptist

Church, takes the vows, then two years later is found in bed with the wife of the Police Chief on the eve of the christening of said chief's first grand-daughter. Goddamn' nuisance fathers, sometimes.'

'I wouldn't know,' said Kathy, quietly.

'So since the name Polk will only ever be worth so much shit in Louisville for years to come,' Danny continued, 'I decided to get the hell out of it. Head east . . . New York . . . Boston. Rich, bloated, self-possessed, so pleased with themselves if they could only get up their own assholes they'd be the happiest people on earth. Understand? However – and this is the big one – boy, have they got money. There are *slums* in Baltimore that make Louisville look run down by comparison. So my thinking goes like this: start a business, rub up against money, hope some of that money rubs off against you. Good plan, eh?'

'All except one thing,' observed Kathy. 'We are sitting in he most run-down car in the world in the bleakest spot this side of the Urals and I didn't hear any of that come into your scenario.'

'That's because you don't understand how much the Americans love the Irish.'

'Or because you're not explaining it to me.'

'It's all down to conscience, see? All those Irish emigrants, generations back, landed on the east coast of the USA. Their descendants made a pile and still feel they owe the Irish something. It's all mixed up in their heads. Some of them have their hearts in the right place, some are just crazy bastards who think that by paying for a killing in Northern Ireland they're doing the homeland some kind of favour. They're really sad. I'm not part of that.'

Kathy was shaking her head. 'You've lost me again.'

'Simple. Second part of the Great Plan. I become an Irishman!'

'An Irishman?'

'Get a bit of Irish. It's the way to get on over there. Chairmen of big companies will kill to get an Irish secretary. If you're called Siobhan, you're through the door before they ask if you can work the computers. It's like a fashion accessory, having something Irish about you. Smart, see.'

'So, when you've got this smart, desirable Irish gloss, what do you do with it?'

'Morrissey's Cars!' he said, as if it were the most obvious thing in the world. 'I want a big fleet of cars in all the East Coast cities: New York, Washington, Boston, Baltimore. That's what this is all about. With Danny Morrissey at the head of it all. A real big shot.' He put the bottle to his lips and took a deep, confident draught of the Guinness to wet his lips, dried by the blast of what Kathy thought a load of hot air.

'Why can't you have *Polk's* cars?' she asked crisply. 'Who cares what the cars are called?'

'I've told you . . . it's the Irish, the blarney, call it what you will. If you've got a bit of it about you, you're one step ahead of the rest.'

'Sorry,' said Kathy. 'But where I come from, we tell jokes about the Irish.'

'Then more fool you,' he replied, lecturing her now. 'I don't mean no disrespect, but Ireland is no joke and if you believe it is you'd better do some deep thinking before you go and sit behind that big desk at the ChipCo factory. This is serious stuff round here. Have you heard of the Celtic Tiger? The economic pussy cat that's been quietly sleeping by the peat fire for most of the last fifty years and has suddenly woken up to let the world know that it's alive and roaring. Hey, this country is booming, living standards have never been so high. And sure, there's people still living with a pig in the back yard but it's because they want to and not because they can't afford to go to the butcher to buy their bacon. Jokes about the Irish don't work any more.' He paused. 'Of course, I know Ballymagee's a bit different, because of the factory and all that.'

'Different, how?'

'Well, let's say that if the rest of Ireland is roaring like a tiger, this place is bellowing like a pride of lions. You'll find out.'

'So what do I call you, if I'm ever in one of your cars again?' she asked, intrigued more by Danny than Ballymagee.

'You can call me *Mr* Morrissey when we're out on business. Nice and formal, very businesslike. And I'm Danny all other times.'

'And what *other* times might there be?'

'Well, the one thing I've learned about this place is that it's like the weather. You never know what's going to turn up.' And he turned and gave her a broad grin.

Through the steamed-up windscreen Kathy spotted the head-lights of a car, approaching very slowly.

'You didn't explain why you're in Ballymagee?' she said, still trying to unravel the enigma.

'Because there's one charter flight a week into here from Boston,' he said with a sigh. 'Bringing the pilgrims to the shrine. It's the cheapest fare across the Atlantic. I could afford to get this far and no further.'

'Do you plan to stay?'

'Sure. This is a great place for me to establish myself. Learn the nuts and bolts of running taxis. And there's ChipCo. All you executives coming in and out all the time. I guessed you'd need transport now and again.'

'And what do they call you in the town? Are you Danny or Raymond?'

'Oh, there I'm Danny. They think it's a bit of a joke. I've only been here a month but they keep trying to teach me these Irish sayings and I take it all in. I was in the pub last night and this feller comes up to me . . .' she noticed the brogue was infecting his tongue again. '. . . and he asked me if I'd heard the expression, "Fur coat and margarine sandwiches". Know what it means?'

Kathy shook her head.

'Delusions of grandeur! She's all fur coat and margarine sandwiches. Get it?'

She nodded

'He's a daft bugger of a gobshite. Understand? All mouth and guzz-eyed? Gobshite – he taught me that. And guzz-eyed. Great words, huh?' He turned to Kathy, carried away by his enthusiasm for the new-found language. 'Do you know what a hand shandy is?' Before the words had left his lips he regretted them. He blushed, words of apology pouring from his mouth. 'Geez! Not the sort of thing to ask a young lady you don't know when she's all on her own in a car with you. I'm sorry.'

Kathy noticed he was blushing. 'And are you making a good job it so far – becoming an Irishman?' she asked.

'I get my leg pulled, I have to admit. They say they've never heard Irish like it before. Some say it's an accent all of my own makin'. Well, it is, isn't it? I'm an American.'

A car pulled up alongside them and out of it poured a large, middle-aged woman, closely resembling a bull and carrying a length of rope. With barely a word of introduction, she got down on the wet ground as if she did this every day of her life, threaded the rope round the least weak point of the car, and tied a knot which would have held the *Titanic* against a harbour wall.

And that was Kathy McGuinness's big entrance into Ballymagee. She arrived outside the Crowley House Hotel, two hours too late for dinner, hauled ignominiously by Mrs Flynn's old Vauxhall. Even so, Danny's first duty on arrival was to run round to the passenger side and open the door for her to get out. He carried her guitar case to the reception and told her there would be no charge. She felt in her pocket and stuffed a twenty-pound note into his hand.

'I didn't catch your name, miss. It might be useful if you travel with Morrissey's Cars again.'

'Fat chance,' she replied. 'But Kathy McGuinness.'

'Kathy!' Danny beamed. 'Short for Kathleen, I bet?'

And the last she saw of him that night he was tripping lightly down the steps of the Crowley House Hotel like a puppy who had found a bone, singing to himself, ' "I'll drive you home again Kathleen . . ." '

2

Life had been much simpler for Kathy Foley when she did not have to pretend she was called Miss McGuinness, when she had to tell no lies nor weigh every word in case her true identity was revealed in an unguarded moment. Anyway, McGuinness seemed such a formal name, stiff and starchy, not like her at all. But it had been her own silly idea, she was forced to admit, and now she must live with the consequences.

One morning, six weeks before, when she was still Miss Foley, Kathy's dreams were shattered by an insistent, rasping buzz in her head. Still half asleep, she struggled to place the sound on the musical scale. A D perhaps, or an E – certainly not a middle C, she thought, muddled by the cruelly intrusive sound. Disorientated, she thought it might be the first note of a Billy Joel tune, one of the songs she always played to send herself to sleep. *Piano Man* perhaps? She loved that song, and every time she heard the introduction wanted to grab a harmonica and join in. She liked the mouth organ; it was simple yet powerful. Dylan had inspired a generation with his. What else could you carry in your pocket that might one day change the world?

The note that was ringing in her head grew louder, broke off, and then returned with more ferocity. Now it came in short bursts, which hurt more. Wide awake by then, she suddenly realised it was the front door.

It was 8.30 and she had overslept. Not even the rumble of the London rush-hour traffic making its way through Earls Court had woken her. She pulled back the curtain and saw, five floors below, her mother's large metallic-bronze Mercedes blocking the road; the arrogant, uniformed driver refusing to move an inch to allow a harassed woman with an overfull carload of children to get through to the school round the corner. The buzzer went again. Kathy grabbed the handset which was part of the remote control lock on the shared front door.

'Hi, Mum! Sorry,' she shouted, trying to sound cheerful and alert, and pressed the button to unlock the front door. She now had the time it took her mother to ascend five floors in which to look as though she had been up for hours awaiting her arrival. It would have been futile to attempt deception, no point to it at all – Mother was never fooled. Kathy opened the front door of her flat and heard a voice on the stairs.

'Put everything back fifteen, will you? I'm going to be late,' Kathy heard her bark down her mobile phone. 'And ring my daughter's office and tell them she will be late in too.'

'Oh, Mother!' gasped Kathy as she came into view on the landing. 'You're *not* wearing fur?'

'Just a little, darling. I do love it.' She stroked the brown pelt of some endangered species which decorated the collar of her woollen suit. 'And everybody these days assumes it's fake. Anyway, I didn't have it killed – it was dead already. All I did was take it off the peg.' Pure Mother, thought Kathy. So long as she's one step removed from the slaughter, anything's all right by her.

Leonora Foley, the sort of woman who expected mountains to come to her rather than to climb them herself, arrived on the top landing feeling breathless, possibly due to the heavy make-up caked on her skin.

'When your daughter's all grown up, you don't expect to have to get her out of bed in the morning,' she announced frostily, foregoing any pleasantries. Kathy headed for the bathroom.

'Grab yourself some coffee, Mum,' she shouted above the hissing of the shower. Her mother took a glance at the unwashed mugs lying on the table and ignored the offer.

'It's a tip! A bloody tip,' Leonora Foley declared. 'Do you want me to get contract cleaners in for you or something?' She strode across the sitting room, stumbled over a fallen music stand and nearly put the spike of one of her heels through a CD which was lying, without its case, on the floor. She picked it up as if it was excrement and held it at arm's length while she tried to read the title. 'Billy who?' she muttered, disgusted, before tiptoeing round the room with no comprehension of life in the wilder environment her daughter inhabited; she trod lightly as if this were a jungle with danger lurking beneath every footfall. Eventually, she came to the wardrobe.

'I'll get you something out for the office, darling,' she announced and pulled on the door. Unexpectedly, a heavy black guitar case fell from a great height across her ankles and Leonora gave a squeal. Then she was assaulted by a cascade of sweaters which fell in a heap at her feet. From the top shelf slithered a tangle of hi-fi cables, a shower of unboxed cassettes and something a mother was surprised to see in her grown up daughter's wardrobe – a poster of a pop star. By the time the avalanche had stopped, Leonora looked as if she had been drafted unwillingly into stocktaking day in a charity shop.

'Is this that Billy chap again?' she asked, reaching for the poster. 'He's a bit old for you, darling, isn't he?' she observed, holding her head on one side, trying to assess the figure with the dark glasses, close-cropped hair and beard.

'He's only fifty,' Kathy responded. 'Just about old enough to be my father,' she added mischievously.

'Leave off, will you?' said her mother, and threw the poster on to the bed.

Kathy started to sing the first few notes of *Piano Man*, but broke off when she sensed her mother's frosty mood. She had made the mistake of mentioning the 'f' word: father.

'Billy's great, even if he is a bit old,' said Kathy, trying to break the frigid atmosphere. 'Have you heard the way he sings? Sometimes there's so much feeling in the way he says the words, it's as if he's aching to tell you he loves you. Or that's what I think anyway. It's like he means every word.'

'Darling, I've had enough real live men tell me they ache for me,' replied Leonora haughtily, 'and I'll tell you this: none of them *ever* means it. Anyway, a young woman your age is better off getting the real thing quavering in their ear, instead of hearing it all from a loudspeaker.'

'Is this the time-you-settled-down speech, Mother?'

'What the hell do you think you're wearing?' Leonora asked, suddenly noticing the concertina creases in Kathy's black suit which had been lying, unfolded, on the back of a chair. 'You can use my account at Harrods any time. Get some new stuff. You look like a bundle of rags!'

'This "bundle of rags" is the last lot of stuff I bought on your account, Mother dear.'

'Well, if you cared for them a bit better, they might not look like a set of workmen's overalls. I hate to sound like the Chief Executive right now, but looks count for something at ChipCo. I speak not only as your mother but as your boss. Get yourself tidied up!'

Kathy drew a broad-toothed comb through the tangles in her long, black hair and with the other hand drew up the zip on a hastily unearthed and less creased skirt.

'What day is it?' she asked her mother, confident that Leonora would have forgotten as usual.

'I'm fifteen minutes late,' she replied impatiently. 'And it's Thursday. Now move!'

'Just Thursday?' asked Kathy.

'All day!' replied her mother, and together they left the flat.

No sooner had the doors of the Mercedes closed than Leonora Foley barked into the carphone, showing it no mercy. She placed a call to European HQ in London which was less than half a mile away, almost within strident shouting distance. She summoned accountants, executives, brand managers and personnel to an unscheduled meeting at eleven that morning. Then she rang the press office and told them to release the news along the lines she had discussed with them, but not before eleven-thirty, and she wanted to vet the press release herself.

'Make the coffee too, will you?' Kathy put in sarcastically, knowing it was the sort of remark only a daughter could get away with. Unabashed, Leonora continued to bark into the phone. She would only give one interview, and it *had* to be to a network. She would give American interviews in the late afternoon, allowing for the time difference.

'America? Do I get to know this news?' enquired Kathy, when her mother eventually pushed the off button. 'Or shall I wait for the press release to find out what my own mother's up to?'

'We did a deal,' snapped Leonora. 'I got you a job at ChipCo *if* you promised there would be a glass wall between us professionally. I can do without any arguments, today of all days. You have made me fifteen, if not twenty minutes late already. You'll be called to the meeting like everybody else and will find out then.'

'Mummy,' said Kathy girlishly, 'you said "today of all days". What day is it?'

'Thursday,' replied Leonora, crisply. 'Thursday, all bloody day.' For five minutes, neither of them spoke.

'How are things in world-wide development anyway?' asked Leonora when she had recovered her temper.

'Pretty much global and developing nicely,' replied Kathy cheekily.

'It's where I started,' said her mother wistfully, a reminiscent smile being her first visible emotion of the day, apart from anger.

'And look at you now,' Kathy replied.

They hardly said another word to each other for the rest of the journey, Kathy reckoning it was best to keep quiet in case that hideous fur on her mother's collar started to stand on end and the old cat raised its hackles for a proper fight.

These all too frequent moments, when her mother distanced herself, made Kathy yearn for a father to talk to. Never having known him, she now had an imaginary dad: he was as real to her as if he were alive and seeing her every day. She held conversations with him, asked his advice, sometimes felt his arms reach out to hug her. She even knew how he looked. He had wide eyes, like Billy.

His real identity was a mystery, a secret which Leonora Foley had never revealed to anyone, not even to Kathy. Despite the insistent probing of the curious press, no hint was ever dropped, nor any clue ever given. No one came forward to claim the distinction of having melted the icy exterior of one of the coldest woman in business. Was it any wonder, thought Kathy, that if she came across an older man who spoke to her, even if it was a pop star, she would listen? And a dad would never have forgotten what day it was, as her mother seemed to have done.

On the top storey of the chilly, glass-clad ChipCo building, set symbolically above all the people who worked there, was the boardroom. By contrast with the ChipCo products which were snazzily packaged in bright, bold colours – glossy little packets of comfort food screaming at you for attention – the boardroom was an uncomfortable, sombre place designed as if to some rule that stated the more frivolous the product, the bleaker the headquarters must be. The cold, pinched atmosphere there was catching and staff thought twice about cracking a joke in case the person above didn't get it and marked them down.

Two suited men pressed their faces to the window. The younger, more fresh-faced of the two looked eager, jabbing his nose against the glass like a child peering into a sweet shop window. The older man glanced at his watch and then looked down at the street, thirteen floors below.

'That's her, in the bronze Mercedes,' he said, in a rather fey voice. '"Boadicea's Chariot" we call it.' He wiped his neatly trimmed moustache on an ironed and perfumed white handkerchief pulled from the breast pocket of his close-fitting grey suit. 'Bloody invincible, she is. I've sat next to her in this boardroom for fifteen years, worked alongside her for thirty, and I've still to get one over on her.'

'I didn't know, Mr Metcalfe, that Chief Executives and their deputies were in some kind of contest?' put in the younger man daringly.

'You're new here, Toby dear. You'll learn. But you're right, it's not a contest. Nevertheless she always wins, game or no. And no bad thing either. She's made some smart moves over the years, has Leonora Foley, and that's why we've all got good jobs today. But just because your pocket's full of loot, doesn't mean your balls don't hurt when someone's twisting them off!'

Ted Metcalfe flashed the younger man a broad, salacious grin, and went and sat in the chair next to the one which Leonora would occupy. For safety, Toby stayed by the window, watching the car door open. He saw Leonora get out, pausing theatrically for a moment like a diva making her entrance. Then she strode across the pavement and he lost sight of her, but reflected in the glass building opposite saw that the door had been pulled open by a uniformed man standing to attention, as if she were royalty.

'Some woman!' he gasped. 'Just look at the way she strides into the building. Powerful or what?'

'Power? That woman's got so much of it she shits authority. Make sure it doesn't land on you,' warned Metcalfe.

'Why are you telling me this?' asked Toby, surprised at his boss's frankness. 'I'm just the new lad in the press office, and here's the deputy chief executive rubbishing his boss to me.'

'Two reasons. First, because you are an honest-looking kind of lad. I like that.' Ted gave Toby another flash of that louche grin of his. 'And second, because it's all about to change. There's a glimmer of hope that my life might be peaceful for the first time in thirty years when that woman finally fucks off. So what I think about her won't much matter any more. It will be old news, and the press office isn't into that, is it? Anyway, this is off the record, understand? If one word of this leaks I'll set *her* on to you. Ever had a Dobermann hanging off your arse?'

Toby turned back to the window and looked down at the street. Only when Leonora was in the building and the glass door had closed behind her, and not until then, did the other door to the car open and out stepped a younger woman.

'Hey, who's the bird?' asked Toby. 'I'm sorry, the young woman,' he added apologetically.

'Some fuckin' press man you are! Has she got black hair, clothes like a bundle of washing, and a vacant expression on her face?' The younger man nodded. 'Then that is Miss Kathy Foley, daughter of our beloved leader.'

'So *that's* what she looks like. I've heard talk about her. Great to work for, apparently. They say there's a real buzz in that department of hers. Global Development, isn't it?'

'Global shit all, that's what she is,' sneered Metcalfe. 'I got that bloody job for her to get her mother off my back. Ever heard of positive discrimination? Nepotism? Well, that's what it looks like when it's on its hind legs.'

'Looks quite good fun to me,' said Toby, watching Kathy every step of the way. He noticed she did not have the self-assured walk of her mother and, rather than brave the marbled hallway, took the more modest side entrance.

'She may have talent, she may not. But I don't intend to let her or anybody else here find out. If anyone thinks I'm seeing the back of one bitch, only to have another member of the family move up a rung, they're wrong! She's being groomed by her mother. Moulded into her own image. Mother, you see, can't believe that anything as perfect as herself could ever again sit at the head of this table, so she's hoping to create her own double. Trouble is, the daughter's as much like her mother as Mickey Mouse is Pythagoras. Run a business? The girl couldn't run for a fuckin' bus. Best someone trips her up before she tries and does some real damage.'

'But she can't be any threat to you,' Toby remarked. 'If I may say so, sir.'

'You flatter me, dear boy. But she's a Foley, and that's that. One of them is enough for one lifetime.' He changed the subject, sensing the aura which heralded Leonora's arrival on the top floor. 'I hope that press release is just what she wants,' remarked Metcalfe, glancing at the paper in the younger man's hand. 'Or you may find your reproductive ability severely curtailed. If you're into that sort of thing.'

The lift's arrival could just be heard through the closed boardroom doors, which then blew open as if a whirlwind had pushed through them. Leonora Foley appeared towing behind her a frightened secretary to whom she was giving dictation on the move. Somehow, thought Toby, the room seemed bigger for her being there, as if some force field accompanied her. It was as if the whole building had suddenly been plugged into it.

'Morning, Ted,' she said vaguely in Metcalfe's direction and blew him a half-hearted kiss. 'And who the hell are you?' she demanded, staring at the younger man.

'This is Toby from the press office,' said Metcalfe. 'Don't they breed them young and lovely these days?'

'For God's sake, leave him alone,' sighed Leonora, and turned to Toby. 'I read the press release in the lift. *Two* spelling mistakes. Rewrite it!' She crumpled it into a ball and flung it across the table at him.

The young man's eyes became blurred, unable to focus on the screwed-up press release over which he'd slaved for hours. His only thought, the one which caused his scrotum to shrivel until it was microscopic was that she was going to meet the press while she was wearing fur. Real, bloody fur!

Kathy's arrival at Global Development, by contrast, was like a warm ray of sunshine emerging from behind dark clouds. Her presence was not electric like her mother's. Or if it was, it was more electric blanket than paint stripper. Someone once said that working alongside Kathy was like having a big sister around; there was always a joke, a laugh to lighten the depressing chore of selling potato crisps to countries of the world which didn't want them, didn't need them or couldn't afford them. So, in the interests of raising life on to a more enjoyable plane, and with Kathy's collusion, the rules were broken in Global Development. Rules about not having their own coffee machine, putting down their own carpet, playing music while they worked – Billy Joel songs formed the background to many a working day in Global – all the dictats forbidding such things were ignored. Global had its own table in the staff restaurant from which giggles and merriment flowed endlessly, unlike the other tables where the staff dined quietly, like nuns. That was why everyone wanted to work in Global.

'Don't forget you've got to be upstairs at eleven, Kathy,' shouted he secretary fondly.

'And don't you forget it's Thursday, Ellie,' Kathy called back excitedly. At that moment a depressed-looking youth scurried in, his head low.

'Peter, bad night?' Kathy asked as he brushed past.

'I'm fine, thanks,' he replied, and took off his coat before settling down to work. She was worried about him; she worried about all of them.

Slowly the room filled with young, fresh faces – Kathy's international sales team. She knew them all, treated them as individuals, had the unbusinesslike habit of getting to know them as if they were brothers and sisters in a family she never had. Telephones were lifted and conversations begun in Portuguese, Spanish, German and Italian. 'Any luck, Kevin?' asked Kathy of a lad who sat chewing his pencil, struggling.

'It's difficult,' he replied. 'I'm trying, but I don't think we're ever going to sell many in Rwanda.'

Kathy patted him on the back and gave him a smile. 'I'd go for the easier ones first. Try Oslo.'

Ellie the secretary interrupted Kathy by prodding her in the side and nodding at her excitedly. It was the cue for the smile to melt from Kathy's face and she assumed a look of mock indignation. Conversations dried, telephones were replaced, the room fell silent, all eyes turned towards the door. It opened and in stumbled a young girl, panting for breath.

'You are *twelve* minutes late,' Kathy shouted, doing her best to sound menacing. 'This is your first proper job after college so it might be as well for me to remind you that ChipCo is not here for your convenience, Miss Fawcett. Punctuality is of the essence!'

'I've done my hours, Kath . . . I mean, Miss Foley. Honest, I have,' she stuttered.

Kathy was not to be deflected.

'Only by *work* can we make a *better* life for ourselves.' It was a hell of a performance.

The girl, not knowing which way to turn, looked like someone who had stumbled into a bad dream. Everyone in the room stared at her sympathetically but no one said a word.

'I have two options,' announced Kathy, adopting that hard edge to her voice copied from her mother. 'I can either dismiss you straight away . . .' Her face set, she paused, and then suddenly the frown vanished, the threat melted away to be replaced by a look of merriment. '. . . or I can wish you *Happy Birthday*, you daft devil. Come here and let me give you a hug!'

Cries of 'Whoopee!' went up and the hapless girl did not know whether to weep or protest. A party popper exploded which sparked another cheer, then through the door came a blond youth bearing a large iced cake ablaze with candles.

'Hang on, Chas!' ordered Kathy, and everyone paused. She sprinted across to her desk, opened her soft leather briefcase and pulled from it a mouth organ. She polished it briefly on her skirt, ran up and down the scale, shouted, 'OK, everybody! One . . . two . . . three . . .' As the first few notes of 'Happy Birthday' were recognised the entire office joined in till the crescendo rose through all thirteen floors, possibly as high as the boardroom. Just another day in Global Development. Much fun had by all; not many potato crisps sold to distant continents.

Kathy had just played the last note, happy that the girl's birthday had been duly noted and celebrated, when the door opened again. This time it was a face she did not recognise. While the others gathered round the cake, cutting it, handing out birthday presents and ignoring the insistent ringing of the telephones and pleas of the customers, Kathy went across to the new arrival.

'I'm sorry,' said the young man, 'but I'm Toby from the press office.'

'Bad luck,' she said, smiling back at him.

'It's about your mother,' he said diffidently.

'She's all right?'

'She is, but I might not be. It's just that, well, everyone says *you're* approachable . . .'

'Unlike Mother?' interrupted Kathy, raising one eyebrow.

The young man was struggling. 'It's just that there's an important press conference, and . . . she's wearing fur! Real animal fur. If any of them spots it, it'll be all over the papers. I'm sorry,' he added, 'but this is my first big press conference. The chief's sick. If this goes wrong for me . . .'

'Why should I care?' asked Kathy, teasing him.

'Because if I get the push from the press office, there's no chance of my ever moving down here to Global Development, which is where I'd really like to be. It's the best. Everyone says so.'

Kathy smiled and winked. 'Care for some sponge cake?'

Half an hour before the press conference was due to start, while Global Development were clearing paper plates and sucking crumbs from out of computer keyboards, Kathy was summoned to Leonora's office. Kathy thought she knew why. Her mother must have remembered. Better late than never.

'You were right, darling,' Leonora enthused, bothering for a change to get up from behind her semi-circular desk and sit with Kathy on the deep leather sofa opposite. 'I should have told you this morning. It's just not fair to let your own flesh and blood learn such an important piece of news at a press conference. Especially as it affects us both personally.' No, this was not what Kathy was hoping to hear.

'Is this what's known as a change of policy, then?' she asked, spurning the overplayed affection in her mother's voice and behaviour.

'Listen,' Leonora's eyes widened till they sparkled, 'I've been offered Acting World President, based in Boston USA. For at least six months while Oscar Bertram has his prostate done.'

'Bertram's got organs other than a calculator for a brain then?' replied Kathy, unimpressed.

'Aren't you happy for me, darling?' asked her mother plaintively.

'Good career move, I guess,' she replied distantly.

'And very good for you, too,' added Leonora, sidling towards her. 'From the President's office, I may well be able to find you a better job than in that pokey little department you're stuck in. It was a good start, I know. I had fun there too, years ago. But it's time for you to move on.'

'I want others to decide when I'm ready for promotion,' Kathy snapped. 'I don't want any leg up from my own mother. Do you realise how much effort I have to put into persuading people to forget that I'm your daughter? Short of plastic surgery and a name change, I'm beginning to wonder what else I can do.'

'Why should you want to? What's wrong with being the daughter of the Chief Executive?' Leonora asked incredulously. 'There's always jealousy in business, darling. Learn to rise above it, eh? Now, I start in Boston a week on Monday.' She stood up and paced around the office, intimate moment over. 'You can have the use of my car and driver while I'm away,' she announced briskly. 'Move into my flat if you want.'

'Mother,' Kathy sighed, 'ever since I came to work here I have longed to travel on the Tube like everybody else. I don't want to live in Curzon Street, I like it in Earls Court. Riding in the back of that bloody Mercedes makes me sick. Not just travel sick, but deep down in my stomach sick. Sick like you'll never understand. I just want to be normal. I want people to judge me on what I can do for myself, not mutter all the time that I'm only here because of who I am.'

'Well,' Leonora replied resignedly, 'it sounds as if the sooner I'm out of the way, the better.'

Kathy stroked her arm.

'It's not like that, Mum. I'll miss you, of course. But just leave my working life be, please. And have a great time in Boston. We'll talk.'

Both women got up and kissed and Kathy rested her head briefly on her mother's shoulder. She felt the tickle of the fur and remembered the hapless young man from the press office. It had taken guts for him to come down like that, to ask the boss's daughter for help. Real guts. Kathy pulled away from her mother's embrace.

'You know,' she remarked casually, 'I'm having second thoughts about that fur. It really looks good. To hell with political correctness.'

'You think so?' Leonora, beamed and began stroking her collar.

'And even if it makes you look that bit older, it's well worth it,' said Kathy. 'It adds dignity.'

'Older? How much older?' gasped Leonora. 'Screw dignity!'

'Hardly any older at all. Only a little bit.'

'Funny,' replied her mother, 'I was just thinking it wasn't quite suitable. I might change.' And she swept out of the room, her thoughts comfortingly on herself once more and no hint on her lips of the two words Kathy most wanted to hear.

Happy Birthday. That was all. She was twenty-nine today.

Strangely, despite her mother's indifference, Kathy missed her when she finally left for America. For all her faults, her bullying, her interference in Kathy's life, her arrogance, her inability to play a maternal role, Leonora was still family and now Kathy was left with no one to talk to outside of Global Development.

It could have been worse. They were a great bunch of kids –

young, ambitious, enthusiastic – if immature in some cases. But they looked to her for support, and just because she had nowhere to turn for help did not mean she should not help others. The novelty of coming to work alone (which she could have done before had the offence caused to her mother been worth the trouble) was enjoyable. Kathy felt more confident within ChipCo, feeling that now people might judge her for herself and not as a poorly cast clone of her mother.

If buildings were able to breathe, that monolithic slab of glass and marble which was ChipCo HQ would have sighed with relief at Leonora's departure. It brought to an end a reign of, if not terror, then something close to it. Every move, every minor cog that shifted in the gearbox of that building, had been under her scrutiny. Now it was Ted Metcalfe's toy to play with, and he had plans to move his soldiers around.

The day, after Leonora's departure, Kathy had taken her entire team out to lunch. It had been a cracking morning's work by all of them, especially young Chas who had tied up the ends of a Japanese deal which would double the ChipCo presence in the Pacific. It was a great coup for the kid to pull off. He'd done it by persistence, a certain amount of courage, a bit of cunning, and a huge dollop of moral support from Kathy who had urged him on at every step. He deserved lunch; they all did. After his second bottle of white wine, Chas, aided by his mates, scrambled on to the table, ripped off his jacket, and declared to the entire restaurant his undying love for Kathy. As all the blokes did sooner or later.

Ellie didn't go to lunch. The secretary drew the short straw and instead manned the telephones while the others drank the wine bar dry. It was she who took the call from Ted Metcalfe which had a slightly intoxicated Kathy knocking on the door of his office at four that afternoon.

It was strange to see someone else behind her mother's desk.

The room felt smaller with Metcalfe in it, diminished somehow. He was over-friendly, Kathy thought, striding across the office to offer her a seat, and asking if she wanted tea. She wanted him to get straight to the point.

'You won't mind Toby Hart being here?' he asked. She turned and saw the young man from the press office, sitting in the shadows in the far corner of the room. Kathy threw him a wink.

'Press matter, is it?'

'It will be big news if you say yes,' replied Metcalfe, beaming. 'Straight to the point, Kathy. I've admired your work for a long time . . .' the man from the press office nervously crossed and uncrossed his legs '. . . and have always thought of you as being one of the people who will climb the ladder at ChipCo, right to the very top.' Toby fumbled with his pen, avoiding anyone's eye. 'The fact that your mother is pretty important here has nothing to do with it, I assure you. You are outstanding in your own right, I believe. And I want to give you a chance to prove it.' Toby, remembering his less flattering description of Kathy only two weeks before, went pale. It was like watching a lamb fall into the jaws of a wolf.

'This is all a bit of a surprise, Ted,' said Kathy.

'The biggest is yet to come. We've got a plant in Ireland at a place called Ballymagee.'

'I've heard of it.'

'As a factory it's fine but it could do better. There are production hiccups, workforce getting a bit idle, management a bit smug. Needs a fire lighting under it, get it roaring again. It was once one of our most profitable plants. In fact, much of the prosperity of this company is based on what happened out there in the 70s.'

'I've heard Mother talk about Ballymagee.'

'I'm not surprised. What she did there became a legend in this business. But that's in the past. The future of Ballymagee is in your hands now, Kathy. I want you to be its new Chief Executive with my full authority to do whatever has to be done to turn that place round and pull it out of the mire it's sliding into.'

'I love Global Development,' she said, after a little thought.

'And you'll love Ballymagee too,' replied Metcalfe. 'It will take time, of course.'

'It's a major promotion,' Kathy observed. 'They'll assume Mother's had something to do with it.'

'I agree. That's why he's here.' Metcalfe nodded towards Toby Hart. 'To make sure none of this gets in the papers. He's going to be our *anti*-press officer for a change.' Toby nodded.

'So far as Global is concerned, I will tell the team that I'm sending you on a six-month world tour, assessing markets. If we give them a date for your return, they'll believe that.'

'I would have to tell Mother, of course,' insisted Kathy.

'Would you?' asked Metcalfe, pursing his lips. 'Think about it. As soon as she hears you're going to Ballymagee, she'll never leave you in peace. She'll be trying to pull all the strings, just like she does when she's here. Especially with its being Ballymagee. She'll want to relive all those old glories. Tell her if you want, but think about it carefully first.'

'So what do you want me to do?' enquired Kathy, trying to weigh her options.

'It's up to you,' he replied, leaning forward in his chair to press home his point, 'but if *you* want to make a name for *yourself*, you won't mention a word of this to anyone. Just go over there quietly, get on with the job, make a huge success of it, and then we can shout it from the rooftops.' He paused to study her face. 'Kathy, you're looking at me as if I've just offered you a prison sentence. It shouldn't take more than six or nine months. You'll be back here for Christmas.' He turned to Hart.

'Any problems keeping this quiet?' he snapped.

'Er, my guess, sir, is that the local press in Ballymagee will notice something. And the name Foley is very well known in ChipCo. I agree we want to keep it out of the financial press in case it hints at any instability in the company, a lack of confidence in the Irish operation.'

'And in the factory, Mr Hart? It would be better if this weren't gossiped about. Word might get across the Atlantic, you see, to Boston. Contrary to what you were probably taught, you will soon learn that it is often the job of press officers to know a great deal but to keep that knowledge entirely to themselves. Understand?'

'Yes, sir.' Toby clicked his pen and put it in his inside pocket, missing at the first stab. He glanced up at Kathy, and felt sorry for her all over again.

'You could always change your name,' he suggested. 'You don't have to be Foley.'

'It's a possibility,' she conceded. 'Then at least no one would be able to say I was my mother's puppet. I'd be judged for what I did and not what I was called.'

'Very true,' Metcalfe nodded, encouraging her. 'Any ideas?'
She shook her head.

'McGuinness . . . I always think that's a good Irish name,' he declared, as if the thought had just crossed his mind. 'If you call yourself Guinness they'll think you're part of the brewery. But *Mc*Guinness, now that's different. Try it.'

'Kathy McGuinness,' she said aloud, and enjoyed the sound of it all the more for its no longer being her mother's name.

Kathy's mind raced. She got up from the chair, imagining life outside Global. No Chas getting drunk, no Ellie sneaking in birthday cake on every occasion. To be replaced by what, and where? On the plus side, perhaps she was being churlish questioning the move; it might be the answer to her prayers, a chance to stand on her own two feet, shed the burden of only being known as her mother's daughter and prove she was her own woman. But she'd miss Chas. He made her laugh. They all did.

'Any thoughts, Kathy?' asked Metcalfe.

'I'll try it,' she replied.

'*Trying* isn't quite good enough. I want better than that, and I know I shall get it, Miss McGuinness.'

3

It was June 1970, and the hit tunes of the day were blaring from a tinny loudspeaker on a dockside in Wales, in a futile attempt at providing entertainment in a distinctly unsociable setting. Peter, Paul and Mary's *Leavin' on a Jet Plane* had just been locked in fierce battle with the roar of the wind which, although mild, was battering the tin shed which passed here for a departure building. Judy Collins had fared no better with *Both Sides Now*. Young Leonora Foley, sitting in a corner on her rucksack, hoped that the hypnotic pulse of Motown music might soon come blasting through and win the war for the crowd's attention. It might quieten them down a bit.

Setting out on her first job after university as a newly recruited ChipCo researcher, she had stuffed a couple of hundred pounds – almost a month's wages – deep into the pocket of her jeans. When she saw the motley collection of people who filled the departure shed at Pembroke Dock, she stuffed the money even deeper. A ragbag of individuals were waiting for the night ferry to Cork: drivers, hitch-hikers, a few families, tramps, and a forlorn brace of nuns who strutted around like distraught penguins used to chilly isolation and not enjoying this hot house of raucous company.

'The English will not keep me from my homeland!' declared a drunk, who might as well have been speaking to a wall for all the interest the other passengers showed in his outburst. 'I must be free to return to the auld country. I must arise and go now,' he intoned, to little effect.

With a dock strike imminent, he was not the only one in a state of agitation. Leonora had bought a copy of that day's *Daily Express* and read how the new Prime Minister, Edward Heath, in power for just a month, had put the army on standby to keep the ports of Britain open if the strike went ahead. This had fuelled panic and queues had built up on the approaches to all ports, particularly the ones to Ireland as home-loving people tried to get themselves back to their families before the docks closed on them.

It was six-thirty in the evening, and there had been jostling at the ticket office in which Leonora had nearly lost her heavy rucksack. Overstuffed with sleeping bag and clothes, it was no asset in a scrum. Luckily, her employer had bought her a ticket which guaranteed her access to the ship; but for such a junior member of staff they had not paid for a cabin for the overnight crossing. Anxiously, she had asked around and was told not having a bed for the night was no problem – there was plenty of room on deck.

A party of lads – bricklayers judging by the dusty state of their overalls and the encrusted handles of trowels jutting out of backpacks – had taken to relieving the tedium by drinking themselves into oblivion on Watney's unappetising Red Barrel beer at the stand-up bar in the corner. Now they were getting noisy and making their own entertainment by insulting the other passengers. One of them asked a nun for a kiss. She gave him a smile of such benevolence and saintly understanding that it cut through his alcoholic confusion and humbled him. But less magnanimous women with children were beginning to move away, crowding the quieter part of the departure shed in which Leonora was sitting on her rucksack. They were united in one thought: when would the ship ever leave? They were so near to getting aboard and away from England, but until that man with the gold braid on his cap lifted the barrier, they might as well have tried to walk across the Irish Sea. Babies cried, drunks screamed, and a hapless young officer threaded his way carefully through the crowd telling as many people as could hear him that, as the ship was full, (to make the crossing more comfortable) it would be delayed by two hours more while a summer gale blew itself out in the Irish Sea, Leonora had no stomach for water at the best of times, and any hint of a rough passage was the worst news. The music came round once again to *Leavin' on a Jet Plane*, which seemed the most inviting option at that particular moment.

To pass the time, she decided to change some of her English pounds into the Irish currency of which she didn't even know the name. She stood at the counter, emptying her pockets of six-pences, half crowns and two-shilling pieces, only to be told by the surly man behind the desk, who had watched her struggle for some time and not bothered to say a word, that they only exchanged notes. She slipped him three five-pound notes and took a fistful of grubby currency in exchange. To a girl unused to the ways of the world outside home and college, and now with a pocket full of money which she could not fathom, this was beginning to feel like the edge of the world.

Going to Ireland was probably a waste of time, she had to admit to herself. The whole trip was pointless. You didn't get the best research jobs when you'd been in a company for six short months; you got the dead-enders that gave you experience but rarely bore fruit, the lousy jobs no one else wanted to pick up, the bottom-of-the-barrel tasks that others had risen above. No one in ChipCo really thought there was anything to be gained by opening a crisp-making factory in the far west of Ireland. ChipCo was doing well enough at evangelising its snack food business around the world without having to undertake mis-sionary work in the wilds of a backward island. Why bother? There were still parts of industrial Britain which had not been

redeveloped after the second world war, and many of those were
on the doorsteps of big cities with three-lane motorways running
between them. What could Ireland possibly offer? Everyone
knew that it was at heart a peasant country; pigs in back yards,
empty beer bottles in pockets, and those not brought to their
knees by booze crouched in endless prayer, slavishly muttering
Catholic devotions. Or that's what Leonora had been told
anyway, mostly by people who had never set foot further west
than Manchester to see George Best play. Men might just have
walked on the moon for the first time, but the west of Ireland
was still one small step too far for most people, and too much
like a giant leap for a company such as ChipCo.

And besides there was the violence. The girls she worked with
at ChipCo had warned Leonora to be careful for her life. Murder
and bloodshed loitered there on every street corner, they told
her, as if they knew anything about it. Most of these uninformed
gossips garnered their understanding of world affairs from the
gabbled bits of news which were sprinkled sparingly and un-
convincingly between the records on the newish Radio One.
Although it was true that army commanders that week in
Northern Ireland had warned that anyone throwing petrol
bombs would be shot, and that only the week before there
had been a gun battle between 1500 British soldiers and IRA
snipers, it did not mean that the whole of Ireland was under
martial law. Leonora understood that, but the ignorant did not
draw any distinction between the widely reported events in the
North, and the quiet, slumbering corners of the South about
which little at all was heard, and to one of which Leonora was
bound.

Two hours passed and there was still no sign of any movement
on the dock. The ship, the *Isle of Inishboffin*, flags blowing
horizontally, cracking in the fresh breeze, tugged at her mooring
lines as if she wanted to be off; impatient, like the crowd, for

home. Leonora had been propped against the wall using her rucksack as a cushion, and was beginning to nod off, hypnotised by the hum of the chatter around her. Then, for no apparent reason, a cheer went up. The more vigilant had kept their faces pressed against the windows looking for any sign of movement on the ship. When they spotted the crane starting to move, they roared with delight and their joy quickly spread. Loading began. Cars were driven on to a heavy sisal net and then plucked from the quayside by a crane, dangling precariously over the water while their anxious owners stood on the dock, watching, holding their breath. The cars were lowered precariously into the hold. Smartly, the empty net was flung back ashore and the process repeated. Everyone reckoned half an hour and they would be on board.

After thirty minutes, with still no movement of that barrier, they guessed something was wrong. It fell to the unfortunate second officer, looking as though he feared for his life, to announce it would be at least another hour before the gale had blown itself out.

Impatience was rife. The drunks could take no more and started to brawl. Leonora heard the sound of breaking glass and was thankful to be in the quieter part of the building. But the restlessness soon spread, and within minutes children who had sat quietly sucking their thumbs, or dozing in their mothers' arms, started to bawl. Even the nuns looked less composed than they had an hour before.

'Now be quiet with yer, yer little gabby-guts,' said the harassed woman who was sitting next to Leonora, two children under three in her charge. 'Do you hear them drunks over there?' she added, disgusted. 'Crawsick, the buggers will be in the mornin'. I should think they'll have to sweep 'em off the ship when we get to Cork.'

'It's been a long wait,' said Leonora, sympathetically.

'God, it has that. I'm so hungry I could eat a farmer's arse. And that's the truth.' Then another child started to bawl which set off a baby a few yards away, but at least the sound of the drunks was now eclipsed.

'Is it always like this?' asked Leonora,

'I should think not or I'd never be coming east again, I can tell you that. They say there's a strike on. We might never get home before Christmas if we don't go now. That's what my sister said, anyway. It's all that Mr Heath's fault. She lives in Camden Town, so she knows all about these t'ings. I don't bother meself with the news all that much.' She started to bounce the baby on her knee, shushing and cooing to it.

'A boy?' asked Leonora.

'A boy he is. And just like his father – all mouth when you least want it. He's called Kieran.'

'How do you do, Kieran?' said Leonora softly, taking hold of his tiny hand.

'And you'd be English yourself?'

'Yes. First time in Ireland. If I ever get there.'

'Ah,' sighed the woman, 'it will be worth the wait. And where would yer be goin', when yer get to the other side?'

'I'm heading for County Mayo. Is that far?'

'It's far enough,' boomed a man's voice. 'But it's God's own country when you get there.'

Leonora let go of the baby's hand and looked up. With the light behind the man, it was difficult to make out his features. He was no dwarf, that was for sure. 'So you know Mayo, do you?' she asked, craning her neck to get a better view of his face.

'I know enough of my own bit, and I don't give a damn for anybody else's,' he said proudly. 'Forty years I've been on God's earth, and he's never tempted me anywhere else.'

'Except to England?'

'If my cousin hadn't done the daftest thing and gone and got his self married to an English girl, I'd never have set foot in the place. But it's a duty to go to your own cousin's wedding.'

'When was this?'

'It's tomorrow,' replied the man. 'But they say there's a strike coming and I may never see home again. God, I thought, I'd better get out of this hell hole of a place and back to somewhere I know. My cousin will get along fine without my good wishes.'

The man knelt beside her and started to waggle a finger or two at the grumbling baby. He had a weathered dark skin, but if it was true that he was forty, was showing few signs of his age; just a crease or two at the corners of his blue eyes, and the slightest fleck of grey in his jet black hair. She watched his fingers teasing the baby; they were a working man's pair of hands, rougher skinned than his face, the fingernails chipped. But gentle with the child. He wore a shapeless tweed jacket, elbows thread bare. Into one pocket was stuffed a rolled up flat cap. All he carried with him was a brown paper parcel tied with string.

'Now, there's no need to be makin' that fuss, yer little gabby-guts,' he said to the child sternly. 'Would yer like a little tune to help yer off t' sleep? Would yer?'

Hypnotised, the child watched his every movement as the man dropped his waggling fingers and reached deep into his inside pocket. From it he pulled a shiny tube with a wooden end which he placed to his lips and blew gently: a tin whistle. He played a few notes, enough to attract the baby's attention away from the canned music hissing from the tinny speakers. The babe was not the only one sick of hearing a strangulated Peter, Paul and Mary. The crowd of exiles wanted a memory of home to carry them through the long hours of waiting; some kind of inspiration to reassure them that the vigil was all worthwhile. Heads turned towards the whistle player – adults as well as children – and conversations stopped. He played the first few notes of a tune which seemed to be instantly recognised by everyone except

Leonora. Lips started to move, and out of nowhere a chorus materialised. It spread through the crowd like flames through kindling, till there was not a soul untouched by it, even the nuns. Leonora tried to catch the words: '. . . *with people all working by day and by night . . .*' As the crowd gained in confidence, the singing became louder till it rose to a crescendo. '. . . *but for all that I've found there I might as well be, where the Mountains of Mourne go down to the sea.*' They clapped and applauded the whistle player, slapped him on the back as if he was some kind of hero. Even the baby tried waving its hands together in appreciation.

'Powerful stuff, is music,' said the man, nodding in the direction of the bar. 'God, if it didn't take those lads' minds off their drink for a while.'

'Where are the Mountains of Mourne?' asked Leonora.

'I'll be damned if I know,' replied the man. 'But they're not in County Mayo, I can tell you that for sure. Or if they are, they're a well-kept secret. Well, goodbye,' he said cheerily, and slipped the whistle back in his inside pocket and melted into the crowd.

Then, as if a bell had been rung to signal the start of a boxing match, the concord of the singing disappeared as quickly as it had arrived, and everyone went on the offensive as the barrier was finally moved to one side. Figures who had been on the ground for hours were suddenly on their feet and pressing, commando-style, towards the ship. No one was immune from the unseemly struggle to get aboard, the nuns carried along like bubbles in a fast-flowing stream. Leonora looked out for the man who had played the whistle but he had vanished. Rucksack on her back, she joined battle, pressing forward with the others, making for the ship as if it was the last lifeboat to leave a sinking Britain.

Access was by a narrow gangplank, which was the reason for the crush. It swayed as Leonora stumbled up it, and rose and fell a little as the ship yielded to the bilious swell which was creeping into the harbour. She felt sick already. She knew little about ships and was not even certain which was the front or back. She was trying to work out which side of the deck to pitch camp, having seen the throng of people who were making for the few seats in the upstairs saloon. It was June, she told herself; she would be warm enough inside her sleeping bag so she found a spot against a bulkhead, not far from the rail and with shelter from the wind provided by a lifeboat which was hanging from davits above. Luckily there was a light, and when she had settled down against her rucksack, she started to read her book again.

The seaman whose job it was to let go the for'ard mooring lines almost tripped over her outstretched legs as he scurried to uncleat the ropes.

'Get yerself crubbed up, or someone'll kill themselves fallin'' over those grand, long legs of yours!' he shouted, grinning as he grabbed the end of the rope.

Slowly the ship gathered speed. Leonora felt comfortable, no sickness at all. But Pembroke Dock is well within the shelter of the huge natural harbour of Milford Haven, and it was half an hour before the ship met the real sea off St Ann's Head. It was a different story then. The bow plunged like a bucking horse as it battled its way into the heavy sea left by a summer gale. Leonora's stomach rose and fell with it till it could take no more. The exhaust from the fans which ventilated the kitchens blew along the side deck and the air was filled with the smell of hot fat. Within minutes, she was on her feet, clutching the rail, leaning over the side, retching.

She puked for a good fifteen minutes. Feeling easier then, she went back to her cosy little spot by the bulkhead, thinking the worst was over. But the motion of the ship became no more gentle as it pushed its way, against the will of the sea, westwards towards Ireland. Feeling dazed, she stumbled again to the rail of the pitching ship and leaned over as far as she dare, watching the heaving water race past thirty feet below.

She felt hands grab her round the waist and despite the sickness stood bolt upright.

'For God's sake, you'll be over the side before you know where you are. That's how people are lost at sea, you know.'

It was the whistle player. Once she was safe, his hands left her waist and dropped back into the pockets of his tweed jacket.

'Have yer tried a stiff drink, to get yer t'sleep? If yer can close yer eyes you'll not feel the motion of the ship. That's what Father always told me. He did a bit o' fishin' out of Bellmullet, although he was no man o' the sea.'

'I couldn't face a drop of anything,' spluttered Leonora. 'But thanks.'

'Well, I can't be leavin' yer here,' said the man. 'Yer'll get the cold of yer life. Look at yer, frozen and shiverin'. It's always cold on the sea, June or no June.'

'Actually,' said Leonora, feeling safer and less sick, 'I'm glad I've seen you again. I want to know about Mayo.'

'And how were you thinking you might get there?'

'Bus?' she replied, innocently.

'Bus! Which bus?'

'I guess the bus from Cork up to Mayo.'

The man laughed out loud. 'I can tell you've never been to the west before. There are no buses, ever, to anywhere you want to go. You get on the first, and that might take you a bit closer. And then when you get off that there'll be another. That won't take you where you want to go either, but it'll take you somewhere where there's another bus. And so it goes. And if God is good to you, you'll get there in the end.'

'And if God's not good to me?'

'Ah, he's good to everyone wanting to go to Mayo.' And the

man gave a broad grin. 'Looks like I should be doin' the gentlemanly thing and takin' yer up to Mayo meself.' Leonora was again overcome and turned away, clinging to the rail of the ship. She was sick for a few moments, and when she recovered, was disappointed to find the whistle player had gone again, seemingly blown away.

No, she was wrong. That was him, walking boldly along the side deck of the pitching ship with the powerful, long stride of a fit man. She sat down, feeling a little better. She knew she had a map in her rucksack and dug deep till she found it. She tried to unfold the map against the wind, but the breeze filled it like a sail and she had to fold it again so it showed only the far north-west corner and not the overview of the whole country. She sat for a few minutes, trying to absorb it.

'When I see that bit o' the map, me heart leaps. It does.' He was behind her again and came to kneel beside her, a cup of hot tea in each hand. 'Try it. You'll feel the better for it. Before you know where you are you'll be after a full Irish breakfast. Black pudding an' all.'

'Oh, please,' groaned Leonora. But she sipped the tea. 'It's sweet.'

'Ah, but not as sweet as the way my mother makes it,' replied the man. He sat down slowly, balancing the cup of tea in his hand, and ended up, either by accident or design, close enough to her so that she could feel the warmth of his arm through his jacket where the sleeve pressed against hers. Not wanting to be quite that close, she used the excuse of refolding the map to move away from him a little.

'Ah, now you've got that map open at the right place.' He took a deep breath, as if he could smell the scents of his native land coming up from the paper. 'Have you ever been to the edge of the world, eh?' he asked. 'Because you've only got to set foot on the Mullet and you might as well be as far away as those poor devils who were sent to the moon.' His bent finger came to rest on a crooked spit of land, joined only to the bulk of Ireland by the thinnest of threads. It faced the Atlantic, cowering, as if bracing itself for the ocean's fury.

She noticed his hand resting on the map. 'It's crooked, your finger, just like the Mullet!'

'The Mullet bends all of us to its will, even down to a little finger,' he replied with reverence. 'I spent time there with my father, fishing. That's why I'm not too bothered by the sea. And I'll tell you a thing – there's not a tree to be seen there! Can you imagine that? God, the wind up there blows so fierce that nothing can face it. Some say it's bleak. I think the whole place is wonderful. Peaceful, yer know? There's bits of rock you can stand on that the scientists say have been there for two billion years. It's the sort of place a man can be on his own, and feel he's standing right next to God. Just over the horizon, past the breakers, is where I think he must be. Somewhere next to heaven, that's the Mullet.' He paused, eyes focussed on the horizon, blinked, then looked back at Leonora. 'I'm rambling on now,' he apologised.

'Homesick?' she asked.

'I'd say I was. I've been away a whole week.'

'A *week*!' cried Leonora, mocking him.

'Well, six whole days if I'm honest. And I shall be pleased to be back under my own roof with my mother's cookin' inside me.'

'No wife?'

'Ah, I trained meself out of all that nonsense. You see, when I was a lad I had it in mind to be a priest, and so I put all thoughts of women behind me. And that's where they stayed.' He took a deep swig of his tea.

'This place you call the Mullet,' said Leonora, 'is that where you live?'

'I would if me mam would let us. But the family's been in the same spot for three generations now and she doesn't feel like movin', not with my father down in the graveyard. She wouldn't want to be leavin' him alone. Anyway, it's not far, the Mullet. I can see it in the distance. We live just outside Ballymagee. I know my way around and I've got to an age where I might get lost if I go anywhere else.'

Leonora laughed. 'You're only forty!'

'True,' he replied. 'But it's been a hard forty.' He changed the subject. 'You're looking better for the tea,' he remarked, noticing a bit of colour returning to her cheeks. 'But you'll need . . .' he broke off to fumble in his inside pocket and withdrew a small flask from which he unscrewed the top '. . . a drop o' Irish whiskey! Put you right back on yer feet, it will.' He put the flask to his mouth and took a gulp, wiped the top on his sleeve and passed it to Leonora. She took it from him and raised it to her lips. The bottle was still warm where his lips had been on it and she pressed the flask hard to her mouth. She took a swig, and spluttered at the strength of it.

'I should have told yer,' he said. 'It's a drop o' home made. Anyway, yer look all the better for it. Now, I'll be wishing you good night and a safe journey.' He took the flask from her, put it back in his jacket and sprang smartly to his feet, walking away without so much as a backward glance.

The *Isle of Inishboffin* smacked the quayside at Cork City as if greeting an old friend. It was an extra hour late due to the rough weather and a general lack of urgency on the part of the ship's crew; but the last five miles up the harbour in the flat water had been a blessing to an exhausted Leonora, who recovered her composure and braved the ladies' lavatories only to find the floors awash in vomit. She splashed fresh water on her face, shut the door quickly behind her, and would have tried some of the tea in the cafeteria if the smell of sick wasn't still trapped in her nostrils. She thought she'd get something at the bus station instead.

It was a long, soggy walk through Cork City, and her first taste of the relentless dampness which is the hallmark of the Irish climate even in high summer. A fine drizzle hung in the air, swirling round, looking for somewhere to land. It was not weak enough to be fog, nor sufficiently strong to be called rain, but potent enough to soak through your clothes. It was a real dampener.

Leonora had an appetite, a craving to fill a stomach she had repeatedly emptied the night before, and was thankful to see a cafe with steam on its windows and the smell of frying bacon oozing through the ventilator, even at six o'clock in the morning. There were two taxis parked outside, and a fish lorry. Inside, it was warm and the steam made it even damper than outside but that did not bother her. After that ship, it was a refuge.

'A large cup of coffee and a bacon sandwich, please,' she said, mouthing the words as if she was in a foreign land where English was hardly spoken.

'Soft day,' said the man behind the counter, wiping his greasy hands on his stained apron.

'Soft?' enquired Leonora.

A voice behind her interrupted before the cafe owner had time to answer. 'You'll get used to softness by the time you've been here a week.' She recognised it and was startled, yet at the same time comforted, to hear it again. It was the whistle-player.

'When we say soft we mean it's damp. And it usually is damp. So if you say it's a soft day you'll never be far wrong. Unless the sun's out – but that doesn't happen often. Now, if you sit down and get that lovely bit o' bacon in yer, yer can tell me how yer plan on gettin' to Mayo?'

'Are you following me?' asked Leonora, half joking.

'Now wouldn't that be an Irish thing to do? You're the one

that doesn't know the way, and I'm the one who does. So why would I be following you? Do you think we're stupid? Now, how are you going to get to Mayo?'

'I was thinking of asking at the bus station.' She wiped away the molten butter which was dribbling down her chin.

'You're a bright girl, all right. But if you were really bright, you'd sooner be talking to a lamppost than askin' yer man in the bus office how to get anywhere.'

'But there must be a timetable,' Leonora insisted.

'There was one, but nobody could ever keep to it. Not if you're goin' as far as Mayo. Anything could happen between here and there, see. I've done it in six hours, and then I've taken three days.'

'Three days!'

'There's the pilgrims, see. There's a shrine up in the north where Our Lady appeared, so they say. She was all in floods of tears according to those who saw her. And all these folk come and say their prayers and tell her their troubles. Well, how can God be expected to take care of the Mayo bus if he's got that lot to listen to as well? Ah, give the man a bit o' peace, I say.'

'Look,' said Leonora, wiping more butter from her face, 'will you help me find my way to Mayo?'

'Did you know, you're a filthy eater?' remarked the man.

'Look the other way, then,' she replied sharply. 'Now, Mayo?'

'It's possible I could help you. You can get very lost. We do lose a few every year. It would be a shame, though, to lose one as pretty as you. Even if you still have butter on your chin.'

'You can play that whistle of yours and I'll follow you,' she joked, wiping her face on her sleeve. 'You can be the Pied Piper of Mayo!'

'Ah, me whistle's only for emergencies, and I don't think we're desperate yet. But I'll show yer the way, as best I can,' he offered in a gentlemanly way. 'I can't remember the last time I took a walk with a young lady. It will be a pleasure.'

It was seven long, rambling, bone-shaking hours to Bally-magee. It was a journey of great suffering, a real pilgrimage to test the faith of anyone who had placed theirs in the bus service. In one lonely spot, just short of Athlone, a flock of bewildered sheep blocked the road for half an hour, unimpressed by the proposed passage of the bus. This was enough of a delay to the already extended journey and was compounded by the fact that the driver knew the farmer and there was ten minutes' more banter before the bus was back on the road. The single-decker rattled and gasped at every hill, engine screaming, pleading for mercy every time the driver attempted anything over thirty-five miles an hour. There was no defined system of bus stops. Instead, the driver seemed to know each and every one of his passengers and even went so far as to make a detour of a mile so an old lady would have less of a walk with her shopping.

'It's going well,' said her companion, turning round and addressing Leonora through the gap between the seats in front. He had hardly spoken a word to her all journey. All she had seen of him so far was the back of his shapely head and robust neck bobbing as the bus bounced over the rutted roads.

'This is good?' she replied, feeling slightly sick again.

'I've known worse.'

It was late afternoon when the bus rolled into the town square in Ballymagee and parked at the foot of the gaunt slab of a building that was the Catholic church. From the tower a single bell tolled. It was six o'clock – the Angelus.

'Well, that's it,' shouted the bus driver, having parked conveniently opposite a bar on which his eye had come to rest. 'I think we'll call that a day,' he said, licking his lips. 'And if there's any of you want to go any further in the morning, well, we'll see what we can do.'

'So near, and yet so far,' sighed the man. 'I live three miles further on and I'll be damned if I'm walking it tonight.'

'You mean, that's it? He's not taking us any further?'

'Wild horses wouldn't drag him back into that driving seat. Not with his beer waiting for him. Not that you'd want to be driven by that rascal when he's had a skinful. He's bad enough sober. So, here you are. Mayo, as promised. Now, what will you be doing for the night?'

'I expect I'll have to find a hotel,' Leonora replied.

'And you'll waste your money doing so. I think I'd best take you to a little place I know.' Leonora hesitated. 'Don't look so worried. It's my Auntie Sheila's. She's got one of them bed and breakfast places where people stay the night. They tell us that one day the place will be teeming with tourists, though God knows what they'll come to see. But hell, if it's not comfortable is Auntie Sheila's. And breakfast's fit for a king.'

'I'll pay,' insisted Leonora, wanting to make her position clear.

'You will as well. Auntie Sheila never gave anything away. I'll carry your rucksack.'

Ballymagee was not a large town and they could have walked from one end of it to the other in half an hour. So, in less than ten minutes they were outside 41 Benwee Avenue; a fine stone house originally built for the manager of the local bank in the days when such a man was a vital spoke in the commercial wheel of the town, and probably English. It had a porch with a large glass-panelled door, tall front room windows set symmetrically to either side. In its heyday, it must have seemed like a palace amidst the squat and modest homes of Ballymagee with their mean little windows designed to keep out the worst of the weather while containing any heat. A sign in the window of number 41 offered 'Bed and Breakfast', under which had been written in proud, black letters: 'Television Room Now Available'. The man rang the doorbell and a dog yapped. After a short wait, the inner door opened and out came an elderly but sharp-eyed woman in a pinafore, hands floured, and wearing a look of resentment that could curdle cream.

'I wasn't thinking of taking anyone tonight,' she snapped, speaking with such haste that Leonora could only catch one word in four.

'But you'll take me in, Auntie Sheila, surely? Or you'll never hear the last of it from me mother.'

The woman looked up and peered into his face, screwing up her eyes till she was certain.

'My God! Padraig Tierney. Pat! I haven't seen you in Ballymagee since your father's funeral.' She threw her arms around him, liberally flouring his shoulders with her powdery hands.

'There's not much drags me away from Mayo,' said the man, 'but our cousin Tommy's gone and got his self married in England. Damned fool! And now the bus won't be takin' me all the way home tonight. And I'll be beggared if I'm walkin'.'

'Well, you're welcome here, and that's for certain.'

Leonora coughed and the woman noticed her for the first time.

'Pat! You haven't gone and got yourself a nice young lady now, have you?' she gasped. 'And such a pretty girl too. Look at that lovely black hair. Is she Irish? And those eyes. I can't wait to tell your mother. Has she got the telephone in yet? Now what's your name, young lady?'

'Leonora. Leonora Foley.'

'Ah, you're from England too.' The excitement in her voice dropped at hearing a clean-cut English accent. 'It's lovely to see you anyway, Irish or not. Now how did you meet? Are you courting, eh?' Leonora blushed.

'It would be more than I was worth to have a fine young lady like this on my arm,' Pat said gallantly. 'No, she's comin' to Ballymagee and I'm showin' her the way. That's all there is to it.'

'Ah,' said the woman, disappointed, 'and your mother would have been so pleased for you. She worries about what will happen to you when she goes. Oh, well, there'll be tea in half an hour. I'll show you to your rooms.'

Upstairs, the bedrooms were arranged to either side of a long corridor wallpapered in bright red roses. There was a smell of mothballs, and an aspidistra looking as sad as Jesus on his cross. There were two bathrooms, one halfway down the corridor, the other at the far end. The woman showed Leonora to her room first. It had a single bed with a dark green eiderdown across it, an open fireplace with a few dried flowers arranged in the grate, and a dressing table on which stood a Bible next to a large mirror which had lost some of its silvering. There was a one-bar electric fire, switched off.

'There's as much hot water as you want. You'll be after needin' a bath,' she said to Leonora, pointing to the bathroom door halfway down the corridor. 'And your room's opposite, Pat. Now, be down in half an hour, both of you.' Pat thanked his aunt before closing the room of his door behind him.

He lay on the bed, so tired by the journey that he did not bother to remove his boots or jacket. He gazed at the cracks in the ceiling. They were not unlike a map of the Mullet . . . he would soon be home.

He shivered a little, got up to close the curtains, and thought he might have a bath to warm himself up. But as he took off his jacket and started to remove the stud from the collar of his shirt, he heard the bathroom door opposite close, followed by the sliding of the bolt. Then came the chuckle of water from the tap. Out of curiosity, he opened the door of his room no more than a couple of inches till the glazed door of the bathroom opposite could clearly be seen. Leaving his door ajar, he went back to his bed and lay down, watching the rising steam from the bath begin to cloud the already frosted glass in the top half of the door. Then, despite the efforts of the steam and the glass to conceal it from him, he saw a blurred image of Leonora's partly naked body.

In the swirling vapour, it looked as if she was floating in a cloud. He could just discern her slender arms undoing whatever was holding back her long, black hair, and then he thought he saw her toss and shake her head to free her black mane. The steam thickened, but not sufficiently to render entirely invisible the tantalising outline of her body. He had seen nothing as perfect in his life before. She raised her arms again and in one movement pulled over her head the shirt she was wearing and became naked from the waist upwards. To his shame, he raised himself up on his elbows and thought he could see her bend over the bath and dabble her hand in the water to take the temperature. Then, as if anticipating the therapeutic caress of the hot water in the tub, he could make her out standing near the bath, enjoying the sight and smell of it before she took the plunge.

As the steam in the bathroom thickened, it formed vertical streaks of condensation on the frosted glass which gathered and ran from top to bottom down the pane of glass, like bars which were keeping her from him. Finally naked, she turned by the door and her body came into some kind of focus. Padraig caught a glimpse of her in all her youthful, female beauty. It was a blurred image, like the work of an impressionist, yet what he saw he relished, and what the steam and the frosted glass kept from his eyes, he imagined. And when the sight of her had been replaced by the sound of her splashing like a playful child in the water, he felt filthy for what he had done and sprang to his feet and slammed the bedroom door. It was a shameful thing to do, he knew, and he screwed up his eyes tight and asked God for forgiveness.

He was barely at the end of his prayers when he sensed the door of his room slowly opening. It was a light hand on the door knob.

'Your tea's on the table,' said his Aunt Sheila in a stage whisper. 'And I don't bake fresh bread for you, Pat Tierney, to lie up here all day while it goes cold on the table. And the young lady had better be sharp too.' She was a wise old bird was his Auntie Sheila, he thought. Had he detected a narrow-eyed glance, fraught with meaning? Did she guess what little game he had been up to? Was it a look of encouragement or of warning? He was none too sure.

Still ashamed of himself, Pat was hardly able to speak a word to Leonora. Certainly through most of the meal of fried bacon, eggs and soda bread spread with thick helpings of butter, he had little conversation in him.

'You're quiet,' she remarked. 'I expect you're tired.'

'I am,' replied Pat. He continued his answer in his mind, yet kept his mouth shut. He wanted to say: I am tired of being on my own, with no one but my mother, living at the ends of the earth. It is self-inflicted, though. If I had not harboured fanciful notions of being a man of God, urged on by my mother who shared the not uncommon ambition in these parts of having a priest in the family, I would not have let girls of my own age pass me by. Then I might not have been be a lonely man now. But he said none of it.

'Lonely?' asked Leonora, out of the blue.

'Me?' replied Pat hastily, fearing she had been tuned into his private thoughts.

'Of course not *you*. Ballymagee – is it a lonely place? There doesn't seem much life in it. Probably the loneliest place I've ever been,' admitted Leonora, feeling homesick.

'Why do you need company for what you're doing? All that *research*, or whatever it is.'

'Everyone needs company, Pat,' said Leonora, bashfully looking down at her plate, realising that it was the first time she had spoken his name. 'People who say they don't are fooling themselves.' She looked up. 'And I'm grateful for yours right now.'

He still felt soiled by having spied on her and any overtures of friendship by her made him feel worse. He changed the subject.

'So what's your business here anyway?'

'Potatoes. Boring old spuds,' admitted Leonora. 'Nothing more interesting than that.'

Pat put down his knife and fork and leaned forward earnestly. 'But there's nothing more interesting than the potato,' he declared. 'It is a wonderful thing, the way it grows and multiplies beneath the ground. All you have to do is dig it up and boil it, and it will save your life. All the food your body needs is there within that potato. Did you know that?'

'*Everything* your body needs?' asked Leonora, teasing. He did not rise to it.

'My family has lived and died by potatoes. They are indeed a serious matter. Have you heard of the Great Famine?' She nodded. 'It killed three generations of my family over four cruel years. We know about potatoes here. We thank God we never have to suffer the blight any more. It was a wicked infection, spread through the potato crop year after year, reducing fine potatoes to putrid pulp. And in doing so condemning the families who were depending on them to certain death.' His eyes did not blink, his voice did not falter, the words came straight from the heart. 'But although the blight is forever behind us, we remember those who died because of it. We can never forget them.' He took a mouthful of bread, ripping the crust with his teeth.

'I knew it was good potato-growing land up here, in places anyway. We at ChipCo are looking for similar areas to develop. We make potato crisps.'

'I've heard of them,' said Pat, chewing on his bread. 'I don't call them proper food. Waste of a good tater. They sell them in the pubs, all right. But they're not for me. All you need to get the best out of potatoes is to wash the little beggars, and boil 'em, and then they're as good as the finest feast money can buy. So which places will you be looking in, for your areas to develop?' he asked, with a snide edge to his voice.

'I haven't a clue. That's why I was sent here, to have a look around.'

'You'll learn nothing by looking, I can promise you that,' he said. 'But if you needed showing, then that's a different matter. I can show you an area of land where the potato grows like no other place on earth,' he said proudly. 'It's as if the finger of God reached out at planting time and blessed that patch of soil. There's nowhere else like it for growing. It's sacred to me. The crops grow free from disease, warmed by the kiss of the wind which blows from the ocean, swelling in the rains till they are a crop of unimaginable proportions and emerge like the finest gems. They have the look of the golden apples of the earth about them, I swear they do.'

'A patch,' asked Leonora, 'or more than that?'

'Two thousand acres, no less,' replied Pat, slowly and proudly. 'So they say. I'm not one for the figures myself. But that's how big it is, and a little bit of it's mine. And my father's before, and his before him.'

'That's a lot of land,' remarked Leonora, trying to calculate the potential yield of potatoes from such a vast area.

'It *is* a good deal of land. Of course, it's not all put to potatoes. There aren't enough of us to grow them. The soil just lies there.'

'Waiting to be developed?' She was making mental note.

'I don't know what it's waiting for. I've never asked it! But it's a miracle to have such a patch of rich soil in the middle of the moors and the peatbogs of Ballymagee at all. And so it's like the goose that lays the golden eggs – we don't bother it all that much.' He shrugged his shoulders. 'You'd think there was nothing there unless you knew where to look. I've had those geologists or whatever they're called up there, and they did explain it to me. Something or other to do with the Ice Age but I'm blessed if I understood them. I just know there's no better land in the whole of Ireland, if not the world, for growin' taters.'

Aunt Sheila burst through the door at that moment carrying a huge tea brack large enough to feed an army. 'You haven't been to 41 Benwee Avenue if you haven't had a slice o' my brack. I'm famous for it.' It was a large fruit loaf looking like a jewelled crown, bursting with raisins and currants, glazed across its well-baked top.

'The tea was very filling already,' Leonora apologised.

'Well, the damage is done then. You'll take no harm by having a slice. Another cup o' tea will wash it all away. Anyway, there's always the dance if you want to work it off. It's Thursday night. All the youngsters in the town will be there.'

'I'm no dancer, and I'm certainly no youngster,' muttered Pat.

'But your girl is,' said the woman, nodding at Leonora.

'She is not *my* girl,' insisted Pat

'What sort of dancing?' asked Leonora.

'Oh, dancing, you know. Jigs and things. And I dare say a bit o' that pop music. But Father Flynn, he doesn't like the pop at all except Dana. I think she's won his heart over a little bit. Made it flutter. He goes quite red at the mention of her name. So proud we were of her the other month! Ah, she's grand. But that's as far as Father Flynn goes. Except I've seen him tap his foot to the Dubliners.' She cut into the brack and it fell apart, bursting with dried fruit.

'Well, as I'm here,' said Leonora, 'there's no point in just looking at potatoes. I might as well get to know the place. That's if I can find a young man to escort me to the dance,' she added mischievously.

Both women looked at Pat. He blushed. 'Ach, I'm no dancer.'

'That you are!' snapped Sheila. 'I remember you at Cousin Finbar's wedding. Dancing the night away, you were.'

'Then that's decided,' said Leonora.

'Good thing too.' Sheila grinned with satisfaction. 'Half-past eight at the church hall and I'd polish your shoes, *both* of you. And remember your manners, Pat. It's rude to refuse a dance. And that goes for you too, miss, although I dare say you'd be excused for not knowing, being English.'

Leonora did her best to eat up the leaden slice of tea brack then went to get changed. Her rucksack did not contain much. In fact, she had brought little more than a pair of jeans to add to the couple of sweaters and plenty of stout socks. She was expecting to be tramping, booted, across muddy fields looking at soil and potatoes, not doing herself up for a night on a dance floor. For make-up she had just powder and a smear of lipstick.

She had brought one short tight skirt which would have passed without remark down the Kings Road in London, or worn to a concert by The Who. With the skirt, she wore an old pink sweater which had shrunk a little in the wash and now clung to her tighter than was intended. She knew it was too revealing, but there was nothing else. She met Pat on the front doorstep.

'Is this all right?' she asked.

'God, I'd say it was fine from where I'm standing. But, hell, what the others will make of it, I've no idea.'

They walked down Benwee Avenue, across the market square and past the grey Catholic church alongside which stood the hall. They joined others heading in the same direction. The other girls, Leonora noticed, were dressed as if the war had just ended; long dresses hung well below the knee, overcoats with belts were fastened tightly to deter intruders. They had sensible flat shoes, stockings, and kept their eyes modestly cast down. The young men were wearing the nearest thing to a suit they could manage and looked uniformly uneasy. A priest, Father Flynn she presumed, stood by the door like a moral guardsman, protector of the ladies' virtue. Alongside him was a constable from the Garda to remind the dancers that if any breaking of the laws of God went unnoticed, the guardian of the laws of the land would be quick to spot them. The prevention of conception by unnatural means was against the law, and so the combined presence of priest and constable provided the town's sole prophylactic.

'Good evening,' said Father Flynn to Pat, who was hoping to shuffle past unnoticed. The priest took a long look at Leonora's outfit, and drew in a short breath. He was on the point of making a remark when Pat spoke.

'Father,' he mumbled respectfully.

'You're an unfamiliar face on dance night. And in church for that matter,' the priest replied curtly.

'It's my mother,' Pat lied. 'It's too far for her to come to Ballymagee these days.' Father Flynn gave Leonora a cold look. 'And this is my friend, all the way from London,' Pat added.

'Yes, she would be,' he said, looking at the hem of her skirt. 'You're welcome, both of you.' Leonora did not feel the courtesy came from his heart.

Once inside, she had no idea of the etiquette of the dance and so she followed Pat towards the green benches which stood in two rows, one down each side of the hall, pushed back against walls painted in cream gloss. There was a gasp from two wide-eyed young women as she took a seat next to Pat. Women were to sit on one side, men on the other, he explained, and shooed Leonora across the room. She went and sat with the women and said a timid 'hello'. They replied politely but with little warmth. The younger girls giggled at the boys opposite, being viewed like cattle in a sale ring, hoping to catch an eye. Nervously, Leonora kept smiling. Two boys, who looked hardly fifteen but were as bold as brass, thought she was smiling at them and winked back at her. She blushed. The priest, who had come inside to share a cup of tea with a nun, told the giggling boys to behave themselves. Such rowdy behaviour would not be tolerated.

Through the door stumbled two dishevelled men, one unshaven and carrying a tired-looking set of drums; the other wore a suit whose trousers had been meant for a man a good six inches shorter. He carried a square black box which he dumped on the stage, opened it, and extracted a piano accordion which he slung on his shoulders with a groan. The keys were yellowed, and some of the black notes were missing. 'Good even'. We're the White Heather Boys,' he said mechanically, and launched into a jaunty Irish foot-tapping tune with no more ado. He looked as though he was playing it in his sleep. The other man was still struggling to erect his drums, fighting the several pints he had already consumed. Eventually he joined in halfway through, slightly behind the beat.

Not a soul moved on either bench. The boys looked at the girls, who looked back at them. Some girls gave piercing glances at individual boys, willing them to their feet to dance. But nothing happened. It was the cheery nun who eventually broke the ice.

'Now!' she shouted. 'Kathleen Crowley, you can dance with your brother. Come on, Joseph. On your feet!' And a weary-looking lad shambled to the middle of the floor for the unpromising prospect of his sister's company for the first dance. One or two other couples, most of them related to each other, were cajoled on to the floor by the persuasive old nun who finally put her arm through the priest's and dragged him on to the floor too.

'So, you'll all follow me, and that will be that,' shouted the nun and nodded at the man pumping air into his accordion.

'Yes, Sister Catherine,' said one of the younger girls resignedly. Halfway through the jig, another shabbily suited man appeared in the doorway, burped and excused himself, and headed towards the stage, somewhat unsteady on his feet, dodging the dancers as best he could. From inside a black plastic bag he pulled out a fiddle and a bow, placed them under his chin and joined in.

The icy atmosphere was so thick it would have taken the fires of hell to melt it, or certainly more than the heat generated by the White Heather Boys. Everyone eventually danced, even if it was at arm's length, but with little passion or pleasure. The more coquettish young women made a play for the few attractive young men. But it was as if they were animals in a zoo who could only meet each other with bars between; there was no closeness. The priest and the constable saw to that.

It soon became clear there was another problem. The eyes of all the men were focused on Leonora, and not on the girls from the town. They were looking at her legs, revealed by the short skirt, and her breasts, fully displayed by the tight pink sweater. They had never seen a woman in public with so few clothes, except on the beach. In their minds, they were all begging her for a dance; she could read that in their eyes and knew it was rude to refuse. But to which one should she nod back? There was the engaging young man with floppy ears but a kind face, like a rabbit, or the serious but handsome one with eyes as dark as the night. Then there were the giggling boys, wet behind the ears, trying their luck for a bet. Eventually Pat, whose eyes had not left Leonora, asked her for the next dance. Every woman in the room watched them, as if he were the Prince Charming of Ballymagee with whom all the would-be Cinderellas would have given their back teeth to have had a dance.

Pat behaved perfectly. He did not try to fondle or grab her as they flung each other around when locking arms, as some of the lads might have done. When the White Heather Boys finally ran out of steam, he thanked her politely for the dance, she thanked him, and they both resumed their seats on either side of the room. This time when Leonora spoke to the woman sitting next to her she got no reply. She tried to start a conversation about the weather, then the music, but no one would be seen speaking to her. Curiosity about the visitor had turned to jealousy.

After a short interval, the White Heather Boys returned sheepishly from behind the curtains, looking like men who had secretly slaked their desperate need for a drink in the vestry of the adjoining church. Leonora saw a door marked 'Toilets' and, taking her opportunity to disappear before she was grabbed for the next dance by an intimidating lad with a vertical cliff-face of a forehead, excused herself.

The door opened on to a dim corridor which smelled of cheap disinfectant and was painted in the same cream gloss paint as the hall itself. There were two doors, one on either side, and she went in the one marked 'Ladies'.

Once inside, the door slammed violently closed without any help from her. Standing behind it was a young woman, taller than Leonora and about the same age. But she wore no make up, her clothes neither looked nor smelled fresh, her teeth were yellowed and chipped, hair hardly combed. She took a measured pace towards Leonora, her eyes unblinking, her breathing heavy. A cubicle door opened and another young woman appeared, face expressionless, eyes staring. Leonora backed away till she felt the washbasin digging into her back.

'What do you mean, comin here and dancin' wi' the men?' said the first woman. 'Look like a tart, you do,' added the second, grabbing hold of Leonora's short skirt and tugging it. 'And I bet there's no knickers up there, either. I know your sort. There's not a hint of decency in you. Look at you!' The woman spat the words, and eyed her up and down in disgust. Leonora felt filthy.

'He asked me to dance. I didn't offer or anything like that.'
But the women were in no mood for any explanation.

'It might be all right to tart yourself around like that on the streets of London, but not here. Not in a skirt like that. It's as short and sweet as an ass's gallop. Look at it! And your lovely coloured lipstick.' The woman stabbed her grubby finger on to Leonora's lips and rubbed it hard from corner to corner till the lipstick was smudged. The finger smelled of fish. 'Who do you think you are, comin' here and takin' our men with your filthy little ways?' She rubbed her foul finger across Leonora's mouth in the opposite direction. 'What can a whoor like you do for a fine man like that, except take him away from his own folk and make his life a misery when he's had enough o' gettin' 'imself between your legs? Leave him be, for one of his own kind.' Leonora tried to get away, make towards the door, but the girl raised a muscled fist and warned, 'I'll lam yer.'

She winced at the strength of the woman's grip, her other hand now tightly gripping Leonora's upper arm. She pleaded to be released. Instead, the woman buried her nose in Leonora's hair, took a deep breath and remarked, 'Ah, what lovely scented soap you must use on that fine head of hair. Let me give you a little something to add to it.' And she cleared her throat till her mouth was full, and spat the phlegm forcefully on to Leonora's scalp, raising her arm till her hand hovered over the spot. Then she forced Leonora's hand down on to her silky, black hair, and made her rub it in.

'We're very keen on the latest fashion here,' said the other woman. 'We like the latest hairstyles. Have you seen this one on the posh streets of London?' And she grabbed Leonora's slimy hair so tightly that she yelped, and despite her pleading they parted it and tied it tightly in a double knot on the top of her head, pulling it hard so it could not come undone.

The two women looked at each other and gave smiles of

satisfaction. Leonora, sobbing now, fell to the floor in a heap.

'We can't leave her like this,' said the first. 'It wouldn't be proper to have a fine head of hair looking like that. I think we'll give her a good shampoo to restore those lovely looks of hers.' Leonora pleaded again to be left alone, lying on the cold, smelly tiles of the floor. She felt a woman on each arm now, taking hold of her wrists and dragging her towards a cubicle. When she was in there, one leaped up and stood astride the toilet seat, grasping her head by the knot they had made in her hair. The other put her hand over Leonora's mouth so that her screams could not be heard and then they pushed her head first into the pan till her mouth was below the level of the unflushed lavatory water, and pulled the chain. Then they let go.

'No charge for the hairdressing today,' joked one of the women, drying her hands on the back of Leonora's pink jumper, and then they left her in a crumpled, sodden heap by the stinking base of the stained lavatory pan.

Back in the hall, Pat was trying to catch a glimpse of Leonora but no matter where he looked he could not spot her. He was worried about her. He noticed two women emerge through the door marked 'Toilets' and watched them sit down opposite him, laughing loudly at each other. One looked at him long and hard, head tilted slightly to one side, the faintest of smiles on her lips. He thought he saw her nod, which he took as an invitation which would cause offence if refused. So, despite her grim appearance, he got to his feet and asked for the next dance.

After Leonora had finally got to her feet, unscrambled the knot in her hair, washed the spit from it and been sick in the lavatory pan, she staggered, terrified and bedraggled, back into the hall, a trail of water dripping behind her. The first sight that met her eyes was one of the women who had done this to her, dancing in the arms of Pat Tierney, grinning with satisfaction.

Pat was the first to spot her standing in the doorway, sobbing.

He ran to her and the woman he'd been dancing with stopped and laughed out loud. The dancing came to a halt in mid-tune, the fiddler stopped playing, then the accordion player. Silence. The priest stood by, suspicious but not judgmental. Blood was thicker than water here. He merely turned his back on Leonora and stared reprovingly at the woman he knew only too well to be responsible for this. He offered no comfort to the visitor, and neither did anyone else. Instead, he waved his hand at the White Heather Boys to continue, and they struck up *When Irish Eyes Are Smiling*, the tune to which Pat led Leonora out of the hall and into the night.

At 41 Benwee Avenue, Auntie Sheila had long since gone to bed. Pat all but carried the distraught Leonora the half mile from the hall, and when they arrived at the house took her quietly through to the kitchen, trying hard not to disturb his aunt. He made a pot of strong tea in a serious-looking brown tea pot, and while it brewed fetched a blanket from the sofa in the front room. Leonora slipped quietly up the stairs to remove her clothes, and wash, and get the vile filth from her hair and the taste of lavatory water from her mouth. She reappeared as the kettle came to the boil, looking more composed and draped in a blanket from her bed. Pat beckoned her to the high-backed wooden chair by the fire, and draped around her shoulders the blanket he had taken from the sofa. They decided the glow from the embers was bright enough and did not turn on the electric light in case the clunk of the switch woke Aunt Sheila. Then Pat poured the tea, gave it plenty of sugar, and threw another lump of peat on the embers of fire, hoping it might catch.

'I can't understand what I did wrong,' said Leonora in bewilderment, staring into the fire. 'All I did was dance with you. No more.' Pat knelt on the floor next to her chair.

'I'd say you were unlucky, that's all,' he explained in a voice little more than a whisper. 'I'm not much of a one for fathoming women, but I'd say it was jealousy. I don't know the women of this town very well, but I dare say this place knows those two well enough. Will you be going straight back to London now? Has this spoilt it for you? It would be my duty to escort you all the way back to the ferry, if not all the way across the Irish Sea as well,' he said gallantly, still whispering. To make it easier for her to hear, he leaned nearer to her, till he was closer to her than he had ever been to a woman, except on the dance floor. 'I don't want you to think that all sons and daughters of Ireland behave in such a way to visitors,' he apologised. She smiled and lifted her arm from underneath the blanket to stroke her finger along his cheek.

'You are a very kind man,' she said softly. 'So long as you stay with me, I shall feel safe.' Pat grabbed her finger and kissed it, and then her hand, followed by her wrist, and finally he smothered the length of her arm with kisses given as quietly as he could, till he came to the bruises where the women had grabbed her.

'I can't bear to see you marked like this,' he said, looking at the flesh which was beginning to turn purple. 'You are the most beautiful, perfect thing that has come into my life ever. And it's my fault you're damaged now.'

She leaned forward till their heads were together, and kissed him on the lips. His arms folded behind her neck, and nothing would have parted them. Except for the creaking of Aunt Sheila's bedsprings above which caused them both to freeze, and then giggle like children at their own naughtiness.

Neither made a move till Aunt Sheila had finished her gyrations and the house was still again save for the slight crackle of the peat in the grate which was beginning to spark into life. When all was quiet, Pat moved on his knees till he was in front of her and then leaned forward as she grabbed his head and it came to rest on her lap. She stroked his hair and fingered the hollow in the back of his neck at which she had stared for so many long miles on the bus. Then she ran her fingertips behind his ears till he was nearly insane with lust for her. As he raised his head, the blanket she was wearing parted, and he could see even in the faint glow from the fire that she wore nothing beneath it. Nestling in the shadows, in a land which he had never before explored, he saw all her beauty She did not make any pretence of modesty or try to hide herself. Instead, she cupped his face in her hands and kissed him deeply. He groaned out loud, and she shushed him for the bedsprings above were on the move again. Trembling to remove his belt, he fumbled like a schoolboy and she loved him all the more for it. She slid forward till she was perched on the edge of the chair, then captured him. Showing him the way was the kindest thing to do. And so he moved deep into love with the only woman of his life.

The next morning, fearful of what Aunt Sheila's analytical eyes might deduce from the satisfied but guilty expression on both their faces, they left soon after dawn, leaving a note of apology and saying they had to catch the early bus. Pat took Leonora to his home in Ballymagee, introduced her to his mother who lived in a whitewashed cottage amidst a jumble of old farm buildings which housed a few chickens, two cows and a calf, the hay in a stack by the back door, a milk churn leaning by the gate awaiting collection, and a fine clamp of potatoes standing proudly beside the lean-to next to the kitchen door. Leonora booked herself into the only hotel, or pub really, called the Crowley House Hotel. It was damp and cheerless but sufficed. The main hazard of living there was the mountainous fried breakfast which she was expected to scale every morning. She and Pat made daily forays into the hinterland of Ballymagee, sometimes making love behind abandoned buildings on the peat bog out of sight of the passing milk lorry, or the pony cart taking a churn or two of milk to the local creamery.

In three weeks, Pat Tierney learned a lot about love, and Leonora Foley learnt even more about potatoes. She discovered that within a few miles of this rundown township was a workforce only too ready for steady, well-paid employment. Around them, commercially unexploited, stretched a vast area of rich soil thrown up by some geological freak which had made it the deep, fertile, well-drained loam that potatoes liked best. In the evenings, before seeing Pat, Leonora made notes, drew up plans and lists of recommendations to take back to London. She had secretive conversations with the indiscreet local solicitor about the price of land; a big-mouthed man, he told her the names of all the poverty-stricken farmers whom she knew would snatch her hand off at the slightest offer she cared to make.

Lying in bed at the Crowley House Hotel she came up with a daring plan. It was outrageous or inspired. Either way, it would make or break her reputation at ChipCo. She would write a report recommending Ballymagee for massive investment and development. It could become the jewel in the crown of ChipCo; truly a factory for the seventies.

The company, she felt sure, would be welcomed with open arms here. And she would be part of it, and could be near Pat and enjoy both him and the fruits of her labours. Leonora scribbled long into the nights; numbers and graphs and population figures she had got from the man at the Post Office. By the time she came to leave Ballymagee, she had filled three exercise books with notes.

Although her greatest wish was to be beside Pat, somehow ambition and professional pride got the better of her, and to her surprise Leonora eventually had no regrets at packing her bags and getting on board that lonely bus for the long journey back to England.

'I shall be back, my darling Pat,' she had scribbled on a note, which she folded so his mother wouldn't see it and pushed through the door of his cottage while he was away up the hill, cutting turf. She did not want a tearful goodbye for she would be back soon and then things would be different. She would put this place on the map, and no Ballymagee woman would ever dare spit in her hair again.

4

The promise Leonora had made to Pat was worthless. She never came back to Ballymagee. No sooner had she presented her ambitious developmental ideas to ChipCo than they were snatched from her for the more experienced to implement. She would have felt disappointed at having her baby whipped from her like that, had she not found herself with a real baby to handle and somehow slot into her career structure. ChipCo, realising the worth of the woman, allowed the child barely to hinder her relentless progress. It was a management problem, and Leonora solved it like all the others she faced: by delegating.

So young, she was already soaring towards the corporate stratosphere without a backward glance at boggy Ballymagee, which had been her launching pad. But the young woman they nicknamed Miss Midas had touched the place and that was good enough to turn it into gold. It meant that thirty years later, Kathy, hell-bent on proving she had more about her than just her mother's name, was the first Foley to set foot in County Mayo since Leonora had scribbled that farewell note to Pat. Not that she intended to boast of the fact that the Foleys were back in town. The name was the first thing that had to go.

Kathy woke on her first Monday morning in the Crowley House Hotel, telling herself over and over again that she was now Kathy McGuinness. *McGuinness*, she repeated, trying to drum the unaccustomed name into her head so that she would automatically take notice whenever it was mentioned. It was like a dog having to learn to answer to a different call, against all its instincts. She had nearly made a mistake the previous night when, tired after the flight and that tortuous taxi ride, she had eaten in the restaurant and come within an ace of signing the bill in her real name. She would have to deal in cash in future. But getting cash might be a problem, she suddenly realised, if she had to sign a cheque in her real name. She was in Ireland now, and her name was *McGuinness*.

The Crowley House Hotel was better than she had been led to believe. The chef, she was told, was Italian and prone to unlikely experiments with wild mushrooms; she had been expecting the inevitable greasy mixture of lamb bones and carrots they called Irish stew. In fact breakfast was continental though if she'd wanted the 'full' Irish breakfast, including the famous black pudding, she was welcome but they would have had to get someone in specially to cook it, there being little call for it these days. There was a vegan option at every meal. They had a portable fax which she was welcome to use in her room, if necessary, and a terminal by the reception if she needed to connect a laptop computer to collect e-mail. All the rooms had satellite television, eighty-five channels. It was as well-equipped and sanitised as a Holiday Inn in any of the world's commercial centres. Kathy had been expecting a glorified pub.

'Good morning, Miss McGuinness.' It took her too long to respond. She would have to be sharper. It was the manageress: suited, smart and cool with her.

'Welcome to Ballymagee,' she said briskly, smiling with her mouth but not her eyes. 'We're always pleased to welcome folk from ChipCo. Congratulations. It's big news round here.'

'Big news?' replied Kathy, genuinely surprised.

'It is. And it's good news.' The manageress paused and looked down her nose. 'At least, we all hope it is. My name's Crowley, by the way. Can I get you a car to take you to the plant?'

'Which car would that be?' asked Kathy carefully.

'Ah, I see from the look on your face that you've met Morrissey's Cars. But there's not much call for taxis. Most people have their own. I dare say you'll be getting one too. There's good bargains to be had at the moment, so my uncle tells me. He's Crowley's Garage, just behind the superstores.'

'There seem to be plenty of Crowleys in Ballymagee,' Kathy remarked, lightly.

'Fewer than there used to be,' the other woman replied pointedly. 'We have had a notable loss lately, I am sorry to say.'

'I think I'll walk.'

'Fifteen minutes, right through the town. You can't get lost. Follow your nose is what I always tell people. Will you be in for dinner?'

Kathy hadn't thought. 'I suppose so. It's home now, isn't it?'

'And that's very much how we'd like you to think of it, Miss McGuinness,' came the reply with practised professional insincerity.

Ballymagee was little more than one long street, interrupted by a market square alongside which stood the grey fortress of the Catholic church. As the Crowley woman had promised, you only had to head for the smell of cooking to find the factory, for the odour of hot oil came hurtling down the street as if it was trying to catch the last bus. Kathy tried to walk as upright and confidently as she could. Her mind was on her agenda for the first day: meeting senior managers, a factory tour, and then it was up to her. When the glad-handing had finished she would have to start making her mark.

She paused, her eye caught by the gleaming showroom which belonged to Crowley's garage. She had not expected to find Mercedes in such numbers in a backward place like this. Was it the football pools they had all won or the Lotto? A car horn sounded behind her. It was not the confident bark of a hooter that meant what it said, but a hesitant little upstart of a horn, possibly with a loose connection. She turned, and the stark, white letters *Morrissey's Cars* filled her view like a scene from a bad dream of the night before.

'How yer doin'?' shouted Danny, winding down the window.

'American or Irish are we today?' replied Kathy.

'We're whatever the customers want. To be sure we are,' he said, switching violently from mid-American to stage Irish. 'Do you need a lift?'

'It's all of three hundred yards,' she replied. 'Is there any chance of getting that far in your fine car?'

Danny, laughing as she waved him on, wound up his window and signalled an apology to the growing queue of traffic behind him. Strangely, Kathy felt happier about life for seeing him again. She dived into a newspaper shop and bought a copy of the local newspaper, the *Tribune*. 'How much?' she asked, cheerily. No reply. The old woman behind the counter was staring at her. Was she deaf? The woman had a nervous tic which grew more rapid as she looked down at the paper, seemingly mesmerised.

'Well, I'd say it was a good likeness of you,' she said eventually. 'In the paper. On the front page. Ah, you're big news here, you are. It makes a nice change from having a picture of a mucky old Bishop or a nasty farm fire. Welcome to Ballymagee.' It was the second welcome Kathy had had that day, and she was yet to discern any real warmth.

The woman broke off and her face stiffened. The nervous tic became still as she reached out for a plastic fly-swat, the size of a fish slice, which she kept within easy reach by the till. When a large, fat bluebottle ceased its droning and came to rest on the top of a pile of newspapers, she brought the swat down upon it, determined it would not live, and spread its fatness all over the front page, in particular across the picture of Kathy's face. It was a fly of such proportions that rather than be reduced to a blob, like most flies are by swatting, this one revealed its sickly, individual inner organs which stretched, when flattened, all the way from Kathy's left ear in the photograph to the bottom right-hand corner of her lip. Kathy instinctively raised her hand to wipe her mouth, as if the fly had been swatted on her.

'I hate the damned things. Lousy bloody flies! And by the time you leave here, you'll loathe them too.' The woman was breathing rapidly, looking truly frightened now. 'There's never good news in Ballymagee when the flies are buzzing around. Remember that.'

Kathy, thinking the woman must be mad, took the *Tribune* on to the street and unfolded it. There, in the centre of the front page, beneath a headline which read 'McGuinness Now in Charge', was a picture of her, hastily snapped in London, she remembered. It wasn't very flattering; her face looked a touch podgy, she thought, and her expression was ineffectual – not at all commanding as an incoming manager's should be. She heard the door of the shop open behind and turned round to find the woman, soiled fly-swat still in hand, calling after her.

'Pardon me, miss,' she blurted. 'It's nothing to do with me, but you look like a sensible sort of woman. So I'm going to tell you that there's no reason to fear anything. And what happened to Percy Crowley, God rest him, was just a terrible accident.'

She wiped the fly swat on her broad backside, and was about to resume her station by the till when Kathy asked her, 'He was the last manager, wasn't he, Percy Crowley?'

'He was. If he was still with us, I imagine you wouldn't be. But God has his ways.'

Kathy walked the final few yards to the factory gate, and tried to remember what she could about Percy Crowley. According to the files he seemed a competent manager, kept profits and production at a reasonable if not spectacular level. Did the woman mean he was dead?

The factory leaked steam like an old express engine. From

where Kathy stood by a small brick gatehouse, she could hear the rattle of machinery, see the fork-lift trucks loading pallets of boxed crisps on to lorries, ducking and diving but never colliding. The building in which the crisps were manufactured was clad in green plastic-coated steel sheeting which helped it blend with the landscape behind of moorland and distant blue hills. The tall chimney, which was so high that atop it was a warning light to deter planes arriving at the airport, was made of shiny aluminium or perhaps steel. It made the factory the sole focus of attention locally, dwarfing the tower of the Catholic church and placing ChipCo above God in Ballymagee, which was just about right.

The factory offices were much older, built of stone, and looked like an old school or perhaps a hospital of the basic kind with which Florence Nightingale would have been familiar. It had the bleak façade of a poverty-stricken institution. Even ChipCo's chilly marbled London towerblock was cosier than this.

'Are you expecting a taxi, miss?' asked the security man on the gate, wearing his peaked hat to the side as if it were a farmer's flat cap. 'Because that daft taxi driver just went through the gates and he said to be sure to tell you he'd arrived safely.'

'It's our joke,' replied Kathy. The man looked unimpressed. 'Is he Irish?' she asked, pretending not to know, trying to find out what others made of Danny Morrissey.

The man laughed out loud. 'He's about as Irish as that Volvo car he drives. And his accent's about as broken down, I would say. Ah, but he's a good laugh in the pub. We've got a saying here that "You won't be stepped on if you're a live wire". And that lad's a live wire all right. With a drop o' beer in 'im.'

There was no reception desk on the other side of the heavy oak doors. Instead, a hand written sign invited her to press a button, which Kathy did. It produced a rasping buzz followed some while after by the impatient sliding back of a frosted glass window.

'Oh, God,' exclaimed a woman, obviously caught by surprise. 'And there was me looking for you arriving in a car, and all.' She was wearing a plain dress beneath a hand-knitted cardigan, both pockets stuffed with used tissues. She had flat-soled shoes and walked as if her feet were bad. She talked without fully opening her mouth, covering it at times with her hand like someone embarrassed by the state of their teeth. 'I'm Jean,' she said, offering a swollen, arthritic hand. 'Pleased to meet you, Miss McGuinness. I'm your secretary as well as the receptionist. I do the paperwork for the chief engineer 'cos he's not too good at that sort of thing, and I have to help out with the wages too.' The woman was blathering. 'Then there's the typing. There used to be another girl but she could never figure the computers so she went to work in her father's shop, and a fine shop it is. If you're needing a new dress or anything then I'll tell you where it is. They have all the latest fashions. They've just got a lot of stuff in from Bond Street. That's in London, you know.'

'Sounds expensive,' remarked Kathy, sensing she ought to be impressed.

'Before things went wrong at the factory, people were making fair money. They couldn't spend it without travelling the two hundred miles to Dublin so the shops came here.' Together they went up the stairs. Slowly, on account of Jean's bad feet.

Kathy was disappointed with her office. It was lined in wood-effect hardboard and had thin vinyl floor-covering made to look like tiles. The overall effect was cheap. It stank of cooking oil and cigarettes, and was equipped only with a scruffy wooden knee-hole desk, the edges of which were deeply scarred by someone's habit of balancing cigarette ends on them. Down the right-hand side were a set of drawers; the other side of the desk consisted of one cupboard and was locked.

99

'I'll get you the key,' said the woman. 'I meant to clear it before you got here but I don't know where the time's gone since the funeral and that. It seemed, you know, disrespectful to clear his things away.

'Look, Miss . . .'

'Jean, please. Call me Jean, Like Mr Crowley did.'

'I know nothing about his death. All I was told was that he'd gone. Retired, I assumed.'

'It was one of those things,' Jean sighed. 'He wasn't the first to fall victim to the drink, and I dare say he won't be the last. It's always been a bit of a problem in these parts.' The woman pulled yet another tissue from up her sleeve and blew her nose. 'I'll make you some tea,' she said, after blowing hard.

Through the frosted glass partition between her office and Jean's, Kathy could see the outline of an electric kettle pressed against the glass. Next to it was a bottle of milk.

'No. I'll make *you* one,' she insisted.

'That would be terrible! The new manager, on her first day, making tea for the staff. Jesus, what would they say?'

Kathy plugged in the kettle and when it boiled, brewed the tea in a large brown teapot. Two girls burst into the office in quick succession with the determined look of gossipers, but on seeing the new manager brewing the tea went pale and scattered like chuckling hens.

'There's no need to be scandalised,' Kathy shouted after them. 'Even managers can brew tea, you know.'

'It was a shock, Mr Crowley dying. I'd worked for him for fifteen years,' Jean explained, sipping her tea. 'He was like a father to me. To all of us, really.'

'A father?' said Kathy.

'Yes. A father figure. Can you understand that?' Kathy shook her head. 'He would scold you and chase you and make your life hell, but if you were truly bothered he was the first to put an arm round you and tell you everything was all right. That's what fathers are for, isn't it?'

'I suppose so,' replied Kathy bleakly.

'He's been dead and buried six weeks now, but we still can't believe he's not with us. We've wanted his spirit to remain in the place, you see. And with you coming it's as if the spell has been broken and we're having to wake up from the bad dream and come to terms with the fact that he's gone.'

'I had no idea,' said Kathy. 'No one told me.'

'I don't suppose head office knew or cared,' replied Jean bitterly. 'I'd sometimes have to ring them up for something or other and I'd get the feeling they'd forgotten we even existed. It didn't matter, though, as long as we had Mr Crowley. He would see us all right, we knew that. Yes, he was really a father to us.'

'It's going to be a hard act to follow.'

'I wouldn't try. Just be yourself. This place has to start over again, and it might as well be now.' Jean blew hard again.

Kathy went over to the large leather chair and as she sat down, the springs groaned as if she had dropped heavily into the lap of Percy Crowley's ghost. 'Now to business,' she announced briskly. 'I've got meetings with the senior managers at eleven, yes? Then a tour of the factory?'

Jean looked sheepish and stared into her teacup, not able to look Kathy in the eye. 'That's what it says on the paper I sent you, indeed.' She started to bite her lower lip. 'But the truth is, there aren't any managers at all.'

'No managers?'

'No. We just get on with it. If there were any problems, Mr Crowley sorted them all out. You see, he'd worked his way up through maintenance and packing, did a spell in sales and purchasing, and knew the business inside out. He could even put a new tyre on a truck if he had to. He didn't mind. He was that sort of man.'

'There are *no* managers?' asked Kathy incredulously. 'But I've seen the staff listed. There's a sales manager, potato purchasing manager, maintenance supervisor . . .' Her voice was rising as she recited the list.

'Ah, there's a maintenance supervisor, all right. That's Jack. He understands all the pipes and things. Dangerous work it is, hot oil and all that. Always says the place could go up like a bomb if he wasn't careful. So we put him in charge of the oil. He's a good man.'

'*We* put him in charge?'

'It's not for me to say any more,' replied Jean defensively. 'I dare say it will all be explained to you in time.'

'And do you think anyone will be kind enough to explain to me exactly what my job here might be? You seem to have everything worked out quite nicely. Where do I fit in?' Jean missed the sarcasm.

'I'll try and find Jack. If there's anything you want while I'm away, just ring 9 and a girl will be up. There are no secrets here. Everyone knows as much as anyone else.'

Except me, thought Kathy.

The phone rang. Jean had vanished. Kathy picked it up and said a cautious hello. The voice asked who this was. She replied, 'It's Kathy Fo— McGuinness. Kathy McGuinness, the new manager. Can I help you?'

'Ah, you're welcome to Ballymagee,' shouted a cheery voice at the other end, trying to make itself heard above a clatter of machinery. 'This is Jack Crowley, the maintenance supervisor. How are ye?'

'Fine,' spluttered Kathy.

'Grand, grand,' he replied jovially. 'I'm up to me neck in oil here. We've lost number six feed pump on the first fryer. I'll be a bit late. Is that all right?'

'Of course,' replied Kathy, and as she put the phone down the door opened and Jean returned. 'Was that him on the phone?' she asked.

'It was. He rang to say he had trouble with the feed pumps. He might be late. I'm sorry, Jean, but I didn't catch your surname?'

'Crowley,' she replied proudly. 'Jean Crowley.'

'There seem to be a lot of Crowleys,' Kathy observed. 'And Jack. Did I hear him right? It's Jack Crowley?' Kathy was also remembering the woman in the hotel, and the name above the Mercedes garage. And now Jean.

'More Crowleys in Ballymagee than currants in a fruit cake, and about as nutty, that's what we always say,' she replied with a giggle.

'And Crowley, the manager who died?'

'Uncle Percy Crowley, he was. You'll have met his sister, Auntie Nancy. She runs the newspaper shop. She rang and told me she'd seen you.'

'And Jack Crowley, the engineer?'

'He's a distant cousin. I'd have to sit down and work it all out. It gets a bit complicated.'

'And Crowley's Garage?'

'Another uncle.'

'Anything that isn't Crowley?'

'Aye,' replied Jean, sadly. 'This office. It's Crowley no longer. It's McGuinness now. And it may be no bad thing either because we've still got some o' them old-fashioned typewriters and the man who fixes them says it's always the letters that make up "Crowley" that wear out first. Shall I show you round? If Jack's number six feed pump is on the blink, he'll be some time. It's a hell of job if he has to get the flange off the secondary chamber. Tight as hell they are.'

'I don't know what feed pumps are?'

'They stand between life and death, they do. Instead of heating the oil for the cooking directly, we have a grand system of passing superheated oil through pipes, and those in turn heat the oil that does the frying. It stops the oil ever burning directly. But it means that the oil that does the heating is wicked stuff, viciously hot and under pressure because of the feed pumps. If anything parted there would be a fine spray of searingly hot oil sprayed everywhere, and if it caught light this whole place would go up like a bomb. That's why the feed pumps are so important. It's the stuff of nightmares.'

'Is it safe?' asked Kathy.

'Oh, very. You'll see steel doors all over the place. They slam shut at the first hint of fire, seal it off, stop the whole place going up. Or that's the theory, anyway,' explained Jean.

'You seem to know a lot about feed pumps, and everything really.'

'I told you, there's not much we can't turn our hands to. That's the way Uncle Percy liked it. And we did too. Now, we'll start at the potato store.'

The potato storage area was the size of an aircraft hangar with the solemn atmosphere of a cathedral. It was dank and gloomy and divided by high walls into large bays, like transepts, some of which were empty, others piled thirty feet high with countless tons of potatoes. There were bright bulbs hanging from the high roof which cast sharp-edged shadows on to the concrete floor. It smelled of earth and reminded Kathy of walking through a dense, chilly forest kicking up natural smells of soil and vegetation with her feet. Apart from the gentle rumble of a fan and the flutter of the wings of a startled pigeon, it was deadly quiet on account of the insulation which kept the potatoes at an even, cool temperature. They seemed at peace.

'There's four hundred tons in each bay,' said Jean proudly. 'All grown within fifteen miles of here. You'll know about the golden triangle of land where potatoes grow like no other place on earth? Magic it is. The farmers have only to look at their land

and the potatoes appear. Or that's what it seems like anyway. We've had geologists here and all, but they've got no answer. It's just like the farmers say, perfect for taters and that's all there is to it.'

'I heard about the land. Very special.'

'It is,' replied Jean. 'And although those folk in their smart offices in London sometimes forget it, the whole company owes its prosperity to that lump of land where potatoes grow just for the asking.' They both paused to look up, paying homage to the tons of potatoes towering over them. Kathy thought they might look threatening if you were not used to the sight. She breathed in the cool air again till it filled every bit of her lungs, and shivered.

'You can't smell anything funny, can you?' asked Jean, looking suddenly anxious.

'Why do you ask?'

'Because the smell is the first clue when something's going wrong. You'll have heard we've had problems? Well, this is where you first find out about them. Here in the potato store. And it starts with a smell. There's others can explain it better,' she said, trying to dismiss the subject and move on.

'How many tons a year do we use?'

'About thirteen thousand.'

'And how many of those come from local farms?'

'All of them, of course,' replied Jean, surprised that such a question need be asked.

'And these problems . . . ?' enquired Kathy.

'Not for me to say,' replied Jean, trying to head towards the door.

'What do you mean by a smell?'

'You'd best ask the others.'

From the chill of the potato store, they went to the warmth of the cooking rooms. Here, the paper-thin slices of potato were carried by a conveyor through shallow pans of cooking oil, heated in turn by those pipes through which superheated oil passed, fed by the pumps on which work was now being done. Hanging at strategic points were foam-filled fire extinguishers, and fire-proof suits which could quickly be donned in case the worst should ever happen. It was dangerous stuff, they all knew, and if it were to ignite it would be like standing in front of a military flame thrower. It would mean cremation for all of them. That was why Jack Crowley took seriously any problems with the oil, and only paused briefly to shake Kathy's hand as she went by, saying he would see her later for a longer chat.

Fried, dried and flavoured by an electrostatic machine which caused particles of tasty powders ranging from Crispy Bacon to Pacific Prawn to be attracted to the bland slices as they hurtled by, the now cool and flavour-enhanced crisps were conveyed to a packaging machine which weighed them, sorted them by size, and dumped the precise amount of product into each dazzlingly shiny bag. It was an engaging process to watch.

'Foley!' declared Jean, out of the blue, as they crossed from the factory back to the offices.

'No, McGuinness,' insisted Kathy, reactions perfect. 'You must be confusing me with someone else. I'm Kathy McGuinness.'

'I know that,' replied Jean. 'It was a Foley who came here in 1970 and discovered the place. There was nothing here then. Amazing, isn't it? All this from one good idea that girl had then. Have you ever met her? They say she's a big shot at ChipCo, but she never comes here now. Never seen her. I've come across her name on the bottom of memos. But you'd think she'd come and see us sometime. I mean, I would. If I was responsible for this, I'd have been so proud. Have you ever met her . . . Leonora Foley?'

'Bumped into her once or twice,' replied Kathy truthfully.

It was beginning to drizzle as Jean and Kathy clattered across the yard between the factory and the offices. They used the back door; a dank little entrance which led into a long, drab corridor, the floor of which was paved with stone flags.

'This is a funny place,' remarked Kathy. 'It gives me the shivers.'

'And you're not the only one,' said Jean. 'Used to be some kind of workhouse or institution. It's got a history. I don't know exactly what it is, but I have my suspicions it's not a very nice one.'

Kathy's office was as drab as she remembered it, and even duller now the sky was clouded over and rain was running down the greasy windows.

'There's one thing you'll have to explain to me. If there are no managers, and your Uncle Percy took all the decisions himself, even changing tyres when necessary, who are all these people on the staff list that London headquarters firmly believe work here?'

Jean looked sheepish. 'Well, if I'm honest, I would have to admit that I am most of them. I wrote all the letters which Uncle Percy dictated to me, and I made up the names and the signatures. It was simple, really.'

'It's also dishonest.'

'No more dishonest than those people at ChipCo taking all the credit for the success they are now, and not admitting how much they owe to Ballymagee. They never give the place a second thought. That's what I call dishonesty.'

'And what about the wages? Where are all the salaries of the people who didn't exist?'

'I didn't steal them, if that's what you're suggesting.'

'I don't think for one minute you did,' Kathy reassured her. 'But I have to know.'

'I suppose all this will get back to head office and we'll get the sack,' said Jean sadly.

'Not necessarily. I was sent here to put this place back on the rails, not go telling tales. If the plant has been compromised I shall have to do something. If you can convince me that what you've got here works, I might say nothing at all.'

'Then I suppose you might as well know,' said Jean. 'We put all the money in a kitty and divide it between us. There were four senior managers' salaries which came to about a hundred and eighty thousand pounds a year. Well, there's seventy people employed, so we got an extra couple of thousand or so each.'

'For how long?' asked Kathy incredulously.

'Six years at least. Except the first year when we started a syndicate and played the Lotto with it. But we never won enough to make it worthwhile.'

Kathy sank back into the old leather chair. The ghost of old Percy Crowley groaned again, as it did every time she sat down.

'And so you know all our little secrets now. And if Uncle Percy hadn't been so ground down by the way things kept going wrong, through no fault of his, he'd never have taken so much strong drink and driven off the road in the dark into the bog, God rest him.'

'I'm speechless,' said Kathy, shaking her head.

'Will I cancel the welcome?' Jean asked, casually.

'*Welcome*? What welcome?'

'The whole factory wanted to meet you and I thought it best done out of hours. So we've booked the back bar at the Crowley House Hotel for tonight at eight. They'd all like to see you.'

'So why should you cancel it?'

'Well, I thought you might be straight back to London, knowing what you know now. I realise this has put you in a difficult position.'

'On the contrary, it has put me in a unique position. I am the manager of a factory that needs no managing.' Kathy started to chuckle. 'As I never wanted to be a manager in the first place, you could say I've landed on my feet.' She laughed out loud at the thought.

Jean was about to go when Kathy stopped her. 'In all seriousness, I want this place to keep going. You want it to succeed for your own reasons, and I have my reasons too. Different ones. It doesn't mean we can't be on the same side.'

For the first time since they had met, Jean looked relaxed.

'The rain's getting heavier,' she observed. 'You'd best have the taxi back to the Crowley House. If you want a good car, my uncle can . . .'

'I know,' Kathy interrupted her, 'he can sell me one. Crowley's Garage would that be?' Jean just nodded and closed the door behind her. Alone now, Kathy was uncertain what to do next. Should she ring head office, speak to Ted Metcalfe, put him in the picture? Should she sack the lot of them? If she did she was sure to get Ted's backing, for she had been given total authority to put this place back on track.

Which raised another question in Kathy's mind: exactly what was the problem with this factory? Hints had been dropped, heads shaken despairingly, but no further explanations offered. Expecting there to be some kind of management structure, she had intended to ask for a report, have someone conduct a study, get an overview by forming a working party – do all the things they did in London when things went wrong. But the entire consultative team was herself, a secretary called Jean, a man called Jack who was up to his armpits in cooking oil, and a workforce most of whom seemed to be called Crowley.

Kathy looked at her watch. It was time for lunch. She would make do with an apple and the inevitable packet of crisps. In the schedule she had intended to follow, she had set herself the target of making her mark on this place, commencing at 3 p.m. sharp, but now she decided to postpone that by twenty-four hours. Instead, she would study what figures there were and try to make her own assessment of where the place was going wrong. She swung the leather chair round till the seat was parallel to the desk, and with a brief apology to the memory of the man she now thought of as her own Uncle Percy, hoisted her legs on to the desk and settled down to read a bundle of reports. She was still there at five that afternoon when Jean knocked politely on the door and reminded her that eight o'clock was when the staff would gather in the Crowley House Hotel.

'I need help with interpreting these reports,' she called. Jean made for the door, like a mouse who senses the cat moving in for the kill. 'Jean! Did you hear me?' Kathy insisted, raising her voice a little.

'I think they explain themselves,' suggested the secretary diffidently.

'They don't explain a damned thing. It's quite clear that every so often, and for no reason that anyone can fathom, something stops production, and suddenly. No warning, no clue that it's coming. It takes at least forty-eight hours to get over that stoppage, but each time production never seems quite to get back to the level it was before. It's as if there's an almighty hiccup, and the factory never gets its breath back.'

'I'd say you'd got it just about right.' Jean tried to make for the door again.

'But I need to know what causes it and what can be done to stop it. So, what is it?'

'It's not for me to say. It's just one of those things that happens and whatever we might try and do, we can't prevent it. There's some say it's the hand of God, punishing our wicked ways in deceiving people about how we run this place. I pray to God He'll give you strength when it happens.'

'But what *is it*?' Kathy insisted, hitting the desk in exasperation with the flat of her hand.

Jean was saved by a knock on the door, which opened to

reveal a boiler-suited figure with a mischievous smile on its face.

'Well, if it isn't my own little unicorn. Mr Morrissey, the famous taxi driver!' said Kathy. 'And wearing a boiler suit with the logo of my company across the breast pocket.'

'I can explain, Miss McGuinness,' stuttered Danny, surprised by her sharpness.

'It had better be good,' she snapped. Jean looked shifty and excused herself.

'Well, you see . . .' He broke off. 'Do you want this in Irish or American?'

'I don't bloody well care so long as you explain whether you drive cars or work for me, here in this factory?'

'Well, I'd say I did a little bit of both, that I would,' he replied in best Irish. 'I drive the lorry that collects from the small farms. Unless the taxi is needed and then I drive that. Either way, I'm on the road all day.'

'But who are you working for? I just want a simple answer,' insisted Kathy. 'I'm desperately trying to understand who works here and who doesn't. It's not a lot to ask.'

'Ah, that's simple,' replied Danny, dropping the Irish accent. 'We all work for each other here. It's one big happy family. Haven't you worked that one out yet? Now, will yer be wantin' a lift to that grand hotel, or not?'

'I want a lift, and a large drink.'

'And would the drink you're havin' be with the driver who's takin' yer home, by any lucky chance?'

'Lucky for the driver or for me?' replied Kathy, melting somewhat in the fast-flowing stream of heavy Irish charm.

'Let's just say, the luck o' the Irish will be on one of us,' he replied with a twinkle in his eye.

Despite her pledge that this would never happen again, Kathy found herself once more in the passenger seat of the wonky Volvo.

She did not speak much on the short journey back to the hotel. Instead, she looked at the passing shops, understanding now the affluence of this place. It all stemmed from ChipCo's money which they'd diverted for their own purposes.

'There's nothing wicked about what they do,' said Danny, reading her thoughts.

'It's fraud,' said Kathy, having made up her mind.

'A bit naughty, perhaps,' replied Danny. 'But it works in everyone's interest. ChipCo's factory keeps on running, after a fashion, and so in London they can forget all about it – which seems to suit them. They pay a very small cash price for that. On the other hand, the town does well out of it. It's like a life-support machine, that factory. It keeps the whole place alive. But I can see it must all come as a surprise to you.'

'It's not the money that worries me. I want to know what it is that keeps going wrong in this place. It's clear from the figures that things trundle along fine for a while – not spectacular, but not disastrous either. Then it's as if someone pulls the plug and the place comes to a grinding halt. It takes forty-eight hours to get over it, but things are never quite back to the same level as before. It is as if the place is bleeding to death, very, very slowly. What is doing it?'

'Or *who*?' said Danny. 'The hand of God is still held to be all powerful round here. And what the Lord giveth, the Lord taketh away. And some days he takes away whatever it is that makes that factory work.'

'You can't believe that?' exclaimed Kathy.

'You can if you live here long enough. Anyway, I'm the son of a Kentucky Baptist preacher. Just 'cos he couldn't keep his hands from up the skirt of the police chief's wife, don't mean I've forgotten all them dangblasted sermons I was forced to sit through.'

'But why will no one tell me what happens? Do you know?'

'I sure do. But it ain't up to me to say. I promised I'd keep my mouth shut. It's a factory matter. I just drive a taxi and hear what I hear when I take people around. And I keep that to myself.'

'Do me a favour, Danny. For the sake of the factory, tell me what you know?'

He turned to her. 'Now, Miss McGuinness, if you're needin' a little company at tonight's welcome party, I'd be happy to escort you and introduce you to as many people as I know – which is all of them,' he boasted. The Volvo came to a halt outside the Crowley House Hotel.

'Do we have a deal?' asked Kathy, before opening the car door. 'About breaking your rule of silence and telling me what the hell's going on?'

'My father, when he was preaching, always said that a promise made before God was made forever. But as keeping promises to God only got the old bastard in deeper and deeper shit, I guess there's something to be said for breaking them here and there, if it's in a good cause.'

'Does that mean you'll tell me or you won't?'

'Well, here we are,' announced Danny. 'The Crowley House Hotel. You can settle up later.' He sped away, giving no reply to her question.

Her bedroom was warm, a safe haven. Kathy ran a deep hot bath, poured in a cocktail of salts and scents and slowly lowered herself into it. She leaned back, letting her long black hair trail in the water and float upwards. She stared at the ceiling, trying to fathom the strange events of the day.

She closed her eyes for a moment, trying to remember the figures, attempting to spot some pattern, a clue to the funda-mental problem. If there had been more people to talk to, managers for instance, then she could have pumped them for information. But those options were closed. If she were to report back to Metcalfe what she had discovered, then without a doubt there would be a purge, leaving the people of Ballymagee with no living of any kind. By letting her even halfway in on the secret, they had shown remarkable trust and it was too soon to betray it.

She slid a little deeper into the bath to warm the parts of her which were becoming chilled and in a hazy, slumbering, rambling way became convinced she had a solution. The problem with the factory was that it was too cold. Everyone there was permanently shivering; it was damp, uncomfortable, made everyone ache with the chill of it. She felt chilly at the thought of the place and rubbed her hands over her body to move the blood around. Colder and colder the factory became till it was icy, frost hanging from every ceiling . . .

There was a loud crash; a sharp report like a gunshot which woke her from her dream. Realising that time had passed, she lifted herself up to try and see the bedside clock. She had been asleep in the water for an hour and the bath was now freezing; the lather had evaporated and those parts of her skin which were not wrinkled, were goose-pimpled and bitterly cold. She got out as quickly as she could and wrapped herself in a towel. There was another crash. A pile of plates, a saucepan falling to the floor? No, it was a purer sound than that. It came again, a little louder, followed by a metallic hissing which she recognised as a cymbal being struck. Someone was trying to play the drums. God, her welcoming party!

Already she could hear a lively murmuring from the bar below. She got into her clothes as quickly as she could. It wasn't formal, she hoped, jeans would have to do. Somewhere, stuffed into that guitar case which she had not yet bothered to unpack, was a clean sweater. There was a twang followed by a crackling which she guessed was the sound of an electric guitar being coaxed into life. Something about the sound of live music uplifted her. She could hear a succession of cars drawing into the yard, and chatter as people came through the front door.

Realising all of them were coming to see and meet her, she crept down the stairs, hoping they might open beneath her feet: anything other than having to face this. It was all a mistake, her coming here. If they'd left her alone she could still have been in Global Development, sitting drinking in a wine bar right now with her mates, laughing at the ridiculous life they led selling potato crisps to the world. Now she was no longer just one of the many dragged along by the corporate engine; she was the driver and her job was to keep all these people and the factory on its rails, and send them the right signals.

She took three deep breaths and opened the door. Instantly, the room fell silent. The drummer dropped his sticks, the guitarist ceased strumming, the lad behind the bar let go of the beer pump, and everyone with a glass in their hand put it down and looked in Kathy's direction. It was like a new animal arriving at the zoo – everyone wanted a glimpse of the creature. One or two of the men got to their feet, thinking it was the right thing to do. She stared back at a mixture of faces: old and young, bloated and drawn, weather-worn and fresh. She tried to read their expressions. She did not sense hostility, just curiosity.

After what seemed like an age, there was murmuring from a couple of tables as conversations were resumed and the spotlight was off her; which gave her a sense of relief till she realised they were talking about her, weighing her up, wondering how much she knew and what she was going to do about it.

Suddenly, she saw Danny, standing at the back of the room, a pint of stout in his hand. People were looking at him too.

'Is it the leprechaun you are today?' shouted a local, switching in mid-stream to stage American. 'Or is it Danny the cowboy riding into town, eh, pardner?' There was a huge roar of laughter.

'Give us a bit o' that good ol' Mayo accent, Danny boy,'

shouted another. 'God be me witness, it's the strangest Mayo sound I've ever heard.' They laughed some more.

'In Mayo, you'd pass for a Kerry man, I'd say!' shouted someone.

'Or even an eejit from Cork,' someone added. 'All gab and guts!'

'I'll be one of you all, a true Mayo man, when I get my tongue round your lingo, that I will to be sure,' Danny replied, joining in the joke in his best confused Irish accent. Then quickly changed the subject. 'And I would ask you to welcome Miss Kathy McGuinness, and wish her well in her new job!' he bellowed.

The men stood, the woman remained seated, and those with glasses in their hands raised them nervously in Kathy's direction.

'Thank you,' she announced to the room. 'No speeches, but . . .' and she looked towards the lad behind the bar '. . . a drink for everyone. And thank you again.'

There was another cheer and an old man with kind, watery eyes leaned across and said to her, 'Those are the first words I've heard you speak, and I'd say you'd already got the hang of the way we like to talk. We appreciate a sentence with the words "have a drink" in it. It's something that lad's never understood.' And he nodded towards Danny. Kathy shook the old man's hand. 'I'm retired now,' he said. 'I'd been in that factory since the day it started. And, you know, seeing you there reminds me so much of that Foley girl thirty years ago. I shall never forget her. A real beauty.'

Conversations resumed, the uncertain tuning of the guitar continued, and Kathy fought her way through the room to where Danny was sitting, now alone.

'Thank you for breaking the ice. It was a kind thing to do.'

'You sure looked relieved,' he remarked. 'Did you think they were going to lynch you or something? This may be the west, but it ain't that wild.'

'I was wondering.'

'You've nothing to worry about. You passed the test.'

'Test? I didn't notice one.'

'Good. I didn't want you to. Perhaps I should give up this taxi driving and get a job as a shrink, like they have in California. All those head doctors. Hey, they make real money over there.'

'And when exactly did you delve into my mind, Dr Morrissey?'

'In the taxi from the airport. You see, they were all terrified who you might be and what you were going to do when you got here. They went through all the staff records and couldn't find a McGuinness anywhere. So they got suspicious. As you're beginning to learn, there's one or two what you might call "special arrangements" been made over the years and so they wanted you checked out. I told them you were fine. So it was decided Jean would come clean with you. In fact, I went further than saying you were just fine. I told 'em I quite liked you.'

Kathy spied Jean at the far end of the room. Kathy nodded and smiled, and the secretary smiled back at her.

'You said what?'

'I told them I quite liked you, actually. You seemed a good ol' gal.'

'I'm flattered to be well regarded by a taxi driver from Louisville. Even if I am still uncertain whether he works for me or for himself, or if he's an Irishman or an American.'

'I'll tell you,' replied Danny, moving closer to her like a man with a great secret to impart, or else a desire to be closer to a woman. 'We're all working for each other. Look around you at these people. They're the best: they're not cheats, or idle, or crooked. All they want is someone who can give them back what they think they're in danger of losing, which is that Goddamned crisp factory. What's wrong with it I don't know, and neither do they. But all these people here sure as hell hope *you* can find out.'

He lifted his glass of stout to his lips and took a deep draught, looking at her sideways while he swallowed.

There was a roll on the drum which gave rise to another cheer from the room, followed by a strident chord on the electric guitar. A middle-aged man whom Kathy recognised, but could not quite place, approached the microphone.

'That's Jack Crowley. Maintenance, remember?' Danny whispered to her. Jack stood in front of the mike and coughed lightly into it to see if it was working.

'If it's broke, Jack'll never fix it,' came a cry from the room followed by a belly laugh or two.

'Now,' shouted Jack, needing no further amplification, 'it's going to be a grand Ballymagee welcome to Miss McGuinness, and no mistake. Have yer got yer squeeze box handy, Michael?' he shouted at a lad sitting by the makeshift stage which had been built out of a few planks resting on upturned, empty beer crates. The boy opened his concertina wide to fill it with air, and as he pushed the two ends together and made the notes with his fingers, it took no more than three of them before his audience recognised the first line of *The Wild Rover*. They listened as Jack Crowley belted out the first verse, and could hardly be contained when they got to the chorus. Some stood to give extra force to the '*no, nay, nevers*', and collapsed back into their seats while Jack did the second verse. By the time he got to the fourth, the room was warming up like a furnace with a fine draught under its fire. When Jack sang, '. . . *and when they've caressed me as oft times before, I* never *will play the wild rover no more*', the plastic chandelier shook as every voice in the room gave the final chorus. And when it was over they cheered and applauded themselves and begged for more.

'If they're like this after the first song, what's it like when they've warmed up?' Kathy shouted in Danny's ear.

'I'll tell you a thing,' he said. 'When the evening shift finishes and the rest of 'em pile in here, you sure as hell better plug those ears of yours. When this lot get goin', I sometimes think you'd hear them back home in Louisville.' And he sidled his way towards the bar.

After an hour of singing and drinking in which Kathy had shaken so many broad and muscular hands that her wrists and fingers ached, the tunes were subtly changing. There was less of the Irish about them. They had given *The Rose of Tralee* all it was worth, and *Galway Bay* and *The Green Hills of Clare*, but when Jack Crowley came back on to the stage, he had different music in mind. There was a roll on the drum which brought the room to attention. 'Jack will now sing his party piece!' shouted the accordion player, and nodded at him, saying, 'You start and I'll follow.' The room knew what was coming and braced themselves.

Jack stood up and took a deep breath. He licked his lips like an operatic tenor coming on to the stage before his solo. He opened his mouth, and in a perfectly judged pitch sang, '*And now the end is near, and so I face the final curtain . . .*' By the time he had got to the end of *My Way*, the room was putty in his hands. They did not applaud till the very last echoes of his final note had faded away, and then they stamped their feet and roared. And when the applause died, Jack was awash with people wanting to slake his thirst.

'It's your turn, now, Danny boy,' he shouted across the room. Danny was sitting next to Kathy who gave him a deep dig in the ribs which propelled him to his feet.

'Ah, hell. I ain't so good at this sort o' thing.'

'Rubbish, boy. Open your mouth and let's hear it,' came a shout from the back.

'Will anything do?' he asked.

'So long as it's decent!'

Danny looked around the room as much for inspiration as

119

anything, and his eye fell on the old upright pub piano. It was a battered elderly brute which had been scarred by countless pints of stout without a thought for the music it could make if brought to life by talented fingers.

'Does it work?' Danny shouted to the lad behind the bar.

'Sure it does,' came the reply. 'Hit the keys and a sound comes out. It's dead simple.' That got a laugh from the room. Danny pulled a stool from under the table and plonked it in front of the piano. He lifted the lid and found most of the keys present. Some of the black ones looked decidedly wobbly but he would have a go.

He took a deep breath and played the first chord, then a cascade of notes, and as soon as the tune started, Kathy felt a shiver run from the top of her head down to the tips of her toes, as if a feather had been run lightly down the length of her bare back. It was *Piano Man*, Billy Joel's song. She loved it, knew every word, hung on every phrase like life support.

'Stop!' she shouted, and the room went quiet as Danny took his fingers from the keys. She felt in her back pocket, but there was nothing there. Had she brought a bag down with her? She hadn't.

'Wait! All of you,' she insisted. 'I'll be back in a minute. Danny, don't you play another note till I'm back.'

Speculation filled the room like stout filled the glasses to overflowing. They heard her sprint up the stairs, cross the creaking boards of the landing, go through the door of her room and across it, where she paused. Then the footsteps started again; back across the floor of her room, through the door which they heard slam behind her, across the creaking boards again and then pell-mell down the stairs. Breathless, Kathy burst into the room to a round of congratulatory applause

'I don't know what you've gone for, girl, but you're keeping us from our music.'

She sprang up on to the impromptu stage, wobbling a little as the beer crates shifted, and gave Danny a nod. She placed her harmonica to her lips, and took a deep breath. She gave another nod, and Danny played the same chord again followed by the cascade of notes, or as many as he could manage with so many keys loose. After a few bars she joined in, and between them they had the room's undivided attention. Kathy hit every accompanying note perfectly. A volcano could have erupted under the Crowley House Hotel at that moment, and no one would have shifted. They were entranced as Danny arrived at the words, and sang in a smooth and tuneful voice, *'It's nine o'clock on a Saturday, the regular crowd shuffles in . . .'* He knew every word as well as Kathy. Between the verses she was ready with her harmonica and accompanied him as well as Billy Joel himself could have wanted.

While Danny played and sang, she watched every move of his skilful fingers, each nod of his head as it marked time with the song. She liked the way his hair flopped forward, the casual and relaxed way his eyes closed at the emotional bits, his lack of embarrassment in singing this song and meaning it. So struck was she by his performance, she almost missed the next solo but came to her senses just in time.

The applause, the cheering, the adoration lasted minutes, rising to a crescendo as Danny rose from the stool, joined Kathy on the wobbly stage, took her hand, kissed it lightly and bowed. An encore would have been guaranteed had a late arrival not broken the spell. Like a stone through a pane of glass, the coming of the man they called 'the Monk' shattered the high spirits of the evening.

Dressed in a long, black woollen coat – the one he wore whatever the weather, at work or at play – he stood in the doorway, clearly surprised to find a crowd in the usually quiet bar. His hair was pure silver and could have passed for a halo had there not been a less than angelic expression on his face. He carried a black walking stick in his right hand made from a stout piece of wood cut from a hedge. He leaned on it as he made his way across to the bar, limping slightly and wearing the pained look of a man whose joints ached. He lifted the walking stick, banged it on the bar and started to order a drink, but was overcome by a coughing spasm which forced him back on to a bar stool. The lad behind the bar made no effort to help him or ask if he was all right or what he might want to drink.

The icy silence of the crowd started to melt as low conversations were resumed. No one paid the man the slightest attention. Except Kathy. She got up and went across to him and waited till his coughing subsided before asking, 'Would you like a drink? I'm buying tonight. Something to help your cough, perhaps?'

The old man looked up. 'And who the hell are you?' he asked, not returning the warmth of Kathy's smile. 'From the factory, aren't you? Another fucker from ChipCo. Keep your bloody drink.' He dragged his nose along the sleeve of his black coat, sniffed deeply and wiped his wet lips on the back of his hand. 'I'd drink the water from the bloody drains before I'd take a drink with you lot. God, if I'd known you'd all be here, I would never have set foot in this bar tonight. The curse of the devil is on you all!' he bellowed, and picked up his stick from the bar to rise uncertainly to his feet.

'And who the bloody hell are you?' he roared at Kathy, indignant that she had dared speak to him.

'Kathy . . . Kathy McGuinness.' The name 'Foley' was so close to her tongue that it nearly slipped out, but she saved herself in time. 'I'm the new manager at the factory. I don't think we've met?' She stretched out her hand. The room watched for the old man's next move. It would be significant; like a meeting of east and west in the old days of the Cold War. A handshake now would mean more than a thousand words.

She left her hand in mid-air, waiting for it to be joined by his. At first his arm twitched as if being pulled by a string which was compelling him to raise it, yet at the same time a greater burden of bitterness kept it pinned firmly by his side. Kathy sensed him trying to weigh her up. His look was not the kind a man gave a woman casually. It was not seductive yet neither was it distant. It was warmer than polite but stopped short of joy. The expression on his face, in fact, was at odds with his manner, and it made her shiver. Watched by the disbelieving crowd, his hand finally rose to meet hers. As they touched, the room fell completely silent.

'I'm pleased to meet you, Miss McGuinness. My name is Pat Tierney and I wish you personally no harm. But may your bloody factory *rot in hell!*'

He dropped his hand, picked up his stick, turned and limped towards the door, slamming it behind him. The accordion player took this as a cue to break the ice and pulled a massive volume of air into his instrument. He started to squeeze *Stand By Your Man* forcibly out of it and was barely a couple of notes into it when every voice in the room joined in. The old man was forgotten.

As the final chorus was expelled from the lungs of the exhausted crowd of ChipCo workers, Danny came across to Kathy, whose hand was being shaken in turn, vigorously and warmly, by everyone in the room. When the last person had gone he spoke.

'Seein' as you live here, you won't be needing a car to take you home. Pity. Got a taxi service I can highly recommend.'

'I can just about get up one flight of stairs without the services of a chauffeur,' Kathy replied.

'We do a carry home service as well.'

They both laughed.

Kathy was about to make for the stairs, heading for her room, when she stopped and turned, as if a daring idea had just crossed her mind.

'Perhaps I do need a cab!'

'I know a driver who would take you to the ends of the earth,' replied Danny, gallantly. They went round to the car park where the tired old Volvo was resting against the back wall of the hotel, windscreen drenched in a heavy dew. Danny had to churn the engine for a full half minute before so much as a spark could be produced by the damp electrics.

'That man who came into the bar . . . "the Monk" you called him?' enquired Kathy.

'Yeah. Miserable old guy. I was sure surprised when he shook your hand. Say ChipCo to him and it's like saying Jesus Christ to the devil.'

'What's his problem?'

'No idea. Goes way back. Someone, somewhere did him wrong and he's never forgiven the place. He writes letters to the local papers saying the whole thing should be shut down. He hates the Brits running it. Doesn't think they've got any right to be owning land and factories in Ireland.'

'He's a republican?'

'It's nothing political, I think he's just off his head. They say he's got this old grudge and it's destroyed him. He's not dangerous, if that's what you're thinking.'

'It was the last thought in my mind. You sound as though you know him?'

'Yeah, sure. I get on with him. But I'm not British and I don't work for ChipCo, so he doesn't give me a hard time. Yeah, I get on with the old lad. He puts the kettle on. We talk about nothing much. I take notice of the way he phrases things and uses words, learn a lot from just listening to him ramble on. I avoid talking about ChipCo and that way he doesn't have to lose his temper.'

'He didn't look an unkind man, or not to me anyway,' probed Kathy.

'No, I wouldn't say he was. Just bitter, that's all. Hey! Where's this drive goin' to take us? Is this a big fare I can look forward to, or a quick trip to the end of the high street for a bag of fries?'

'Does the old man live far away?'

'Ten minutes, up the hill.'

'Then that's where I want to go,' Kathy declared.

'You've got the whole of this beautiful part of Ireland, a crowd of grand folks all dying for your attention, and you want to follow that miserable old bastard up the hill? What in hell's name for?'

'Because of the way he shook my hand,' she said. 'He took hold of it with a greater gentleness than any miserable old bastard, as you put it, might be expected to do.'

'It's all in yer imagination,' scoffed Danny. 'And if yer go followin' every guy who shakes yer hand, yer'll be gettin' yourself a reputation, sure you will.'

'And when the moment came to let go, he held on for a fraction of a second,' she continued, undeflected.

'Dirty old devil,' muttered Danny, with a hint of jealousy. But Kathy didn't hear him.

'And that's when I thought I caught sight of a different man behind the mask.'

'Mask?'

'Yes, mask. He might appear grumpy and bitter. But I'll bet you he's not, deep in his heart.'

'And how would you be gettin' deep in his heart to find out, eh?'

'By having you drive me up the hill, for starters.'

'It'll be pitch black,' protested Danny. 'You'll see nothing. And the place is a real tip, anyway. I could take you somewhere more interesting. Prove your theory some other time. I could show you my Billy Joel CDs,' he added temptingly.

'Up the hill, please, driver! I just want to see. I'm curious, that's all. Dead curious.'

Danny, Kathy admitted to herself privately, ten minutes later was dead right – this was a crazy thing to do. On the journey she tried to decide exactly what it was that had prompted this unlikely trip. The attraction of opposites, perhaps? Or was the clue in the touch of his hand, which to her had felt charged with unusual significance.

They arrived at two gateposts built out of breeze blocks once painted a clean white. A galvanised gate hung limply from one hinge.

'This is it,' announced Danny. 'I told you it was no great place.' Kathy got out of the car and took a deep breath of the air.

'But it's a marvellous place to live,' she insisted, feeling an urge to embrace her surroundings, as if they had a freedom about them which the town did not. 'The air is so clear tonight.' She looked up and followed the line of the shimmering Milky Way across the starry sky. 'I can smell the sea,' she said, taking another breath, 'and the peat burning in that cottage. It's so sweet you could almost drink it. Is that where the old man lives?' she asked, looking towards the low cottage.

'I told you it was nowhere special.'

'But it's perfect,' insisted Kathy. 'And it proves I was right about him.'

'Don't prove nothin' to me,' grumbled Danny.

'Well, it's clear to me,' insisted Kathy. 'No one with evil deep in their heart could live in such peace as this. This is the home of a kind man, I promise you. It's halfway to the clouds, out of this world. Don't you get a sense of being elsewhere? As if this isn't in the same part of Ireland as Ballymagee?'

'You wouldn't think that if the wind were the other way. Then you get the cooking smells drifting over. It's like sitting on top of the chimney here. Then I suppose you'd be sayin' he was a foul, stinking old sod.'

Kathy was not listening. Instead, intoxicated by the place, she was breathing the air ever more deeply, remembering the lingering touch of the old man's hand, trying to recapture the electric feeling.

'Is that what makes him so angry?' she asked, coming to her senses. 'The smell from the factory?'

'Nope,' replied Danny. 'He's kind of learned to live with that. It's something deeper. But, as I say, we never discuss it. I never talk to him about ChipCo.'

Kathy turned and looked down the valley towards the factory. It was brightly illuminated by floodlights which created a dazzling yellow haze in the air. What arrogance, she thought, intruding on such a peaceful spot as this. Yet at the same time, she had to concede, it might be considered a beacon of wealth for those who lived around it.

'Take me back to the hotel, will you, Danny?'

'You had enough up here?'

'No, I wouldn't say I had,' replied Kathy, 'but enough for now.'

5

A week later, two board meetings were held: one in Ballymagee, the other in Boston, USA. One started with a smile, a cup of tea and slice of the indigenous fruity bread, the other with a draught of pure fear. The meeting in Ballymagee was called for no real reason other than that Kathy thought she ought to have everyone round a table within her first few days in the factory. There was no agenda, no resolutions to be discussed, but plenty of cups of tea.

In Boston, on the other hand, it was Leonora Foley's first ever chance to sit at the head of the immense boardroom table in her capacity of Acting World President. The tigress was at last running the zoo. On one side of her sat the company secretary, who defensively kept his eyes fixed on the table except when he was making notes. To her right was Ted Metcalfe who had flown over from London especially for the meeting at her invitation. He had greeted her like a long-lost friend with kisses on both cheeks, embraces and protestations of 'missing you' and other lies designed to make her believe his life was empty without her presence dominating the London office.

For this debut, cast for the first time in the role of world player, Leonora had embraced power dressing like a python crushing limbs: New York tailoring, French perfume, Italian accessories. But this was mere outward cladding; the deadliest weapon was her mind, which everyone round the table knew outshone theirs. Except Ted Metcalfe, who'd always believed he could better her if he bothered to make the effort. Today he did not even bother to sharpen his wit or polish his armour: he was small fry compared to the corporate heads of Asia, North and South America and Europe. She would not be out to impress him. In fact, he privately wondered why he was here at all. London was a branch office compared with this lot.

Down the middle of the table, where other companies might have had flowers or carafes of water, ChipCo had plates of potato crisps, freshly opened but unlabelled. There was Thai Spice with Lemon Grass flavour, Pacific Oyster and Sea Salt, Caribbean Jerk, and Frankfurter and Mustard. It was not just the crisps that were there for testing, but the people as well.

'Shall we taste, gentlemen?' Leonora invited them as if they had any other option. If she had told them to stick their heads in a bucket, these guys would have obeyed.

'You may take notes,' she added, 'and we'll discuss them first on the agenda.' They reached towards the dishes and picked up individual crisps with the reverence of priests handling Communion wafers.

'Of course,' smarmed an Italian, the European marketing chief, his new Gucci loafers creaking as he got up to reach the dishes on the far side of the ridiculously large table, 'it is always a great pleasure to taste. It is the most satisfying aspect of my job.' He dipped his fingers into the crisps like a child at a birthday party.

Some tried to impress by approaching the task like a wine tasting. A Californian with a bright red shirt and the intense expression of a man who might be electing a Pope, took tiny nibbles and spat them into a wastepaper bin before taking a sip of water after each and moving on. 'Mmm, really good!' he moaned after the Frankfurter and Mustard, as if it were sex. Metcalfe watched, amused, but didn't bother to try any himself. Then he saw Leonora giving him one of her irritated looks, and made a half-hearted attempt at tasting a couple of crisps, but no more than that. He too spat them out.

'Hey, buddy. What's wrong with the chips?' shouted a New Yorker, head of east coast marketing. 'Why spit 'em out? You Brits got philosophical problems with taking a good mouthful of anything, eh?

'I like to taste and assess, not indulge in a feeding frenzy,' replied Metcalfe condescendingly.

'And I like to imagine what the customers will do,' replied the New Yorker, 'and that is stuff them as far down their throats as fast as they can till the whole packet's empty in less than half a minute. So, you don't go in for any of that fast down the throat stuff in the London office, eh?' he asked salaciously. Metcalfe glanced at Leonora.

She tapped on her glass with her gold ball point pen, and like well-behaved schoolboys the men resumed their seats. As they were making themselves comfortable, Leonora leaned closer to Ted Metcalfe and said, 'You didn't bother to put much effort into the tasting.'

'I've made up my mind already.'

'Don't be too smug,' she warned, before gazing around the table and opening her notebook. It was the first hint Ted Metcalfe had that this might be a less than cordial occasion. She addressed the entire room.

'I'd like comments, please. I don't have to tell you all that keeping ahead of competitors in the flavour game is the only way to win in the end. So, I want to hear your views.' She swung menacingly towards Ted. 'How does London assess them?'

Despite his apparent nonchalance, he was ready for her. 'Far East is in at the moment, very fashionable destination with kids. So the Thai will go well. The oyster tastes like prawns, and anyway most people think oysters give you the shits . . .' There was smothered laughter at this.

'I thought they were an aphrodisiac,' remarked Leonora. 'Although perhaps you're beyond such things, Teddy dear.' She wore the least benevolent smile he had ever seen on her face.

'Frankfurter?' she asked.

'Bland.'

'In what way?' Leonora quizzed him, like a barrister on the offensive.

'The mustard doesn't come through. Just tastes like pork sausage. Nothing out of the ordinary.'

This was all so much time-wasting. Leonora had made up her mind before she even came through the door, he knew.

'Assuming there are no political contra-indications concerning Thailand . . .' she glanced across at the head of the Asia operation who shook his head '. . . then I think we should go ahead to the developmental stage with the Thai flavour. Oysters simply aren't sexy enough.' They all laughed dutifully. 'And the Jerk and Frankfurter simply didn't work for me.' She looked accusingly at Metcalfe. 'Those two rather ordinary ideas were from the London office.'

They were, he reflected, dreamed up while you were still in charge of London, you fat-arsed old bitch. Get your high heels out of my throat, Leonora. But when he opened his mouth all that came out was a limp, 'I think we can do better.'

'I *want* better,' Leonora commanded. And they moved on.

'There are certain factories which are under-performing,' she announced, and the men around the table started to finger the crotch of their trousers like schoolboys awaiting a ticking off by the teacher. She listed a plant in Australia where figures were four per cent below target, Santiago had been wobbly but had stabilised, the German figures were disappointing. The Italian spoke up.

'There has been much industrial unrest. It was never going to

132

be easy starting in East Germany. Unification has been a terrible problem for them. Things will settle down.'

'If I have to rebuild the Berlin Wall to make that factory pay, then I shall be happy to do so. Understand?' barked Leonora. The Italian nodded his head and the nervous creaking of his Guccis could be heard again from under the table.

'Which brings us to the London figures.' She turned to Metcalfe, eyes blazing like a welding torch. 'Are you happy with them, Ted?'

It was a question to which he could have no correct answer, not knowing whether she thought they were good or bad. They were an indifferent set of figures, he had to admit, but not spectacularly lousy. It was that blasted Irish factory that brought down all the averages.

'Yeah, I think I'm happy with them. Of course, there have been hiccups.'

'Oh, hiccups, are they?' remarked Leonora, an edge to her voice. 'Indigestion on a massive scale, I would have said.'

'Well, you would know, Leonora, having left London only a couple of weeks ago.'

She stood up, straightened her skirt and strode across to the window till she had placed herself goddess-like between the men and the sun, casting a long shadow across them.

'The problem, Ted, has arisen since I handed over to *you*, which was at least a month before I left. *Your* figures, not *mine*, are so much shit. Oh, I know – it's been one problem after another and none of them poor little Ted's fault. Just bad luck . . . Well, I don't buy any of that, and I'm not going to sit over here in Boston and watch everything I worked for in London be pissed away.' He tried unsuccessfully to explain about Ireland, but she bit back.

'No explanations, no excuses!' she barked. 'Get back to London and sort it.' She sat down like a spent tornado and the men felt a chill after draught blow through the boardroom.

They went through the rest of the agenda at top speed, no one wishing to cross swords with Leonora Foley. She had made her first mark as Acting World President, and most of the bruises were on Ted Metcalfe.

'You didn't have to do that,' he said, drawing her aside as the others were leaving.

'Someone had to get their bollocks chewed today. Sorry it had to be you. But I meant it. Every word. Get those London figures back on track, whatever it takes. I'll be back in six months' time and I've no intention of walking into some kind of disaster area.'

'You know what the problem is,' he persisted. 'It's the Irish plant. It's prone to disastrous interruptions. It should be closed down and all those Paddys put back in the bog where they came from. Or are you still sentimental about the place?'

'You don't get to sit behind this desk if your mouth and mind are ruled by your heart. Of course I'm not sentimental. I'd be sorry, yes. A lot of this company's success is based on what we did in Ballymagee. But if it's got to go, it's got to go. Who's running the place these days, anyway?'

'New girl,' Metcalfe replied in all honesty. 'Name of McGuinness.'

'Do I know her?'

'Yeah, you've met.'

'She can't have left much of an impression. There are too many nonentities in this company. Time-servers. McGuinness? No, never heard of her. Where did she come from?'

'Global Development,' replied Metcalfe.

'Then Kathy must know her.'

'Actually, she recommended her.'

'That would figure,' Leonora sighed. 'If you want to get rid of her, do.'

'And if the whole factory has to go?' enquired Metcalfe.

'Then it has to go. Don't get me wrong, I loved that factory and was proud of it. I don't suppose you can imagine me shedding a tear at the thought of its closing, but I would. But if you're going to make me cry, Ted, it had better be worth it.' She gave him the tightest of menacing smiles and swept from the room with the arrogance of a wild cat leaving behind some mauled remains.

Just before her sharp finger prodded the button to summon the lift, Leonora turned back to Metcalfe and shouted, 'By the way, have you seen Kathy lately? She never seems to be at home. Is she all right?'

'She's fine,' he replied. 'On a special assignment. I'm just broadening her horizons. I'll tell her to give you a call.'

'Thanks for looking after her, Ted. That's really kind.' Leonora smiled, and for the first time that day looked human.

Jean Crowley made the tea for the board meeting in Ballymagee. It was less of a meeting really than a get together of old friends. Jack the maintenance man was there, and someone called Paddy who 'helped out with sales' came too, although what sales he ever achieved was a matter for some debate since all the output of the factory was shipped directly to the mainland for sale and distribution from England. There was also Molly, a rotund lady with her ginger hair tied in a bun who looked like a severe seaside landlady. She was there to speak for the workers, if they should need speaking for. Kathy sat behind her desk feeling more like a babysitter than an executive. She thanked them all for coming and Jean handed round the tea in china cups and saucers, since it was a proper meeting the like of which they'd never had when Percy Crowley had been running things.

Kathy tapped her pencil on an empty glass, as she had seen her mother do at meetings to attract attention.

'Ah, that's a lovely note. So pure, don't you think?' said Jack,

135

quite missing the point. When the chatter came to a stop and the stirring of the tea had finished, Kathy spoke.

'I'd like to understand the decision-making process here,' she said, trying to introduce an air of formality. 'How are problems solved as they arise? What structures are in place to deal with them?'

They looked blankly at each other.

'If I might explain,' said Jean softly. 'If there's a decision needs to be taken, then what we do is, sort of, take it. And that's it done.'

'But are the decisions taken on the basis of any overall strategy?'

'Sure they are,' boasted Jack, through a mouthful of fruit bread. 'All decisions are based on the need to keep the factory running. Simple, eh?'

There was no arguing with that. 'What about business development? Who's in charge of forward planning, machinery replacement, implementing new ideas coming from London?'

'Well, I suppose I am,' confessed Jean bashfully.

'But you're the secretary. A good one,' Kathy added, hastily, 'but still a secretary.'

'True. Receptionist as well. But I'm the one who opens all the letters and reads all that nonsense that comes from London.' Jean's nerves were getting the better of her and she gabbled, 'And if any of it seems a good idea to me, I tell the rest. If it sounds like just another load of old rubbish, I usually chuck it in the bin. I've never missed anything really important. Every single word gets read, I promise.'

Kathy took a deep breath. 'And technological developments?'

'Ah,' exclaimed Jack. 'Now, you're talking to the right man here. I do all that. I keep abreast of all developments and upgrade the equipment when necessary.'

'Good!' declared Kathy, sensing a breakthrough in understanding. 'And how many major changes since the plant opened in 1975?'

'Just the one,' he replied. 'We had a new machine for putting the flavours on. All electrostatic and that. Sure, it was a grand new thing once the girls got used to it.' There was a giggle from Jean, and Jack smiled back at her. 'I have to admit in the early days they wound the knobs up a bit far and the smoky bacon tasted as strong as a fire in a pig farm. But when they'd got the hang of it, sure it was fine.'

'And when was that machinery upgrade?' asked Kathy.

He took a sharp intake of breath. '1977.'

'And there's been nothing new in this plant since then?' she said in disbelief.

They looked at each other and shook their heads innocently. Why should there have been anything new? It all worked, didn't it?

The door fell open and an unkempt young man, bursting out of a tweed jacket and wearing stained rubber boots, dropped into the room, just managing to restrain two bundles of files which he was holding beneath each arm.

'I'm so sorry. Michael's the name. I do the books.'

'Michael . . . er . . . ?' asked Kathy.

'Crowley. Michael Crowley.'

'Of course,' she observed under her breath. Mike's job, he explained, between apologies, was to keep the books and records up to date. But he had a herd of fine cattle up on the hill and was never available on market days or during the calving season. So he had to apologise in advance because he might turn up to meetings or he might not. Today, the vet had kept him waiting, and he apologised again.

'So how are the figures?' she asked him. 'Do you have a breakdown?'

'No, it was the vet who had the breakdown, just coming up

the hill. His clutch cable went, poor feller. And there's me in a hell of stew, wanting to get here and fifteen cows to inject.'

'I meant a breakdown of the figures,' said Kathy patiently.

'Ah, the figures. Yes, they're good. There's no breakdown there. I'd say they were very good. As good a set of figures as I've ever seen. They're fine, so they are.'

'Can you be a bit more specific?' pressed Kathy.

'Specific?' He seemed uncertain of the meaning of the word.

'Like cost analysis, cash flow, current account, productivity figures.'

'Ah, we sort of get a feeling, don't we, when things are going well?' He looked at the others for support and they all nodded back in agreement.' And you get a sort of instinct when things aren't going as you'd quite like them to be. So that's when we do something about things. Whatever those things might be.'

'And Mr Crowley's role in all this?'

'Which Mr Crowley would that be?'

'Mr Percy Crowley, the late manager.'

'Well, old Percy, God rest his soul,' said Jean piously, 'he was a grand chap and very fond of the salmon fishing, you know. And we didn't keep him from it too much if we could help it, did we?' They shook their heads in agreement.

'So if I understand you all correctly, every decision taken about the running of the factory was done on the say-so of the people in this room. That was the sum total of the factory's management?' Molly, the fierce-looking woman who had not spoken so far, raised her hand.

'Not quite, if I may say so.' Her voice was softer than her stern expression. 'Often the workforce had an idea or two to throw in, and very useful they were too when it came to understanding those memo things which came over from London. Well, Percy didn't have time for all that readin', so anything Jack or Jean hadn't got round to, we used to read it ourselves in the tea breaks and pass opinion. It was rare for Mr Percy not to take notice of us. Trusted us, he did.'

From where Kathy was sitting, it was like the curtains being drawn back on some kind of black comedy.

'We could have told them that the flotation on the Singapore Stock Exchange would come to no good,' Molly continued blithely.

'You knew about that?' gasped Kathy in disbelief. 'That was the disaster they managed to hide from the British press.'

'Well, they didn't hide it from *us*,' said Molly smugly. 'Stood to reason it was going to be a flop. The offer price was too high. We all said so. No one in their right mind would have bought at that price.'

'Ridiculous, it was,' added Jack. They all shook their heads dolefully.

'May I ask who wrote the monthly report for the London office?' enquired Kathy, treading carefully through this mine-field of revelations.

'Sometimes it was me,' confessed Jean.

'Not always,' added Molly sharply. 'When your mother was bad and you stayed at home with her, that nice Mrs Cadogan from packaging wrote it. Ever so nicely she put it. All them words and figures. Made up, of course. We knew what London wanted to read and so we gave it to them.'

'So, what would you like my job to be?' Kathy asked. It was meant sarcastically but they took her question at face value.

'Well, we'd like you to have a nice time while you're here,' said Jean, and they all agreed enthusiastically.

'And help us to keep things going as they are, if you'd be so kind,' added Jack.

'And that's about it,' said Molly.

'But it's not,' said Kathy, shaking her head. 'I wish it could be. I've never been made more welcome anywhere I've been, and the last thing I want to do is to offend you all. But I've been sent here to do a job, and getting that job done means changing things. It can *never* be the same as it was when Percy Crowley was in charge.'

'But why ever not?' said a disbelieving Molly.

'Because London believes that this factory is underperforming. It appears to be prone to disruptive breakdowns for reasons I have yet to understand. They want that sorted, and they want me to be the one who sorts it. I *have* to change things because if I don't solve the problems there are here, I'm not certain the factory will even exist this time next year.' She paused while that sank in. 'Nothing has been said, but I know the way their minds work.'

They looked at her like children scolded by their mothers for no reason that they understood.

'Close us down? They couldn't!' declared Jack. 'What else would we do? There's nothing in Ballymagee but potatoes. Potatoes are our living, our lives. It would be like signing our death warrant.'

'I understand that,' said Kathy sympathetically, 'but London won't. That's why we've got to get to the root of the problems. So, are any of you going to tell me what the trouble is with this factory? I need to know. I've looked at the figures but they show only the result of the problem, not the problem itself. I'm like a doctor who can see the scars but doesn't not know what caused them. I *must* know,' she pleaded and stabbed her finger emphatically at the desk. They bowed their heads, avoiding her eye.

'It is not something of which we ever speak,' said Jean Crowley formally, as if giving evidence.

'But you *must*,' said Kathy, exasperated.

'No, we must not, beggin' your pardon. It's already enough of a curse without fresh life being breathed into it by idle gossip.'

'It's highly likely that within the next few weeks it will happen again,' added Jack sadly. 'It strikes without notice, as if the finger of the devil has pointed straight at this factory and blighted it. It's a punishment, we believe, for our decietful way of running this factory. We know full well the sinfulness of what we do. And our curse is the price the Lord exacts. So we bear with it, and pray it will not last long.'

'You must understand,' said Jean, 'that not many generations ago in this part of Ireland, hundreds of thousands died because the potatoes failed them in the Famine. It was wicked. And what would those ancestors of ours, who died of hunger, disease and starvation, what would they think of us, whining about a stoppage of a mere day or two? No, we owe it to their memory to live with this, and thank the Lord it is no worse.'

'Did you lose family in the Famine?' asked Kathy.

'I did, so my great-grandmother used to tell me. Every relation on my mother's side of the family perished. We have no idea where they were buried.'

'And the same with our branch of the family too,' added Jack. 'There's no family alive today in these parts which wasn't ripped apart by the cruel years of famine. It started here in 1845 and it was not until ten years later that the potatoes grew properly hereabouts.'

'So you can see,' said Jean, 'why a little suffering isn't much to us. It reminds us how lucky we are, and how close we can be to disaster. But never so close as our families who died. It reminds us to be duly humble, and thankful to the Lord for all he has given us.'

'Amen,' they chorused.

At five-thirty a hooter blew to mark the end of the day shift, and Kathy usually took that as her cue to leave the factory for the day and make her way back to the Crowley House Hotel. Today the telephone on her desk rang as well. It was Jean. Kathy had enough on her mind and wanted no more.

'I see young Danny's outside with his car,' said the secretary. 'Will you be havin' a lift back to the hotel or walk down the High Street as usual? Hello, are you there?' she asked again, getting no reply.

Kathy was deciding. Not whether to walk or to ride, but if the company of Danny might not be just what she needed at this moment. She wanted to get away from all ridiculous notions of curses, morbid memories of long-dead ancestors, sentimental notions of the will of the Lord.

'Yes. Tell him I'll be down in five minutes.' Having checked her face and flicked a comb through her hair, she marched out towards Danny's waiting Volvo.

'So,' she said, having fallen into the ripped and unsupportive upholstery of the car, 'what goes on here, apart from crisps and potatoes and the occasional sing-song in the back room of the Crowley House Hotel? What other life is there? Because right now I'm looking for some.'

'Ah, well now . . .' he started in his best Mayo accent.

'Danny,' she pleaded, 'give it a rest. I'm up to here in leprechauns.'

'Life around here? Well, I ain't found none yet. This place makes the suburbs of Louisville seem like up town Las Vegas. I wouldn't be expecting too much more than you're gettin' already. Now, if you want to do a taxi driver a favour you can ask him to take you to Galway. They say there's a bit of life there. Then, of course, there's Dublin! Five hours away. But don't let me talk you out of it. It's a one hundred and fifty pound fare each way and I'd be sure as hell glad to drive you.'

'In this? You must be joking. We'll stick closer to home. How about *your* home?' Kathy said forwardly. 'I'm sick to death of the four walls of my room in the Crowley House Hotel. The food's fine but there's a limit to the number of times I can eat salmon before I feel the need to swim up a river and spawn. And there are only so many occasions on which you can have a conversation with a member of the Crowley family before you go stir crazy. I want a *change*. I am desperate for a *change*. I want *you* to ask *me* round to your place. For a *change*! No more than that.'

The penny had a long way to travel, but eventually it dropped. 'Sure, you're welcome. But it's a hell of a tip, I warn you. You won't find the home comforts you get at that smart hotel of yours.'

'I'm up to here in comfort. It's time for a little humanity in my life again.' Kathy turned to him and grinned. 'And you're the nearest thing to it I've seen so far. I'll try and make the best of a bad job.'

Danny dropped her at the Crowley House Hotel so she could shed her corporate uniform of skirt, blouse and jacket, the casting aside of which was the best moment of Kathy's day. Regaining her grey sweater and jeans was like recapturing her own life. For colour she grabbed a red silk scarf and tied it loosely round her neck. By the time she came tripping out of the hotel, free from the burdens of management, Danny was drumming his fingers on the steering wheel. He'd tried to insist that he went home first to tidy the place and then drive back to the hotel to collect her, but she would not allow him.

'I want to see it as it really is. In all its glory!' joked Kathy. 'Unless there's anything, or perhaps any*one*, you don't want me to see?'

'Problem,' he announced. 'There's no food. Not even any milk. I gave the last to Lucinda.'

'Lucinda?'

'The cat,' he explained. 'She's fat but cute.'

143

'Too much milk, probably. We'll stop at Crowley's and get some food in.'

'You're planning on eating at my place too?' he exclaimed.

'Where else?' said Kathy. 'I am asking you, as a friend, for shelter. I want somewhere else to be for a while. I'm frightened. Scared of these people. I know they want to be friendly, but all this talk of curses and the will of God and the work of the devil is really getting to me.'

'Ah.' He nodded. 'I wondered when they'd get on to all that crap.'

Danny drove up to the house in which he lived. The address was 41 Benwee Avenue. 'Are you sure you want to be seen goin' in here with me?' he asked politely.

'Should I have a Crowley as chaperone or something?' asked Kathy. 'Anyway, the damage is already done. Mrs Crowley in the shop saw me buying two of everything and spotted you sitting in the car outside. That's as good as telling everyone in the town. Her fluttering eye started to go crazy with the excitement. If it had wings it would have taken off.'

From the back seat they hauled plastic carrier bags containing several bottles of beer and what was left at the butcher's counter – chicken legs. There was also a loaf a bread and a sad-looking ready-to-bake apple pie which looked as limp as Kathy felt.

She paused to look at number 41. 'Some house,' she remarked. 'All of it yours?'

'Hell, no,' said Danny. 'It's in several flats now, but I'm the only one staying here at the moment, so the place is as good as mine. Most people who come to Ballymagee are from ChipCo and can afford better than this hole. Still, there's worse places. Each flat's got an upstairs bedroom and bathroom and you're supposed to share the downstairs kitchen and sitting room. Quite a place in its day, I guess. All that stone and those big windows. I heard tell it was a bed and breakfast place, till the old girl died. That's when they made the flats.'

They walked together up to the front door.

'It feels welcoming,' said Kathy. 'You know, it's almost as if I've been here before.'

'Well, I would have thought you'd either been here before or you hadn't. And that's all there is to it.'

Kathy dropped the shopping on the table and started to explore.

'You've got a real fireplace in the kitchen. Must be cosy in the winter.' Then she bounded up the stairs. 'Hey,' she shouted. 'Not very modest, this bathroom of yours, with glass in the door.'

'Don't seem to matter so much when you're on your own,' replied Danny, bewildered by the energy which Kathy was expending on peering into every nook and cranny.

'What's opposite?' she shouted, and turned the handle of the door. 'Oh, your bedroom. I see.' And she shut it quickly behind her and came back downstairs where she found it chilly and damp, and smelling of Lucinda the cat.

'I'll get the camp fire going in the kitchen,' said Danny

'*Camp* fire?'

'Yup. You've got to remember we Kentucky boys have a bit of cowboy blood in us, you know. Not far from where my family hail from the great Daniel Boone himself set off to open up the west. He fought the Indians, and the weather, even his own folk. But he made it. And when I first set foot in Ballymagee, that's pretty much how I felt – opening up my personal frontiers.'

'Do you want me to whistle the theme from *The Big Country*, or something?' suggested Kathy.' Though, to be fair, it is like frontier country round here, isn't it? Wish I had a bit of that cowboy blood in me.'

'But you're a McGuinness. They must be made of pretty strong stuff. It's a common name. You find lots o' people in the same place with the same name and it usually means they're a pretty influential bunch.'

'Then the Crowleys must be very influential round here. There's tons of them.'

'Hey, know what?'

'What?'

'I call 'em the Creepy Crowleys. I reckon they're all a bit weird. Harmless, but real weird.'

Danny put down the matches with which he was trying to light the fire. It was built of crumpled newspaper on which he had placed some roughly cut lumps of peat. Kathy sat down in an upright chair by the cracked 1940s tiled fireplace, watching Danny on his knees trying to make an impression on the inert lumps of peat.

'I can never understand how lumps of soil burn,' said Kathy. 'They're pretty big lumps, too.'

'They make them neater, and probably drier too. But I don't pay for anything if I don't have to. I usually just pick up a few lumps as I do my rounds.'

'Rounds?'

'Ah,' said Danny guiltily. 'It's a bit of a sideline of mine. As well as doing the collections from the bigger farmers with proper contracts, I drive around buying potatoes off the smaller farmers who don't have contracts, and sell them on to ChipCo. Suits them and it suits me. It just about covers the cost of the diesel to run the old truck I borrow from Teddy Crowley at the garage. And it pays for my beer. And that's it.'

'Perhaps you shouldn't be telling me this. Sounds against company regulations to me.'

'Just one of so many dodgy things that go on round here,' he replied.

'Have you tried blowing on the fire?' she asked, wanting to forget all about ChipCo. 'Give it a bit of a draught. Have you any bellows?'

'Only the ones in me chest,' said Danny, playfully beating his breast like a gorilla.

Kathy got up from the chair and kneeled down beside him on the dusty hearth rug. 'I'll show you,' she said, and pursed her lips. 'Do it like this. It's important to get the proper shape to achieve the maximum effect.'

'I aint goin' to argue with that,' replied Danny, pursing his lips as she had. 'Then you blow,' she said softly, pointing her face towards the fire and aiming her breath at the base of the lumps of turf, provoking the slightest hint of smoky combustion. She looked like an angel, and Danny was entranced by her profile until annoyingly it was obscured by her black hair falling across her face. He reached out one finger and hooked it back so he could study her again. She did not notice.

'Look! It's getting hotter. Can you see the red bits? There'll be a blaze soon.' Kathy looked up at him. 'You're not helping,' she scolded him. 'Now blow on it too or we'll be here all night, shivering. Come on, *blow*!'

To his surprise, it worked. The redness spread through the fire till the sweet smoke started to rise up the chimney, and eventually the draught took over and neither of them needed to blow any more. Satisfied, Kathy rested back on her heels and gazed into the flames. Danny's eyes were fixed on her. Two fires had just been kindled.

'It's the first real thing I've done since I've been here, lighting that fire.' She was still staring into the fledgling flames. 'The rest of the time I've been living out a managerial charade behind that desk. Nothing real at all. No achievement.'

'Glad the fire's cheered you up,' he said softly. 'At Morrissey's Cars we like to provide a complete service to our customers.' His joke broke her trance and she sprang to her feet. 'So, food?' she asked.

'Do we have to talk about food?' he asked, hoping their moment together by the fire might last.

'I'm starving.'

'Then it's chicken legs.'

'Sounds dreary.'

'I can always take you back to the Crowley House. They've got a very full menu.'

'Chicken legs don't sound *that* dreary,' she said quickly.

'Hey, you've offended me now!' He was teasing her. 'It sure does a guy's manhood no good to hear he don't know how to cook a lousy piece o' chicken. And him from Kentucky too.' He was in cowboy mode again. 'You never heard of the famous Colonel Sanders, miss? He taught the world to cook chicken.'

'A relation of yours?'

'I cook chicken as if he were my grandpa,' boasted Danny, reaching for a rusty frying pan on a shelf above the old gas stove.

'I can't work you out,' said Kathy, bemused. 'I don't know if you're an American being an Irishman, or an Irishman being an American.'

'Ever met an Irishman who can cook fried chicken?'

'Seriously, you confuse me.'

'Try seeing it from where I stand, and you'll soon be as mixed up as I am.'

'There you go,' said Kathy, banging her fist on the arm of the chair. 'You can shift continents in the middle of a sentence.'

'The man who shifted continents!' joked Danny, flexing his muscles and posing like a weightlifter, before grasping the frying pan by its black and greasy handle.

There followed an interlude where fat was put in the pan and melted over the gas. The chicken legs were rubbed with flour to which had been added a few herbs and spices mixed according to what Danny said was a secret Kentucky recipe. When Kathy fished out of the waste bin an empty sachet of Southern Fried Chicken Ready-to-Use Spices bearing a Crowley's price tag, they both broke into helpless giggles. To accompany the chicken were tinned baked beans. And while the floppy apple pie crisped in the oven, they cracked the tops off two bottles of beer and squatted cross-legged in front of the kitchen fire, cowboy-style, their dinner in their laps.

'I want the lights off,' said Kathy. The days were long and it was not yet fully dark outside and so together with the glow of the fire there was enough light for them to see their food. 'I want to imagine we're on our way to discover the west like that cowboy you mentioned.'

'Daniel Boone?'

'Yeah, Boone,' she said, in a far away voice. 'And we're in a clearing in the woods, just you and me, and there are wolves all around. But we've had to stop and eat 'cos we haven't eaten for days.' She dropped her fork on to her plate. 'And we need each other for protection from the rest of the world.'

'That would be nice,' agreed Danny.

'How old are you?'

'Twen'y-eight.'

'You're just a kid,' said Kathy. 'I'm twenty-nine. So why are two bright nearly thirty year olds sitting here, playing at cowboys, when we could be beating up the world?'

'Cowboys was your idea,' replied Danny.

'You mentioned them first. Anyway, it's how I feel. Ballymagee's like some kind of frontier town where strangers get ambushed.'

'Hey, those people really got to you today, didn't they? You shouldn't take so much notice. They're friendly to strangers, sure enough. But you'll never be one of them, so don't even try. Keep 'em at arm's length. That's what I do.'

'But they won't tell me about this stupid curse they keep going on about. They won't say a word,' she protested, exasperated.

'I've seen it. It's grim. But it's no curse. It's just that it's got a certain symbolism. It means something to them that it doesn't mean to me, or to you for that matter. They explained it to me once and couldn't believe it when I just sort of shrugged my shoulders. Didn't speak to me for days afterwards. But it don't seem nothin' special to me. They think it's all mixed up with the potato famine. But, hell, that was a hundred and fifty or more years ago. It's crazy! Do you want some more beans?'

There was a dampness around Kathy's eyes, he noticed, brought on by what he guessed might be true fright. But the reflection of the flames in her tears only made them more jewel-like.

'You'll deal with it fine if it happens,' he said, trying to reassure her. 'And if it doesn't, you've saved yourself an awful lot of worry.'

Kathy brushed her eyes with the back of her hand. Her hair had fallen across her face again. Danny reached out a finger as he had done before. This time, she noticed.

'I think I'd better be going.'

'Now you're insulting my manhood again.'

'How so?'

'By leaving before the apple pie! Back home, if I got out of the house before Mom's apple pie had hit the table, it would be the end of family life. Pie is to be taken seriously. So stay where you are!' he ordered her. He got to his feet and went to the kitchen. As she heard the oven door open, the unmistakable scent of charred pastry filled the downstairs rooms.

'Your mother's quicker on her feet than you, is she?' Kathy joked.

'Aren't all mothers?' Danny shouted back at her. 'What about yours? Isn't she smarter than you?'

'Yup,' admitted Kathy. It was the first time any thought of Leonora had crossed her mind since she had been in Ballymagee. It made her wonder what her mother would do in this situation: close down the whole factory, sack the lot of them, bring in an emergency management team, having declared the whole place out of control?

'What would you do, about the factory?' she asked Danny as he handed her a well-crisped slice of apple pie.

'Hey, I'm a taxi driver and occasional potato haulage man. Those are questions for you to answer. You're the Daniel Boone figure round here. I'm just one of the cowboys.'

The pie filling was hot and she blew on it as she had on the peat. While it cooled she glanced at two posters fixed to opposite walls of the kitchen. One proclaimed 'Welcome to Louisville', with a bold picture of the Ohio river and cameos around it of Louisville's famous sons – Thomas Edison, Tom Cruise, Victor Mature. On the other poster was a smaller and less flamboyant portrait of W.B. Yeats, his grey mane combed backwards, thin-rimmed spectacles on the end of his nose, and a tie loosely knotted in a bow round his neck. All in all, a consummately literary-looking gentleman with an understated charisma that easily outshone the brash offspring of Louisville.

'If I were a psychologist, which I'm not,' mused Kathy, 'I would say you were not happy in Ireland. If you were, the picture of the Irish poet would be bigger than the poster of home.'

'Then we can all be grateful you're *not* a psychologist, because the Louisville poster is the only one big enough to cover the damp patch where Mrs Donovan has her bath next door. Yeats may have been a literary giant but Mrs Donovan is a giant of a woman, and when she gets in that bath it overflows with such a tidal wave it takes a poster of a big city to cover it. All right?'

'Do you like poetry?' she asked, still staring at Yeats.

'I ain't sure what the guy's on about. But when I told the folks back home that I was coming to Ireland, they said I'd know his poems back to front before I'd been here a fortnight. They said he was the heart and soul of the nation, gave it back its literature and all that.'

'Try one on me then,' said Kathy. 'From memory.'

Danny took a deep breath and psyched himself into his Irish accent:

> ' "*I will arise and go now, and go to Inisfree,*
> *And a small cabin build there, of clay and wattles made:*
> *Nine bean rows will I have there, a hive for the honey-bee,*
> *And live alone there in the bee-loud glade.*"

'Er, that's it,' he admitted.

'It's a bit short!'

'Oh, there's more. But I'd have to look it up.'

'And that's the sum total of your understanding of Irish literature, and you a student of it?

'It's not easy,' protested Danny. He reached out for a small book lying on the mantel-shelf beneath a well-used service manual for his Volvo. 'There's some good ones in here.' He flicked through the pages. Kathy was on her knees again, blowing softly on the lumps of peat, trying to revitalise them now that the best of the heat was out of them. He was enjoying the touch of her shoulders against his legs while he stood, turning the pages, watching her creating a gentle breeze with her carefully pursed lips. 'It's about a guy who goes into a hazel wood, cuts a stick, ties a berry on the end of it and puts it in a stream to catch a trout.'

'Luck of the Irish!' she remarked.

'Hey, the next verse is about you, sort of,' said Danny. 'The guy brings the fish home, right? Then it goes on:

' *"When I had lain it on the floor*
I went to blow the fire aflame . . ."

'Like you're doing now, get it?

' *". . . But something rustled on the floor,*
And someone called me by my name:
It had become a glimmering girl
With apple blossom in her hair
Who called me by my name and ran
And faded through the brightening air . . ."

'Spooky, don't you think? There you are, blowing the fire aflame, rustling on the floor.'

'What, like a dead fish?' said Kathy, in mock indignation.

'No, like a glimmering girl with apple blossom in her hair.'

'So what happens next?' asked Kathy unromantically. 'Does he chase the girl or barbecue the fish on the fire? Which wins, love or hunger?'

'Love, of course. Love always wins in these Irish things. Love or death.' Danny dropped to his knees till he was beside her, then raked his fingers theatrically through his hair till it was swept backwards. 'Do I look at all like Yeats?'

'Not in the slightest. You look like a cowboy. I know an Irishman when I see one, and whatever you do or say, I only ever see an American.'

'Eyes can play tricks,' muttered Danny

He leaned forward and undid the silk scarf around her neck, fingering the knot so gently that when his fingers accidentally touched her neck, Kathy tingled. Having removed the red scarf, he put it round his own neck and tied it in a bow, like Yeats in the poster. 'Am I getting there?'

'You need the thin-rimmed glasses too,' she giggled. 'And

another thirty years on you. You're too fresh-faced, Danny boy.'

'For God's sake, we're dealing with imagination here. Poetry and all that! If you can't imagine a pair of glasses, how the hell are you going to dream yourself into being the girl who minutes before was a fish on the end of a line?'

'Finish the poem,' she urged. Danny coughed and recited:

> ' *"Though I am old with wandering*
> *Through hollow lands and hilly lands,*
> *I will find out where she has gone,*
> *And kiss her lips and take her hands".'*

He reached out and rested his hand on Kathy's. She stifled a giggle. 'Don't spoil it!' he scolded her.

> ' *"And walk among long dappled grass,*
> *And pluck till time and times are done*
> *The silver apples of the moon,*
> *The golden apples of the sun."*

'So there,' he declared, with a sigh.

'I can see you now,' Kathy teased him, 'sitting behind the wheel of a Morrissey's limousine, cruising through Manhattan with a rich widow on the back seat, and you crooning to her about the golden apples of the sun.'

'I can take any mockery,' he replied. 'It will be the making of me, I tell you.'

'Danny,' she said, changing the subject abruptly, 'who exactly was that old man who appeared in the bar the other night? He didn't seem to be welcome there.'

'Here I am, trying to squeeze every ounce of emotion out of one of old Yeats's verses, and all you can think about is some other feller!'

'I don't know why he suddenly came to mind, but he did. Who was he? Tell me what you know.'

'He's one of those "I will arise now" guys. A dreamer. You've seen where he lives, up on the hill. Nine bean rows, and all that. A real one for the bee-loud glade. I don't think there's much harm in him, though. He's civil enough whenever I go to see him.'

'So why was there so much hostility towards him? The room went cold when he came in. It was like pressing a switch and all the friendliness and welcome were shut off.'

'Because they were giving as much as they get. He's made no secret over the years that he hates the ChipCo factory, everything to do with it, and everyone who works there.'

'Why?'

'It's another of the many secrets everyone here seems to know the answer to but won't tell you. So I've given up asking. I just pick up his taters, and that's it.'

'If he hates the place, why does he sell them potatoes?'

'Ah, well,' said Danny, hesitantly, 'that's another of those things that go on that not everyone knows about. See, I buy the potatoes off the old boy and make a point of never telling him where they go. He knows, of course, but he's got to live. And that makes him even more angry, I guess. You see, he's as dependent on the place as anyone else round here.'

'He could sell his potatoes elsewhere, surely?' suggested Kathy.

'Nope. Too few of 'em. Not worth the transport. He's a ChipCo slave like the rest of us though he refuses to admit it.'

'Do they know they're processing his potatoes?'

'I don't think I ever bothered to mention it,' replied Danny, grinning.

'But why do they hate him so?'

'He stood in an election once. It was part of his one-man campaign to get the factory closed on the grounds of "exploitation of the people, British commercial imperialism" all that sort of thing. 'Course, he got himself on television and all that, like the crackpots always do. Hell of a lot of publicity. Drew too much attention to what goes on round here, see? They run things their own way here and don't like folks interfering. He only got one vote and that was his own.'

Kathy leaned forward and reclaimed her scarf from round Danny's neck.

'Anyway, what's so interesting about the old Monk?' he asked as she fumbled with the knot. 'What's wrong with the present company?'

'What's his real name?'

'Pat something or other. Actually Padraig, strictly speaking. I can't recall the surname but I'll be up there in the next few days and then I'll make a point of remembering it, since you're so interested.'

'In the next few days?'

'I guess. He sells me a sack or two a month. Depending on how many he needs for himself. And he's got a pig he fattens, and boils a few to feed it. Any spare taters I buy from him.'

'Will you take me to meet him?'

'He's a mucky, bitter old man who lives in a tip,' said Danny. 'You've seen it. It's no better in the daylight.'

Kathy looked around the room. 'Worse than this?'

'To make up for that very unkind and hurtful remark, you must let me kiss you goodnight.'

'You ask rather a lot, for a chauffeur.'

He reached out his hands and rested them on her shoulders, and as he leaned slowly towards her, started to whisper:

' "Had I the heavens' embroidered cloths,
Enwrought with golden and silver light,
The blue and the dim and the dark cloths
Of night and light and the half-light,

156

I would spread the cloths under your feet;
But I, being poor, have only my dreams;
I have spread my dreams under your feet;
Tread softly because you tread on my dreams." '

'You know more Yeats than you're letting on,' said Kathy.

'I know a lot of things I'm not letting on,' he replied, before kissing her briefly on the cheek. 'I knew, for example, that the book was open at that page and all I had to do was read that poem over your shoulder.'

'You are impossible, Danny boy. Now, do you happen to know where I can get a taxi home?'

6

Kathy awoke thirty-six hours later, uneasy at being back in her Earls Court flat. It no longer felt like home. Far from being the comforting little refuge she remembered, it was dank and musty, smelling of stale air and the accumulated odours of other people's cooking which had risen up the stairwell, crept under the door, collected, and now lay in wait for her. There had been a mountain of mail behind the door which she had had to push against to get in, and the flashing display on her telephone answering machine said there were fifteen messages waiting. She had been away a month, and when she left she'd loved the place. Now she loathed it. And the sheets felt damp.

She looked out of the window, used to the sight of Mayo, but saw only flats, people, a little sky and no horizon. The incessant noise disturbed her. She was used to the gentle hum and rumble of the crisp factory, but the drumming roar of traffic here was threatening. Despite having been in Ireland for such short a time, she could recognise nearly every vehicle which went past her window in Ballymagee. She knew the sound of Danny's Volvo, certainly, and the potato lorries, and the stutter of Jean Crowley's car. They were friendly sounds; these London noises seemed maliciously intrusive.

She had arrived late the night before, on the last flight out of Ireland, and had fallen straight into bed wondering what was so urgent that Ted Metcalfe felt he had to speak to her face to face about it, and not on the telephone. By morning she still had no clue. She reached out for the alarm clock to check the time, but it had stopped when the battery went flat and she had not been there to replace it. Beside it she saw a CD, Billy Joel's face smiling at her from the box. It seemed crazy that only a month ago she had found comfort in a picture of a singer. Schoolgirl stuff. That she now thought the idea ridiculous was a measure of how much she had grown up in so short a time. She looked again at the picture and thought she recognised the slightest hint of Danny in it; in the eyes, perhaps, or the shallow furrows on the brow. She tried to remember the lyrics of some of her favourite songs, like *Piano Man*, but all that came to mind were the silver apples of the moon, the golden apples of the sun – neither of which were shining through the grimy windows of her flat to lift her depressed spirits or dry the dank sheets

She realised she had few clothes here, the water was cold, there was no milk for coffee, and it was a toss up as to whether she should first open the mail or clear the messages from the tape. She could face neither without sustenance, and so put on the clothes she had travelled in the night before to shamble to the corner shop for milk. It was no Crowley's store. Instead of a welcoming smile, she was stared at by a security camera monitored from behind the till by an Asian grandmother who spoke little English. She knew none of the customers, as she would if she were in Ballymagee. The cool-cabinet in which the milk was kept smelt of fish; inside, it felt decidedly warm. Kathy looked at the sell-by dates on the elderly boxes of milk and found them all on the verge of expiry. At Crowley's, milk came fresh every day from a cousin's farm a few miles out of town. She looked at the loaves of bread which were all sliced, wrapped, or so stale that the crust would be impenetrable. She bought a packet of digestive biscuits instead.

Walking back to her flat, she remembered a song which Danny played incessantly on the quavering tape player in his car. It was one of those songs, he claimed, which always got him in an Irish frame of mind. An instant fix of blarney. *'Oh, Mary, this London's a wonderful sight, with people all working by day and by night.'* It was the song of an exile, dazzled by the richness of city life. *'They don't sow potatoes, nor barley nor wheat, But there's gangs of 'em digging for gold in the street,'* it continued. Kathy hummed it to herself and sang the words in her head. When she got to, *'but for all that I've found there I might as well be, where the Mountains of Mourne sweep down to the sea'*, she felt an overwhelming flood of homesickness for Ballymagee, far greater than anything she'd experienced after leaving London. No, this filthy place was no longer home. Let them dig for gold here if they wanted to.

Dipping biscuits into her black coffee, she quickly fanned through the mail and found it easy to deal with. It was either bills or circulars. The bills she stuffed into her bag to take home – a word she now used in the context of Ballymagee – and the circulars went straight in the bin. Except for one which was from an estate agent who was claiming to have a queue of customers looking for flats just like hers. This place felt so alien, so much a part of her previous life, that even if she did ultimately return to London, she would not want to live here again. Thinking she might sell up, she stuffed that leaflet into the bag with the unpaid bills. Now for the answering machine.

All fifteen calls were from her mother. They began with the word 'darling' and ended with 'I'll try again. Or you can call me'. Kathy was not a natural liar, and so had avoided any conversation with her mother in case of difficult questions. They had spoken just once, but Leonora had been too busy for a detailed conversation, which suited Kathy, and they had not spoken since. Mother obviously still had no idea that Kathy was living in Ballymagee. E-mail was the answer, she thought. She could e-mail her mother a note and then her precise whereabouts would remain cloaked in internet anonymity. She would explain that the time difference made it difficult for them to catch each other on the phone, and an electronic note now and again might be the best way of staying in touch. It was efficient and sufficient, both of which should appeal to her punctilious mother.

Or perhaps she should come clean and tell her mother she was in Ireland, following in her footsteps, maintaining the family link with the little bit of commercial history known as the Ballymagee ChipCo plant. What was there to fear in telling her the truth? If she'd believed that her mother might, for a moment, respect her for what she was doing, she would have told her straight away. But Kathy knew she would not be impressed. It had been a recurrent theme of her childhood; marks in exams were good, but never quite good enough. She had won cups for running, but never the Victor Ludorum; her A levels had been fine for the university she wanted to attend, but nothing special; her degree in business studies was adequate, but her mother wasn't impressed. A father, if she'd known one, might have been more generous. She had scraped by in everything she had done, her mother had told her repeatedly. Nothing truly outstanding. Maybe a dad would have been more lenient.

Kathy had studied other girls, especially the lucky ones whose fathers were blind to all their faults. It did not matter if there were harsh words from their mother, so long as the daughter remained the apple of her father's eye. It meant there was more justice, for there was always someone else on the jury not just a mother alone. Nothing Kathy had done so far had made her mother believe she was anything more than adequate, and so until she was able to point a finger at a definite achievement, a head and shoulders above the ordinary achievement, it was better to keep her mouth closed. Kathy had tried to assert herself before and the inevitable deflation always hurt.

She caught the Underground and loathed every stuffy, subterranean minute. Danny would have cheered her up if he'd been here; told her it was worse in Louisville or something. Whispered her a poem perhaps. She looked at her fellow travellers and saw no friends. In fact, she made it as far as the revolving doors of ChipCo HQ before so much as a single recognisable face lifted her spirits.

'Kathy, Kathy!' came an excited call from behind her. It was a man's voice she half recognised. She could hear hurried footsteps break into a run, trying to catch up with her. She turned.

'Chas!' she screamed in delight, recognising her old mate from Global Development. As he drew nearer she stretched out her arms and they gave each other a friendly hug.

'You've got new glasses,' she remarked. 'And your hair's shorter! In love again?'

'Possibly.' He smiled. 'And you're looking good too,' he added. 'A real manager by the look of you. Very serious and proper.' He looked her up and down appraisingly.

'It's all dressing, believe me. How's things in Global? Sold much to Rwanda yet?'

'Things aren't the same. Busy, yes. Sales up, yes. But not so much fun. We need you back.'

'That's kind, Chas. I miss you, really I do. I haven't heard a good joke since I left.'

'That place you're in, Bally-whatever-it-is, is one big joke, isn't it?'

'Now that's a bit below the belt. They're great people out there. You should come and have a look sometime. Be grand to see you.'

'Well, actually,' said Chas, bashfully, 'this new bloke of mine . . . we had half a mind to do a bit of cycling, get fit and all that, and he really fancies Ireland. We might give you a call sometime. Catch up on a few beers.'

'Is he nice?' asked Kathy.

'Pretty special,' Chas replied bashfully.

Chas took the revolving door on the left and Kathy the right. As they spun apart, he blew her a kiss and disappeared towards Global. She wanted to follow him, be safely back in the old days. Instead, she forced herself towards the reception desk.

'Miss Foley! How nice to see you again,' said the perfumed doll behind the desk. Kathy was no longer used to hearing herself called Foley, and it felt unlucky to deny the name McGuinness which had served her well so far. Without acknowledging her real name in any way, she asked for Ted Metcalfe's office and was told to go straight up.

Metcalfe, in shirt sleeves, sat hunched behind his desk. His face wore the shallow look of corporate beneficence of which Kathy had learned to be wary. She knew that at senior management level in ChipCo there was no real kindness, and so anyone with a benevolent expression was invariably lying. There was not even an exchange of pleasantries. Sitting on the couch by the window was the well-groomed young man she remembered from the press office. Toby Hart, wasn't it? Hadn't he come to her for help when her mother was set on wearing real fur at a press conference? He held a pencil, poised to take notes. He'd been halfway to his feet to shake Kathy's hand but Metcalfe just forged straight ahead. Hart immediately sat down and buried his head in his notes, sensing an imminent slaughter of the innocent.

'Kathy. Sorry to have brought you all this way but it will be easier face to face,' Metcalfe announced.

'Easier?' she asked cautiously.

'No beating about the bush. I wanted to give you time to make your mark, but time is not on our side, I'm afraid. I'm coming under a great deal of pressure for swift action. Which is not good news for Ballymagee. Or you.'

'Action?'

'To close the factory,' he said, bluntly.

'*Close* it? On what grounds? Production is running just about on target. Its figures are fine.'

'Fine, yes. Adequate, yes. But not special,' insisted Metcalfe. '*Just about* on target, as you yourself put it.'

'For God's sake, I've hardly been there a month.'

'The pressure is coming from elsewhere,' he said sheepishly.

'From Boston?' Metcalfe nodded.

'From the very top?' He nodded again.

'From Mother?' After a while, there was a slight downward movement of his head which she took to be affirmative.

'I can't believe this,' said Kathy, agitated. 'That factory meant more to her than I did.'

'I don't want to get into family history here,' said Metcalfe, shaking his head warily.

'It's not history we're talking about.' Kathy thought of Jean and Danny, the Crowley clan, all the people of Ballymagee who depended on the factory for their livelihood. 'It's about the people who work for you and depend on you.'

'It's about shareholders too.'

'To hell with shareholders!'

'Now I know you're not your mother's daughter!' Metcalfe sniggered.

'I'll talk to her,' offered Kathy hastily. 'Explain to her what's at stake.'

'It's an option. But think carefully. At the moment your mother has no idea you are there. So far as she and every one on the board is concerned, that factory is being run by a Miss McGuinness.' He leaned forward, elbows on the desk. 'Now I sent you there, Kathy, to make your mark on that factory. I wanted you to go and prove once and for all that you've got the makings of a top-line executive at ChipCo. Go running to your mother now, and some would say that you'd blown it. Up to you, of course.' Hart was swallowing hard. Metcalfe turned to him. 'What are the press implications of closure at Ballymagee?'

Before he could open his mouth, Kathy spoke. 'To hell with the press. What about the people? You have a responsibility to them. You have been their sole source of income for twenty-five years. You can't just walk out on them.'

'Not me, Kathy,' replied Metcalfe smugly. 'It's *you* who is signing the death warrant. You're in charge. Give me figures to prove the place can be turned around and there'll be no reason to close it.'

'How long have I got?' she snapped.

'Four more weeks of uninterrupted production, and continuity of supply and quality. And get the costs down! Four weeks.'

'But the whole place needs restructuring. You can't dismantle and rebuild in a month.'

'Some people might not be able to. Others could,' replied Metcalfe patronisingly. 'I want to know which of the two you are.'

'And if it does close, despite doing everything I try?'

'That would be up to you. But resignation is always better than dismissal.'

'Mother would be furious,' said Kathy, regretting it as she spoke the words.

'You can live in the shadow of your mother or out in the full glare of the real world. This is make up your mind time.'

'Four weeks?'

'Four weeks,' he replied.

Kathy got to her feet and made for the door, not wishing to waste time on pleasantries. Just before it closed behind her, Metcalfe shouted, 'And ring your mother, Kathy. She was asking where you were. Best she doesn't find out the truth. Until you've made a success of it, of course.'

Grinning, he turned to young Hart who was still sitting on the couch, feeling splattered by the blooding his boss had given Kathy.

'Toby, dearest boy, you heard what we agreed?' Hart nodded. 'She'll get her month. And then we'll close the place, whatever. Give some thought to a press release now, there's a good lad.'

'And Miss . . . er . . . ?' said Hart. 'Will there be a release about her resignation?'

'There will indeed.' Metcalfe smiled.

'And will that be in the name of Foley or McGuinness?'

'Oh, McGuinness, I think. The name Foley means too much round here. People might start making connections.'

'The Acting World President may not be too happy,' Hart dared to remark. 'Perhaps I should brief the corporate affairs chief in Boston?'

'I think not. I shall break this to Leonora when it's all cut and dried. Explain to her that the subterfuge was Kathy's idea to show the world she didn't have to use her mother's surname to prove her worth. A pity, I shall explain with great sadness, that her little experiment failed despite everything I did to help her. And that will be one less Foley for me to worry about.

'Do you know the trouble with that family? They're like birds of prey. They wait until you're dazzled by them, then attack you from out of the sun. One less will make for a safer life. I don't underestimate that girl.' He nodded in the direction of the door through which Kathy had just left. 'If I thought she was stupid I wouldn't bother with any of this. But there's just a chance that somewhere within that shapely little body is the same thing that makes her mother tick, and I don't want her discovering it and letting it loose round here. Two Foleys is two too many.'

Kathy should have gone back to the flat to turn off the fridge, reset the answering machine, and check that the door was double locked. But instead, in a state of confusion and panic, she took a cab straight to the airport, hoping to catch the first flight out. Somewhere in the depths of her bag was a piece of card on which Danny had written his phone number at Benwee Avenue. More than anything else, she wanted him to be at the airport to meet her.

Despite the stomach-churning motion of the taxi as it wove amongst the London lunchtime traffic, the thoughts in her head started to settle and become clearer. The panic she felt was not for herself; it was the others she cared about. It might be a blessing in disguise if she were kicked out of ChipCo. But it would be no heavenly act for ChipCo to axe Ballymagee.

She arrived at the airport and found there was a flight that would get her there by evening. Having failed to find Danny's number, she rang Jean in the office and asked her to track him down. Jean told her there was sure to be someone at the airport who would give her a lift, but Kathy insisted she should contact Danny and make sure he, personally, was there to meet her. Having made that clear, she had a large, overpriced whiskey to brace herself for another trip with Aer Shamrock, the airline which had given a whole new meaning to the word turbulence.

The plane was an hour late landing at Ballymagee. Kathy half hoped to recapture the feeling of her first arrival a couple of weeks ago; that she would burst into arrivals and see that ingenuous face of Danny's, smothered in the woolly bobble hat waiting to welcome her. She was even looking forward to hearing those ridiculous tapes and their overwhelming soppiness. But she had not taken many paces on Irish soil before she realised things were different. The woman who made tea did not seem very enthusiastic about life; the girl who took the bookings for the shrine had less of the look of someone making money, and more that of a troubled soul deep in torment. Someone, somewhere, had found the switch marked 'joy' and turned it off.

'Hey,' cried Kathy, spotting Danny sitting by the baggage trolleys. 'Something wrong round here?'

'Ah, it ain't nothin'. It's just that folks get edgy from time to time. No reason for you to catch it too.' He led her to his car, keeping unusually quiet for him.

'Are you sure you're feeling well?' she asked. 'You look like someone who's coming down with the 'flu. You know, low and pale.'

'I told you,' he snapped, 'it's just people round here gettin' edgy. So I get that way too.'

'Sorry,' she apologised, getting into the car, not feeling at all welcome. 'Shall we have some music while we drive?'

'I ain't in the mood. Unless you want some, of course. Customer's always right and all that.'

'Danny,' she pleaded, 'what the hell's going on? I leave here and the place is like one long party. Then I'm away a day and a half and I come back to find the whole place looking like the beer's gone flat.'

Danny stabbed at the tape machine. It spewed the first few notes of a corny ballad before Kathy's finger hit the stop button.

'I'm not getting out of this car till you explain.'

'But I *can't* talk. There's a superstition round here about talking things up, making things happen by gossiping, allowing things to come true by voicing your fears and feelings. It's all fairy tales, but they believe in it. To hear old Father Flynn, you might think that fear of the Lord has pretty much got a grasp on these people – but it ain't nothin' compared with their dread of old beliefs. And this is one of them. You see, if I started chattering about it all now, and it happened tomorrow, and they found out, they'd say it was all my fault. And who's to say they wouldn't be right?'

Mist was clinging to the landscape. Danny flicked on the

wipers to keep the windscreen clear. It was that difficult time of day when the light was fading but night vision had yet to sharpen his wits. He switched on the headlights to help him see the edges of the road through the low-lying mist.

'Do you believe in all that superstition and stuff?' asked Kathy.

'It don't matter if I do or I don't. If you come to live in a community you've got to show respect for its people and the way they live and what they believe in. You wouldn't go into a tribe in darkest Africa and tell them they're crazy for believing in witch doctors, would you? It's all to do with respect. They're a tribe out here, with their own beliefs. Even if between you and me, it's all crap.'

He leaned forward to get a better view through the windscreen, the wipers only serving to spread the drizzle rather than clear it. He brushed condensation away with the back of his hand. Kathy, bewildered by Danny's brusqueness, and tired too, thought she saw a red light in the distance. She squinted to try and focus on it, get a perspective and judge whether it was near or far, but the lone wiper smeared its way across the windscreen and the red gleam vanished for a moment. It was, she decided, not close at all but far away, probably the outside floodlight of a farmyard building somehow made to look red by the moisture in the air. She closed her eyes and wiped them to clear away the tiredness. When she opened them again the relative distances suddenly fell into place. It was not a far, bright light, but a feeble one, and close. She watched it and saw it start to move, swaying from side to side. She shook her head, thinking the flight might have blurred her vision. Then, when she realised what it was, and how close, she tried to shout. But there wasn't time. She grabbed the steering wheel and pushed it to the right, away from the edge of the road.

'What the hell!' cried Danny, fighting to regain control, Kathy refusing to let go. 'You tryin' to kill us?'

'Stop the car!' she insisted. He pumped the brakes and the car slithered to a halt on the wet road.

'Didn't you see the red light?'

'What red light?'

'It was a bicycle. Back there. If we didn't hit whoever it was, we came pretty close. I'm going to check.' Kathy opened the door and put her feet straight into the muddy gutter.

'Are you all right? Is anybody hurt?' she cried into the mist. She could hear a rattle, like a bicycle being righted, and the heavy breathing of someone recently winded. Then she heard the heavy-booted footsteps of someone moving around. At least they weren't dead.

'I'm fine,' came a reply. A man's voice, heavily accented, a local she guessed. 'Though it is no thanks to you that I'm alive and breathing at this moment.' The voice sounded old, and trembled.

As she stumbled along the sodden gutter, mud covering her feet, a figure appeared through the mist, standing, she was relieved to see, by the bicycle. It was the old man they called the Monk.

'You won't know who I am,' Kathy said, 'but I recognise you.'

'And how would you be knowing who I am, young lady?'

'I'm Kathy McGuinness from the factory. I saw you at the Crowley House Hotel the other night.'

'Trying to put an end to me, are you, by driving like a bat out of hell down the lanes, throwing people into the ditch like so much shit?' He spat the words at her.

'That's not fair!' shouted Danny. 'I was at the wheel. Kathy saved you. If it hadn't been for her you'd have been getting a fine view of the undersides of my tyre treads.'

'Ah, so it's you, yer daft young eejit,' he said, recognising Danny. 'Now, if you get out of it I'll be on my way home. And see if I can get there without my life being threatened by bloody ChipCo.'

'No,' insisted Kathy, 'we'll take you home. Danny will drive you.'

'I'm paying no fancy taxi prices.'

'I guess this ride ought to be on me,' offered Danny, hauling the old man's bicycle off the road and pushing it sideways into the boot of the Volvo.

The short journey passed in silence. The old man sat, wordless and dignified, beside Kathy on the back seat.

'You can drop me here,' he said as the car came abreast of the breeze-block gateposts.

'Least I can do is take you all the way there, sir,' said Danny.

'I think you might be more shaken up than you realise,' added Kathy. 'Would it help if I made you some tea?'

'I have had many knocks in my life, young woman,' he said proudly, 'and tonight's is the least of them. I can just about summon the strength to boil my own water, thank you.'

Danny hauled the bicycle out of the car and the old man walked beside it into the gloom. They did not drive off straight away. Instead, they sat and watched him disappear and then, a few moments later, a soft yellow light filled the inside of the cottage.

'It's an oil lamp,' said Danny. 'I've been inside the place a few times. Pretty crude.'

'No electricity?'

'Nope, except for a single bulb which he rarely uses. All the power round here comes from the generator at the factory, see.'

'All the power in the town comes from ChipCo?' she verified. Danny nodded.

'So if the factory closed the place would be without electricity?'

'I suppose it would,' he replied. 'Not very likely though, is it?'

'No, not likely at all,' said Kathy cautiously. 'So what did they do before the factory? They can't have been on oil lamps till the seventies?'

'There was a cable put in by the authorities when "the electric", as they call it, first came in in the forties. But it was old and knackered and always fusing things. The cost of replacement was fantastic, so ChipCo did a deal. They'd supply the town with power in return for which they got government grants and things.'

Kathy looked down at the lights of the town, sparkling before her. The shops, the church, the school, the hall, and of course the factory.

'So the whole place depends on the factory, and not just for jobs?'

'You could say that. The factory's like one of those life-support machines. Keeps the heart of the place pumping, I guess.'

They watched a curtain being drawn across the warm light from the cottage window, and then Danny drove her back to the Crowley House Hotel.

By morning the unmistakable cloud of depression hanging over the town had not dispersed. No change in the emotional weather. Breakfast service in the hotel was unusually slow and surly. There was no banter, only crisp, terse exchanges. With hardly a pleasant word exchanged with anyone, Kathy set off to walk to the factory. The streets were quiet, less bustling than usual. Children made less noise, and behaved in an unusually restrained way on their way to school. She called into Crowley's the newsagent's and found a flustered Mrs Crowley, nervous eyelid fluttering like the shutter of a movie camera, brandishing an aerosol can of fly killer in one hand and a rolled up copy of the *Tribune* in the other.

She was flailing the newspaper through the air, trying in vain to outwit the marauding flies which buzzed and dived, colliding like bullets with the shop window before bouncing back in her

173

direction. They were not tiny upstarts of flies but fat, greedy, obnoxious and large enough for the colours on their bodies to be distinguishable and the buzz of their wings to hold a rasping menace. Mrs Crowley was breathless with the effort of controlling them, though it seemed to Kathy a somewhat unnecessary pastime. It was summer, after all, and vile though they were they were only flies.

'I can't deal with you now,' said the flustered newsagent, stabbing at the air and spraying the aerosol till insecticide was thick enough in the air to make Kathy cough. 'I'd get up to the factory as fast as you can.'

'I just wanted a newspaper.'

'You don't seem to understand, Miss McGuinness,' she said with dramatic emphasis. 'It is happening again, as we all feared it would. It has been five weeks since the last and we have lived in fear of this moment. Now it is upon us again and we must deal with it. We must be strong. We are being tested once more.'

'You make it sound like a plague,' said Kathy, trying to make light of it.

'I can think of no better word,' replied Mrs Crowley in all seriousness.

Urgently now, Kathy jogged along the high street towards the factory, gathering speed. By the time she was within sight of the gates, she could see a small crowd gathering. Breathless, she arrived at the barrier. There was no one to operate it. The security box was empty.

'He's inside, trying to help,' cried one of the women. 'They need all the help they can get. All the menfolk are in there. I'd leave them to it.'

'I am the manager,' declared Kathy. 'Will somebody tell me what the hell is happening?' No one replied. Seeing a small gang of boiler-suited men, clad in masks and helmets, gathering outside the potato store, she made off in that direction, breathing hard, suddenly realising that with every breath she was inhaling the increasingly sickly taint of organic decay. A pair of hands reached out and grabbed her, stopping her in her tracks.

'I wouldn't go in. It's foul. As bad as it's ever been. Let them get it sorted and then I would have a look. Not before.'

Kathy shook herself free and walked cautiously towards the potato store. The women at the gate were watching her every step. She swallowed hard as the rancid odour of putrefaction became stronger, clinging to the back of her throat and turning her stomach. It was the smell of some kind of death. She put her hand to her mouth, and tried not to vomit. If it was like this outside in the supposedly fresh air, she dreaded what it would be like on the other side of the door. A man ran up behind her, offering her a helmet with a visor, and a breathing mask. She took the mask and slipped it across her face, but shunned the helmet and visor.

'I would take it, miss,' warned the man. 'The place is alive with flies. So thick in the air you could cut through it. They're new-born and crazed and have no sense of direction. They'll attack your face and it will feel as if you're standing in a shower of hail. Take the helmet.'

Kathy stood for a moment, listening. She could hear a low-pitched drumming which rose occasionally to a crescendo, then subsided for a while until some stimulus brought it back to life. One of the men accidentally dropped a shovel against the doors and that was sufficient to cause a million creatures to take wing at the same instant. Kathy jammed her hands across her ears, feeling threatened by the drone, and let the man put the helmet and visor on her. Then she nodded to him to open the small, side door. She felt a tug on her arm, more insistent than the last. It was Danny.

'You're a fool if you go in there. Let them deal with it. They've done it before. This is no place for you.'

Pulling the mask from her face, and swallowing hard to prevent herself from being sick, she replied, 'If no one will tell me what happens, I have to see it for myself.' Danny grabbed her arm tighter, pulling her away from the door.

'For fuck's sake, I'm running this place,' she screamed at him, twisting her arm free from his grasp. 'And you are a taxi driver. Remember that. I don't see this is anything to do with you.'

'And *you* have no fucking idea what you are dealing with here,' he screamed back at her. 'You haven't a clue. It isn't safe for you to be in there. They can sort it. Then you can do the rest from behind that desk of yours. But don't try playing the big brave girl round here or you'll get hurt.'

'And don't tell me what to do, taxi driver, OK?'

Kathy slipped the mask back over her face and grabbed the handle of the door. She pulled it open a fraction, and fat, disorientated flies escaped into the wider world, hugging first her clothes, then her legs and hands.

'Are there any lights in there?' she asked.

'They're on,' said the man who had given her the helmet.

'I can't see anything.'

'Too many flies. Thick with them, it is.' He thrust a wide-beamed torch into her hand and looked at her as if to say, Are you going in?

She nodded, he flicked the torch's switch, and she opened the door of the potato store and took one step inside Hell. Above the roar of the buzzing flies she thought she heard Danny shouting, 'Get her back! For Christ's sake, get her back.' His pleas were the last words she heard before the flies awoke to the realisation that something new had come into their lives – a fresh source of food.

The helmet, visor and breathing mask protected Kathy's face, but she felt the creatures land one after another in a continuous stream on her arms, neck and legs. She tried to swipe them away but it only made them more insistent. She waved the torch in the air which was thick with insects, and the beam of light stood out as clearly as if it were being shone through fog. She took a few paces forward, disorientated now, not certain how far she had come. The light from the torch did not penetrate as far as walls or ceilings. Occasionally, she felt the hard lump of a potato under her feet. She tried to remember the store's layout, having only seen it once on that first visit. She imagined the bays, piled to the roof with hundreds of tons of potatoes awaiting processing; in the middle, an open concrete area where the trucks darted in and out as potatoes were shifted around. She guessed that it was on this concrete area she was now standing. As she shuffled forwards, her feet fell on increasing numbers of potatoes and she guessed she was moving nearer to one of the storage bays.

Four more paces and she thought she detected a lightening of the atmosphere, a faint glow where there had been none before, like the lights of a distant town brightening the sky above it. She shuffled towards it, every footfall now becoming more hazardous as the covering of potatoes on the ground grew thicker. Yes, it was a light, and in a brief moment while the insect horde diminished she could make out the figures of three men, clad in protective suits and holding shovels in their hands, staring at her as she appeared from the darkness like a vision.

Her sudden appearance stunned the men into inactivity, which caused the flies to cease their violent flight and settle into less frantic exploration. The atmosphere cleared a little, like fog lifting, and Kathy waved. The motion of her hand immediately caused the nervy flies to take wing once again. She waited till they settled.

At the feet of the workmen she saw what she guessed to be a slimy river of putrefied potato swilling around their feet. It had the texture and appearance of thick soup, the pallid colour of rotten meat, and the stink of deathly decay. She clasped the mask closer to her mouth and nose, hoping to exclude the worst of the noxious stench. She felt her stomach involuntarily contract, but did not submit. The putrid river had its source halfway up the wall of potatoes contained in bay number six. When full it held four hundred tons and she noticed that the potatoes were not far from the top of the dividing wall. Four hundred tons, bleeding to death, rotting, losing all shape and value and turning into a thick, fast-flowing stream of decay. So this, she thought, was what they feared; the curse of which they never spoke. She understood for the first time their terror; how easy it was to believe that this was an act of vengeance beyond anyone's control, as if an evil spirit had entered the potatoes and caused them to rot.

Kathy shuffled forward, filthy matter up to her ankles. The men resumed their work. One switched on a hose and played it across the wall of potatoes in front of him, hoping, he explained, to keep them cool. Another bravely took a spade and started to dig at what he guessed to be the source of the rot. He wanted to get to the core, he explained, shouting as best he could through his breathing mask. And when he had got to the heart he would assess how far the rot had carried. The worst job went to the third man who followed behind, taking individual potatoes and slicing them in half with a knife. If they looked healthy, he was pleased. If he could see no apparent greyness in them, or hint of slime on the skins, he then had to remove his breathing mask and press them to his nose. The first sign of rot was smell. Sometimes a fine potato, sliced to reveal a healthy, succulent heart, only revealed itself to be a traitor when submitted to a sensitive nose.

All three men looked grim. The further they dug, the greater the gush of slime from the decaying mountain. The man with the knife did not even bother to slice them open any more – he could tell just by looking. These potatoes were dead and would be best buried.

They dropped their tools and walked towards Kathy, carefully taking her arms, supporting her as if she were porcelain and leading her back through the agitated clouds of flies, towards the door. She had never been so thankful to see daylight. The priest was waiting to greet them, an old man leaning on a walking stick who introduced himself to her as Father Flynn.

'I came as fast as I could. I'm very sorry. We shall all pray that the potatoes can be saved.'

'I wouldn't bother, Father,' said the man with the spade. 'They're as rotten as Hell in there. There'll be no saving them this time.'

A small crowd had gathered around the doorway, drawn towards the comforting presence of the priest. They waved their hands to scare away any flies which had escaped when the door was opened. A few landed on the bald head of the priest and one of the faithful brushed them away.

'I will say a prayer here and now, if you wish?' Father Flynn said to Kathy.

'The entire potato store will have to be emptied,' announced one of the workmen. 'It usually needs twenty lorries for at least eight hours and all the farmers' diggers in Ballymagee. We need to get them as far away from the factory as we can. Twenty miles isn't too far. We usually spread them out on the bogs and the crows take them.'

'Usually?' gasped Kathy.

'Oh, yes. I'd say we do this at least once every five or six weeks. Did you not know?'

'But first, we'll have to evacuate the place,' explained another workman. 'To get the potatoes out, we open the big doors, and then it's as if you'd taken a sledgehammer to a beehive. Those flies, bellies full of food and energy, come out of that place like jet fighters going to war. The sky is thick with 'em. It wouldn't be safe to keep the factory going. They'd be everywhere. In the packets of crisps given a chance.' The third man, who had been playing a hosepipe on the rotting heap in a grand act of futility, removed his mask and Kathy saw it was Jack from maintenance.

'You never explained it was like this,' she reproached him.

'It was better you didn't know until you had to. But now you do know and have seen it for yourself, you must understand why it is we're so afraid of what this might do to our factory and our livings. At the moment, it happens only every five weeks or so. But who's to say it could not happen every day, non-stop, bringing the factory to a complete standstill and an end to our livelihoods? There's nothing for us here but the potatoes.' He turned and strode back towards the store.

'Hi. It's your taxi driver,' said Danny, misjudging Kathy's mood and trying to joke with her. 'Talking to scum like me, are we? Or shall I get back behind the wheel of the car and sort of be humble, eh?'

'*You* never told me either,' she said, still shaken. '*You* knew it was going to be like this sooner or later and you never warned me. Just let me find out for myself. Bastard! When I make friends I expect them to behave like friends. You *should* have told me.'

'Hell,' spluttered Danny, 'I was only doin' what they said was best. Wasn't my idea to keep quiet.'

'You are on ChipCo property,' said Kathy icily. 'As you are not an employee, I suggest you leave. *Fast.* We'll call you if we need you, but don't hold your breath.' She strode off with out a backward glance.

The factory workers needed no telling what to do next. It was obviously well rehearsed. They made their way home as fast as they could to close all windows and doors to keep out the flies. As soon as the insects had gorged on the bad potatoes, and then bred and multiplied in the heat of the rotting vegetation, they would be off in search of other feasts, invading the town, hiding amongst curtains or in the cracks of doors. Then, unannounced, they would emerge like a second coming and the plague would have moved successfully from factory to home, a victory for the vermin. Someone rang the school to warn them to keep the children in at dinnertime, and not let them out in the evening till they were collected. Extra food would be brought in. The shops were telephoned and advised to put up their shutters. Farmers with diggers were called and the small army rumbled down the main street in well-practised formation, heading for battle.

Meanwhile, volunteers were gathering in the church hall, boiling large kettles on gas rings to make vast pots of thick, strong tea. Women sliced cake and buttered bread for sand-wiches. Those who wanted the company of others could find it here. Father Flynn would be saying prayers later.

Slowly the church hall filled as men and women opted for the company of others rather than maintaining a lonely vigil in their homes.

'How long will it be?' asked one woman, turning to the man standing next to her.

'All day, I should say. I reckon bay number six was full to the brim. Several hundred tons. If we're home tonight, we'll be lucky.'

The woman shook her head, sadly, and sipped on the hot, sweet tea. 'Good morning, Father,' she whispered as the priest moved amongst his people, squeezing any arm in proximity to give comfort.

'Can anyone give me some help now?' shouted a woman from behind the makeshift counter. 'There's been a call from the headmaster. He says he'd rather all the families were together if it's going to take all day, and the wind's blowing the wrong way so the smell will be down on the school before too long. So they're all coming round here, God help us. Beggin' your pardon, Father!'

Back at the ChipCo factory, Jean Crowley was standing on Kathy's desk, reaching as high as she could in order to seal the windows with sticky tape.

'The damned things will get into any little crack and stay there till they're hungry again.'

'What do you do now?' asked Kathy.

'Well,' replied Jean, 'I usually go down the church hall with the rest. It cheers us up.'

'And Percy Crowley, what did he do?'

'Well,' said the secretary, ashamed, 'he always said the best place to be on days like this was in the wide open. And so it often took no more than the buzzing of a fly and he'd be picking up his fishing rod and gone as fast as his legs would carry him. I left a message at home for him when it was all over.'

'And how many times has it happened?'

'I'd say a couple of dozen.'

'A couple of dozen!' exclaimed Kathy. 'But it's in none of your reports. There's no word of it in any of the briefing notes I've been given. Does anybody know about this outside the town?'

'Only the men who drive the lorries and diggers, and they're all Crowleys or close relations, see? So they'd be keeping their mouths shut.'

'But why keep quiet about it? It's a technical problem. Something sends the potatoes rotten, suddenly and with no warning. This place needs a microbiologist or two, that's all. There's no shame in it. It's a problem science can solve. If head office knew, they'd have this cracked in no time. It can't be unique to Ballymagee.'

'I dare say it's not,' agreed Jean, 'but Ballymagee is unique in many other ways. You must understand that although it is one hundred and fifty years ago, we've never forgotten how the potato can turn in a moment from friend to enemy. This place suffered some of the worst starvation in the west. Look at the list of dead in the church hall and you'll see how many came from hereabouts. And here we all are now, making good money out of the potatoes, living grand lives with cars and houses and televisions and everything we could want. All thanks to the potato. So if it is God's will that sometimes the potato reminds us we are still its servants, then we must bow our heads and be thankful for what we have, and not what we sometimes lose when the potatoes go rotten.'

'It's crazy,' insisted Kathy. 'It's pure sentiment, a triumph of emotion over common sense.'

'Of course it is,' replied Jean, unashamed. 'But this is Bally-magee, and it's how we are. But we shall get over this, like we have before, and by tomorrow things will be back to normal. We'll have done our penance. Now, will you be coming to the church hall? There'll be tea there. I'll find Danny and he'll drive you down.'

'Let him be,' mumbled Kathy. 'Give me a few minutes and I'll follow you down.' Just as Jean was about to leave, Kathy shouted after her, 'Do you know where Jack is? I need to be kept up to date.'

'I wouldn't bother. The lads will sort it, and when it's done they'll tell you. Just be thankful you haven't got to do their washing when they come home.'

'But what about the potatoes in the other stores? Shouldn't someone check those?'

'It's an amazing thing, but it only ever seems to be in one store at a time. Never two. It never spreads. That's why we take it as a gentle reminder, and try not to fret too much. If the Lord really wanted to punish us, he'd turn the whole lot rotten, so he would. Now, I'll see you down the hall. Remember the way?'

Alone, sitting behind her desk, watching fat flies land on the windowpanes outside attempting forcible entry, the fragments of a confused picture sorted themselves into some kind of order in Kathy's mind. Now she understood why production figures were never quite what they should be, even though she had seen the factory running at full stretch, an eager work force giving everything they had to the job. It was simple. Every five weeks there was a major interruption such as this one which cost thousands of pounds in wasted potatoes and cleaning costs, as well as loss of production while the factory closed. It took weeks to get over the disruption, import fresh supplies of potatoes, disinfect storage areas, by which time the blight would have struck again. It was like a children's game: no matter how vigorously they threw the dice, the factory never quite got to the top of the ladder before it found itself once again slithering down the back of a malevolent snake. To conceal this from prying eyes outside Ballymagee, the production average was maintained by working that much harder the rest of the time. Praiseworthy, really. And although she was still angry at the way they had conspired to conceal the truth from her, Kathy thought more highly of them because they had done it out of the best of motives.

The people of Ballymagee drew no distinction between themselves and the ChipCo factory. They were as one, and so any fault with the factory was a fault with them. For all the silly management games played back in London – team building, loyalty and interdependence strategies, as they fancifully called them – none of them could ever have forged half so close a bond as existed between these people and their factory. Not that anyone who saw the world from behind a boardroom table would understand that, for they would take just one look at this place and write it off. Perhaps, thought Kathy, the people of Ballymagee were not so stupid in keeping it to themselves after all.

She opened her office door, and put her hand to her face to try and keep out the infectious stench which was spreading into every corner of the building. Outside, a steady stream of lorries, leaking sludge, were roaring by as fast as they dare go, getting the filth out of town as fast as possible. Behind them trundled a farmer on a tractor hauling an elderly spraying machine which was smothering the greasy road with foaming disinfectant. Some of the more adventurous flies followed the lorries but most preferred the warmth of the factory. Eventually, as the lorries got further down the road, the flies tired, to be replaced by flocks of gulls and crows which swooped in delight on the free and unexpected feast.

Inside the church hall tea and cake had worked a magical healing process, and distress and terror had given way to easier conversation. Even the occasional smile. Father Flynn's prayer group dwindled as the crisis passed, and he took the opportunity to sit on a side bench and refresh himself from a small flask carried in his hip pocket.

And then another calming influence spread through the room. It was started by a man in the corner who was whistling a tune to which someone started tapping their foot. A boy took up an empty cake tin, turned it over and started using it as a drum, and soon everyone was clapping their hands to the beat. When another man put down his mug of tea and pulled a tin whistle from his pocket, the impromptu orchestra was complete. Men, women, boys and girls took to the floor and danced to the jig. It was this which greeted Kathy as she opened the door of the church hall. As soon as the man with the whistle saw her, he dropped it from his lips and the child stopped banging the tin. The dancing stopped and they stared at her, trying to judge her mood. Fear or anger?

'Will yer be havin' a mug o' tea in your hand, Miss McGuinness?' shouted a woman from the kitchen.

Kathy smiled, nodded, and took hold of the mug as it was passed to her. Her hand was trembling. She looked around and saw that at the end of the hall was a small stage where children did recitations and performed the Christmas nativity play. She walked towards it, every eye on her as she climbed the three stairs. She looked down at them. Loyal people, she thought; better than ChipCo deserved.

'I just want you to know that I understand how you feel about what has happened today, and I gather it is not the first time.'

One or two hung their heads, ashamed. The rest fixed their eyes on her, weighing her every word. She took a deep breath.

'It is not for me to condemn or criticise. You will have to earn your living here long after I am gone and although every corporate bone in my body says I should do the businesslike thing and close the place down till this problem is sorted, I will not do that. It is not fair to all of you.'

There was a murmur of approval.

'What you choose to believe is your business,' she continued. 'But I will tell you what I believe, and it is that together we can solve this. If we work together, trust each other, we can beat whatever it is that is doing this to the factory. Trust me to go about it my way, please. We both want the same thing, and that is the continued existence of this factory. There is a lot here that headquarters would go crazy about if they knew . . .' The room froze, waiting for her next words. 'But they will not hear it from me.' There was an audible sigh of relief. The women applauded her. 'I promise you one thing,' added Kathy when the clapping had died down, 'we will *not* be meeting here again in five weeks' time in order to recover from another outbreak of the blight. No need to get the kettles out next month!' she shouted to the women in the kitchen. 'Whatever it is, we shall beat it. You will never again have to smell the vileness of the rotting potato! No one in Ballymagee will lose their living because of this pestilence. History cannot be allowed to repeat itself.'

The man who had been playing the whistle leaped on to the stage and gave her a spontaneous hug, so strong she thought it might break her ribs. He thrust his hand into the air to silence the room.

'We always said, didn't we, that Percy Crowley was a gift from heaven for the way he ran things? God bless the man! But who would have thought that we in Ballymagee would be twice blessed? And this time with a beauty like Miss McGuinness.' And he planted a large, wet, tea-flavoured kiss on her cheek before offering her his hand and leading her down the steps.

Kathy made for the door and was just about to leave when she noticed Danny, sitting in the corner, surrounded by discarded coats.

'Well done! Guess you won them round,' he said, looking up at her apologetically from under his bobble hat. 'Took some courage to get up there and speak your mind.'

'Always does when the cowboys have to face the Indians,' she replied, courteously but with no real warmth.

'There's strong stuff in you, Miss McGuinness,' observed Danny. 'I sometimes wonder where you get it from?'

7

In one of those intoxicated, rambling conversations which lasted long into the evenings in the bar at the Crowley House Hotel, Kathy had heard them speak of the Mullet. It was, by all accounts, a beautiful place; a crooked finger of rough land joined by the thinnest of rocky threads to the mainland. To be strictly accurate it was an island now, after the cutting of a narrow canal to save an open sea journey of fifty miles for fishermen wanting to pass from Broadhaven Bay to the north or Blacksod Bay to the south. But there was a bridge, and so it *was* an island, yet wasn't. Anyway, there was water all around it and that was that.

Kathy thought a blast of unsullied Atlantic breeze might clear her head of sickly thoughts of putrid potatoes, and dislodge from the corners of her mind the foul smells of two days before. The detritus in the store had been cleared, the floors hosed and disinfected, and in ten different flavours, crisps were now churning off the production line once again in little shiny bags.

She needed time alone, a break from living on top of everyone from the factory, as bound up with them as if they were all sharing the same bed so that if one rolled over the others must follow. But escape was also becoming urgent for other reasons. She now had just four weeks in which to solve this problem and arrive at a logical, scientific explanation for what was happening. She had made a public promise. To put her mind to keeping it, she took the day off and headed west.

The Mullet seemed as good a place to go as any. It was lovely, they said; wild, but not threatening. The few people who lived there, she was told, were welcoming. If the sun shone, the Atlantic beaches were inviting too. She looked at a tourist map on the desk of the hotel and worked out it was too far to walk – about twenty miles. Not wanting to bother with taxis, and in particular taxi drivers, she enquired if there was a bus. There was, and so she hired from Crowley's Garage a rusty bicycle to get her round the Mullet and stood with it at the bus stop in the market square, suffering the disbelieving stares of passing workers. Factory managers did not ride bikes.

'I want to be dropped about five miles short of the Mullet,' she told the driver of the single-decker bus.

'And where would that be precisely?' he asked.

'Not bothered. I just want to cycle the last bit.'

'Then I'll drop you at Glencastle. Will that do?'

She paid a modest fare and had no trouble finding a seat. There was no one else on the bus.

'You can put your bike across the back seat, if you want,' suggested the driver.

'Mightn't someone want that place?'

'If the day ever arrives when this bus is full, it will be a cause for such celebration by the bus company we'd all be at the party and wouldn't be giving a damn what was on the back seat. There's never more than three people on this bus at a time. The back seat will be fine.'

Kathy trundled the bike to the back of the bus, laid it across the dingy upholstery and walked forwards again to pay her fare.

'I'll be stoppin' off in Bellacorick for a cup o' tea, if that's all right? It's where my sister lives. I bring her the papers every day. She'll make you a cup too, so don't you worry now.'

It would be an exaggeration to suggest that the bus sped away, but it seemed to Kathy to be going at a greater speed than its elderly frame could sustain. She clung on with both hands to the seat in front while gazing out of the window, trying to get a better impression of the countryside than the one she had gathered in those twilit journeys in Danny Morrissey's car.

She was surprised by how quickly the town of Ballymagee disappeared into the distance. For all its self-importance, it was only a tiny blemish on the rolling, barren landscape. The houses and cottages came to an abrupt halt on the town boundary to be replaced by farms worked with expensive new tractors, growing in total two thousand acres of potatoes, sixty or more thousand tons in a good harvest. The farmhouses were no hovels. Some were newly built, Spanish-style bungalows with patios and conservatories, and large, new cars parked outside. The gardens were cultivated to an unnatural degree of tidiness, and the ring of white flowers created by field after field of blossoming potatoes surrounded them like a daisy chain round a child's neck.

Once over the brow of the hill, the town and potato fields disappeared. Peering forward, Kathy saw the bleak, boggy landscape with deep, black incisions running geometrically across it, where the peat had been cut. In places the rain had collected and large, shallow lakes had been formed. The road ran right across the bog, a couple of feet above it. It rose and fell like a rollercoaster where its foundations had been sucked into the sodden ground, leaving other bits high and dry. Kathy felt sick. They passed bus stop after bus stop. No one was waiting.

'That's Drumderg we're just through,' shouted the driver, as if it was supposed to mean something to her. 'We'll be well into Bellacorick in ten minutes. If the weather's clear, she'll see me coming over the top and be puttin' the kettle on.'

'I might have a look round the shops, while you have your tea,' said Kathy.

The driver chuckled. 'If it's shops you need it'll be the next bus back you're wantin'. There's only two houses in Bellacorick, and my sister's in one of 'em. And I'm sorry to have to tell you the other's not a shop.'

'Would you come this way if you were going to Ballymagee from the airport?' Kathy asked, curious.

'You might, if you were going the long way round. It's what I'd call a taxi driver's route. You know, to bump up the fare.'

'That figures,' muttered Kathy. This place had an undeniably familiar feel to it. She had been here before, and not long ago either. It may have been the distinctive rumble of the road under the tyres or the shapes of the dead trees, turned into leafless, leaning sculptures by the relentless Atlantic gales. Then, just as she was beginning to wonder what the Mullet would be like, two leaning gateposts appeared, built out of breeze blocks and with a galvanised iron gate loosely attached. She knew them. This was where Pat Tierney lived.

'Well, we'll be havin' a little ten minutes here. If you'd care for a cup o' tea you'll be welcome.' The driver reached under his seat for a copy of that day's *Tribune*, muttering about the shameful ways of young people. Kathy had read that morning's paper over breakfast, hoping there would be no reports of the problems at the factory. There weren't. Instead, a head of indignation was being got up over three kids who'd flicked the slightest spot of paint over a statue of the Virgin Mary. It was such a small spot that had the woman been a real one and not a statue, she would not even have bothered to take the skirt to the cleaner's. Still, Kathy thought, it made better reading than ChipCo's problems spread all over the front page.

'Is this where your sister lives?' she asked, looking past the breeze block gateposts and along the rutted track to the cottage.

'It is,' replied the driver, proudly.

'Her gateposts don't look too good,' remarked Kathy.

'Bless you, that's not her. God, no! She's on the other side of the road. Don't go mistakin' my sister for the daft old devil who lives up there or there'll be no tea for you, that's for sure,' he said with a smile. The driver led her across the road and between two substantial gateposts, these upright and painted gleaming white, the grass at the edge of the track neatly mown. The cottage was not unlike the one across the road in terms of general appearance, but this one sparkled. The paintwork was fresh, the windows polished. They went into the tidy, back kitchen where the tablecloth was spotlessly white, chairs were arranged neatly, and three willow-patterned cups and saucers, complete with spoons, were laid out. Beside each was a small side plate and knife. In the middle of the table stood a large fruit loaf. The kettle was singing on the hob of the peat-burning range and the air in the cottage was thick with the mingled smells of peat smoke and fresh baking. If someone had set the place up to make a television commercial for Barry's Tea, they couldn't have done better than this. Kathy sat down while the woman, who introduced herself as Janet, poured the tea carefully and precisely. Kathy thanked her.

'You seemed to know how many passengers might be on the bus. Or did you guess and put out three cups on the off chance?'

'Well,' said Janet, picking crumbs off her woollen cardigan, 'if there's more than a couple, I don't usually bother. It gets too much. But if there's just the one person on board, I don't mind. I ring the Post Office in Ballymagee just after the bus has left and he usually tells me how many are coming. He told me you had a bicycle. He'd never seen the manager of the factory on a bicycle before. You wouldn't have got old Percy Crowley on two wheels.' She chuckled. 'He wouldn't have been upright for more than a moment.'

'You know I'm from the factory, then?'

'I do. You're Miss McGuinness.' The woman lifted the plate of fruit loaf and offered her another slice. 'Are you one of the McGuinnesses from Athlone? I thought there was a hint of a

cousin of mine in your eyes. And that fine head of black hair.'
Kathy shook her head. 'Ah, but you're a good-lookin' lass. And
such lovely Irish eyes. I heard you made a fine speech to the
workers.'

'You heard about that?'

'I did. Went down rather well, so they say.'

'Good, I'm glad. I've got to do everything I can to make sure
the factory keeps going, and profitably. Everyone's been so
welcoming it's the least I can do.'

'Well, let's hope they stay welcoming, Miss McGuinness.
They're a funny lot in Ballymagee. They'll take against you as
quickly as they'll embrace you. Like they did to the old man next
door. He's a trouble maker and I wish he were a thousand miles
from here. He's always goin' on about the factory, telling the
people they're slaves to it and should be fighting for their
freedom. All that sort o' rubbish.'

'And what's his problem?' Kathy asked.

'His head. *That's* his problem. Went off his rocker when his
mother died and left him to run the farm. He goes around, gettin'
drunk, shouting in the streets if anyone's foolish enough to give
him a ride into town, boasting that he's a wealthy man to
everyone that passes by – whether they want to hear about it
or not.'

'And is he? Wealthy, I mean?'

'I shouldn't think so for one minute. Just look at how he lives!'
Kathy followed the turn of the woman's head and together they
looked out of the kitchen window, across a boggy patch of land
to the bleak hovel opposite. 'Is that the home of a rich man? He's
an old fool who'd be better dead, the rubbish he talks.'

'But there's no real harm in him, is there?'

The woman took a deep breath and sighed. 'Well, there are
just a few who might be persuaded that what he says is right.
Especially the youngsters who read all about this republican

stuff – armies, politics and the like. These kids aren't happy to have that factory owned by what they think of as a London firm. They don't like being ruled by the British.'

'But this is Ireland,' insisted Kathy. 'Independent Ireland.'

'Not Ballymagee. There's nothing here that isn't dependent in some way for its prosperity on that British-owned factory. So is it any wonder some of the kids ask who's in charge, eh? The Irish or the British once again? Let me be honest with you, Miss McGuinness. The British have a poor reputation round here when it comes to trust. They let our families perish in the Famine. We haven't forgotten that. And I don't suppose you have either.'

Kathy did not understand. Her face registered no reaction.

'Why,' Janet continued, 'there's enough McGuinnesses up on that memorial board. I imagine you were all family once.'

Kathy shifted uneasily, pushing the cup away from her.

'It was scary at the factory the other day. I guess you know all about it? I've never seen people in such an unholy terror.'

'Well,' replied Janet, 'is it any wonder they go into a blind panic every time something goes wrong with potatoes? But you're Irish too, aren't you? You understand. Are you sure you're not from Athlone? Such lovely eyes . . .'

Ten minutes later, the bus was back on the road and ten minutes after that it had come to a squealing halt at a godforsaken bend in the road which boasted two houses on one side, a cottage on the other, and a pub.

'This is Glencastle,' announced the driver. 'It won't take you long to get from here to the Mullet. But if it's all too much, then yer can make a telephone call to O'Regan's bar on the Mullet itself and leave a message saying you'll be wanting a lift back. I leave at four o'clock, but I don't mind waiting ten minutes or so if I know you're coming.'

'And where will you be?' asked Kathy innocently.

'In O'Regan's! Where else is there on the Mullet? Well, cheerio. And safe home.'

The bus left Kathy and her bicycle standing in a cloud of blue diesel exhaust so thick that it took the sea breeze a few moments to disperse it. She mounted and pedalled down the hill, following the tracks of the bus, letting the fiercely fresh air blow through her head. From the top of a rise she could see the sea. It looked grey and unwelcoming, except when sun filtered through a gap in the clouds and then it sparkled as blue as the Caribbean. And that was true of the whole of the Mullet. When the rain-laden clouds hung heavy over the land, when the ditches swelled to bursting point with fallen rain and the tracks became rivers, it felt like an edge of the world where one step further would send you tumbling into oblivion. But when the clouds parted and the rain eased, the golden light transformed it. The browns, greens and purples of the heather moors, the dark gullies where peat had been dug, the colossal, boiling clouds, waiting over the Atlantic Ocean for their turn to drop their cargo of rain, were all touched with magic. Kathy thought of golden apples, and the sun. She remembered Danny reading that line to her. Perhaps she'd been too hard on him. No, she hadn't. Bugger him!

It was tempting to indulge herself in a romantic, idle day of slow pedalling and gazing at the landscape. But the problem of the potato blight had to be solved and she had come here to give it some thought. How would her mother have tackled it? By brainpower, by reasoning, and ultimately by laying down the law. Such was the force of Leonora's personality that she would have ordered the potatoes to behave and they would have obliged. Kathy knew she was not in the same league.

She worked through the problem, step by step. Potatoes, she knew from her training, were susceptible to all kinds of infection; bacterial, fungal, even viral. It must be one of those. Some

196

diseases were more virulent than others, and this one, whatever it was, was clearly hell-bent on hasty annihilation of as many potatoes as it could touch. She figured that although the temperature of the potatoes in the store was monitored – heat being the first sign of impending rot – if the infection took hold with sufficient speed it could achieve in the heart of the four-hundred-ton heap a temperature high enough for multiplication before anyone spotted the thermometer move. So she did not think the problem was lazy monitoring. It all happened too quickly, and once it had taken hold there was no hope. It spread from potato to potato, putrefying them as it went, which made it an ideal breeding ground for flies who may have laid their eggs weeks or months before. The heat hatched them and then in turn rotted the potatoes to give the newborn maggots sustenance. It was heaven for a fly – a perfect bed and breakfast.

The thought of it all, and the memory of the smell which she still carried in her mind, made Kathy feel sick all over again. She stopped pedalling and waited till the wind had cleared her head. She could not work out why it should happen every four or five weeks. Could it be something to do with the weather? Hardly. How could an infection chart the passing of the days so precisely? Of greater importance was what she was going to do about it. She had promised faithfully, in front of them all, that she would solve this problem, and they had believed her. She remembered the moment she'd spoken those words of guarantee from the rickety stage in the church hall. The fear had melted from their eyes like frost from a window under warm breath. She had promised, and now she must deliver.

Her first instinct was to get help from London. ChipCo had some of the finest scientific research in the world at its fingertips. It could be something very simple; as fathomable to a biologist as a headache to a doctor. There might be a quick and cheap prescription which would end it once and for all. They would, of course, need samples, and have to study local working methods. And therein lay the problem. For as soon as outside help was brought into Ballymagee, it would become common knowledge how the place was run and how far outside the conventional rules of management it functioned, and that would be the end of it. Kathy understood now why they had not sought help before. They were fearful not only of the diagnosis and eventual prognosis, but of the examination itself.

Kathy called in at O'Regan's bar to tell the bus driver that she would not be catching the bus, thank you. She had a half-formed idea in her head; a ridiculous notion but a compelling one. She would cycle all the way back and call on the old man they called 'the Monk'.

She was not certain why, and came up with many spurious arguments. The most plausible was that an outsider might give her a fresh view of the potato problem. Being unconnected with the factory, he might have ideas of his own, if she could tease them out of him. But this was not the real reason she was drawn back towards him. It was to do with a certain attraction she felt towards the man, not of a sexual or even romantic kind but totally unlike anything she had felt before. It was a desire to talk to him, to know him, to be near him, hear his voice, feel his presence. She had felt it the first time she'd set eyes on him, despite the circumstances in the back bar of the Crowley House Hotel, and then again by the roadside as she'd helped him to his feet after the accident. She felt she knew him yet at the same time did not know him at all. He was a total stranger yet as familiar to her as if she had known him all her life. She had developed a hunger to meet him which their first brief encounters had not satisfied. It took her two and a half hours of determined pedalling against a stiff headwind before, as dusk was falling, she was once again beside the breeze block gateposts.

The wind rattled the iron gate on its hinge. Dusk had fallen early. Kathy saw that he had lit the same oil lamp she remembered seeing the night she had tried to help him home. She walked slowly along the track, leaving her bicycle leaning against the gate. The looming head of a filthy brown bullock appeared over a sagging barbed wire fence, staring at her with wide open eyes which swivelled as she went past. Its head remained resolutely still till its eye could spin no further, and then the beast walked quietly away. There was a scurrying as three lazy sheep awoke to the fact that there was a stranger in their midst, then a metallic clatter. It was a piece of loose tin, she thought, part of the roof flapping in the wind. Lurking in the doorway were two cackling hens perched atop an upturned beer crate. Kathy rapped on the door but it sounded pitifully faint, so she knocked harder. Nothing stirred. She knocked again.

'Blast you, bloody cows!' came a growling voice from inside the cottage and the door was flung wide open to reveal the old man standing with his collarless shirt undone to the waist, dribbles of dried food down the front. His braces were hanging down. She thought she smelled some kind of drink coming either from him or from further inside the cottage.

'My God! Is it a vision I see before me? Is it an angel itself come down from heaven to appear on my own doorstep!' he cried. Kathy decided the drink was in him. 'And what would such a piece of loveliness be doing in a wild part of the world like this? Do you know who I am? It is me that children in the village are warned away from. And here you are, standing in front of me and not even trembling in fear!'

'I didn't want to disturb you. But I was in the car which knocked you over the other night . . .'

'So you were,' he remarked, moving closer towards her and squinting to examine her more closely. 'But that's not where I've seen you . . . I mean, I saw you there but somewhere else too. Now where would that be?'

'In Ballymagee, perhaps.'

'Your name?' he asked, crisply.

'McGuinness. Kathy McGuinness.'

'I don't know you. I must be wrong. Well, thank you for calling.' He started to close the door. 'As you can see, I am far from death and you can tell them all that when you get back to town. They won't be pleased to hear it.' He chuckled.

'I'm from the factory,' she told him, trying to grab his attention before the door closed. 'I'm the new manager.'

He was about to close the door in her face, but paused.

'You're from the factory! And you have come to see *me*?'

'I thought it was the least I could do, after the other night. They all seemed so rude to you when you came into the Crowley House. It didn't seem fair.'

'They know nothing about fairness down there. They know only about themselves, what they can make, how much they can earn, and the hell with everyone else.'

'Not me,' said Kathy.

'I can open this door an inch further,' said the old man, 'and invite you to step inside. But every nerve in my body tells me that Pat Tierney would be better dead than having anyone from that factory cross his threshold.'

'So why aren't you closing the door on me, Mr Tierney?' she asked.

'Because . . .' he paused. 'Because . . . I don't bloody well know why. My brain must be goin' soft. The rain has got to it and made it rot. I'll be cursed for this. Come in, girl, and close the door.'

She followed him into the cottage. It was warm, but filthy. There was stained newspaper spread across the table in place of a cloth, mugs were unwashed, dishes thick with dried food, old copies of the *Tribune* heaped in every corner, empty jam jars collected in cardboard boxes. Grey shirts, once white, were hanging near the peat fire to dry. With a groan, Pat threw a lump of turf into the hearth and fell back into a soft chair by the fireside, saying nothing.

'May I sit down?' asked Kathy. He nodded, his eyes fixed on her unblinking.

'Drink?' he offered.

'No, thanks.'

'It's special.'

'I've got to cycle back to town. I need a clear head.'

'No,' he said, correcting her. 'If you're going back there the last thing you need is clear vision or you'll perceive the truth of the place. It will become self-evident. Better clouded in drink, I would say.'

'And what is the truth of the place?'

'My views are well known.'

'I would like to hear them from you.'

'Why? So you can try and talk me out of them, win me over, make me one more of the loyal band of ChipCo followers who slavishly follow company laws?'

'You're too hard on them,' she said. 'They're decent people trying to earn a living in a bleak place where there'd otherwise be no work at all. You're not above selling us potatoes yourself, I find.'

'He told you that, did he? Your fancy young man with the taxi. I saw him the other night. That eejit who's dying to be an American. Or the other way round, I've lost track.'

'He is not an idiot, and he is not my fancy man.'

'I offered you a drink,' he reminded her. 'If you can't take a drink with a man you nearly sent to his death, what hope is there of any reconciliation?' Without waiting for her assent, he stood up and pulled two small tumblers from a cupboard above the stone sink and blew into them to disperse the dust. Then, delving deep into a mahogany sideboard, he pulled out a corked bottle, half filled with a clear spirit. He poured a thimbleful into one of the glasses and slung it on to the fire. There was a surge of vivid yellow flame, as if it were petrol he'd thrown. He chuckled as he poured Kathy a glass and passed it to her with a shaking hand. She reached out, and with her left hand took hold of his wrist to steady it while she safely removed the tumbler with her right. Then, when she should have let go, she found herself wanting to hold on.

'Have you tasted the stuff, eh? Real poteen, brewed I'd best not tell you where. But not far from here. Do you know what it's made from?'

'Potatoes.'

'True. Spirit distilled from the fermenting tater. And did you know that it's against the law to brew it, distil it and drink it?'

'Yes, I did.'

'And did you know how many hundreds of thousands died for lack of potatoes three generations back, and how the English had the cheek to ban the stuff ten years before that because they thought it was making the Irish people unruly, when it was the English themselves that were doing that? Did you know?'

'I didn't know that.'

'Where is the McGuinness family from, your part of it?' he asked, changing the subject.

'I'm not sure,' Kathy replied cautiously.

'Not sure! An Irish girl who doesn't know every root and branch of her family wherever in the world they might be? I've never met such a person before.'

Kathy took a sip of the poteen. It stung like pure spirit; tore at her mouth like boiling liquid. When it hit the back of her throat it was as good as caustic, scarring her gullet as it made its way into her stomach bound for the bloodstream where it would soon work its relaxing magic. He smiled, watching her face as she struggled to remain composed in the face of this alcoholic assault.

'Do the McGuinness family not touch a drop of the poteen, then?'

'It seems to have passed me by,' she replied and changed the subject quickly, her eye caught by the sight of an old tin whistle, shrouded in dust, lying on the shelf over the fireplace.

'Do you play the whistle? I play the mouth organ sometimes.'

'Haven't played it in years, damned thing. Last time was on a ship, I think. Never mind. All history now.'

He took a sip of his own poteen, but for any reaction that showed on his face it might as well have been water. 'Aye, 'tis a good drop. And strong enough too. I can make it easier for you?' He reached for the kettle by the fire and offered to pour some hot water into her glass, to dilute the spirit. Thinking it might make drinking easier, she accepted, and was able to take a heartier swig the next time. The hot water made it easier to swallow, but it also gave new life to the warmed, volatile alcohol which found its way even more quickly into every corner of her body, relaxing it. Kathy suddenly felt tired after the cycling, and pulled her legs up under her and rested her head on the cushion, which smelt of cats. Her eyes closed for the briefest moment till she sensed Pat looking at her again.

'Do you know what the people down there would do if they knew you were here with me?' he asked.

'Whatever they might do,' she replied, 'I would tell them that it was none of their business.'

'You would – if you had the time to draw breath before they ran you out of town.' He laughed. 'They think I'm wicked, you see. Some kind of demon. Well, let me tell you, it's not easy playing the part of the devil when you should, in all justice, be cast in the role of guardian angel.'

'And what do you do for the people of Ballymagee that could ever make them believe you were on their side?'

'Ah,' he explained, 'I am the guardian of their consciences.

I am the only one who remembers what they choose to forget.'

'But the Famine was a century and a half ago. Aren't they allowed to turn their backs on it?'

'They may look forward, of course, thinking themselves free from guilt. But there are things in the past for which they can never be forgiven, no matter how many years pass.'

'Things they have done to you?'

'And continue to do to themselves, yes. They haven't the wit to see that they are making themselves slaves of the English once again, as their ancestors did. And, like the last time they turned to the English for help, once they are in any kind of need they'll find they are shunned and left to starve by ChipCo. The people of Ballymagee are no longer the servants of absentee English lords and ladies, but serfs of their modern equivalent – bloody ChipCo.' There was a moment's silence while Kathy gathered together her courage.

'Is it you,' she asked pointedly, 'who is disrupting the factory? Turning the potatoes bad?'

He chuckled. 'Do you think I'm some kind of wizard? Some kind of magician who waves a wand and casts his spell on the place? I don't mind admitting that sometimes I wish I had the power. And I would use it. But when it comes to turning potatoes sour, I fear it's beyond me. You'll have to look elsewhere for your culprit.' He stood up and reached for the poteen bottle and leaned over to offer her another slug of the strong spirit. At the same time, she leaned forward to help herself to a drop of the hot water. Their faces met in the warm firelight which melted away his mask of anger and discontent. She saw a younger happier man.

'What was it that made you so bitter?' she asked gently.

'It's too long a tale, and too long ago to matter now.'

'And why is it all so tied up with the factory? What did they do to you? What was it that hurt so much you still feel the pain?'

'Who says I feel pain? It's only you surmisin' and makin' things up in your silly head. Women are always thinkin' everything's to do with romance.' It was an unconvincing show of indignation.

'I didn't mention romance,' remarked Kathy.

'Is there a love in your life?' he asked.

'No.'

'Has there been?'

'There have been friends, good friends' she replied guardedly.

'But you expect to love again, do you?' he persisted. Kathy nodded.

'Then that's good. But can you imagine if you'd loved only once and found that afterwards you could never love again? Can you begin to contemplate a life from which the heart had been removed?' He took a deep slug of the spirit, then a deep breath, and his face swelled with anger.

'And it's all the fault of the bloody potato!' he cried. 'The stupid, bloated tater!' He threw the glass tumbler towards the fireplace where it smashed against the grate, the poteen catching light and sending sheets of vivid flame the full height of the fireplace.

'Is it fair that the potato should haunt me all my life? It was the potato that took my family in the most cruel suffering ever known in this island one hundred and fifty years ago. And a century later it was because of the potato that I lost my only chance of true happiness. And now,' he waved the bottle of poteen in the air, 'the spirit of the potato is taking my mind too. Destroying it.'

His eyes, fixed on the remnants of the flame in the hearth where the last of the poteen was burning out, started to fill with tears.

'And so perhaps it's not the people of Ballymagee with whom you are so angry, but yourself?' Kathy suggested.

205

'They're no saints, those folks. I'm not excusing any of 'em. Especially the Crowleys. They're all scum to me.' He raised his finger and pointed to a slim book on the nearby shelf. 'Pass that down, will you?' Kathy got up, reached for it, blew the dust off it. It was a prayer book.

'I want to read this to you,' he declared, removing an old, folded piece of paper stored carefully inside the missal. 'But I have not an idea where my glasses might be and so you'll have to hold it closer than that.' He put his arm around first her neck, and then along the upper part of her arm till he reached her elbow, then pulled the paper towards him till he was able to focus on it. He read slowly and deliberately.

'"With regret we have to add another name to the melancholy catalogue of the dead from starvation in this district, in the person of a poor aged man named Padraig Michael Tierney" . . . that was my great-great-grandfather . . . "who, while on his way on Wednesday last to seek admission to the workhouse, expired on the side of the road near Ballymagee within about a mile of the town. When he was discovered life was found to be extinct, and his remains were taken to the warehouse where an inquest was subsequently held upon the body by . . ."' he paused to give emphasis to the words he was about to speak '". . . Michael Crowley Esq., deputy coroner, and the verdict returned of 'died from want'."'

'I'm very sorry,' said Kathy.

'But that tells only half the tale,' explained Tierney. 'My family were trying to work poor land that was owned by some lord or other from England, and the Crowleys were his agents here. Not only did Michael Crowley, deputy coroner, certify the man dead, it was he that killed him. Murdered him by refusing to give him relief from paying the rent when the potatoes were plagued. He could have allowed them to save a little of the oats for themselves instead of being forced to sell them all to pay rents that were far too high anyway. But the Crowleys obeyed their masters in England and did nothing for their fellow men. Do you wonder now why I will have little to do with *that* place,' he stabbed his chapped finger in the direction of the town, 'full as it is of Crowleys to this day.'

'But it was one hundred and fifty years ago. A crime of the past,' said Kathy. 'And the Crowleys lost family too, Jean told me. No one escaped without loss.'

'The Crowleys lost some, true. But not on the scale of loss some families endured. God, many were wiped out entirely while the Crowleys fed themselves on the proceeds of their work on behalf of the murdering English landlords.'

He paused, trying to weigh in his mind whether he should tell her more. He licked his lips, wiped his eyes and said to her, 'Do you know the final insult?' He glanced back at the fragile scrap of paper and read aloud once again. '". . . when he was discovered, life was found to be extinct, *and his remains were taken to the warehouse.*" Do you know where that was? Did you know about the warehouse where they piled the bodies high until they could dig graves in the yard big enough to hold them all? Did you know where that stood? On the very same spot where they built that factory. In the very same place where those people, my people, were buried, they built a works to turn the potatoes, for lack of which they starved, into a futile form of nourishment they call crisps, out of which the Crowleys have made their fortunes.'

'And where does love come into this?' Kathy asked. 'I hear only hatred.'

'Who spoke of love?'

'You did,' she reminded him. 'You asked me about love. Told me you lived a life with no heart in it. Where did that heart go?'

'A woman took it. The usual tale.' He looked at Kathy who had slid down the sofa a little and was now resting her head against his chest. 'She looked not unlike you. A real beauty.' She felt him lean forward as if he were about to place a kiss on her forehead. Before she had time to accept or spurn it, there was a sudden noise behind her as the door opened, bringing a sobering waft of cold air into the cottage. Both she and the old man sat upright.

'Well, caught you two in a cosy moment, eh?' It was an American accent.

'Morrissey. What the hell are you doing here?' spluttered the old man.

'Looks like I'm interrupting somethin' special,' said Danny. Kathy could have denied it, to shut him up, but could not bring herself to. It *had* been special.

'I thought you were coming Thursday,' snapped the old man.

'It *is* Thursday. Perhaps time flew by when you were in each other's arms,' he sneered.

'The boy comes here most weeks for a lesson or two in the Gaelic,' Pat explained to Kathy. 'It saves me having to pay him to take the potatoes down to the factory. Though what use Gaelic will be on the streets of America, I haven't a clue.'

'I'll go,' said Kathy, embarrassed.

'Want a lift?' offered Danny.

'I'm fine,' she thanked him. 'It's downhill to Ballymagee.'

'The truest words ever spoken,' muttered the old man.

With not a care for what Danny might think, Kathy took hold of Pat's hand, leaned towards him, and kissed the old man on the cheek. 'Thank you for seeing me,' she said. 'I think I understand. Really I do.' And finding herself unable to let go of him, even under the disapproving stare of Danny Morrisey, she kissed him again on the other cheek before disappearing through the cottage door.

The old man went across to the window and watched her walk down the track to the gate where she had left her bicycle.

'Will she be safe in the dark?' he asked.

The only other movement on the hillside that night, apart from the grass being buffeted sideways by the wind, was the twitch of the curtain in the front window of the house opposite where the bus driver's sister lived.

8

Ted Metcalfe always enjoyed the company of a neat young man and without any doubt would have had his hands all over the current object of his desire, Toby Hart, the fresh-faced press officer, if his fingers had not been too preoccupied feeding a sheet of paper into his desktop fax machine. It would usually have been his secretary's job, but he was working late and she had left early. He pressed the 'send' button and turned to the young man, sitting in his usual subservient position on the sofa. Ted liked that pose.

'Sorry to keep you here after hours. I'm sure we'll be through soon. You'll have other things to do, I expect. Other people to go and spend time with.' Metcalfe moistened his lips and stroked his natty moustache before asking, 'And what do you do for relaxation? You seem a very physical sort of young man. Like lots of activity, do you?'

'Cycling, mostly. I've got a friend.'

'A special sort of friend?'

'I hope so.'

Metcalfe examined the machine to ensure the fax had gone through.

'Pity,' he said. 'Friends are difficult to find, and I thought I might have found one in you.'

'That fax,' said Hart, trying to steer the conversation from the flirtatious to the professional. 'My head of corporate relations would be concerned if she knew you had sent it without briefing her first.'

'Her?' exclaimed Metcalfe. 'Aren't you sick to death of being pushed around by bloody women? Wherever you turn in this organisation there's one woman or another ready to chew your bollocks off. Easier to talk, man to man, don't you think?'

'It doesn't bother me much. It's just work.'

'It would bother you if you sat where I sit,' said Metcalfe. 'Do you know what it's like for me, working here? What with the fuckin' Foley woman, and that cow of yours in corporate relations, it's like having their arses across your face full time. Well, if that's what happens to turn you on, fine. But it doesn't do much for me, and I wouldn't have thought it did much for you either, having a woman on top of you. Anyway, that cow in corporate relations is due for a move sooner or later. Sooner if I have my way. It will, of course, leave a nice gap in the organisation . . .' He paused to grin. 'And I shall be looking for an able young man to fill the position. Someone with experience, shall we say, at executive level. Do you have much, er, experience?' He played his tongue round the inside of his cheek. 'Seeking to widen your horizons at all?'

'I am looking for professional advancement, it's true, sir,' said Toby Hart, choosing his words carefully, trying not to show revulsion at Metcalfe's unsubtle advances. 'I was wondering how you square the contents of that fax with the promise you gave to Miss Foley – I mean, McGuinness – when she was here a few days ago? You gave her a month to sort things out. Now you're announcing the closure of her factory.'

'Is that a matter for corporate relations?' Metcalfe asked. 'It is more a question of *my* relations with Miss Foley, isn't it?'

'Is it true, what you said in the fax? Has closure been demanded by the full board? I wasn't aware there had been a board meeting in Boston since you spoke to Miss Foley – er, McGuinness,' said Hart bravely.

'We are a clever boy, aren't we? Brains and so pretty too. Well, mind your own fuckin' business, eh?'

'But these are questions the press will want answered. Closure of the Ballymagee plant will make news, certainly in Ireland, and there will be implications for our share price here, if not around the world. It's part of corporate relations' brief to protect the company's share value.'

'But a twitch in the stock price, my dear boy, will be the smallest of prices to pay for ridding this company of a fledgling Foley. There are too many little chicks in this nest, and one less won't matter too much. We'll ride the stock market,' declared Metcalfe arrogantly. 'They'll sell for a couple of days and then worry about something else. The price will drop admittedly, but within a couple of weeks it will creep back up. No problem.'

'And your promise to Kathy?'

'Oh, *Kathy*, is it?' said Metcalfe. 'On her side, are we?'

'I don't take sides, sir. But what's her future, may I ask? It's customary for a press officer to be in possession of the wider picture.'

'Then her outlook is bleak, wouldn't you say?' replied Metcalfe with a smug grin. 'Of course, I shall immediately offer her another position in the company.' He leaned forward across the desk. 'Then I would like you, personally, to make a few discreet calls to the papers – gossip columns rather than financial pages. Just suggest, off the record of course, that she's only being offered another job because her mother is Acting World President. When that gets out there's not a hope in hell's chance she'll be able to accept anything I offer.'

'And what about the people of Ballymagee?'

Metcalfe shrugged his shoulders. 'Do they give a shit about me? Why should I give a shit about them? It was a lousy little factory anyway. We only kept it running because Leonora Foley fiddled the figures to make it look better. Just 'cos she went out there years ago, got herself fucked by some bog Irishman and laid the foundations of her own fortune at the same time, she felt it gave her a licence to do what she liked with the place.'

'She'll go ballistic when she hears you've closed it, if I may say so.'

'No, she won't. She can't. It will be seen as her daughter's failure and any attempts by Leonora to cover up that fact would be too damaging to her own reputation. She may be fond of her only child, but she's a damned sight more fond of herself.'

Metcalfe leaned forward and pulled from the fax machine the document he had just sent. 'I'm rather pleased with this,' he declared, and started to read aloud from it.

' "Dear Kathy,

' "I am under pressure from the board to make dramatic improvements in our western European operations. Despite the valiant efforts you are making, I can see no real progress being achieved in Ballymagee. Therefore, I would like you to start planning for closure. We shall assess the levels of redundancy payments but I have asked the legal department to see if there is any way under Irish law that we can avoid them. I envisage a reduction in production levels in four weeks, and final closure in eight.

' "This matter is to be treated in the strictest confidence and no word passed to the staff till a formal and public announcement can be made. I apologise for sending such a disappointing letter, but you can rest assured that your personal position in this company will be safeguarded.

' "Yours, Ted".'

He turned to Toby. 'Like it? Neat, eh?'

'I'm worried about its confidentiality. That text will be sitting on the fax machine in her office overnight. Anyone passing by could read it. Unless she's the first in the office in the morning, her secretary for sure will have read it. It's hardly the sort of thing even the most loyal employee is going to keep to themselves.'

'Oh.' Metcalfe grinned, leaning back and swivelling round in his leather chair. 'I never thought of that. You mean, there's a possibility that the people in the factory might find out before Kathy does?' he said disingenuously. 'Oh, dear me. That would be a shame. Now, would you like a drink? I know a club where we can be seen together. It's discreet. Are you sure I can't tempt you?'

The next morning, for no reason she could imagine, Kathy awoke feeling happy within herself. It was like love. It obliterated everything else from her mind and induced such a deep sense of relaxation she could have stayed in bed all day and wallowed in it. As it was, it was already nine-thirty and she should have been up an hour ago.

She'd decided it was a good morning the instant she opened her eyes. It was not the sort of jolly feeling you get when the sun beams in through the windows, or when you suddenly remember it's a lazy Sunday morning, but a deeper sense of satisfaction. In fact, outside it was drizzling so it could not have been the weather that had cheered her. It was undeniably the thought of Pat Tierney. For a man whose character had been so blackened by everyone who had spoken of him, how could it be that Kathy found him the most benevolent of men? Not on the basis of anything he had said or done, but because she felt at ease in his company in a way she had never felt with a man before, certainly not with a boyfriend. This was different, and although she did not understand it she knew it felt good.

She would go and see him again that afternoon, if there was nothing pressing at the factory. Take him a cake, bring a little comfort into his lonely life, care for him a little, sit next to him on the sofa again in front of the smouldering peat fire, hoping he might put his arm around her. It had been the best of moments. Kathy had never felt so protected in her life.

She sprang into her clothes and bounced down the stairs, shouting apologies for being late. She'd expected a reply but there was none. She looked behind the reception desk where the phone was ringing. There was no one to answer it. She picked it up and explained who she was, then the line went dead. In the dining room, the place settings for breakfast had been removed early and a note had been scribbled round the edge of a soggy beer mat, propped against a salt cellar. It said starkly, 'Breakfast service finished'. This was unusual. Kathy had been staying here long enough to be part of the family, or so she thought, and they had made it clear to her often enough that she should use the place as her own home, make tea in the kitchen if she needed it. They wouldn't leave her without breakfast, even if they had all gone out. She tried the door to the kitchen but it was locked. The cleaning lady appeared from round the corner carrying a mop and bucket and Kathy asked where everybody had gone.

'From the looks on their faces, I would say they had all gone to hell.' The woman shuffled off again without giving Kathy the usual smile.

She decided she would buy a snack at Crowley's the newsagent's, and a cake at the same time to take up to hill to Pat Tierney's. Jean would make her coffee in the office. It was now nearly ten o'clock and Kathy was later than she'd wished to be. She closed the front door of the hotel behind her and was delighted to see Danny's green Volvo cruising down the main street towards her. It was time for a reconciliation. She had been hard on him, and no longer had it in her heart to be tough on anybody. After all, he had only acted out of loyalty to people in the town who had become his friends. That was understandable.

She flagged him down and he drew up alongside the kerb and wound down the window on the passenger side.

'I'm sorry, Danny,' she said. 'I wasn't fair to you the other day. It wasn't your place to tell me about the problem with the potatoes. I shouldn't have been so cross with you. I really am sorry.'

'If you say so,' he replied, unimpressed.

'Can I have a lift to the factory? Still friends, eh? There's time for a few verses of *Danny Boy* if you've got the tape?'

'The taxi's closed today. I can't help you,' he said abruptly, and reached out to wind up the window. Kathy put her hand on the rising glass to stop him.

'But I just saw you drop a lady on the corner. Of course the taxi's running,' she insisted.

'For some people it is, and for some it ain't,' he replied, winding up the window with such speed that she was only just able to extract her fingers before it closed completely.

Kathy crossed the road and wondered whether to waste time buying the cake or get straight to the factory. Anything could have cropped up. There again, nothing ever seemed to. The most recent crisis had passed and she still had three and a half weeks in which to solve the problem before it was due to recur. She would buy a cake, for the pleasure of seeing what she hoped would be the smile on Pat Tierney's face when he saw it.

She walked up the street and waited to cross. She recognised one or two of the faces behind the wheels of passing cars and raised a hand and flashed a smile, as she did to everyone from the factory. But this morning they did not respond. Instead, they looked through her as if she weren't there. Their faces carried no hint of recognition, their eyes did not flicker from the road ahead. She could have been a ghost for all the notice they took of her.

She went into Crowley's, intending to buy that cake and fresh milk for the tea she would make Pat. The atmosphere here was no warmer than on the chilly streets. Worried that the potatoes might be blighted again, Kathy asked, 'Is it the flies, Mrs Crowley?' The woman was standing behind the counter with the pale and drained look of one who had seen her own spirit leave her body. 'There isn't a problem at the factory, is there?'

'Don't pretend you have no idea, Miss McGuinness,' said Mrs Crowley, in an accusing voice. 'As if flies weren't enough, now we have rats in our midst.'

'Rats? Can't the vermin people sort that?'

'There's rats and there's rats. Now, what do you want exactly?'

'I'll take that cake,' Kathy said, trying to be friendly, 'and a bottle of milk.'

Mrs Crowley went into the chill-cabinet and pulled out a pint bottle. She slammed it on the glass-topped counter with such force it was a miracle that neither of them smashed. Kathy recoiled.

'How much?'

Spitting words like bullets, the woman replied, 'I will not take your money. And may the milk go sour in your stomach. And if the cake is stale to its very core, I will be only too happy.' Then she swept indignantly through the door into the back room.

Shaken, Kathy gathered up the milk and cake, and darted across the road. A car came screeching by, showing no sign of stopping if her step had faltered. It blared its horn and the driver waved his fist at her as if it had been her fault. Two eight year olds hurried past towards the school. She said good morning to them, and they replied 'Cow!'

Kathy sprinted the last few yards to the factory gate where she could always rely on a welcome from the red- faced guard who invariably raised his cap while giving her a smile warm enough to melt the polar ice cap. But this morning he did not stir. His face had lost its colour, and although his eyes glanced in her direction, it was a look as benevolent as the barrel of a loaded shotgun.

She took a few steps towards the office but stopped in her tracks as a fork-lift truck crossed her path at speed, the driver showing no signs of willingness to deviate from his intended path whether she was in the way or not. He gave her a look that could have killed as easily as his speeding truck. Kathy knew the driver, had liked his sense of humour, shared a drink or two with him. It was he, she remembered, who had led the applause that night she'd got up and played *Piano Man*, the night they'd welcomed her to Ballymagee. Now he looked as though he could have mown her down and not thought twice about it. Kathy crashed through the office doors, trembling now

'Jean,' she cried, persisting in her attempts to be friendly. 'Coffee, please. And what's going on? You can cut the atmosphere with a knife. Are the potatoes going bad again?'

'There's no coffee,' replied Jean sharply. 'And the potatoes are fine.'

'Jean, *please*,' said Kathy. 'I desperately need a drink. For some reason the hotel stopped breakfast before I got down.'

'Ah, yes, they rang a few minutes ago. They say they're packing your stuff and they'll send it round sometime.'

'Packing! They've gone into my room and been through my things? Why? Won't anyone explain what's going on here? And where the hell do I sleep tonight?'

'I could make a suggestion,' said Jean sarcastically.

'And what does that mean?'

'It means nothing at all. The hotel said they didn't give a damn where you put your head. It could be in the gas oven for all they cared. And, they said, what do you want doing with that guitar case? I told them to send it round. I thought they might sling it on the bonfire if it was left there any longer.'

'I have been abused, threatened, nearly run down in the street and outside the factory, and now evicted,' Kathy screamed. 'What have I done wrong? Am I going crazy? Have I missed something?'

'I think you've missed nothing. You know what this is all about. You've know all along. Here!' And Jean flung a crumpled piece of fax paper at Kathy. It was Ted Metcalfe's memo. She read it once, shaking her head from side to side in disbelief.

'It says closure in eight weeks,' said Jean. 'It seems to us that such a decision must have been taken months ago, and that *you* most certainly knew about it before ever you set foot here. You were sent to close the place, and that's it. Now we know the truth.'

'Nothing could be further from it. Get me Metcalfe on the phone,' Kathy demanded.

'Get him yourself. And the best o' luck. I've tried already and he's in Frankfurt for the rest of the week. His only message to you is that his memo is self-explanatory.'

'And everyone in the factory knows this? They've seen this memo?'

'I'd say everyone knows by now, in the town as well as the factory. 'Twas my duty to tell them all. Blood, Miss McGuinness, is thicker than water. You'll find that people here give as good as they get. You had our loyalty so long as we had yours. Now that has gone, ours has vanished with it. If I were you, I'd get down to that airport and leave us be. We thought you were our friend, but it turns out you're our deadliest enemy. I'd go now, if I were you.'

'And what makes you so certain I knew anything about this?'

'Because you were seen!' said Jean impatiently.

'Seen where?'

'Not where but with whom.'

'What do you mean, for God's sake?' demanded Kathy.

'Up the hill at old Tierney's house last night. You were seen! That man is wicked, we all know it. He hates this place and would do anything to see it gone. And now we have the evidence that you and he are working together to close the place. It's him, that rotten, miserable old bastard, who's putting a curse on the factory. And now you've arrived to help do his dirty work for him. I dare say you were an answer to all his prayers. Jesus, I bet he's sitting up on that hill, chuckling to himself this morning. Well, I would warn him, if he truly is a friend of yours – go and tell him that people here have had about as much of him as they can take. And he'd better be lookin' over his shoulder.'

There was a knock on the door. Without being asked to enter, a nervous and subdued-looking Danny Morrissey fell into the room, a bundle of Kathy's clothes in one hand and a guitar case in the other. Having decided that it would be safer for her if he maintained some kind of relationship with the Crowleys, he'd tried hard to show no affection or fondness for her. So, against all his instincts, he acted as if he too thought she was the devil incarnate.

He said coolly, 'It's your clothes, from the hotel. Sorry they're not packed neatly and all that. They didn't seem in much of a mood to give them a great deal of attention.' He dropped them unceremoniously in a heap in the middle of the floor.

Danny's apparent indifference was the final straw. Kathy screamed at him, stabbing her finger into his chest so that he was forced backwards. 'It was *you* who told them about Pat Tierney, wasn't it? You told them I was there last night. What other little stories have you made up, eh?'

'I swear to God,' shouted Danny, 'I ain't spoken one word. Not me. Whatever they found out, they got it someplace else.'

'And you expect me to believe that? Great friend you turned out to be.' Kathy turned to the secretary. 'Jean!' she snapped.

'My name is Miss Crowley, if you please.' She crossed her arms.

221

Kathy marched across to her, grabbed her by the shoulders, making her wince, and dragged her across to her desk. 'Sit down,' she commanded. Danny's eyes widened. 'Get on the phone to the whole bloody town and tell them to be in the church hall at six o'clock. I want to talk to them. It's the only way to sort this out.'

'They'll lynch you,' warned Danny. 'I've talked with some of the guys round here, and they're pretty uptight. I'd leave town if I were you.'

'Is that all the brave cowboy has to suggest? Running scared?'

Jean was halfway through dialling when she stopped. 'It's the Irish Countrywomen's Group meeting tonight. They'll be using the hall.'

'Tell the Countrywomen to get the fuck out of it for the night!' screamed Kathy.

Unable to ally himself a moment longer with Jean Crowley, Danny's true feelings got the better of him and he beamed, jubilant now that the new kitten was roaring as loudly as the Celtic tiger itself. He punched the air with his fist. 'I knew there was something in you somewhere, Kathy. And it's sure as hell comin' out now.'

'I have never heard such language spoken in this office!' Jean protested.

'That,' explained Kathy, 'is because there was never anyone *in* this office to say a word about anything. As far as I can gather, Percy Crowley might as well have been a stiff years ago for all he did round here. Now get on the phone! Six o'clock.'

Kathy stormed from the office leaving Jean to combine the action of dialling the telephone with crossing herself and begging for the Lord's blessing.

'Hey, you'll be wanting transport,' said Danny, chasing after Kathy down the corridor. 'The clock's not running today. All rides for free. It's Morrissey's Cars special promotional offer!' he joked. Kathy stopped in her tracks.

'Oh, the taxi's suddenly open for business, is it? Danny, I need to know whose side you're on? I am fast running out of friends in this town and I'd like to believe you were on mine. But when I think how you let it become common knowledge that I went to see the old man . . .'

'I swear to God, I never told them about the old bastard.'

'Which leaves you where?' asked Kathy.

'Guess – pretty much on your side. S'pose I kind of owe you, for not coming clean about the potatoes and the blight. But old Tierney, that's nothin' to do with me.'

'So you're on my side, cowboy?'

'Look, you need a friend in the enemy camp.' He glanced over his shoulder to make sure he couldn't be overheard. 'It's bad enough having to be pleasant to these shitebags without having you think the less of me for doing it. It's all to help you, right? Remember that great song Billy sings: *Only the Good Die Young*? Well, ain't there a line in there that goes: "*I'd rather laugh with the sinners than cry with the saints*"? Well, I reckon these people round here think so much of themselves they're not too sure they ain't saints already. I'd rather pitch in with the sinners. Now, I'll have you out of town real fast. Airport? Local or Dublin?'

'I'm not going anywhere,' insisted Kathy. 'I've called a meeting for six o'clock to explain how I intend to fight the closure. I'll face them. I'm not turning my back on this.'

'You're crazy. They can get real ugly. They're like a sect. Remember what happened at Waco?'

'Don't be ridiculous.'

'Believe me. Threaten them and they come together like a pack of wolves in a way you could never imagine. I wouldn't risk it. Come on, let's get out of town. There's nothin' here for me anyway. Not now. If the factory closes, they won't need no taxi. They'll be back to horses and carts. I'm out of this too. They're all fruit cakes round here.'

'Fruit cake! You can drive me up the hill,' said Kathy, to Pat's cottage. I want to talk to him. I have a cake for him.'

'Now I *know* you're off your head. If they think you've been there again, they'll believe you're plotting something with him. You've no idea how much they hate that guy. Geez, this place is starting to make life in Louisville look real quiet.'

'You said you were my friend?' Danny nodded. 'Then let's be up the hill. Have you seen a cake lying around anywhere?'

'They're gettin' up a lynch mob out there, and all you can think about is cake? What is this? The calorific theory of crisis management . . . just kidding. Here's the damn' cake. Now let's get out of here.'

Danny coaxed the taxi up the hill and parked the Volvo beside the gateposts. Together he and Kathy walked towards the cottage, heads bowed into the damp west wind. Danny walked two paces in front, protectively. There was a trace of smoke emerging from the chimney – the old man was at home. Danny knocked on the door but did not wait to be asked in. Pushing it open, he was met by the roar of the old man's indignation.

'Do they teach you bloody Americans no manners? I can tell you haven't a drop of Irish blood in you or you wouldn't go barging into other people's property. For all you try, you'll never be an Irishman, my boy.'

'We'll see,' muttered Danny, to himself.

The old man was sitting by the fire, boots removed and his bare toes sticking through the holes in his socks. In search of warmth, they were as good as in the hearth. He was holding up that day's copy of the *Tribune*, and declaiming from behind it. 'Anyway,' he continued, the newspaper still between him and Danny, 'it's not a fortnight past since I sent ten stone of potatoes. You know very well there'll be no more for at least three weeks.

So why are you bothering me at this time of day? It's too early for the Gaelic. I have to get in the mood.'

'I've brought someone to see you,' said Danny. The old man dropped the newspaper and let it lie on the floor at his feet. Danny noticed it was open at the financial pages. 'I've brought Kathy McGuinness from the factory. She wanted to see you again.'

'Did she now?' exclaimed the old man enthusiastically, his hands reaching up to comb back his long grey hair with his fingers. He fastened a couple of buttons on the front of his shirt, checked the fly of his trousers was closed, and tidied himself.

'So where is she?' he said, like an excited child. Kathy stepped out of the shadows.

'I've never seen you in the light of day,' said the old man. 'You're even prettier, Kathy. Which is rare, did you know? For the soft light of the oil lamp is a great flatterer. Only true beauty is revealed by harsh daylight.'

'Er, um . . .' mumbled Danny, embarrassed. 'You two look as though you're goin' to get kind of cosy. I'll go check the oil in the car or somethin'. No potatoes, you said?'

'No potatoes, thank you, Danny.'

'Hey, you should get a little more female company. Works wonders for your manners.' Danny glanced at Kathy as he walked towards the door. 'I'll be waiting for you.'

'Something wrong, Danny?' she asked, seeing his downcast expression.

'Got a sneakin' feelin' I just lost you again. But I'll be waiting.'

'Come and sit down,' said the old man. 'Why have you come to see me? To try and talk me round, is that it? Preach the ChipCo gospel, convert me? Is this missionary work you're after doing?'

Kathy laughed. 'I think you're a lost cause. So far as ChipCo's concerned you're beyond redemption. And no bad thing either. I'm not certain there's much about ChipCo that's very heavenly.'

'You're beginning to sound like me, young lady. Be careful.'

'It doesn't matter now. None of it does. I bought you this cake, thought we might share it, get to know each other. But things aren't exactly going my way. I'm under orders from London to close the factory and that's not making me the most popular person in Ballymagee so it's best I leave as soon as I can. The long hello is cancelled, I'm here to say a quick goodbye.'

'Goodbye? you're going?' he whispered in disbelief. 'Leaving me alone? When we've only just met?'

'It's not as though we've known each other very long.'

'What does time have to do with it? Could we be better friends for knowing each other longer? I don't think so. You can sense trust at first glance, and I am rarely wrong. I trust you, Kathy. Anyway, I feel I have known you all my life.'

'Do you?' she asked. He nodded.

'Strange, so do I.' She was thrown by her own admission, and took a moment to get a grasp once again of what she had come to tell him. 'It makes no difference, I've got to go. The people in the town aren't happy. They'd string me up given half a chance. I don't want to run away from this place but I don't see much point in staying.'

'Let the bastards put one finger on you,' he declared, waving a trembling fist, 'and they'll have me to answer to.'

'You're very kind. I want us to eat a slice of cake and have a cup of tea by your fire, so I can remember what it was like to be with you. The gentleness of you that no one else round here has seen but me. I don't want to go away with the idea that being close to you was some kind of dream brought on by that wicked poteen, or whatever you called it. I want to know it was real. I need to feel about you the way I did last night, when I was like a child protected from the world. I need to know it was real.'

He took her hand and kissed it lightly, then clasped her by the shoulders and pulled her towards him. Kathy sobbed aloud, her tears running down his neck like the soft rain on the hills.

'And where will you go from here?' asked Pat.

'To the church hall at six o'clock. I have to address the whole workforce, try and persuade them I haven't cheated them. Then back to London, I suppose.'

'It's all my fault,' the old man declared. 'It had never crossed my mind that it would hurt anyone like you.'

'No, it was my mistake,' said Kathy. 'I should never have come to see you at all, knowing how the people in town felt about you. But I just had to see you again. Perhaps because you looked so helpless and in need of love. I can't explain it . . . But the factory people put two and two together and made thousands. They believe you're behind the problems with the potatoes, and that we're somehow working hand in hand.'

'They'll believe what they wish to believe,' said Pat. 'If it happens to be the truth, then that's more a matter of good luck than their befuddled judgment.'

'If it happens to be the truth?' Kathy repeated, weighing each word.

'Yes. The truth. It *is* my doing, the potatoes. I cannot lie to you. In the middle of the sacks I send down with Danny every four or five weeks, I ensure there is at least one that is riddled with disease. I have a special shed, out the back, where I keep a few potatoes damp and warm under an old sack. It's a breeding ground for disease and that's where my rotten potatoes come from. By the time they have lain in that pile, slowly going putrid, they're riddled with every bacteria and virus a potato ever knew. I'll tell you the truth now: the smell of it sometimes turns my stomach, so bad it is. I pick the most diseased from the pile when I'm making up my sacks to send to the factory, and so infectious are they that as soon as they come into contact with the others, the rot spreads fast. All farmers who sell potatoes to the factory are bound to spray and fumigate them, but I do not. Of course, the factory has no idea that my potatoes are amongst the ones Danny takes down there, or they wouldn't touch 'em with gloved hands. No, they prefer to think I'm doing it by casting spells and muttering oaths or some such. But it was much easier than that.'

'So they were right about you?'

'About me, yes, they were right. But for the wrong reasons. And not about you. You're innocent, and now I'm paying for my crime by seeing you punished for it.'

'But you must be pleased. You've won. The factory is to close.'

'I didn't wish that. It was only to teach them a lesson that I did it, those damned Crowleys. They're the culprits. They have grown fat on potatoes and I thought it would do them good to know what it felt like to go hungry. Of course, they'll never feel the pains of a real death from hunger like my family suffered, but any pain will serve. So I sent their potatoes rotten now and again, just to remind them.'

There was an impatient blare of a car's horn.

'I don't want to leave you,' said Kathy, clasping his arm. 'The last thing in the world I want to do is turn round and go out of that door, never to see you again.'

'Then we could go together,' the old man declared. 'Away from here, now, turn our backs on the place. I would go with you, if you would go with me.'

'I can't flee from these people as if I'm guilty. I shall go, yes, but in my own time. First I have to face them. I've done them no wrong. I can keep all my promises to them. I can tell them that I had no part in planning the closure of this factory, which is true. I can stand before them for the last time an honest woman. Then I shall turn my back on the place.'

She kissed him on the cheek and ran to Danny's car, not daring to look back. It was a quarter to six.

By five to six, the church hall was full. It was as crowded as a cattle market and as bad-tempered and raucous. No one had made any effort to tidy themselves and they had arrived in working clothes or whatever came to hand. It made the hall smell of cooking oil. Children were brought too and the younger ones sat beside their parents, several wailing. Some preferred to stand at the back. Amongst them was a token presence from the Garda, Sergeant Crowley, who kept as much out of sight as he could.

'I have come here tonight in search of some answers,' muttered one man to his neighbour, his unwashed fingers still stained with engine oil. 'My business depends on servicing the lorries. If there's no factory, I'm finished.'

'And so shall I be too,' added a smarter man, dressed in a suit. 'What money will there be to spend on insurance in this town if the factory closes?'

'I think we should demand compensation for the loss of our businesses,' said the man from the television shop. 'I'll sue the damned company, so I will.'

'To hell with your bloody televisions,' said a woman nursing two small children on her knee. 'We can do without televisions, but what are we to do to buy food for the children? Why should we all be forced on to the benefit through no fault of our own? I want to know that!'

'It's all very well for those of you who work in the factory,' said another man. 'You'll all get redundancy. There'll be nothing for us shopkeepers. Nothin' at all.'

'Argh, shut up, Paddy Donovan. The sooner the day comes when we can't afford to buy bread from your miserable bakery, the better for all of us, say I.'

The room fell silent as the Angelus bell sounded. It was six o'clock. Some prayed. When the last bell had chimed, suppressed anger found its release.

'Where is she? Where the hell is the woman? Is she too scared to stand before us? If she is, then we will know the truth of the matter,' shouted a woman.

'If she does not appear,' shouted a burly man on the back row, 'I shall walk the streets till I find her, and drag her here by that long black hair if I have to.' They all applauded, cheering him on.

Kathy walked into the room at that moment. Danny was a pace behind her. He fell back to join the other men on the back row. She walked alone down the aisle between the chairs. Not even a baby stirred. All that could be heard was each footfall as Kathy made for the stage.

She stood up before them, two hundred pairs of eyes peering at her angrily, daring her to address them. She took a deep breath, but had no time to speak even a single word before a barrage of venom hit her.

'We want the truth! Will we close? There are livelihoods at risk here. Do you give a damn for any of us? I doubt it.'

The room rose to its feet and cheered. She did not flinch but instead looked at Danny. He was the only one in the room whose lips were not moving. He could take no more of it. He ran down the aisle and sprang up on to the stage, holding his arms wide apart.

'Hey! You got any fuckin' manners? Just pipe down and listen to what the lady has to say, then you might learn something instead of jumping to conclusions, OK?'

To his surprise, they took notice. He had shamed them into silence. He jumped down from the stage and went back to the rear of the room. The audience settled. Kathy took another deep breath.

'I am very sorry,' she said. 'I give you my solemn promise, in this hall that is part of the house of God, that what I will tell you is the truth.'

'That's what we want! The whole truth and nothing but the bloody truth,' shouted a woman from the middle of the room.

'We'll not get it from *her*,' roared a man, stabbing an accusing finger at Kathy.

'It is the truth that I had no knowledge whatsoever that they were planning closure. I was under orders to improve productivity and make production more reliable. No more than that. This is as much a shock to me as it is to you. Please believe me.'

'It's all right for you,' bawled a woman. 'There'll be a nice job back in London for you. There'll be nothing left for us here.'

'And what about the potatoes?' added another. 'Is that why they're closing us down? Have *you* told them about the potatoes? Is it because of you and your big mouth that they found out, after all the trouble we've gone to to keep it to ourselves? You promised you'd help us. Fat load of bloody help those promises turned out to be.'

'Sling her out of town!' shouted a woman.

'Chuck her in the river!' demanded another.

'She's a lying bitch and will bring us down. Get rid of her!'

An unstoppable flood of hatred was about to engulf Kathy. The sands were shifting beneath her. Every shout threatened to topple her and allow the tide of fury to drown her. She held up her hands in one last plea, one last bid for air before she went under.

'There will be no further problems with the potatoes,' she promised. 'If we can find a way of keeping the factory open, you will not have to suffer the blight any more. I *promise*.'

'We've had enough of your promises,' a woman snarled.

A distinguished-looking gentleman got to his feet next – the only man in the room wearing a suit and tie. He was well known as the town's solicitor and something of an entertainer in the courts when defending the drunk and disorderly of Ballymagee with his precise and poetic way of phrasing questions.

'May I ask something, please?' No one dared interrupt him. The room fell quiet, like a court.

'How can you be so certain there will be no further problems with the potatoes? If you are so sure, you must have found the cause. Logic demands it be so. Might not your promise be more convincing if you explained to us what the cause of the blight was?'

'I know but I cannot say,' Kathy replied, realising it sounded feeble. There was a murmur of dissatisfaction.

'Is it anything at all to do with Patrick Tierney?' asked the man. 'Yes or no?'

She knew the truth, and had promised to speak it. But if she told them it was Pat who'd poisoned the crop, then it was his death warrant she was signing. Where as if she denied it, it could be hers. But why should she feel she owed these people anything? It was not as if their friendship had been anything more than a charade. They had been ready to welcome her as one of them when they thought she was on their side. Once the tide turned against them, they were more than ready to cast her adrift. She'd seen animals behave like this; kittens which would play with you happily so long as they held the upper hand, but threaten them and they soon showed their claws. They were indeed the creepiest of Crowleys; mean-hearted and selfish, fuelled by greed. Animals that acted tame till cornered, then came out fighting dirty. There was something fundamentally selfish about them, Pat was right. She did not owe them the truth right now.

'I can't say,' she replied.

'It is not a clear denial,' said the scholarly lawyer. 'I think that people here will draw their own conclusions from your silence.'

Then a woman screamed: 'You were with him the other night.

232

And again this afternoon!' It was Janet, the bus driver's sister. 'I saw you through my curtains. I couldn't miss you, standing there in each other's arms while the taxi waited outside. Disgusting!'

There was a shaking of heads, and expressions of shock designed to make her feel filthy.

Then Jean Crowley appeared in the doorway and paused. She was holding in her right hand an envelope which Kathy could see bore the corporate logo of ChipCo. It was, she assumed, from London.

'I have this for you,' shouted Jean, bringing the room to silence as she waved the letter in the air. 'It's from a man in something called Global Development. His name is Chas. Does that mean anything to you, Miss McGuinness?'

'I know Chas. Yes, he's in Global.' From where she was standing now, Global Development felt like heaven.

'Well, he was concerned that this letter, whatever it's about, might not arrive safely, so he rang up to check. He spoke to me.' Jean paused. It was like waiting for the clap of thunder when you had seen the flash of lightning. 'The person he asked for was Miss Kathy *Foley*. I told him we didn't have a Miss Foley, only a Kathy McGuinness. The name didn't mean anything to him. I told him you were the only Kathy here. He described the Foley girl to me. I can't think it is anyone but you.'

Kathy's eyes fell first upon Danny at the back of the hall, who looked perplexed, as if trying to work out whether this was good news or bad. The name Foley obviously meant nothing to him. But it did to everyone else, and it was as if a spark had fallen on explosives. A blast was now inevitable.

The first shout was 'She's a liar! We can't trust anything about the woman!' and then the crowd started to press forward. Danny was on the point of dashing forward to haul Kathy from the stage for her own protection, and would have done so had not two heavy male hands clasped each of his shoulders and pushed him to the ground. Kathy watched him crumple under the pressure till he was out of her sight. Her only hope of salvation had just disappeared.

'Please,' she shouted, 'I can explain. There was no deception intended.'

'Are you the daughter of Leonora Foley?' someone shouted. 'I am.'

'Well, if that's not deception, then what is it?' came the angry reply.

Jack Crowley stood up. Out of respect for one of the more senior of the clan, the room hushed. He spoke calmly at first.

'We must acknowledge that we owe Leonora Foley a great debt. It is well known that without her there would never have been a factory, and we'd all have been the poorer for that.' Most nodded in respectful agreement. 'But she too has a debt to repay. For on the backs of our efforts she has built a career and amassed a considerable personal fortune. I believe she now sits at the head of the board in the United States of America. And so, if you add it all up, I think you'll agree that we, over the years, have done more for her than she has ever done for us.' The calm, measured tones faltered. 'And to do this to us now, sending her daughter to do her dirty work, is despicable. We should not stand for it!'

There was a roar of approval.

'Tell us no more of your lies,' came a voice from the floor. 'Get back up the hill to your lover boy, that dirty old beggar. It's all that old bastard's fault.'

'I ask you again,' said the town's solicitor, waiting his moment, 'is Patrick Tierney to blame for the blight? I remind you that you made us a solemn promise to tell us the truth. Perhaps you will now do us the honour of making clear to us whether you know Mr Tierney to be involved. Was he? A simple yes or no will do for reply.'

The clock on the church struck six-thirty. It tolled for Patrick

Tierney when, through her tears, Kathy admitted quietly, 'Yes. It was him.'

Kathy, was now no longer the focus of any interest. Tierney was now the head of the hit list. Danny was able to slide away from the two men who had been restraining him, and were now distracted by the thought of their new quarry.

'We've suffered the insults of that old eejit for long enough,' said the first of the thugs.

'So long as it was just words from his foul mouth, I was prepared to put up with it,' said the other, gathering men around him. 'But now we know for sure that he's responsible for the blight, we cannot let him go free.' The others agreed. The sergeant came across and warned them that illegal action would invoke the severest punishment. Then he informed them he would be out of town for the next three hours, on business elsewhere.

'Tierney's by seven-thirty, all right?' asked the ring leader. The huddle of men nodded. 'He's warned us often enough that for our sins we'll all burn in hell. Perhaps he'll find out what it's like before we do.'

Danny was about to shuffle through the door when he spotted, lying on the floor, the letter from London which Jean Crowley had dropped in the excitement. He edged his fingers towards it, trying not to draw attention to himself. As the tip of his first finger touched the envelope, a draught from under the door carried it an inch further from him. He stretched his arm as far as it would reach; if he moved any more they would be reminded he was there. Then the draught briefly blew the other way as the door opened and he caught the letter. As soon as Danny had it safely in his pocket, he slid away while the angry army made their plans.

What was about to be enacted on the hillside outside Ballymagee was man's work. It was no business of the women, although it was clear that some kind of tacit agreement had been reached by the entire population of Ballymagee. There did not seem to be any dissenters. Before leaving the hall, each man looked at his woman, seeking approval. It was unanimously given. As the raucous gang tumbled out of the church hall, roaring through the streets, a handful of the women were left alone with Kathy.

'What are they going to do to him? Will they hurt him?' she asked, fearing the answer.

'I have a fair idea what they intend,' replied Jean menacingly.

'You're crazy, all of you. Do you know that?' sobbed Kathy.

'We're not that mad,' replied Jean. 'We have to secure our future, that's all. Without the factory we're all done for. We'll do all we can to protect it.'

'This is ridiculous,' protested Kathy. 'You won't be allowed to starve. The Government will help.'

'We want no charity. The Crowleys of Ballymagee have their pride. We've worked for what we have and we'll not give it up now. It's beyond the will of someone in London, or even may I say the United States of America, to close us down. We *are* that factory. To stop it you'll have to stop us first. And that will take some doing.'

'You're kidding yourselves. What the board wants, the board gets. They'll just pull the plug. There'll be no supplies, no technical support, no marketing. You'll collapse within a month. Give in. Take ChipCo's redundancy money. I'll try and see you get a fair deal.'

'We want only one deal. And that's to keep the factory open.'

'I don't see what you can do,' said Kathy, exasperated. 'There's no pressure you can apply. They'll make you redundant and that will be that. The bulldozers can be in before the month is out. There'll be nothing left.'

Jean Crowley ignored her. She looked at the clock and then at the handful of women around her. Some of them Kathy recognised from the packing lines and staff canteen, remembering them not as a malicious horde but as jovial souls happily going about their work, breezing through life. Now they seemed possessed.

'We have half an hour to kill, if you'll excuse the expression,' Jean announced. 'Shall we have a cup of tea, ladies?' Kathy felt more threatened by this politeness than at any time throughout the shouting and bawling of the previous half hour.

'I don't think I'll stay for tea. My things are in the office. I'll go back there,' she said.

'You will indeed,' insisted Jean. 'But only when we say so.' A stout woman moved to cover the door. 'Until then, you'll have tea with us, and when we're ready to allow you to go elsewhere, then you may. Sugar as usual? I am sorry there are no biscuits.'

While the kettle took forever to come to the boil on the slow gas ring, one woman took out her knitting. It was the longest Kathy had ever waited for a cup of tea.

'Where have the men gone?' she asked with trepidation.

'Paying a call. Social, you know. On Mr Tierney.'

'He means you no real harm,' Kathy pleaded.

'Does he not? If that were true he wouldn't be cursing us, poisoning our future by sending our potatoes rotten with his oaths.'

'He's an old man. Confused. It would be cowardly to hurt him.'

'It would be cowardly of us to do nothing. What's the life of one old man set against the lives of all of us?'

'Are you going to kill him?'

'Ah, the kettle at last,' Jean replied. The other women smiled.

The minutes passed in complete silence except for stirring and slurping of tea. 'Well,' Jean said finally, getting to her feet, 'we'd best be getting there if we want to see the entertainment. It will be a great sight, gladden all our hearts. We'd best be on our way now or we shall miss it.'

237

'When will you explain?' pleaded Kathy.

'It will need no explanation.'

Jean grabbed Kathy by the hand to lead her to the door. Once out of the church hall, instead of taking the path down to the road, they turned for the church itself, the huge, grey slab of a building weathered by the incessant battering of Atlantic wind and rain. It was not a joyous sight but functional, workmanlike in its approach to devotion.

As they passed through the doors and faced the altar, each woman knelt and crossed herself. Kathy, not in the mood for holiness, would not have done so had Jean not dipped to her knee too, and pulled Kathy down with her. The cold stone collided painfully with Kathy's leg and she gasped. The wind was rising and the few candles burning in the church flickered. Kathy watched Jean and the others say a brief prayer.

'Does any of you really understand the meaning of sin?' she asked. 'How dare you pray for anything except forgiveness?' But she was ignored.

She had no choice other than to follow Jean back towards a narrow door just inside the main entrance of the church. It opened to reveal a bleak staircase which wound its way high into the tower of the church. They started the dusty climb, displacing spiders and pigeons as they clambered higher towards the clock.

'You know,' said Jean, pausing for breath, 'from up there's one of the finest views of Ballymagee and beyond. The finest in all of Mayo, in fact. We shall even be high enough to see as far as the Mullet. In the direction Mr Tierney lives, you understand.' They could hear the repetitive thud of the clock's mechanism as it ticked away the seconds.

They came abreast with another small door which opened on to a narrow balcony running around the outside of the tower. 'We used to come here when we were kids,' said Jean. 'It wasn't allowed but it never stopped us. I watched them build the factory from up here. Saw the big chimney grow and eventually overtake the tower, and even though I was a kid I worked out there and then that God had His ways but ChipCo could always outdo him.'

Kathy emerged into the evening air. It was clear as crystal and the horizon seemed far away. She looked down, dizzy for a moment because of the height. Not a soul in the town moved. No car sped down the High Street, no child played in a garden, no drunk fell out of a bar, no youth headed for the chip shop, no smoke came out of the factory chimney.

'And would you care to be lookin' over in that direction?' Jean urged Kathy. 'I believe you will see on the hillside there, over the tops of the hills, in the distance is Mr Tierney's cottage. Of course, you know the way well enough by now. You need no telling from me.'

'I can see cars moving towards it,' said Kathy, focussing her eyes on the hillside, and making out the grey outline of the cottage. 'What will the men do?'

'It's a cold night. I dare say they will light him a nice fire, to keep him warm.'

There was a heavy clunk behind them as the long hand of the clock jumped a notch to half-past seven. There was a whirring sound, like the wind, as the machine wound itself up to sound the half hour. Then a resounding strike of the hammer on the bronze bell, so close that it was deafening.

Kathy put her hands to her ears and stared towards the hillside. The echo of the chime had not died away when she saw the first glimmer of what she guessed was a flame. It started like a feeble car headlight seen from a distance, only the slightest trace of brightness. Then the point of light took on a shape of its own, spreading, developing arms and wrapping itself round the cottage. The place was on fire. She wanted to shout, to warn him, to run and save him. Fanned by the wind, the flames

239

reached higher into the sky, and then she saw a burst of conflagration. The flames, she guessed, had reached the straw covering Pat Tierney's store of potatoes.

'You must give him a chance. At least send help – an ambulance, anything.'

'It's such a pity,' said Jean, unconcerned, as if it were a garden bonfire they were watching, 'but looking at that blaze, I'd say no one could survive it. I doubt it will be worth bothering the poor firemen. They'll be away to their tea anyway.'

'It's murder!' screamed Kathy.

'Shame on you. And in God's house, too. It's a terrible accident, I will admit. Be careful, Miss Foley. Accidents are in the air.'

'You're evil, Jean. All of you are evil,' she shouted at the top of her voice to the indifferent town below. 'All you Crowleys are touched by the devil. It's not that old man dying out there in the flames, it's you who are perishing as well.'

'Now you've got that out of your system, my dear, your things are in the office. That's where you shall spend the night,' explained Jean, as calm and collected as if it been a Bonfire Night Guy they had watched being burnt.

'I'm not spending another minute in this town,' declared Kathy.

'You speak as if you had a choice.' Jean tightened her grip on Kathy's wrist and hauled her back down the stairs. 'As I said, you'll go back to your office. You'll be given food and drink, and there you will stay.'

'Until?'

'Until something happens.'

'Are you taking me hostage?'

'Not at all. We are a law-abiding community in Ballymagee. We want you to be safe. In fact, we were so worried after we heard about the fire on the hillside that we thought it best to confine you to the office. That's what I shall tell your mother, anyway.'

'You're bringing her into this?'

'Oh, yes. I shall fax her in the United States the moment we get back to the office. I thought to tell her that her daughter was here, in our care, and if she wanted her back then she was to guarantee the future of our factory. It doesn't seem a lot to ask, in exchange for your own flesh and blood.'

'So I *am* a hostage?'

'No, my dear. You're the factory manager, remember?'

Jean Crowley turned to the others and thanked them, bade them good night as if they had been playing an innocent game or two of bingo together. The air smelled no longer of frying potatoes. Instead it was filled with the fumes of distant burning: charred straw, searing heat, scorched wood. The smell of death.

9

Never had the curtains at 41 Benwee Avenue been drawn so quickly. In fact, such was the haste with which Danny grabbed the grubby material that the rail was on the verge of parting company with the wall. If he had tugged just a little harder, it would have been a disaster. Having closed them, he cautiously parted them a little, no more than a couple of inches, and checked that the street was deserted and no prying eyes watching from the other side of the road. Then he felt safe enough to switch on the light. He didn't like it, it seemed too bright. Something a bit less brilliant might be the thing, so he fumbled behind a pile of CDs and magazines till he found the switch to a table lamp which had a dark shade and suitably weak bulb.

'I can't image what all the fuss is about,' grumbled Pat Tierney, who had been bundled into a chair by the fireplace and told to sit still and keep quiet. 'I've been dragged from my own home with no explanation, thrown into that dangerous car of yours and driven at breakneck speed down the lanes. I've none of my possessions, no clothing, forced to leave behind my best hat and coat . . .' He would have moaned on, if allowed.

'You crazy old bastard,' cried Danny. 'You'd better start gettin' used to the idea that you ain't got no possessions. Not any more.' He parted the curtain again, just an inch, and peered through. Still all clear.

'No possessions? What do you mean?'

'Just that. You've got fuck all, old man. No matter how much you miss that mucky old coat of yours, you've got to ask yourself if you'd rather have that or your life.'

'I've not a clue what you're blathering about. Life? What has all this got to do with life? I was quite happy till I was taken prisoner by you, young man. I'm tempted to ring the Garda. This is kidnapping! I have no wish to be here. And where the bloody hell am I, anyway?'

'They've torched your cottage. Get it? Burnt that shit hole down to the ground. If I'd left you there, there'd have been nothing left of you but ashes in the grate. Now do you under-stand?'

'You mean, the cottage is gone? My home? Everything?'

'Except your life.'

'This is beyond belief.'

'And mine too,' said Danny, pushing Pat into the upright wooden chair by the fireplace. 'There was this message from London they found out about. It said the factory had to be closed. Got them all pretty darned mad, I can tell you. Of course, poor Kathy got the blame.'

'I know all this,' Pat said impatiently, gripping the arms of the chair so tightly that his knuckles went white. 'She told me it was going to happen.'

'That's only half the problem. The other half is you.'

'How so?'

'Ain't it you who sends the potatoes rotten? What kind a screwball are you anyway? And I've got a bone to pick with you,' added Danny. 'Those rotten potatoes must have been in the sacks I carted down to the factory for you. They'll be round *here* with their bloody firelighters next. Thanks, pal.'

'Did she tell them it was me who was blighting the potatoes?' asked Pat.

'She didn't have to. They'd made up their own minds. They still think it's some kind of witch doctor stuff. They don't know about the lousy spuds you had me take to the factory for you. Kathy told me about that. She didn't tell them. But, by telling her, you put her in quite a tricky position. Shitty thing to do.'

'That's the last thing I wanted,' sighed Pat, holding his head in his hands. 'I would no more want to be responsible for hurting her than for causing pain to one of my own. Where's she now? Safe? What have they done to her?' he asked, agitated.

'I ain't sure. I'll wait till things are quieter then see what I can find out. But for the moment we just keep our heads down, right? Don't pick up the phone, go to the window or use the john in the back yard. Piss in the sink if you have to. Just don't move! Understand?'

'I'm more worried for Kathy than I am for myself. Should I give myself up? Would that satisfy them? Save her from any harm?'

'No point. They think you're dead already. And do you know what? They're really happy about that. That's why I made you leave the coat and hat. I stuffed the coat with cushions, put the hat on it and sat it by the fire. With any luck they thought it was you. Won't fool the Garda when they come to look for your remains. But that'll take a day or two.'

'Ah, all the policemen are Crowleys,' said Pat. 'They won't be looking too hard for clues. But Kathy! I care nothing for myself.'

'Look, we're both pretty fond of that girl. I'm on your side. I don't want her hurt either.'

'Do you love her?' asked Pat.

'Yup,' replied Danny bashfully.

'So do I. But we shan't fight over her. Take my hand, boy, and shake it while I thank you for everything you have done for both of us so far. My only regret is that coat. It was the finest. I'll never get another as good.'

'Keep the noise down,' Danny hissed. Pat slumped back in the chair.

'Does the name Foley mean anything to you?' asked Danny.

'It might,' replied Pat cautiously, puzzled that Danny should mention it.

'Well, it may or may not mean anything at all, but Kathy McGuinness isn't her real name.'

'Oh? Is that so?'

'Apparently, she's Kathy *Foley*,' Danny explained. 'Folks around here think it's some kind of deception. Apparently, some hot shot in ChipCo is called Foley. They reckon Kathy's the daughter and it's all a conspiracy.' Pat Tierney looked as though he had been struck a stunning blow.

'She's called *Foley*?' he asked. 'Daughter of Leonora Foley?'

'Seems so. Kathy didn't deny it anyway. Does it all add up to something? Sure means nothing to me.'

'And how old is Kathy?' asked Pat, sounding excited. 'I mean, how old *precisely*?'

'Just so happens she's recently had her birthday – twenty-nine.'

Pat fumbled through some hasty mental arithmetic. It was thirty years, he calculated, since Leonora Foley had been in Ballymagee. Thirty long years in which he had loved nobody, spiritually or physically, since those all-consuming weeks he'd spent with his Leonora who had then disappeared like a dawn mist. And now there was this young woman of twenty-nine years. Leonora's daughter.

'I want you to look at me,' he said urgently.

'Do I have to?' Danny replied.

'This is serious, young man. Now, will you look into my face? Stare at it. Ignore what the years have done to it. Disregard the greying hairs and make them black again. Smooth the furrows and the wrinkles and peel back the damage the drink has done over three decades. Ignore the watering eyes and imagine them sparkling with youth. Smooth the cracked lips till they're as even as silk. And then tell me what you see.'

Danny stared long and hard at Pat Tierney.

'Kind o' tricky. I sure as hell don't see what you're getting at.'

'Look harder,' demanded Pat. 'Do you see anything that reminds you of Kathy? Any small thing at all? A slight hint, a vague resemblance?'

'Of Kathy?' exclaimed Danny, embarrassed. His eyes scanned Tierney's unblinking face which he held upright and motionless for examination. 'Hey,' he announced,' you know she's got that little turn up to the end of her nose?'

'Yes, yes,' replied Pat enthusiastically.

'Well, you ain't got that, that's for sure. But, you know, your eyes are the same shape, and the same colour too. But you don't smell half as good as she does.' Danny pulled back, examination over.

'I believe she is my daughter,' announced Pat with great solemnity.

'No, come on,' Danny gasped. 'Don't be crazy. I know you've been through a lot, but this is just infatuation speaking. It happens to older men all the time. Happened to my dad. They see younger women and get drawn to them. Anyway, be sensible. How does a guy like you have a kid like that when her mother's some hotshot over in Boston?'

'She wasn't always a hotshot,' replied Pat reflectively. 'And once she had a heart of gold. That was what I fell for. But she lost it somewhere along the way. I had heard she'd had a child but I thought it was just malicious rumour. I felt sure that if it were mine Leonora would surely have told me. Wouldn't you expect that?' Danny nodded. 'But I never heard a word from her. Not a note or a call. All I had to live on was gossip. I was never allowed to see my own child. And all these years I have lived with the feeling that there was a part of me which was elsewhere; an offshoot, a branch of me, which had grown and flourished without my ever seeing it. I always believed that, deep in my heart.'

247

'Geez! If it had been me, I'd have demanded to see the kid. Faced the bitch. Told her the kid was as much mine as hers.'

'I was too cowardly. By the time I'd heard she'd had a child, Leonora had been promoted to some grand job or other and it would have meant going all the way to London. And then I might have made a fool of myself. There might never have been any child at all. And I would rather have lived with the thought that it could have been mine, for it was the only child I would ever have, you see. I vowed I would never love a woman again after Leonora. And I didn't.' Pat paused. 'Except for Kathy. I loved her from the minute I saw her and now I know why. She's mine.'

'Ah, shit!' Danny sighed. 'Why does it all have to be so complicated? Why don't I ever seem to be in one of those nice, straightforward boy meets girl and falls in love scenarios? No complications, no bullshit. Just love.'

'We shouldn't be thinking about ourselves at this time,' Pat scolded him. 'We should be thinking of Kathy.'

'If they've told her about the fire, she'll think you're dead,' said Danny. 'That'll sure cut her up. She's hellish fond of you too.'

'Then we must find her. Make sure she's safe,' insisted Pat, trying to get to his feet. Danny pushed him back into the chair.

'I don't want to be melodramatic about this, but as soon as you set foot out of here, you're dead meat. Sit down, shut up, don't move. I'll be back within the hour. By then you'd better have done some thinking about our next step. But at the moment we're both in deep shit, understand? If they find out I rescued you, I might as well stick my head up the chimney and save them the trouble of smoking me out.'

'You're right, of course,' Pat admitted. 'They believe I'm as well cooked as a packet of their miserable crisps. They're not likely to look kindly on my saviour. What will you do?'

'Find out where Kathy is. Now, just sit still and shut up, will yer?' Danny crashed out of the front door, slamming it behind him, leaving Pat by the cold hearth to come to terms with his new surroundings. He ran his hands along the smooth wooden arms of the chair then looked at the cold fireplace and around the room. Had Danny told him the address? Had he said where the house was? Although the kitchen was not what Pat would call familiar, neither was he a complete stranger here. He knew that instinctively.

Copying Danny, he pulled the curtains apart by less than an inch and peered out. It was Benwee Avenue, he knew it well. He had walked along it whenever he'd bothered to come into town for the cattle market. It led off the main street, sure it did. There was no doubt about it. Broken threads of memory started to knit and he looked once again at the chair. He visualised it standing in a cleaner kitchen than this; one with a white cloth on the table and a fire blazing in the hearth. His aunt's house! He remembered how it had looked.

There was only one way to be certain where he was, and that was to check the number on the door. It should say 41. Pat looked around again, less certain this time. He would have to open the door and glance at the number. It would take the briefest of moments and then he could slam it shut and no one would even have seen him. He walked down the hallway and turned the lock till he felt the door give a little. Now, all he had to do was pull. He pressed his ear to the wood, wondering if he would be able to hear footsteps or a passing car. It was deadly quiet. He opened the door far enough to peer round it. His head was hard against the wall and his line of sight restricted and so he had to open it a good couple of feet – too far for safety. Then, when the door was at its widest, he felt something close, so near to him that it felt as though it was touching his trouser leg. He looked down. It was a damned cat. Pat stared at the door. No bloody number. He slammed it shut.

Apart from the chair by the kitchen fireplace there was only one other feature of his aunt's house he remembered. He walked slowly up the stairs and found the remnants of what he re-membered as a longer corridor with rooms to either side of it. The house had changed a lot but the glazed bathroom door was still there, and the bedroom door opposite. He opened it and found the bed still to be in the same place it was thirty years before. He rested on the cold sheets, and remembered the intoxicating sight of the young Leonora Foley seen through the frosted glazing of the bathroom door opposite. It was indeed 41 Benwee Avenue.

'But it's all in the past,' mused Pat, making himself more comfortable on the bed. 'Adventures of thirty years ago . . . There's no point living in the past. No point now in bitterness, only sweetness in the thought of Kathy. My daughter.' His face broke into a smile. 'She's fine-looking, of course. They'll say she gets it from her mother but I feel sure it's from her father's side too.' He ran his fingers through his long grey hair to tidy it. 'Ah, she's a lovely girl. And, I must admit, no thanks to me. But I can make amends now. We can go out together, arm in arm, do all the things that fathers and daughters do. We can joke, and play, and argue no doubt. There's lost time to make up, so much lost time.'

Not many minutes later he fell into a blissful sleep.

The streets of Ballymagee had never been so quiet since the funeral of Percy Crowley, which had had the same status as a day of national mourning. Danny found no one with whom to strike up a casual conversation, no gossip to be had on a street corner, no loud mouths holding forth. So he went first to the Crowley House Hotel where he found the bar empty, which was unprecedented at nine o'clock in the evening in Ballymagee. Not even the beer pumps were switched on – a grave sign. He asked the receptionist, as if it were of no real matter to him, if Kathy was in her room.

'We're neither expecting her nor hoping she'll be back,' said the chilly girl behind the desk. He went next into a bar called Donovan's. It was silent too, except for the ticking of the clock and the grumbling of the barman's stomach. Donovan himself, proudly stroking his gut, said he had heard word that Kathy was now at the factory, although someone had seen her leaving the church, just after seven, with some friends. And, by the way, did Danny know that Pat Tierney was dead? Terrible accident. Good news, eh?

Back on the deserted street, Danny saw the distant embers of the fire, the smoke still rising in the sky. He made his way towards the factory. It was quiet, the air clear of cooking smells, the factory closed for the night. The rats had left the ship. There was one inattentive, surly security man on the front gate. 'They've closed down for the night, out of respect. Poor Mr Tierney,' said the man sarcastically. 'He died, you know, in that terrible fire. Such a shame.' A wolfish grin spread across his face.

Danny saw that the fire escape door which led to the offices stood slightly ajar.

'Taxi service's still running,' he explained to security. 'Got a parcel to pick up. Can I go and get it?'

'And where's your taxi, then?'

'Needed the exercise,' said Danny. 'It's back home.'

'It's fine advert for a taxi service if the driver walks around the place, leaving his car by the roadside. I sometimes think you Americans are stupid.'

'Yeah, we took lessons from the Irish,' quipped Danny. While the dim security man was still trying to work out if this was a joke or an insult, Danny was halfway to the fire exit, and before the oaf on the gate noticed he was inside, feet pounding along the stone-flagged floors. He sprinted up the back stairs, passed the photocopying room which was quiet, and the deserted sales office, and saw through the glass partition a light shining in Kathy's office at the end of the corridor. He crept towards it, dodging the desks and treading warily to avoid the creaking floorboards, taking care that his shadow should not fall across the glass on Kathy's office door. He moved with the caution of a cat burglar.

Then the door opened and out came a woman, moving like an alert farmyard rat.

'Jean!' shouted Danny. She stopped in her tracks, spun round as if caught in the beam of a farmer's torch. She peered the length of the office, trying to work out whose voice it was and where it had come from.

'Jean,' he shouted again. 'It's Danny. Where's Kathy?'

'Oh, why don't you just fuck off, Danny?' she shouted. He couldn't believe he had heard such a word from her lips. The demure, respectable, well-mannered and courteous secretary had actually told him to fuck off. It would have been less of a shock to hear such words on the lips of the priest.

'Get the fuck back in there yourself,' ordered Danny, dashing the length of the room and seizing Jean Crowley by the arm till she cried out with pain.

'Is she here? Is Kathy here? Tell me!' he said, quietly but threateningly.

'She's in the office.'

'I want her out of this place. You Crowleys murdered Tierney, but you won't harm her.'

'Shame on you!' replied Jean. ''Twas a terrible accident. We're all grieving.'

'What do Crowleys know of pity?' Danny spat the words. 'I know more about your family than you think. We'll get this

252

sorted first, then I've old Percy's death to discuss with you lot. But just one word of warning. If you've harmed Kathy, you'll be wishing *you* were smouldering halfway up the hillside.'

With her free hand, Jean opened the door and Danny followed her in. Behind the desk sat Kathy, eyes red with weeping, face distraught. To either side of her sat two burly ladies Danny recognised as more Crowleys.

'Are you all right?' he asked, extending one hand. 'Come on. We're going.' The two unpleasant looking women guards, faces grim, took a step closer to Kathy, blocking her in.

'She'll not be leaving here with you, I'm afraid,' said Jean. 'Don't try to take her away or it'll only result in harm to her.'

'Is Pat all right?' cried Kathy. 'Did he get out in time? Tell me he's alive?'

Danny did the hardest thing he had ever had to do in his life. He lied to her.

'I heard he was found dead. It was a terrible fire. Everyone is saying it was an accident, but we know differently, I think.' He looked at the Crowley women. 'Come on, Kathy. Let's go.'

Jean intervened. 'Miss Foley stays here till we have an assurance from her mother that the factory will not close. I have faxed our demands to her. I'm awaiting a response. In the meantime, I suggest you try nothing which will cause our patience to run out, and result in unpleasantness for Miss Foley.' Danny looked at the two fat thugs to either side of Kathy. They were fierce-looking women, strong too.

'Sit tight, girl,' he ordered her. 'We'll work this out. The Indians ain't beaten the cowboys yet. Got yer bag with yer?' Kathy nodded. 'Then get that ol' harmonica out, and play yourself a tune to pass the time. Something the Crowleys might like. The *Death March*, perhaps.'

He didn't say goodbye or look her in the eye as he left. Had he done so, he knew he would never have had the strength to leave at all. As he ran down the corridor he heard Kathy shouting for him, pleading for help, begging him to go back, her voice cracking. His every instinct was to turn and answer her plea, but instead he left her to the mercies of the Crowleys and sprinted back to Benwee Avenue, taking every chance he could to look over his shoulder and check he was not being followed.

He arrived, breathless, and collapsed in the chair opposite Pat who had spent the hour Danny had been away going through the piles of newspapers lying on the floor. It looked as though there'd been a paperchase through the house. Loose sheets of newsprint were draped over every chair and piece of furniture.

'She's all right,' gasped Danny. 'They've got her in the office and they say they're goin' to keep her there. What they want is an assurance from her mother that the factory won't close.'

'They have a bloody cheek, the people of Ballymagee. Murderers, and now blackmailers. Let them rot.'

'Then Kathy will rot with them. They intend to hang on to her till they get what they want. Look, this is getting too big for us. There's two of us here who both say we love that girl. Doesn't sound like any excuse for sittin' on our arses, doin' nothin'. Shall we call the Garda?' asked Danny.

'No point. They're all related, piss in the same pot. You'll find the officers are otherwise engaged. I've made complaints before but nothing ever happens.' Pat paused for a little and picked up a page of the newspaper, much to Danny's irritation. He didn't see this as an opportunity for a little light reading.

'Is it true that if the factory is saved from closure, then Kathy will be allowed to go unharmed?'

'That's what they said. They've faxed Boston with that demand.'

'ChipCo will never give in. It's no more than terrorism.'

'Yeah, but they've got Kathy. Leonora Foley's daughter.

That's got to swing it their way hasn't it? And the company won't want a scandal, so the factory's safe for at least a year or two.'

'I wouldn't be so sure. There's never been any evidence that there's anything other than a calculator behind Leonora's breastbone. Certainly not a loving heart.'

'But for Christ's sake, it's her *daughter*!' exclaimed Danny.

'And she's *my* daughter too. It is my responsibility to act as well as Leonora's. I have been reading the newspapers,' said Pat.

'Glad you found time for a little relaxation,' observed Danny, looking at the sea of newsprint spread around the room.

'It may well be that I am in a position to buy the factory from ChipCo.'

'Say again?'

'Are you deaf, American boy? I may be able to buy the whole fuckin' dump.'

'You sick in the head? Has all this business cooked your brain or something?'

'If it were mine,' Pat continued, unabashed, 'it would be up to me to decide whether it closed or not.'

'How are *you* going to buy a fucking crisp factory?' Danny mocked him. 'Don't waste my time.'

'Do you know how many millions I'm worth?' replied the old man, grinning with satisfaction. '*Several*, possibly. I have been looking through your newspapers trying to work it out, but I'm not so good at the figures and I couldn't find a pencil anywhere.'

'Is this some kind o' leg pull?'

'It is not!' replied Pat indignantly. 'In gratitude for what I'd done for Leonora Foley in helping her find the ideal place for her factory, I was given shares in ChipCo International. Thousands and thousands of them. They were a very little company at the time, it was early days for ChipCo. I got the first allocation shortly after she went back to London, and then, about a year later, another lump, bigger than the first. I never knew why. Possibly she was paying me to stay away. She would have had the baby by then, see, and probably there was no room for anyone else in her life. She was buying me off.'

'Ever spent any of this money?'

'No. Not so much as a penny. I have a man in Dublin who says he's a stockbroker, though I have no clue if it's true. He has written over the years to tell me that there have been takeovers and dividends and things, and God knows what else. I've got a rough idea of how many shares there are and it's enough. They're not shares in this factory, see, but in the whole bloody international set up, so he tells me. He does all the paperwork for me, insists I give him all the letters and things. Which is as well,' mused Pat, 'otherwise the whole lot would have gone up in smoke by now.' He chuckled to himself. 'He came to see me once. Asked me what I'd do with all the money if ever I sold the shares. He couldn't believe that I took no pleasure in what he kept calling a "substantial holding". Except that I admit now and again to looking at the price of ChipCo shares and seeing them rise and rise towards the heavens, and then looking down on the poor bastards who work in the factory, and the Crowleys who think they've all been so clever. When it's me, who doing nothing at all, has been the clever one all this time.'

'And what exactly are you going to do with this loot if you cash in the shares?'

'Spend it, Danny boy! Invest in ChipCo Ireland. Buy a controlling interest in the factory.'

'Buy – the – factory!' said Danny incredulously.

'I shall if I want to. It will mean telephoning Dublin and finding this stockbroker man and telling him to get on with the job.'

'Got a number for the guy?'

'No. It's gone up in flames. But I remember his name is O' Leary.'

'That narrows it down, I don't think,' said Danny. 'This is crazy. You don't just go out and buy a factory like a new car.'

'That's true. But I've been reading the financial pages of the *Tribune* for years now and I know all the tricks they get up to. I shall have to buy fifty-one per cent of the shares of the Irish division of ChipCo. It's a separate company from the rest, see? Once I have fifty-one per cent, I can give the orders.'

'Will it work?' asked Danny.

'It depends how much my shares are worth. Only Mr O'Leary knows the answer.' The telephone rang. Danny picked it up and in a businesslike voice said, 'Morrissey's Cars. Can I help you?'

It was Jean Crowley, talking now in her cool, professional secretary's voice.

'I would like to order a taxi,' she said. 'A Leonora Foley is arriving at the airport tomorrow afternoon at five o'clock. Will you bring her to the factory, please? And one more thing, Danny.' The professional tone slipped a little. 'Keep your big mouth shut, eh?'

'You can rely on a fully professional service from Morrissey's Cars,' he replied slamming down the phone straight afterwards. 'You Crowleys have got some shit comin' your way!'

He looked at the clock. Then a thought occurred to him. 'You bloody old fool,' said Danny. 'It's Friday night. Tomorrow's Saturday. Your O'Leary won't be in his office on a Saturday, will he?'

'But we can't leave Kathy with them for two whole days. I'm worried about her.'

'She'll hang on till her mother arrives.'

'Her mother?'

'Yup. The great Leonora Foley's about to breeze into town. There'll be some arses kicked, I guess.'

'I wonder if I shall see her,' said Pat. 'I wonder how she looks – if she has the same black hair, the sparkle, the smile that made me love her . . .'

'For God's sake, this is no time to be sentimental. You can sleep on the couch,' said Danny, pushing piles of newsprint aside.

'Do you have a drop of the mountain dew? The poteen?' asked Pat.

'Get some sleep, old man. Tomorrow will be a busy day.'

'And what are you planning to do?'

'First things first. Kathy's got to know that you're safe. She'll be desperate. Then we're going to have to get serious about your death.'

'Uh?'

'A funeral! Someone's got to organise your funeral. Now, how would you like it? Anyone special you'd like there? Any particular prayers? Father Flynn do for you, or do you want me to try for the Pope himself? Remember, you are well and truly dead. Stiff as a board, fried as a Kentucky Chicken – and the congregation of that church are going to want to make it one hell of a party.'

'I know,' said Pat. 'They could dance on my grave, and just as they were getting into their stride, I could rise up from it and grab that miserable Jean Crowley by the ankle! Frighten the shit out of the old cow, so it would.'

'I've got things to fix,' said Danny. 'Just play dead, remember. And quietly!'

10

The following afternoon, Danny drove with great solemnity to the airport to collect Morrissey's most important customer ever: Leonora Foley, Acting World President of the ChipCo corporation. Only the Pope himself would have taken precedence and even then it might have been a close-run thing.

Danny had spent most of the morning polishing the Volvo in a futile attempt to get some gloss on to the tired paint. He swept the inside, removing the ground-in dirt and straw which had clung to Pat Tierney's boots as Danny dragged him from his intended funeral pyre. He even went so far as to apply sticky tape to the gaping holes in the seat covers, such was the importance of this passenger.

He had put in a call to the factory that morning and was surprised to be allowed to speak to Kathy. She seemed collected and calm under the circumstances, until Danny told her that her mother was about to hit town and he was going to collect her. 'Can you take her the long way round, like via Moscow or something?' Danny thought it a good sign that Kathy was up to humour. He asked if she had been told when they would allow her to go free. Under no circumstances could she leave till they had spoken with her mother, they had told her. She urged him not to worry about her and even blew him a kiss, saying she would play a tune on the mouth organ and think of him. 'What tune?' he'd asked. '*When Irish Eyes are Smiling*,' she'd replied with heavy sarcasm.

Pat Tierney stayed in bed at 41 Benwee Avenue, tucked up like

PAUL HEINEY

a bristly hedgehog trying to sleep. He was under strict orders not
to move. He had woken once or twice and wondered where he
was, confused by not seeing the familiar damp walls of his
cottage, nor the customary pile of dirty washing-up in the sink,
hearing no crowing from a cockerel perched on the kitchen
window, no rattling of the tin on the roof where the wind tried to
part it from the walls. It wasn't home, for sure. But neither was it
unfamiliar to him.

When sleep finally let go of him he remembered with some
satisfaction where he was. He raised his head from the pillow
and looked across at the bedroom door. It was open, as it had
been that night thirty years ago, and he could see the glazed
panel in the bathroom door opposite. He was a man of forty
again, seeing Leonora's body dimly through the glass. The vision
in his mind's eye was as clear as if it had been yesterday that he
had feasted on the sight of her. He wondered what he had done
wrong, and why fate had deprived him not only of her, but of his
child too. Why had he been singled out for a lingering torment
like this? Would it have been better if he had never found out
about Kathy, and gone to his grave in peaceful, untroubled
ignorance?

No, he had set eyes on his child, flesh and blood in his own
likeness, and she was the most beautiful creature he had ever
seen. If he never saw her again, he would be content with that
memory. Indeed, he did not dare to imagine he would ever see
her again: it would be tempting fate. The gods, it seemed to him,
were determined to tease him endlessly; first with Leonora and
then with Kathy.

But this time, thanks to Danny, he might have outwitted
destiny and would live to see his beautiful Kathy again. He
would hold her, kiss her, apologise to her for his absence all her
life, praying to God she would understand and forgive him. He
could have risen from his bed there and then and proudly

260

waltzed down the street, boastfully shouting her name, declaring her to be his beloved only child. Which would, of course, have been suicide. So instead he lay looking at that frosted bathroom window. The young Leonora was only a memory, as fleeting as the clouds of steam in which her body had been bathed. But Kathy was real. Pat chuckled delightedly to himself before closing his eyes and going back to sleep.

Danny was sitting in the Volvo parked by the passenger terminal, drumming his fingers on the steering wheel, waiting for the plane to disgorge its exalted passenger. It was time, he thought, to face the depressing fact that there was no room in Kathy's life for him. Christ, what would she want with two new men in her life? She was a bright woman, would eventually marry one of her own kind when the novelty of discovering her father wore off, and live a sensible life with tidy kids, not much love perhaps, but lots of loot. That's what always happened to women like that – the boardroom romance. He couldn't compete with big money and status, not yet. A shitty old Volvo wasn't a lot with which to woo a girl. He would lose her, he knew it. Which was a shame because as well as all the other things he loved about her, she was a damned good harmonica player.

He noticed flags flying at the airport; the Irish Republic, the European flag, a Union Jack out of politeness, and next to them a ChipCo flag, larger than the others, as if the corporation had nation status. Danny decided enough time had passed since the landing of the plane to allow the Foley woman through baggage and customs, always assuming she hadn't been delayed by a state welcome; or perhaps the government had sent some humble ministers for her to walk over as she stepped on to Irish soil. If this woman really was the Queen of Chips, Danny bet himself she was salt-and-vinegar flavoured. He straightened a vulgar floral tie which he had bought for pence at a charity shop, and fastened the middle button of an ill-fitting blazer which had also come cheap. It was free, in fact; taken in lieu of a fare from a drunk who had run out of cash. The drunk swore it was his, but Danny had never been sure. Anyway, no one had asked for it back.

He went through the main airport door and could have dropped dead when he saw Leonora Foley, standing by the shrine booking desk, tapping her foot, looking like an ageing angel who had just discovered bad temper. For a fleeting moment he thought it was Kathy. Ignore the age and the attitude and peel away the heavy layer of make-up, the poise, eyes and hair were identical. Hell of a pair o' peas to find in one pod, thought Danny, braving himself to apologise.

'Ach, God, I'm sorry,' he said, in his best blarney. 'It's usually a good twenty minutes from touchdown to arrival. They must have had their skates on, that they must.'

'It's quicker with no bags. Now, to the factory. Are you the chauffeur?'

'Well, more private hire, really,' he said apologetically. 'But I do my best.'

'That's what I remember about this place,' snarled a jet-lagged Leonora. 'Everyone doing their best, but being basically useless. And ungrateful too, it would appear from what's going on here. Come on, let's get this sorted and then I can get back to civilisation.' She got into the Volvo with a look of such disgust that Danny wondered for a moment if some of the soot left by Pat Tierney was still clinging.

'Stop that necklace rattling, will you?' she snapped, seeing the rosary beads hanging round the rear-view mirror. 'And how much do you know about this nonsense that's been going on?' she asked, clinging to the back of the driver's seat as the car lurched away from the airport.

'Pretty well all of it.'

'Would you like to share it with me? It appears my daughter is being held some kind of hostage. What rubbish!'

'I think you ought to know that a man is dead, missus. Possibly murdered. The people your daughter's caught up with ain't stupid either.'

'Please,' said Leonora, 'let's not get over dramatic. People aren't *killed* in Ballymagee except when they're drunk in the street and get run over. As for Kathy, well, it was news to me that she was here in the first place. Trust the damned girl to bite off more than she could chew!'

'I wouldn't be too hard on her. She's trying hard to make her mark.'

'Well, she should have come to me for advice first.'

'I'd say that was the last thing she wanted to do.'

'What?'

'Come to her mother. It's the last thing she'd be doin'.'

'Why, for God's sake?' asked Leonora.

'Ach, not my job to give yer answers to questions like that, missus. You haven't even asked if she's safe, if I may say so.'

'You may *not* say anything of the sort. That is a matter between me and my daughter. Blood is thicker than water after all.'

'But not thick enough to prevent you closing the factory over her head, eh?' said Danny, watching her in the mirror and gauging how far he dare go with his cheek.

'Close the factory? Who's closing the factory? I'm not. I told them to tighten the whole place up. It's flabby, it's fat and unfit, and needs trimming. But *closing*. Who thinks I gave orders for the factory to close?'

'You'll find that's what most people think.'

'Well, I shall just tell them it's untrue. My word should be good enough. Then I can get Kathy out of here and that will be that. It'll maybe teach her to talk to her mother before plunging into the deep end without taking swimming lessons first.'

'You don't rate the girl, do you?'

'And you do?' replied Leonora haughtily. 'I do so hope she's not getting attached to a driver of a seedy car. I am sure you are a very nice young man, but Kathy deserves better than someone from the bogs of Ballymagee. So don't get any ideas.'

'Oh,' said Danny, bristling, 'I heard that thirty years or so ago, the local lads weren't such bad catches for girls who came out to set up factories. Very fond of getting between the sheets with the lower forms of life round here, some of them were. Or that's what I heard anyway.'

'How *dare* you speak to me like that? *I* am Acting World President!'

'I don't care if you're the feckin' President of the Universe. You've got a daughter in that factory who needs help, and on present showing I don't think you're the one to give her it. Missus, you suck,' he announced, giving way to an Americanism. 'That'll be eight pounds fifty. The factory gate's over there.'

'Drive me in,' insisted Leonora.

'Get out and walk.'

'You'll never get another job in ChipCo,' she said, as she flung a ten-pound note at him.

'That could be the best thing that ever happened to me. I don't care if ChipCo vanishes up its own arse. But I do care about Kathy. So get your backside in there and do something useful for your daughter for once in your life.'

Leonora Foley's attempt to step out of the car like a queen was thwarted when her foot landed deep in a puddle of the waste water left after the swilling clean of the foul potato store. She cursed the place. In her expensive, and now stained, high heels, she wobbled towards the factory and got as far as the torpid figure on security. She announced herself as Acting World President. 'And I'm Mickey Mouse,' he chortled. Then he rang

Jean Crowley to tell her that some loud-mouthed trollop had come to see her. He turned away so that Leonora could not hear, then said she looked like 'a painted old tart'.

'That must be Leonora Foley,' confirmed Jean.

'Bugger me! Is that what yer look like?' exclaimed the guard, turning back to a by now seething Leonora.

She strode past him as if he were scum. She would have looked like a storm trooper going into battle were it not for the wobble as she stumbled in her damp shoes. Tailored Boston couture, complete with pearls, did little to prevent her from looking ridiculous in the rugged setting of Ballymagee.

'Kathy!' she shouted along empty, stone-floored corridors, as if calling to a wayward child. 'Where are you?'

'Another floor up, Mrs President,' shouted Jean Crowley respectfully from the upper corridor. Short of breath, even shorter of temper, but fuelled by rage, Leonora headed towards Jean like a guided missile. Her mouth opened to demand to be taken to Kathy, insist the factory start up again, and then order a mass dismissal of the troublemakers. But something about Jean stopped her dead and stilled her tongue. The women came to a halt a few feet apart, weighing each other up like boxers spoiling for a fight.

For the first time in her life faltering in her stride, Leonora could not work out what it was about Jean Crowley that put the fear of God into her. No mere servant, no humble woman cheaply dressed in man-made fabrics and working as a secretary in a ChipCo outpost, should be able to stop a well-dressed, supremely confident Acting World President in her tracks, but Jean Crowley did.

Breathless, Leonora stared at her, pondering, then she remembered.

'Are you from Ballymagee?' she asked.

'I am, and proud of it.'

'Have you lived here all your life?'

'I have.'

'And thirty years ago you would have been a young woman?'

'I don't see . . .' said Jean Crowley, becoming impatient.

'I do, very clearly. I see that mean little face of yours, in the church hall, the night I danced with a man called Pat.' For the first time the invincible Leonora could remember, she felt threatened as she faced this old foe. 'Was it you who spat on my head, or one of your charming friends?'

There was a pause before Jean spoke, which told Leonora that she was right.

'I'm sure I would never have done such a thing to a superior,' Jean lied. It was when the Crowley woman opened her mouth and Leonora saw those chipped, yellowing teeth on parade, that she was convinced.

'You were the boss, then. The girl who wanted all the men under your control. Didn't want anyone else moving in on your patch. How many more women did you spit on?'

'I'm sorry, Ms Foley. I think you are mistaken.'

'I think not. Those evil, jealous eyes of yours still stare at me in my worst nightmares. Did you know that? Would you ever believe that a secretary in a bloody hole like this could haunt a World President? Quite an achievement. Look at that turned up mouth of yours that tries to smile but only sneers. That foul little mouth could only belong to a truly nasty woman. I've often wondered what I'd do if ever I met you again. Run for my life, I thought, like I would if I'd come face to face with a witch.'

'Thirty years ago? With the Tierney son?' asked Jean coolly. 'Was that you? The one who danced with him in the church hall that night and made him look happier than any woman had ever made him look before? Was that really you? Then I'm sorry for what we did. We were silly girls then.'

'I doubt you're the slightest bit sorry. But what was so special

266

about him anyway?' asked Leonora. 'He was nearly twice your age.'

'The same thing that made him attractive to you, I imagine. He was twice your age too. He was a fine man, strong, and knew his own mind. Grown up. Not like the lads in the town who just wanted to grab any girl for the excitement of it. Pat was a gentleman, I always thought. And not unhandsome.'

'Then it's a great shame you were no lady. How many more of his friends did you abuse? Did you do the same to all the others who dared cast an eye on Pat Tierney?'

'There were no others after you. Don't think that all the women in the town didn't try and catch his eye, because they did. Some would have killed for the man. But you soured him. Turned him against all women. He wouldn't give any of us a second glance after you'd had your hands on him. And how did you repay him? You turned your back on the man, and broke his heart. It died broken, did you know?'

'Died?'

'The other night. There was a terrible fire in his cottage and the poor man burnt to death, God rest his soul.'

'Pat is dead?' asked Leonora, in disbelief. It was not within her makeup to display any vulnerability. But at this moment, with the news of Pat Tierney's death and the spectre of the Crowley woman before her, Leonora's outward show of confidence evaporated and she felt as lost in the world as on the day she first arrived in Ballymagee, as frightened as on that night thirty years before.

'I must see Kathy,' she insisted, collecting herself.

Jean Crowley led her down the corridor to an office at the end. She opened the door and there was Kathy, looking frail and apprehensive. Her expression reminded her mother of her own reflection when she had looked in the mirror the night they had attacked her. Two sombre, bloated women – one of them

possibly an old accomplice who had held Leonora while Jean
Crowley abused her – were standing guard, and looked to Jean
for guidance. She gave a nod of approval and they allowed
Kathy to cross the room and fall into her mother's arms.

'My darling, are you safe?'

'I'm fine,' said Kathy through her tears. 'But terrible things are
happening here. Get me out, please. They killed a man called Pat
Tierney and made me watch while they did it.' Leonora glanced
at Jean Crowley, who made no attempt to deny it. 'He was a
dear old man who lived on the hill alone and never did any harm
to a soul. They killed him because of the blight. Just because he
dared to mess up their precious bloody potatoes, they killed
him.'

'This is all nonsense,' insisted Jean. ''Twas a terrible accident.'

'Are you expecting me to believe that none of you have it in
you to commit violence against another human being?' Leonora
asked, looking first at the other women and then at Jean
Crowley, who at least had the good grace to hang her head.

Leonora looked at Kathy. 'I know of Pat Tierney,' she
explained. 'He was an old friend, from way back, the days
when I first came to Ballymagee. I was very fond of him once.'

'I loved him,' said Kathy, 'as if we were part of each other.'

'Like a father, perhaps?' suggested Jean Crowley, throwing an
accusing look at Leonora.

'Yes, like a father,' agreed Kathy, relieved. 'Exactly that! Like
the father I never knew and always wanted. How did you
know?'

'It might be worth asking your mother that question,' suggested Jean.

'Is he my father? Is it true?' She looked at her mother, who did
not speak, but Kathy read confirmation in her guilty expression.
Now she understood the complex attraction she had felt towards
Pat Tierney, and for just a moment forgot the horror of the night

before, of watching helplessly while his cottage was consumed by flames. But in a heartbeat, elation turned to despair. Her real father had been taken from her. The elusive, mythical figure whose company she had craved throughout childhood and adolescence had briefly become real. She had touched him, spoken to him. And now that she wanted to reach out and touch him again, he was as far beyond her grasp as ever. Distraught, she dropped into the chair behind the desk and fell back in it, sobbing.

'It's all your fault that he's dead,' she said to her mother through the tears.

'No,' replied Leonora, glancing sideways at Jean Crowley. 'Others seem more culpable than I am.'

'*You* ordered the factory to close. *You* started the panic that ran through this place. If they weren't so afraid of what might happen without this bloody potato factory to support them, they would have put up with Pat for the daft old man he was. Instead, they panicked. You caused that.'

'This is the second time today I've heard this story about my ordering the factory to close. First from that retard of a taxi driver . . .'

The door opened, and as if on cue Danny barged into the room. When he was angry, he didn't bother with the blarney.

'Beggin' your pardon but I guess when you're hearin' your name being taken in vain, you kind of prick up your ears, right? So this retard of a driver had better tell you what he knows.' Ignoring everyone except Kathy, he went to the far side of the desk and knelt down next to her, speaking only to her.

'Kathy, listen to me. This isn't your mother's fault.'

'Whose bloody side are you on?'

'Yours is the only side I want to be on. Listen. The letter that Jean brought into the hall last night, the one addressed to Kathy Foley instead of McGuinness . . .'

'It's all history now,' said Kathy.

'It was from a guy called Chas in London. Know him?' Kathy nodded. 'I want to read a bit of it to you. It begins:

' "Dear Kathy.

' "When we met the other day, I told you I had a new boyfriend. Well, he's called Toby Hart and he's in corporate relations. We were on a date and he started telling me how Ted Metcalfe had tried to chat him up, and how it had nearly made him sick. Well, it would, wouldn't it? Then he told me that Metcalfe had boasted how he had set up this woman called Kathy so as to get at her mother. He said Metcalfe had sent you to Ireland and fixed things so that before you had a chance to stand on your own two feet, he would pull the rug from under you.

' "Sorry about the mixed metaphors and all that – long day. What's more you did Toby a big favour once. Something to do with your mother and a fur collar. Does that make sense?

' "Anyway, thought you ought to know. Take care.

' "Love, Chas, X X X".

'Guess that sort of clears the air, eh?' He folded the letter and handed it to Kathy. Then got to his feet, bent over and kissed her on the forehead, and made to leave the room. 'I'll say goodbye before I go,' he said over his shoulder.

'Go where?'

'Anywhere. Emigration they call it, don't they? Find work some place. That's what you do, isn't it, when the potatoes give out? History repeating itself, I guess. Get the hell out of it, sing a mournful song about the homeland far away, and then I'll be an an Irishman to the core. Guess I'll have achieved everything I came here for.'

The door closed behind him before Kathy could stop him. She

heard his footsteps recede along the corridor and was wondering why he had not gone as far as the stairs when her mother spoke.

'I don't suppose he'll be much of a loss.'

'Is there anyone else you'd like to remove from my life, Mother, while you're here?' said Kathy sarcastically.

'None of this is anything to do with me. It was your juvenile idea to come here, not mine. I could have warned you this place was trouble.'

'But it wasn't,' replied Kathy. 'It was simple. This could have been my home, near my father. I could have been making my own way in life, not bobbing along in your wake.'

'That's not fair! I've given you everything I can.'

'On the contrary, I'm not certain you've given me anything except a few moments of your precious time which, I dare say, you begrudged. You sent me to schools I loathed, put me into jobs I didn't want, pushed me up the ladder when I wanted to climb by myself. But all that is nothing compared with what you did to my father. Let's not think about us. Think about *him*. What it must have been like to have had a child and not known it. To go through life thinking, but not being certain, that there was a part of you elsewhere in the world that didn't even know you existed. Yet that child was craving to meet him, to hold him and hug him. Imagine that. And now he's dead. He came so close to me, and because of the legacy you left to Ballymagee, now we're separated forever. You'd no part in his death, Mother, but that doesn't mean your conscience is clear.'

The telephone rang.

Jean Crowley picked it up. After saying hello, she listened for a while and then said in a reverential voice, covering the mouthpiece to drown out Kathy's sobs, 'Yes, Father. I understand. I'm sure that will be appropriate. And what time would the Mass be? And the Confession? Thank you for calling, Father. I'm sure all the town will want to pray at a time like this. Goodbye.'

271

She replaced the phone.

'That was Father Flynn,' she announced. 'He's to hold a special Mass in view of the sad death of Mr Tierney. He will hear confession at six o'clock. The Mass will start at seven. He assumes you will both want to go.'

Leonora sighed. 'Yes, I remember this place. It's all coming back to me now. Always blame someone else when things go wrong. Never your fault. Put it all down to the will of God. Light the bloody candles and chuck the incense around and everything will be all right.'

While Kathy and her mother had been locked in the office, negotiating with the Crowley woman and her cronies – the Crowley Cronies, he liked that – Danny had crept into an empty office next door. The weeks of training had paid off. The hours spent learning the rhythms of the Mayo accent, the reading of Yeats, the gruelling listening to Irish tenors, all the input he had suffered in order to make himself an Irishman, suddenly came good. He had done a perfect impersonation of old Father Flynn down the telephone. Even the priest's smoker's cough with which he managed to punctuate his speech had sounded authentic. It had been a virtuoso performance and Danny quietly thanked God for letting him get away with it. Then, with renewed confidence, he picked up the phone again and starting ringing key people in the town, asking them to spread the word that a special Mass was to be held. Finally, he rang Father Flynn's, just to check that he would be away that night, at his sister's, as usual on a Monday.

Never in any Catholic church had there been such a false display of grief and mourning as in Ballymagee that evening. It was a spectacular show of two-facedness. Everything about the congregation's demeanour, from their slow mournful walk to their downcast faces, would lead an outsider to believe they were gathering in heartfelt grief. But Jesus on his cross above the altar did not look down on one soul in the body of that church who was not involved in that fire on the hillside above the town. Even those who had stayed behind, not attempting to restrain the frenzied mob, bore some responsibility. No one in Ballymagee could have washed their hands of this crime had Pat Tierney really been dead.

The Garda had told the *Tribune* that so intense had been the conflagration no remains had yet been found, and it would be some weeks before a forensic conclusion could be reached. It was, however, far from certain that Sergeant Crowley had even bothered to call in any experts. He might just as easily decide to let the matter drop and record it as a tragic accident. He could always find a cooperative doctor in the town to sign a death certificate. If a Crowley asked for one.

The church bell tolled, and with no noise from the factory to mask it, its ringing could be heard in the office buildings where Kathy and her mother had spent the afternoon trying to come to some agreement which would allow the factory to continue, and Kathy to go free.

'There's nothing to stop us from saying a prayer here and now,' said Kathy. 'We don't have to go to church if we don't want.'

'Church is better!' announced Danny, breezing through the door. 'The car's outside. I'll run you down there.'

'I couldn't sit with those people, nor kneel in prayer with them,' said Kathy, surprised to see him again so soon.

'Thought you'd left town,' muttered Leonora. 'And don't think I'm going to church either,' she declared, pointing at Jean Crowley. 'What, get down on my knees with the likes of her?'

There followed a quick spat between the two women who sounded like hissing cats. Their clash gave Danny a chance to catch Kathy's eye. 'Get down to church!' he hissed at her. 'For Christ's sake, go to church!' he urged, as loudly as he could without the other women hearing.

She could think of countless reasons not to go. The memory of the devouring flames, the terror of facing the angry towns people in the church hall, the sick sensation in her stomach when she thought of their smug faces gathered to pray. Sinners, murderers! But if Danny Morrissey said she ought to go, then perhaps she should. She had trusted him from the moment she fell into that ridiculous taxi on the night she'd arrived in Ballymagee, and despite everything that had happened, she trusted him still. Kathy had only made two real friends in the time she had been here. One was dead, the other was Danny.

'I'll go to church, Mother,' she announced. Danny breathed a sigh of relief. 'But I won't go as a hostage. I'll go on my own.'

'That will be in order,' said Jean. 'But we will need a little insurance.' She nodded at the two fat women who moved across the room and stood like gauleiters to either side of Leonora.

'This is scandalous,' she shouted. 'Do you all know who I am?'

'The sooner you realise that you are nobody in this town any longer, Mother, the sooner this will be over,' said Kathy. 'They've won. Give in.'

The Volvo pulled away from the front gate of the factory, low on its rear springs with the two fat women insisting on travelling to either side of Leonora. Kathy sat in front, next to Danny. Jean had said she would walk.

'Father Flynn said to tell you he was hearing confession,' said Danny.

'That's for the rest of this town rather than me, isn't it?' replied Kathy.

'Could say that. There again, it's one of the sacraments, you know. Part of the faith.'

274

'Not my faith,' said Kathy. 'I've no faith at all. And never will have, now.' Danny sighed again, exasperated.

'Then have faith in me,' he said, giving such emphasis to each word that she could not ignore his plea. 'And go to confession.'

'Very unusual,' observed one of the fat women, 'for confession to be held at such a time of day, and just before a Mass too.'

'Sure is,' said Danny. 'Special times we live in, ain't they? Anyway, old Flynn's gettin' on. Confused old bastard.'

'All the same, very unusual,' said the woman, unimpressed.

When they arrived at the church, Danny got out of the car as fast as he could, sprinted round to the front passenger door and opened it for Kathy, leaving the three in the back seat to struggle with the loose door handles. Walking at great speed, dragging Kathy along with him so as to leave some distance between her and the others following behind, he told her, 'Get into that bleedin' confession box and prepare yourself for a shock. When you come out, don't look any different from when you went in. Just sit down in the church. Cry a little if you can manage it.' She looked at him as if he was crazy. 'Trust me . . . for Christ's sake, trust me. Get into the confessional, say, "Bless me, Father, for I have sinned", and take it from there. Now, *go!*'

He pushed her through the heavy doors of the church, and then pointed her towards the dark oak confessional. Kathy had never liked the atmosphere of Catholic churches, and in particular disliked this one. The chilly concrete edifice was as cold as the grave. It had been from the tower of this very church that she had seen her father consumed in flames and so, to Kathy, it was the least godly place on earth.

The confessional was a grim, upright coffin of a contraption; completely alien to a non-Catholic like Kathy. It was ornately carved, and partly draped in a moth-eaten green velvet curtain. She pulled open the door and stepped into the darkness. It smelled of tobacco, Father Flynn's she guessed, and slightly of sweat. And it was cold. The light was very faint and all she could see of the old priest was the vague outline of his face through the narrow slats in the wooden screen which divided them. She thought she saw a beard, and didn't remember Father Flynn as having one; neither was he coughing, which was unusual. She sat down on a hard stool and tried to remember what Danny had told her to say.

'Bless me, Father, for I have sinned.'

'You have committed no sin, my dear one. You have every reason to stand before God and claim to be pure in spirit. Which is more than the bastards gathering out there can say.'

It was the voice of Pat Tierney, from the other side of the screen, as clear as if he were alive, thought Kathy. Was it a hallucination or a cruel illusion? she wondered. Or another wicked trick?

'It's me, Kathy. Pat, truly it is,' he said, and then she knew it was real for there was love in his voice, she could feel it.

'Is it really you?' she asked, begging for confirmation. She pressed her hands anxiously against the screen, trying to make it give way. Only her finger tips could penetrate the gaps between the wood. Then she felt the old man's rough fingers stroke them. 'Kathy, my love,' he said, 'I'm sorry to have frightened you. It wasn't my idea. I wanted to walk down the street and look them all in the face, show them I was alive. That I have defied them and their murderous intent. But young Danny was right. They really would have killed me if I'd been stupid enough to do that.'

'But the fire,' she said, bewildered, clutching at the screen, face pressed against it, trying to get closer to him to reassure herself that this was no ghost. 'I saw you die.'

'You would have done, had it not been for Danny. He's a good lad. He saved me. Saved me for you, Kathy. You're all that matters in my life now.' He paused. 'I have something to tell you.'

'Yes?'

'I'm your father.'

'I know.'

'Your mother – did she admit it? Did Leonora tell you I was your father?' he asked excitedly, hungry for confirmation. 'Did you hear those very words on her lips?'

'Can there be any doubt in your mind?' Kathy asked. 'I'm as certain that you're my father as it is possible to be about anything. Can't you feel there's something special between us? Didn't you know that from the moment we first saw each other? I did. I didn't know then what it was, but I know now.'

'And does it make you happy?'

'Happier than I have ever been.'

'I'm sorry for the last twenty-four hours,' said Pat. 'It's all been out of my hands. I had to do what young Danny told me. He loves you very much, you know.'

'When can I talk to you properly?' Kathy pleaded. 'As father and daughter, together?'

'When I have finally put the fear of God into those sinners out there.' Pat started to chuckle. 'Then we can begin our lives again. Bless the Lord, they're in for the shock of their lives! Now, Kathy, I want you to be a brave girl for your old dad, and wipe that relieved expression from your face. I can't see much of you, girl, through this blasted screen, but I can see you're a sight more cheerful than when you came in. I want you emerging from this confessional box distraught. Can you do that? Some tears would help. Give me more time. Is your mother here?'

'Yes.'

'Sitting at the back? Then I want you to sit at the front. The best seats in the house for this one performance only. Keep calm but distressed as well, if you get my meaning. Now, get some cryin' done, girl, and make your father proud of you.'

Kathy pretended to herself she had just lived through a dream, that Pat had not spoken to her from the other side of the screen but was really dead, ashes on the bare hillside. She would never see his face again. She started to cry.

'Good girl,' he whispered. 'Now I must be gone. Time to face the enemy.' She heard the priest's door open, and as soon as it had closed behind him she opened her door and brushed the velvet curtain aside. Her face was awash; tears ran in twin channels of grief down her face. Only three people in that church knew that they were tears of relief and not despair.

As she walked down the aisle, the congregation was beginning to fill the pews. She must show emotion now; her father had said so, and fathers know best. As she passed the pew where her mother was sitting, Leonora reached out to comfort her. Kathy ignored the gesture.

She sat in the front pew, as he had said, and fell to her knees about to give thanks for Pat's safe delivery. But fearing these creepy people might have powers of mind reading, she stuck with the show of grief and prayed for a recently departed soul. No need for any of them to know it was not Pat Tierney's.

The greatest test of Kathy's composure came when she looked up and saw, sitting at the organ dressed in a long, black cape fastened at the waist with a broad leather belt, none other than Danny. He gave her the subtlest of winks and she tried to devise a way of smiling back at him in acknowledgment and thanks, without in any way letting up on her mask of despair. She stared hard, daring to think fleeting, thankful thoughts, and hoped the message had been safely received and not intercepted.

The sound of the clock striking seven, the same bell that had tolled for Pat Tierney's supposed passing chilled her rigid. The congregation went still and not a muscle twitched as the priest emerged from the side vestry, his face hidden under a white hooded cape. He bowed towards the altar and crossed himself, and the congregation did likewise. The priest then made the slightest of nods in the direction of the organ, which was Danny's cue. He started to play.

He may have got as far as seven notes, possibly even a dozen, before there was angry shouting from the body of the church. 'This is blasphemy. And in God's house! The Devil is amongst us!' He was playing the unholy melody to Billy Joel's *Piano Man*. 'Stop, whoever it is! Is he drunk or drugged?' Two men made their way towards the organ, intent on stopping him.

The priest turned to face them, drew back the hood of his cape and bellowed: 'Stop! Forgive the boy. He knows no hymns.' Then he chuckled.

There was a scream, an ear-splitting howl of horror from the mouth of Jean Crowley, loud enough to put fear into the hearts of everyone for ten miles around. It was infectious, causing panic and fear to spread through that church like flames hurrying through Pat Tierney's cottage. There was no priest, no Father Flynn. Instead, draped in the priest's robe, was a ghost come back to haunt them. It was Pat Tierney.

He ripped off the vestments, leaving himself clad in his familiar, mucky clothes of greying shirt and woollen trousers, and left the gleaming white robe in a heap in front of the altar before walking to the foot of the steps. He held out his arms, Christ-like, and addressed them all.

'Shall we pray? And if so, who do we pray for?'

'Are you a ghost?' screamed a woman. Faces paled, women started to cry out in fear. The only one who remained untroubled was Kathy Foley, sitting perfectly composed in the front pew, beaming.

'Sit down all of you, and shut up!' bellowed Pat. In their bewilderment, they obeyed.

'I'm sorry to disappoint you all but I had no appointment with death, and the one you presumed to make for me I could not keep.' He spoke with such force that the pigeons in the tower took flight.

'Sit down,' cried a man. 'This is the house of the Lord. You're no priest.'

'Do not, sir, presume to remind me of the dignity of this place. If there is anyone who has lost sight of what is right and wrong in this town it is all of *you*. Not me!' Pat stabbed his finger at them, voice gaining in strength, amplified by the resonance of the church. 'There's not one man here who hasn't come within an ace of being a murderer, whether he struck the match or merely watched it done.' Next he looked accusingly at the women. 'And you all allowed the men to go up the hill to light that fire, and said not one word that might persuade them from their murderous mission.' He stared pointedly at the trembling figure of Jean Crowley. 'You are all guilty!'

'We should finish the job we started. We're not to be meddled with, nor brought here to play your games,' came a defiant reply. 'Let this be a lesson to you, Tierney, that the man who tries to upset our livelihood can never live amongst us.'

'I have news for you all. From now onwards, you all play *my* game.'

There were murmurs of scorn and disbelief.

'Listen!' shouted Pat, but they took no notice. Sensing things were not going their way, Danny crashed his fists on to the keyboard of the organ till a ferocious, discordant sound rattled the windows and caused the candle flames to shiver. It sounded like a musical expression of the wrath of God, and stunned them all into silence.

'You can have your bloody factory, and a fat lot of good may it do you! It can run for as long as you wish, churn out crisps until eternity, and you can continue to make yourselves fat on it.'

'Is this some kind of joke? Who are you to be telling us when to open and close the place? ChipCo gives the orders,' shouted Jean Crowley.

Out of the corner of his eye, Pat spotted Leonora Foley nodding in agreement with her.

'My dear Leonora,' he called out to her, 'this may not be the proper time to convene an extraordinary meeting but since I shall soon be the major shareholder in ChipCo-Ireland, we might as well talk business.'

'He's drunk,' shouted Leonora. 'Crazy,' shouted another. 'Let's get him now, while we have him, and finish the job,' cried a third. Pat's precarious rein on his temper beginning to give way, he turned towards the altar and grabbed the first thing that came to reach. It was a heavy metal candlestick which he weighed in his hand for a moment until it was properly balanced then flung it into the congregation, aiming for the rabble-rouser who was calling for his death. It hit the man full in the chest and forced him back against the pew where he sat, winded and gasping at the pain.

'Never been more sober, my dear Leonora. As you see, my aim was perfect. Now, all of you *listen*!' The congregation sat transfixed by fear and shock as Pat addressed them. 'When the stock market opens I shall own 51% of the shares in this factory, so nice Mr O'Leary, my stockbroker in Dublin, tells me. So don't answer back to your superiors, any of you. Nor you, Leonora.'

'We don't understand, Tierney. Explain yourself,' shouted Jack Crowley. 'How the hell can you own the factory? It's ChipCo's.'

'For a few hours longer it is, that's true. Then it's mine. Let's just say I saved up, like a kid, and bought myself a toy. Now I intend to play with it.'

'I don't believe a word of it,' shouted Jean Crowley.

'Then ask Leonora Foley. Ask her about the worthless shares

she showered on me thirty years ago. I was tempted to wipe my arse on the lot of 'em, at the time but I'm damned glad I didn't 'cos they're worth a fortune now, aren't they, Leonora?'

Heads turned towards her, seeking confirmation of this apparently ludicrous story. They could hardly believe it when she nodded agreement.

'So what will happen? That's what we want to know,' shouted one of Pat's congregation.

'Oh, ready with the questions now, are we all? Not so ready the other night when you had matches in your pocket, and paraffin to pour over my cottage. I don't remember getting much of a chance to have my say then.'

'Have it now. Say your piece,' shouted Jack Crowley. 'If this crazy story about you buying the factory is true we want to know what our futures will be.'

'It would give me the greatest of pleasure,' growled Pat, 'to keep you guessing for as long as possible. To watch you squirm with fright, fearing the good days were gone forever. I could make up a new rule. I could say anyone may have a job at the factory, providing they're not called Crowley. How would that do?' He stooped to pick up the priest's robes which he had dropped by the altar.

He paused for a moment. 'But there's jobs for you all. I'm not a vindictive man. We'll forget all this and carry on as if nothing happened, shall we?'

You could have counted to a hundred in the silence that followed. Pat moved towards the door of the church, the robe in his hand.

He was about to leave when Jack Crowley spoke again.

'If you're prepared to put this business behind you, and keep us in our jobs, then I think there's a future for all of us here in Ballymagee.' Every person there nodded. Pat smiled.

'And there you go. Proving what a spineless crowd you

Crowleys are! How you will turn and follow anybody who can guarantee you your factory. There's nothing else in your lives, is there? No loyalty, no values, no standards, no guilt, no shame, no sense of right or wrong. You're a truly worthless lot. You can all have your jobs, and I hope you suffer for them in this life or the next. Suffer like my family did on the long, lonely walk to starvation when all they needed was help from the Crowleys, and it was not forthcoming. I should cast you all loose in memory of them, let you sink in the bog to scrabble for rotten potatoes to feed your families on, like mine did. I should let you suffer, and die of want. But I have found happiness in Ballymagee, and so the place cannot be entirely worthless.'

Leonora interrupted him. 'This takeover will have to be discussed. The board hasn't met – there are implications for the share price, and the costs of restructuring.'

'Are you feckin' deaf, woman?' he bellowed. 'Have I not just said that I've found happiness after all these years? And all you want to prattle on about is the bloody share price. You selfish bitch, Leonora Foley. Shall we share our news with our new-found friends?'

He took a deep breath, strode back to Kathy, took her by the hand and pulled her to her feet. Danny, watching from his seat in front of the organ, played more softly this time. It was still *Piano Man* but no one objected. 'May I introduce my daughter, Miss Kathy Foley? Ain't she a grand girl?' And arm in arm, Pat and Kathy walked down the aisle leaving the congregation aghast. The moment they hit the pavement outside, the music came to an abrupt halt as Danny, a true taxi driver at heart, sensed a fare and ran out to his car.

Kathy pulled herself away from Pat and embraced Danny on the front steps of the church, thanks pouring from her as rapidly as tears had flowed an hour before.

'You won't go, Danny. You won't leave town, will you?' she pleaded with him.

'Don't see much future for me here . . .' Kathy hugged him again, and kissed him.

'There's every future for you here,' said Pat. 'This town needs young men like you. Honest, decent ones. Not more bloody Crowleys. Anyway, they wouldn't have you back in the United States. You're one of us, now.'

'Possibly,' said Danny. Unable, Kathy noticed, to look her in the eye.

Jack Crowley came out of the church and took Pat Tierney's hand. 'I doubt we can ever apologise properly, but if you are true to your word, you will have our undying thanks. And please believe that our shame will be deeply felt.'

Pat pushed his hand aside. 'And our very best wishes to your daughter,' Crowley shouted as an afterthought, though it didn't make Pat think any the better of him either.

'Much as I would like a ride in Mr Morrissey's famous car,' he said, 'I think Kathy and I will walk back to *our* factory. Eh, Kathy?'

So they walked, hand in hand. Cars hooted in salute; hands which had never before stirred on seeing Pat Tierney, rose in greeting.

'I am going to do something very naughty,' he announced, a wicked glint in his eye. 'Do you know that mad old woman, another bloody Crowley I dare say, who runs that newspaper shop?' Kathy nodded, sensing mischief. 'I'm not sure the old cow was in church. Teach her to have proper respect for the dead, I will. Watch me.'

Pat crossed the road and stood outside the shop. He waited till Mrs Crowley's attention was taken by the newspaper she was idly glancing at, and then tapped on the window. When she turned, he pressed his face as hard against the glass as he could and shouted, 'Mrs Crowley, I'm back from the dead! The ghost of Tierney come to haunt you!' She stared, speechless, at the horrific image of his contorted face pressed against the glass but, remarkably, her nervous tic did not even flicker. It showed no sign of life, not even the slightest tremor, so petrified was she.

Pat pulled away, opened the door, marched into the shop and kissed her on the cheek. Whereupon she screamed until she was hoarse. 'You've met my beautiful daughter, I do believe,' he said proudly, and closed the shop door behind him, leaving Mrs Crowley dumbstruck.

Kathy and her father had not gone much further before they spotted, on the other side of the street, Jean Crowley hurrying along, head bowed like a broken woman.

'Jean,' shouted Pat. 'Will you come over here and talk to your new boss?'

From the other side of the street she shouted back at him, 'I've spent the greater part of my life crossing the road to get out of your way. I won't break that habit. Don't think you have the respect of everyone round here.'

'Jean Crowley, you are about to witness the first act of the new owner. You are sacked! Feckin' well sacked, fired, kicked up your miserable bloody arse. Piss off, woman!' Pat punched the air, and even Kathy could not hide a smile.

Once the mischief was out of Pat's system, tiredness took over. 'I shall have fun for a few minutes more,' he said, 'and then I shall go back to Benwee Avenue. Danny will let me lie down for a while. Then I must find somewhere to live. I suppose I could buy that house. It's where your mother and I first made love, you know. It's part of our family history. I'll have a sleep there and then we can plan our lives afresh. It'll be a new beginning.

'In the meantime,' he said in mock seriousness, 'you have my full authority to make whatever management decisions are necessary for the profitable running of my factory.' Then he kissed her and turned off down Benwee Avenue. Kathy went to find Jack Crowley, to tell him to get the factory up and running. Potatoes needed cleaning, slicing, frying. The steam would be rising from the chimney within the hour; half an hour after that the oil would be hot and the clean Atlantic air tainted with the smell of frying potatoes. The people of Ballymagee would be reunited with their potato crisps, and be happy once again.

11

While Pat Tierney slept the deep sleep of a contented man upstairs at 41 Benwee Avenue, Danny sat uneasily in the upright chair by the kitchen fireplace, deciding what to do next. His heart wanted one thing, his head another. His first wish was to stay with Kathy, wherever and forever. But he was beginning to feel like an intruder at a party; an uninvited guest at her emotional reunion with her father. So he'd decided he would go elsewhere, turn his back on the place and on Kathy, and start again. Perhaps Morrissey's Cars wasn't such a good idea after all. Anyway, the Celtic tiger would probably have stopped its roaring by the time he made it back to Boston, and the hotshots would have laughed at him with his Yeats and his phoney Irish eyes a' smilin'. It could happen. Prosperity could vanish in the time it took to down a pint – it had happened in Ireland before. It had happened in the factory, hadn't it? They'd had all they could have wished for, and then it was taken from them. No wonder they still believed in Acts of God. The Irish were like children who kept having the fanciest of baubles dangled in front of them, allowed to touch but very rarely to them keep. Danny felt he knew a lot more now about being an Irishman.

There was a knock on the door. He opened it to find a dishevelled Leonora standing on the step, looking far less regal than when he had collected her from the airport forty-eight-hours before. The Queen had lost her throne, in Ballymagee anyway, and was now no better than the rest of them. Life amongst the commoners did not come easy to her.

'If it's the taxi you want, I'll be right with you.'

'Not yet,' she replied, though not in the strident tones Danny associated with her. She seemed tired and deflated somehow. 'But I shall want a lift later.'

'Then if it's Kathy you're after, she went up to the factory.'

'No, I've said goodbye to her. I wanted to see this place again. And to thank you.'

'Thank me?' he said, surprised to be on the receiving end of a compliment from Leonora Foley.

'It was a good thing you did, bringing Kathy and Pat together. A kind thing. I'm sorry for what I might have said about you.' It was clear, even to Danny, that words of apology were not her customary stock in trade.

'Best come in,' he offered, a little embarrassed. Leonora did not step in straight away.

'Kathy told me all about you. We spoke about a lot of things while we were locked in that office together. She told me you'd come over here to get a bit of Irishness about you.'

'Yeah,' said Danny, avoiding her eye.

'Which is odd,' she continued, 'because I've listened to a lot of Americans and a load of Irishmen, and it seemed to me you're more Irish than anything else. That's a faultless brogue you've got there.'

'Then it's a great compliment to Pat,' said Danny. 'We chatted a lot about being Irish, about living up to the image of the rascal, layabout and drunk. And we used to condem the people who saw all Irishmen as stereotypes. And then we thought about the Crowleys. And, do you know, they're all bloody rascals, lay-abouts and drunks! So we had a drink on it, and that was that.'

'And now you're finding it hard to slip back into being an American, aren't you?' she asked pointedly.

'Sure as hell I do sometimes.'

'Sure – as – hell – I – do?' Leonora repeated his words.

'Watched a lot of cowboy movies, have we? Or American soaps? Got the American from the television, perhaps?'

'I'm sorry, ma'am, but I ain't sure any more what you're on about,' he said, flustered.

'I think I'd better come in now,' she said. Danny nodded, and led her down the hall to the kitchen.

'It's lovely to see this place again. It's very special to me,' said Leonora, making herself comfortable.

'This place? Ain't nothin' special so far as I can see,' said Danny, trying his best to sound American again.

'It was to me,' said Leonora wistfully. 'I don't think it's had a lick of paint in thirty years. What happened to the woman who lived here? She was Pat's aunt, did you know that? It was a bed and breakfast place then.' She saw the upright chair by the fireplace, and smiled. 'And that chair's still here.'

She walked across to it and sat down, enjoying its embrace as she rubbed her back against the uprights and stroked the arms, running her fingers with the grain of wood which had been worn smooth over the years. She closed her eyes. 'Pat was a man of nearly forty that first night, but he acted like a boy of eighteen. Anxious and a little frightened, I guess. Innocent of women, he must have been. He became a wonderful lover, my true love, in the weeks after that. I shouldn't have left him. But there was always business to do, never time for me to come back to Ballymagee.

'You're fond of Kathy, aren't you?' Danny nodded. 'Then don't let her make the same mistake I did. It's very easy to miss the things that matter when you live your life in a hurry. Always speeding somewhere, never slowing down to grab what's important. Then what happens is that you reach out and realise it's gone. Tell Kathy that, will you? She won't listen to me, and I can't blame her for it.'

'Pat's asleep upstairs,' said Danny. 'Do you want me to wake him?'

'Too late. Years ago there might have been some point. No, I didn't come here to say goodbye to him. I came to thank you for all you've done for Kathy. And if it's to you she reaches out, for God's sake don't let her fall out of your hands.' There was a brief silence.

'Will you tell her?' asked Leonora then, fixing Danny with a hard stare.

'Tell her what?'

'Tell her why you're as about as American as a pint of stout. Explain to her why a kid who says he was born in Kentucky speaks with an accent straight out of a Hollywood movie. And why, for someone who has supposedly been up here to learn the Mayo accent, you speak Irish with the lilt of a man born and bred in County Cork?'

Danny still said nothing.

'I came through Cork, you see, the first time I came to Ireland. It's a softer, slower way of speaking. The accent is thicker, the words are swallowed – harder to understand for a stranger. I was so terrified, I suppose, to be alone in a strange country that my every sense was hyper-alert. And whenever I hear just a trace of that Cork accent, I still shiver a little because I remember how nervous I was the first time I heard it, and how I met Pat and he showed me the way to Mayo, and I taught him how to make love.' She caressed the arms of the chair. 'And it's a touch of a Cork accent I hear on your lips.'

Danny sighed with relief at having his secret discovered. The American act was getting harder to keep up, the deception wearying. He had conducted the double bluff for so long that he was no longer certain whether he was a lad from Cork, Mayo, or fresh from Kentucky.

'Some people did notice. I just laughed it off,' he said with a smile, relaxed now he could confess. 'They enjoyed making fun of me, telling me if I started sounding like a Cork man, I'd grow as daft as one. It made them laugh, not suspicious. Do you think Kathy will mind?'

'That's something for you to find out, not me,' said Leonora. 'But I would like to know exactly what kind of game you're playing? I may not have been the greatest mother, but she's still my daughter.'

Danny took a deep breath. All attempts at an American accent had now been abandoned and he spoke from the heart, with the voice of his native County Cork.

'It was old Percy Crowley. He was my mum's eldest cousin, so he was.'

'So your mother was a Crowley?' asked Leonora. Danny nodded.

'When old Percy died, we always thought it was odd. You see, they said he'd died of the drink. Well, none of us had ever heard of Percy takin' a drop o' the stuff in his life, so we thought it mighty strange. But there again we didn't. Because he used to write to my mother, telling her that the Crowleys of Ballymagee were gettin' above themselves and how he'd have to do somethin' about it eventually. I think he must have just got to the point of spillin' the beans to head office when he met with his "accident". They always were a creepy lot, the Crowleys up here. We never trusted them. So for my old mam's sake more than anything else, I thought I'd at least try and find out the truth. And I came up here, playing at bein' an American, cos' if there's anything that doesn't look out of place in the west of Ireland, it's an American pretending he comes from the auld country.'

'And what will you do now?' asked Leonora.

'Go home to Mam, I suppose. Nothin' much more for me up here. Let old Percy rest in peace. There's nothing I can prove. I don't suppose Kathy will be too impressed when she finds out I've been lying to her all this time about who I really am.'

'I think she's impressed enough,' said Leonora, with a touch of sympathy now.

There was a creaking of wooden floorboards above which caused them both to pause and look up at the ceiling. Pat was obviously turning in his sleep. When he had settled and the room was quiet again, Danny said boldly, 'And what about you, then? If we're uncovering each other's secrets, I might ask why you never told Kathy who her father was?'

'Because I knew only too well who that father was, and it *wasn't* Pat Tierney. I'm pretty sure I was pregnant when I came out here. There was a party a couple of weeks before I left London. We were all young and stupid and got drunk. You know the sort of thing. It was a one-night stand with a guy called Metcalfe – Ted Metcalfe. He was a slime bag then, and he still is. Gay, actually. He was using me as his one last opportunity to make it with a woman before he decided to start chasing men seriously.'

'Metcalfe from ChipCo?' asked Danny.

'The very one. The same one who fixed for Kathy to fall into a trap of his own making. Some father, eh?'

'Will you tell her?'

'No. Nor Metcalfe either. Nor Pat. I've thought about it. But now, for the first time, I've been able to give her something she really wants and needs. I've given her what she believes to be her father and I can never give her anything better than that. To take it away would be cruel.'

'But she'd be living a lie, thinking all the time that old Pat was her dad?'

'She wouldn't be the only one surrounded by deception, would she?' replied Leonora, with an accusing look. 'Pat's close enough to being her father. It's all a game of roulette, isn't it? It could just as easily have happened that first night in Ballymagee, in this chair, as on the floor of Metcalfe's camp little flat in

Notting Hill a week before. All a matter of chance. Where's the harm in her believing Pat was the man? He'll make a fine father, and she'll be a good daughter to him.'

The boards above creaked once again to the movement of Pat Tierney in his bed. Leonora waited till he had settled again and threw an affectionate glance towards the ceiling. Then she got up and patted the arm of the chair as if bidding it goodbye. 'Well, thank you, Danny,' she said. 'Will you drive me to the airport now?'

The Volvo set off on its well-rehearsed journey to the airport. Upstairs, at 41 Benwee Avenue, in the bedroom where he had first set eyes on Leonora's naked body, Pat Tierney was awake and weeping. Finally he sobbed uncontrollably. Cruelly, fate had woken him when Leonora banged on the front door and once again he been been unable to prevent himself from spying on her, as he had that night thirty years before. He had heard every word she had said to Danny, and knew that he was not Kathy's real father after all. It was a disappointment of the cruellest kind. There had never been a greater joy in his life than thinking that Kathy was his; he had been happy beyond the meaning of the word, and proud too. But she was not his, never had been. She was somebody else's child.

Pat had led a life into which there had been only two brief episodes of pleasure. The first was thirty years ago, with the young Leonora; the second the few pitifully brief hours of thinking Kathy was his child. Leonora had robbed him of the first and now had taken the second from him too. He would soon be seventy, he reasoned. What chance that such happiness would ever come again? No chance at all. No point in going on.

He rose from the bed, not bothering to tidy his clothes or straighten his wild hair. He tried to remember the words of the precious newspaper cutting from the *Tribune*, now lying burnt to dust in the charred remains of his home. He spoke the words aloud, as best he could remember them, as he strode down Benwee Avenue towards the factory, crying openly, not caring who saw him or what they thought. Over and over again he recited the words as if they were a prayer.

'With regret we have to add another name to the melancholy catalogue of the dead . . .' It was the last time, he thought, that the story of the long, hungry walk of his ancestor would ever be heard. Several people spoke to him as he made his way across the town, asked him if he was all right, did he need a doctor, he looked pale, could they help? This unaccustomed kindness was bought with his money. Those blasted shares! Suddenly, Pat's muddled thinking left him and he saw clearly what he must do. There was no doubt in his mind. The whole business of the factory, of Leonora and Kathy, had clouded his judgement, confused his ambitions. He had, for a brief moment, forgotten that before he departed this life he'd promised himself the Crowleys would be taught a lesson.

'Who will remember now the wrongs that have been done by generations past?' he said to himself. 'Who will be left to remember the long, hungry walk of Padraig Michael Tierney? No one if I am gone. Perhaps, after all, it's time to put the legend to rest. Let Padraig cease his long walk through all our lives.'

He reached the factory forecourt. The security man stopped him, recognised him and then apologised, afterwards welcoming him to the factory. 'All yours now, Mr Tierney, sir.'

'Do you have a match? I'm in great need of a smoke,' said Pat casually. The guard handed him a box and wished him a good day.

'Do you know where you are – what this place is?' Pat asked.

'Always been the factory so far as I know,' replied the guard, 'ChipCo through and through,' he added proudly.

'Does its history mean nothing to you?'

'Well, I suppose it's famous for its crisps, you know.'

The man knew nothing of the warehouse where the bodies had been piled; where, on 4 April 1847, Padraig Michael Tierney's body had been hauled; where 'life was found to be extinct' and Michael Crowley, deputy coroner, had declared he had 'died of want'. No one remembered, only Pat Tierney. But he was going to ensure that no one would ever again forget.

'I would like you to do something for me.' He beamed at the security guard on the gate, trying to disguise his nervousness. 'Will you please ring Miss Kathy Foley, she's in her office, and ask her to come to your box here, and wait for me. Tell her she is under no circumstances to go back into the factory till I come out. Those are my orders as owner of this place.' The guard picked up the phone and Pat heard him talking to Kathy as he strode towards the main doors. He overheard her argue with the guard, query the instruction.

'Tell her!' screamed Pat, momentarily losing his cool. The guard blanched and passed the order on to Kathy.

Pat loped along the stone-floored corridors of the old building. 'Padraig Michael, I have come to give you your eternal rest,' he bellowed, voice cracking with emotion as he forced the words through his tears. 'I hold your memory sacred, Padraig. You will never be forgotten here. Never!' Office doors opened as he ranted, nervous faces peered around them to watch him stumbling along the corridor then taking the door through to the factory. No one dared approach him. He looked like a man possessed.

Pat followed his nose, seeking out the source of the smell of hot oil which he had inhaled for the best part of thirty years. He had forgotten how vile it was, how it had maliciously crept up the hill towards his old cottage, day after day, to taunt him. It was the smug scent of the Crowleys at their greedy work. Pat staggered on till, fortuitously, he came across a sweating Jack

Crowley, standing by a searingly hot fryer, wearing his boiler suit, a greasy spanner in one slippery hand. It could not have been a more perfect meeting. The hand of God had brought them together, Pat decided.

'Mr Crowley,' he said, offering his hand, apparently in friendship. 'It's time I understood what you do here. Will you explain it to me?'

Crowley was surprised by the old man's sudden interest. 'Well, sir,' he said, finding words of respect did not come easily, 'the superheated oil travels up these pipes. Don't touch!' he shouted as Pat reached out. 'It's not only superheated, but under pressure too.'

'And what would happen,' asked Pat casually, 'if the couplings worked loose? If those nuts and bolts over there were undone?' He pointed to a heavily engineered joint on one of the pipes carrying the superheated oil. It was three feet away but radiated an intense heat, and the sound of bubbling oil could be heard rushing through it.

'Well, the pressure of the oil inside the pipe would first of all distort the rubber gasket. Once that gave way it would allow a fine spray to come through. It would be very dangerous, like a huge aerosol can – volatile and highly flammable. Deadly. I'd be out of here like a bloody shot,' joked Jack.

'Undo the nut and bolt with your spanner,' Pat ordered him calmly.

'Not on your bloody life!' said the maintenance man, assuming Pat was pulling his leg.

'Life! What did any of you care about life?' His anger flared anew eyes bulging until they appeared to have doubled in size. 'When did you give a shit for my life, or the lives of the Tierneys a hundred and fifty years ago? You Crowleys have done nothing to deserve life.'

With a thump to Jack's chest, Pat pushed him backwards. As

he fell, his hand reached out for the pipe carrying the super-heated oil. Unfortunately for him the length of pipe for which he grabbed to steady himself was an uninsulated length. It felt as if his hand had suddenly been pressed on to the lid of a furnace. To silence his screams, Pat pulled him away from the pipe, took the large spanner from his hand and gave him one precise blow to the head. The screams of pain stopped. Jack Crowley crumpled to the ground.

Pat stepped over him without a glance. He took a deep breath and was once again in control of his emotions. He could reason with himself now, account for his actions. He wiped the blood from the spanner and held it up to one of the nuts holding two sections of pipe together.

'I would never have done this,' he said aloud, 'if I had any good reason to live. If I had my Kathy that would have been cause enough. But I have nothing at all, so I have nothing to lose.'

He started working on the nuts and bolts. They were tight. He sweated in the heat, losing his grip on the slippery tool, nearly fainting in the sweltering air. After a few turns of the nut, he could hear a hissing sound. The gasket had given way. Pat waited till he could clearly make out the fine spray bursting from the seal. It looked like the rain that came down over the tops of his beloved hills and fell softly on the patch of land where, every year, whatever the weather, on 2 April he planted his potato seed. Pat paused for a moment, wondering about the crop, whether the fire had destroyed it? If not, who would harvest it now? Did it matter? Perhaps it was time for the Tierneys to forget about potatoes. Let them lie in untroubled ground. He would join them soon. Ashes to ashes. He reached into his pocket for the matches, and struck one. It did not even have the chance to burst fully into flame, so fast did the vaporised oil catch light, free its energy and form a ball of flame with Pat Tierney at its epicentre. There was not even time for him to scream.

12

It was a terrible accident, they all agreed. An awful mishap. No other possible explanation crossed anyone's mind. Of course, if the security guard had been capable of putting two and two together, he would have realised that Pat Tierney's asking for a match followed by a factory fire minutes later was more than a coincidence. But all the guard's energy had been expended on restraining Kathy, who had stood at the factory gates as Pat had ordered until hearing the explosion. It had taken the strength of an ox to prevent her from rushing to his rescue then.

If anyone still sought a cause for the fire, they decided they had no further to look than old Jack Crowley who was getting on in years, less certain with his tools, taken with the drink most likely. A terrible accident. And how unlucky for Pat Tierney to be visiting his factory at the time. An awful shame.

The rest of the talk was all of lucky escape. Had not the heavy fire doors slammed shut at the first hint of the conflagration, then the entire factory would have been razed to the ground. Had not the factory been running at below its capacity, dozens of workers nearest to the blast would have perished. But most were at home, relieved at the thought of a stable future free from the burden of the deception they had perpetuated to disguise the problem of the blight. No, it could have been much worse. Just two deaths – Old Tierney, who was a bit of joke anyway, and Jack Crowley who would be the only one to be deeply missed.

But those who saw past the immediate realised that now the outlook was far from secure and the future of their factory was once again uncertain. Tierney had promised them it would be theirs as soon as he could make the financial arrangements. But how far those arrangements had gone no one knew, and who outside Ballymagee would ever believe that an old man, a virtual hermit who had come down from the hills, would be able to make them a gift of an entire factory? It was like a dream, and such fantasies hardly ever came true.

Kathy thought about none of these things; only of her dead father. On the morning following the accident, as she walked the few miles from the Crowley House Hotel to the ruins of his burnt-out cottage, she remembered Pat's warm embrace, his affection for her, the joy of discovering him. She took deep breaths of the fresh Atlantic air, and looked at the distant Mullet which he would never see again. She knew she would cry one day, and from the bottom of her heart, but for the time being she was composed. For a few brief moments she thought she might reach the brow of the next rise in the road and see his cottage still standing; her father in his field with a hoe in hand, tending his precious potatoes.

In her pocket she carried a letter of condolence written on behalf of everyone who worked in the factory and pushed under her door that morning at the hotel.

Dear Miss Foley,
We are deeply sorry that your father died in the terrible accident at the factory and the entire staff express our heartfelt sympathy. He showed himself to be a man of good heart.
Of course, you will need time to consider the future of the factory but we hope you will give us an indication before too long. I am sure the entire town will want to attend the funeral as soon as the date is known.

Kathy had to laugh. Pat had had his funeral already, hadn't he? Wasn't that when he had appeared before them, clothed in priestly robes, and shocked the living daylights out of them? She laughed at the thought of them returning to the church for a second wake, biting their fingernails, fearful this might be get another of his little tricks and that his bony old hand would rise from the coffin, or his body materialise out of thin air. Then she remembered that this time it could not possibly, and she wept.

On the walk to the cottage she thought about what she should do for the best. It would be easy to turn her back on the whole place and flee. No one would criticise her for that. She could melt back into ChipCo, having failed to prove herself as strong as her mother. Would that be seen as failure, not being as good as Leonora at running things? What did management skills count for anyway if you were talentless in the motherhood and general human-being departments?

No, Kathy decided. To be truly successful would be to solve the problems of the people of Ballymagee, and not her own. After all, the Crowleys and their followers had no motivation other than the preservation of their jobs and way of life, which was far from opulent. They had not stolen or defrauded on a grand scale, but merely to conceal a problem of which they had an instinctive and understandable fear – the failure of the potato. True, a little cash had gone into their back pockets when it rightly belonged in the corporate coffers, but that seemed a relatively trivial crime.

Although rarely spoken of, the race memory of the potato famine of a century and a half before must have been an ingredient in their muddled and panicky thinking. It could not have been a mere desire to hang on to the second car, the summer holiday in Spain, and all the other trappings of modest wealth that forced them to the point of attempting to murder an old man in his cottage on the hillside. Their fear must have run deeper than that.

ChipCo was not without guilt either. It had brought prosperity to a benighted patch of rural Ireland, given its people a taste of a life they could never have imagined, and then let them live in fear that it would all be taken away from them. That was the action of a bully, not a benefactor. Almost a repetition of the way the English had snubbed the hungry Irish when the potato failed them one hundred and fifty or more years before. No, all things considered, these people needed help not punishment.

But Kathy could not let the passing of her father go unmarked. Somehow, he must be remembered. As he had clung to the legend of the long, hungry walk of his ancestor, Padraig Michael Tierney, so these people must be made to remember Pat, for all he promised to do for them, for a generosity of spirit that was almost beyond her understanding. There must be a proper memorial.

Her walk brought her to the two gateposts, which looked sadder than she had ever seen them. On the windward side, nearest the burnt-out remains of her father's cottage, smoke from the fire had blackened them. She walked along the path which led to where the front door had stood. The cattle were gone. It was a lonely little ruin. She looked around the blackened plot, kicking over charred bits of timber which had once supported the roof. There was no hint of it now, except for the crumbling rafters which lay on the ground and over which she trod carefully. But in her mind's eye she could see it as clearly as if it were still there; the comfort of it, the welcoming embrace of the room which transcended Pat's apparent frostiness, the ease with which she'd felt at home upon entering.

Kathy kicked the rubble. She hoped she might find a memento, a keepsake, a token she could keep close to her for the rest of her life. But the only thing she unearthed with the toe of her shoe was the glass bottle of poteen. Somehow, for all the explosive nature of its contents, it was intact, if a little sooty on the outside. She picked it up, unscrewed the top and breathed in the distilled spirit of the potato which had once fired her father.

She was about to abandon her half-hearted search of the ruin when beneath the charred remains of the sofa something caught her eye. It glistened in the black debris, like a jewel amongst the filth. A flash of bright light reflected from it as if pleading for her attention. It looked metallic, silvery, perhaps a piece of plumbing, a tap or something. She bent down and found herself grasping the end of a tin whistle. Kathy wiped it with her hand till it regained its shine and then placed it to her lips and blew. It gave a pure, single note. She placed her fingers over the holes and, breathing carefully, almost managed a scale. It sounded sweet yet lonely. The mournful sound broke the dam of her tears.

She wept for several minutes, then heard a distant, mechanical sound which she knew only too well – the uncertain chug of Danny's Volvo. She did not want him to find her less than composed so placed the whistle where she could retrieve it and grabbed at the bottle of poteen. She unscrewed the top, put the bottle to her lips and took a deep swig. Then she wiped her lips and eyes, and straightened her hair. She brushed the dust off herself, ready to face Danny.

She had not expected to see her mother as well.

'Someone in the village said they'd seen you headin' this way. Sorry to disturb, and all that,' Danny shouted from the car apologetically

Kathy was not listening. Instead, she was watching her mother extricate herself from the front seat like a woman appalled by such a conveyance. Balanced on ridiculously high heels, Leonora rushed over to her, arms outstretched, ready to embrace and comfort. Kathy, by standing perfectly still and showing no willingness to reciprocate, sent a signal which even her mother eventually received, and Leonora dropped her arms awkwardly.

'I'm so sorry to hear about Pat,' she said. 'I got as far as London, and turned back as soon as I heard. I'm so very sorry.'

'Is this sympathy or apology?' asked Kathy. 'Because if it's apology you're too late. The one you should be saying sorry to is dead.'

'Kathy, please,' her mother begged.

'It's a pity you didn't bother to make the journey twenty or more years ago. Not a lot for a man to expect of a woman who's having his child.'

'I can never have your father's forgiveness for what I did,' faltered Leonora. 'All I can do is beg for yours.'

'At least he has no problems now. We're the ones left with a mess to sort out,' said Kathy.

'It can all be cleared up. We'll appoint a new manager here. I've been giving it some thought. There'll be a job coming up in New York – I can fix it for you, if you want it? There'll be others if you don't fancy that. Someone else can come in here now and conduct an orderly closure of the factory.'

'No,' Kathy declared. 'The promise must be kept. My father gave his word that the factory would belong to the people and it must become theirs. You can't descend on them god-like, as ChipCo did, transform their lives with a wave of your commercial wand, then just take it all away again. Because you have the power to make dreams come true doesn't give you the right to trample on them when you feel like it. No, the factory must stay.'

'The board won't wear it. They'll insist it closes. It's the figures. They just don't add up.'

'And the people?' Kathy retorted.

'They're nothing but thieves. Murderers even. They took you hostage, for Christ's sake!'

'Only from fear,' said Kathy. 'The factory must stay. It's the heart of this community. Don't break it, like you broke my father's.'

'Well,' said Leonora impatiently, 'I suppose Pat did have those shares if he says he did. That would all have to be looked into, of course. I doubt he made a will or anything. But we could ask lawyers to offer an opinion as to whether you would be the beneficiary. If so, the money from selling his shares would be yours to do with as you wished. If you wanted to buy the damned factory, I'm sure the board would be only too happy to unload it on to you. It's a dead duck.'

'Excuse me,' said Danny who had made his way quietly across from the car. 'Can I throw in a thought?'

'What you know of company and inheritance law would be of enormous value to us, I'm sure,' replied Leonora sarcastically.

'Well, seems to me that if Kathy is to inherit from her father, then someone's goin' to have to prove they're related. And the only person who can do that is her mother, isn't that so? Which means you,' he said, looking Leonora straight in the eye. 'You're goin' to have to stand up in court and swear Pat Tierney was Kathy's father. Now, I assume that would be no problem for you?' He did not blink once but kept his eyes locked firmly on Leonora's.

'Of course it would be no problem,' she replied, flustered. 'But the publicity would be damaging. Not just for me, of course,' she added disingenuously, 'but for Kathy as well. A real embarrassment.'

'So you're thinking you might *not* be able to swear Pat's Kathy's father?' asked Danny. Kathy tried to interrupt but Danny stopped her. He was like a hound after a fox; he was chasing an idea.

'Well, not in public anyway,' said Leonora, eyes downcast.

'So without your declaration that Pat was her father, there's not much chance of Kathy's seeing any money. They'll say Pat died without heirs and the Government will take the loot. Which leaves the problem of a missing few million with which to buy the factory.'

'Yes,' agreed Leonora. 'That rules it out. And a good thing too. Always was a daft idea.'

'I mean the people to have that factory, Mother,' insisted Kathy, glancing at Danny and suddenly realising the direction in which this argument of his was going.

'Guess we need to find some wealthy benefactor,' said Danny, eyes fixed on Leonora as he tried to corner her with his argument. 'The sort of person who wouldn't miss a few million, has loads of shares they can sell and amends to make in this community. Someone who was quite prepared to cast these people aside like so much shit, but now feels they want to say sorry instead.'

'Someone who sees such a personal sacrifice as a lasting monument to a former lover – the father of her child,' added Kathy.

'It would wipe me out!' said Leonora, horrified, as she grasped their argument. 'It's ridiculous!'

'You'll bounce back, mother,' chuckled Kathy.

'Yeah, it's crazy,' agreed Danny. 'Far simpler just to go to court, put your hand on the Bible and swear that Pat was Kathy's dad and it can all be sorted legally.'

'We all have our little secrets we wish to keep, haven't we, Danny?' said Leonora, attempting a feeble fight-back.

'Not all worth several million quid though, are they?' he replied.

'Take me back to the airport.' Leonora made for the car. Looking back over her shoulder, she said, 'I'll arrange for a transfer of funds of some kind. My lawyers will be in touch. You win, both of you. Have the bloody factory! Give it to the people. Do what you like with it. Just let me turn my back on this place forever.'

'Leave it to me, mother, to clear up the mess,' shouted Kathy accusingly. 'Nearly thirty years ago you sowed the seeds of destruction and look at the outcome: a broken-hearted old man is now dead, a panicked community has been driven to the point of committing murder, a daughter has lost her father. *You* couldn't sort this if you wanted because it takes heart when all you have is money. So we'll have some of that money, and you can leave us to do the caring.'

Danny followed her towards the car, opened the passenger door, and waited for Leonora to take the hint that she was not wanted here any more.

'You'll catch the next Aer Shamrock flight, Mother. Remember to get a good sniff at the cabin crew,' laughed Kathy. 'They're wearing a much better class of perfume these days. You might recognise it.'

'You can come too. It's not too late to put all this behind us,' pleaded Leonora.

'No,' replied Kathy. 'I'm staying. With Dad.'

While the taxi made its way to the airport, Kathy took one final walk around the ruins of Pat's old cottage. Amidst the destruction and the deathly pall that hung over the place, one element was still thriving. She noticed a fine crop of potatoes had burst into full leaf, green heads full of vigour, no sign of disease, no reason to expect anything other than a bumper crop. She knew enough about potatoes to know that it would not be long before the green shoots burst into flower and then for a few days the field would be awash with blooms. Then the long, slow withering process would begin when the leaves curled and died, the stalks lost their moisture and turned limp till they shrivelled in the sun. The plants would look dead to the world. But beneath the soil would lie the crop. The gift of the potato plant was not the withered mass it left on the surface, but the treasure that lay hidden, waiting to be harvested.

And so, that autumn, six months after Pat Tierney had planted his potatoes, a platoon of people gathered on the patch of land which had once been his home. Jean Crowley was there, and the Crowleys from the hotel, and the woman from the shop on the High Street whose fluttering eye was no better, and anyone else called Crowley who lived in Ballymagee. They came with baskets to hang on their arms, and bottles filled with tea or stronger drink. Danny was there, too, joining in the party mood, wielding a giant pot of freshly mixed whitewash which he was daubing on the gateposts to make them smart again. The cottage was slowly being rebuilt. The roof would be on within the week, Kathy and Danny hoped, and then they would be able to move in together. 41 Benwee Avenue had been bought by a property developer and was to be pulled down to make way for a supermarket car park, and cohabitation at the Crowley House Hotel was not the easiest of things to achieve. The sooner they had a place of their own, the better.

In exchange for the factory, which now belonged to the people of the town, Kathy had insisted there was a small price to pay. Every year at potato harvesting time, the people of the town must come up the hill to the land where Pat Tierney had grown his crop, and get down on their hands and knees to harvest what she and Danny would plant in his memory. And while doing so they should think kindly of her father. That was all. An annual act of commemoration. How it would have amused him, she thought, to see the Crowleys on their hands and knees, scrabbling across his land. But they were unexpectedly good about it, and entered into the spirit of the occasion, saying that next year they might make a bigger party of it. And even when their hands fell upon the rotten, slimy tuber which is at the heart of every ripe potato plant, they did not mind. Even when the occasional fat fly sniffed the putrid mass and came to feed on it, it no longer held any fear for them. For this rotten tuber had once been the healthy parent of the crop which gave everything to the next generation.

It was a good crop that first year, nearly twenty tons to the acre. Pat would have been overjoyed. When the Crowleys had gone cheerfully back to town to start the night shift at the factory, Danny and Kathy walked across the field again, kicking the clods of earth, picking up the few potatoes that had been missed.

'Are you sure you want to live here? I mean, up here on the hill where he used to live?' Danny asked.

'It's the only way I can stay close to him and guard everything he held precious – the potatoes and his land. It's all he ever cared about, and it will do for me too. And I want to be with you, and love you, and live here with you in the cottage we've rebuilt together. To play silly tunes on the harmonica, have kids, grow potatoes, even get a decent tune out of Dad's old whistle. That's if you can ever give up thoughts of making it big back home?'

Danny had been living that lie too long. Now was the time to tell her about himself, apologise for the deception.

'There's something you ought to know.' He closed his eyes. This was going to be hard. 'I'm a bit of fake,' he confessed.

'A *bit* of a fake!' exclaimed Kathy. 'You're a *complete* fake. You've fooled everyone, you know. That Irish accent of yours is so good these days that you'd pass for an Irishman anywhere. The American's gone completely. They'd never let you back in now. Dad must have done a good job of teaching you, even if it is the funniest Mayo accent anyone's ever heard. No one would believe you were an American. Irish through and through they'd say you were.'

She paused from potato picking to straighten her back. 'Who'd have thought it?' she declared with a smile of satisfaction on her face. 'I've fallen for an Irishman!' Suddenly she thought of her mother. 'I suppose it runs in the family. Falling for the Irish, and having their kids.' She laughed out loud.

One day, Danny knew, he would have to tell her the truth

about himself. But it was more difficult to decide whether he would explain to her that Pat Tierney was not her father. In the months following Pat's death in the factory, Danny had cast his mind back to that night at 41 Benwee Avenue when Leonora had sat in the kitchen chair by the fire, and in that strident, penetrating voice of hers, explained to him that the old man was not Kathy's father. Those creaking floorboards above . . . Had Pat heard every word? Was the factory fire no accident but suicide? Danny had no way of knowing and since his suspicions were incapable of being resolved, thought it best to kept those particular ones to himself forever.

But if he was ever going to tell Kathy about her true parentage it would have to be now. The longer she spent remembering and mourning Pat as her father, the greater a part of her he would become. Danny thought about it for a brief moment, looked at the smile on Kathy's face as she enjoyed the irony of the thought that she was not only following in her mother's footsteps by falling for the blarney, but following her father's between the furrows. She looked so happy. Danny said nothing. Instead, he took up a fork and dug into the soil, teasing a vast golden potato to the surface.

'Planted some good seed, for an old Monk. Damned good seed,' was all he said to her.